MW01200841

PRAISE FOR CHARLES MARTIN

"*The Last Exchange* is somehow equal parts page-turner, heart-breaker, and hope-dealer. Another brilliantly written novel by Charles Martin."
—ANNIE F. DOWNS, *NEW YORK TIMES* BESTSELLING
AUTHOR OF *THAT SOUNDS FUN*

"The adrenaline-pumping third entry in Martin's Murphy Shepherd series (after *The Letter Keeper*) explores human depravity and the healing power of love. Series fans will snap this up."
—*PUBLISHERS WEEKLY* FOR *THE RECORD KEEPER*

"Very few contemporary novelists have found acclaim within mainstream and evangelical markets, but Charles Martin is among them. [*The Letter Keeper*] hinges on the Scriptural message of forsaking the found in order to seek the lost, a theme Martin brings to poetic and brilliant life."
—DAVIS BUNN, WRITING FOR *CHRISTIANITY TODAY*

"Martin follows up *The Water Keeper* with this heartrending, action-packed chapter in the saga of Murphy Shepherd . . . Those familiar with the series will appreciate the emotional punch this rip-roaring adventure packs."
—*PUBLISHERS WEEKLY* FOR *THE LETTER KEEPER*

"Martin excels at writing characters who exist in the margins of life. Readers who enjoy flawed yet likable characters created by authors such as John Grisham and Nicholas Sparks will want to start reading Martin's fiction."
—*LIBRARY JOURNAL*, STARRED REVIEW, FOR *THE WATER KEEPER*

"*The Water Keeper* is a wonderfully satisfying book with a plot driven by both action and love, and characters who will stay in readers' heads long after the last page."
—*SOUTHERN LITERARY REVIEW*

"*The Water Keeper* is a multilayered story woven together with grace and redemption, and packed tight with tension and achingly real characters. This one will keep you turning pages to see what else—and who else—Murph will encounter as he travels down the coastline of Florida."
—LAUREN K. DENTON, *USA TODAY* BESTSELLING
AUTHOR OF *THE HIDEAWAY*

"In *The Water Keeper* Charles Martin crafts a compelling story with skill and sensitivity. Current fans won't be disappointed; new readers will understand why Charles Martin is on the short list of contemporary authors I recommend above all others."

—ROBERT WHITLOW, BESTSELLING AUTHOR

"Martin explores themes of grace, mercy, and forgiveness in this sweeping love story . . ."

—PUBLISHERS WEEKLY, STARRED REVIEW, FOR SEND DOWN THE RAIN

"Charles Martin never fails to ask and answer the questions that linger deep within all of us. In this beautifully told story of a prodigal coming home, readers will find the broken and mended pieces of their own hearts."

—LISA WINGATE, NATIONAL BESTSELLING AUTHOR OF
BEFORE WE WERE YOURS, FOR LONG WAY GONE

"Martin weaves all the pieces of this story together with a beautiful musical thread, and as the final pieces fall into place, we close this story feeling as if we have witnessed something surreal, a multisensory narrative for anyone who enjoys a redemptive story."

—JULIE CANTRELL, NEW YORK TIMES AND USA TODAY
BESTSELLING AUTHOR OF PERENNIALS, FOR LONG WAY GONE

"A beautiful story of redemption and love once lost but found again, *Long Way Gone* proves two things: music washes us from the inside out and Charles Martin's words do the same."

—BILLY COFFEY, AUTHOR OF STEAL AWAY HOME

"Martin's story charges headlong into the sentimental territory and bestseller terrain of *The Notebook*, which doubtless will mean major studio screen treatment."

—KIRKUS, STARRED REVIEW, FOR UNWRITTEN

"Charles Martin understands the power of story, and he uses it to alter the souls and lives of both his characters and his readers."

—PATTI CALLAHAN HENRY, NEW YORK TIMES BESTSELLING AUTHOR

"Martin is the new king of the romantic novel . . . *A Life Intercepted* is a book that will swallow you up and keep you spellbound."

—JACKIE K. COOPER, BOOK CRITIC, HUFFINGTON POST

"Martin's strength is in his memorable characters . . ."

"Charles Martin is changing the face of inspirational fiction one book at a time. *Wrapped in Rain* is a sentimental tale that is not to be missed."

"Martin spins an engaging story about healing and the triumph of love . . . Filled with delightful local color."

THE

KEEPER

ALSO BY CHARLES MARTIN

THE

KEEPER

A Murphy Shepherd Novel

CHARLES

MARTIN

THOMAS NELSON
Since 1798

Published in Nashville, Tennessee, by Thomas Nelson. Thomas Nelson is a registered trademark of HarperCollins Christian Publishing, Inc.

Published in association with The Christopher Ferebee Agency, www.christopherferebee.com.

Thomas Nelson titles may be purchased in bulk for educational, business, fundraising, or sales promotional use. For information, please email SpecialMarkets@ThomasNelson.com.

Scripture taken from The Holy Bible, English Standard Version. ESV® Text Edition: 2016. Copyright © 2001 by Crossway Bibles, a publishing ministry of Good News Publishers.

ISBN 978-0-8407-2247-8 (hardcover)
ISBN 978-0-8407-2248-5 (epub)
ISBN 978-0-8407-2249-2 (audio download)

Library of Congress Cataloging-in-Publication Data

CIP data is available upon request.

Printed in the United States of America

25 26 27 28 29 LBC 5 4 3 2 1

For Charlie, John T., and Rives

Because the needs of the one outweigh those of the ninety-nine

PROLOGUE

Somewhere on the dark web in an encrypted chat room:

MAN 1: "Money received. Target address?"

MAN 2: "See attachment."

MAN 1: "Security protocols?"

MAN 2: "Same package."

MAN 1: "House schematics?"

MAN 2: "Same."

MAN 1: "Target?"

MAN 2: "Three. And I want them all."

MAN 1: "Collaterals?"

MAN 2: "The mother. Hands off. Not to be harmed."

MAN 1: "Dogs?"

MAN 2: "Yes."

MAN 1: "Trained?"

MAN 2: "Very."

MAN 1: "Father?"

MAN 2: "Away."

MAN 1: "Secret Service?"

MAN 2: "Make a statement."

MAN 1: "Define 'statement.'"

MAN 2: "Leave bodies."

MAN 1: "Orders following extraction?"

MAN 2: "Photographed. Then taken and held at this address until further notice."

MAN 1: "And once there?"

MAN 2: "Keep them alive."

MAN 1: "Any restrictions? I need to be specific with my men."

A pause.

MAN 2: "The spoils of war. Enjoy the fruits of your labor."

MAN 1: "Much obliged."

MAN 2: "Pleasure doing business with you."

At 2:00 a.m., the blacked-out Suburban exited the asphalt onto a dirt road, at which time the lights were killed. A mile and a half later, six men exited the SUV and walked single file through a half mile of twenty-year-old pines. Aided by Trijicon night vision devices and thermal viewers, they stepped over or around infrared motion detectors and laser alarms, "speaking" through hand signals. A drone hovered a thousand feet above, allowing the man connected to the voice in their ear to monitor the heat signatures of the special agents guarding the compound and its occupants. The eye in the sky told them when to wait, when to walk, what code to punch, and where to step to avoid the cameras.

Reaching the edge of the field, two of the six lay prone behind Christensen Arms Modern Precision Rifles chambered in .300 Win Mag. While one member of the team ranged the target at 875 yards, the shooters dialed 7.03 MILs of elevation into Schmidt & Bender PMII optics, acquired a sight picture and superimposed the crosshairs on the target, pushed the safety to the fire position, then awaited the order. Following a seven-second countdown, both shooters pressed the trigger at zero, sending 210-grain solid copper projectiles out the muzzles at 2,804 feet per second, which reached the targets downrange 1.3 seconds later carrying 998 foot-pounds of impact energy.

Of the twelve remaining agents assigned to this protection detail, seven died in the next ninety seconds.

Once inside the home, the operatives donned gas masks and slipped felt outer soles over their boots, climbing the stairs in relative silence. Landing on the second floor, they stopped at the master bedroom, snaked a hose between the door and the floor, and opened a tank valve. They would not kill her on purpose—although when she woke, she would wish they had. Ninety seconds later, having neutralized occupant number one, they approached bedrooms two, three, and four, where each team snaked a small thermal viewer into the room to verify the condition of the occupants.

And the location of the three Belgian Malinois.

The existence of the dogs had never been leaked to the press and no pictures existed. Their presence was highly protected information.

The first camera proved dog number one was asleep. The dogs in rooms three and four were not. The first dog received a suppressed subsonic round from a Glock 47. The second dog heard the rustle of the camera, jumped off the bed to investigate, and sniffed the strange tube, which released a gas, rendering dog two just as incapable as dog one.

Two teams entered the rooms, placing masks over the noses and mouths of occupants two and three, which startled them, forcing gas into their lungs. Two seconds later, a hypodermic needle was inserted into each neck. Sleep followed quickly.

The problem came at door number four. Neither the occupant nor the dog was asleep. Another tube was placed beneath the door. Another valve opened. A minute later, both the occupant and the dog slumped over, followed immediately by an injection into the occupant's neck. Using facial recognition software embedded in their phones, each team scanned the occupant's face and awaited confirmation. Once received, they exited in unison, finishing dogs two and three with suppressed rounds.

While the eye in the sky monitored their retreat along with the heat signatures of the five remaining agents, one member of each team shouldered an occupant and the other covered their retreat as they returned down a hallway, down two flights of stairs, out a side door, and back across the field. That's when the eye alerted them to an agent exiting the bunk-house just prior to shift change. He was met with nine rounds from a suppressed Daniel Defense 300 Blackout. Returning through the pines, the team retrieved both precision rifles, placed the occupants in the back of the SUV, then drove nine minutes to a private airport where each occupant was stripped, scanned, blindfolded, gagged, zip-tied, photographed, and placed in one of three different planes.

Four hours later, the video was sent.

PART I

"... He who enters by the door is the shepherd of
the sheep. To him the gatekeeper opens."

—John 10:2–3

CHAPTER 1

16 HOURS EARLIER

The snow blew sideways, carried on a brittle, cutting wind. Dusted dark coats, glasses, gloves, and umbrellas stood in stark contrast to the perfect rows of white headstones rolling off into the fog. In my life, I'd found myself in many places where I never wanted to be again. This was one of them. Arlington National. Not because the dead aren't worth our greatest respect. They are. These are the best of us. Chances are good I'm writing this and you're reading this because of those lying there.

But today was different. Today we'd add one more.

Today, we'd officially bury Bones.

It'd been a month since I watched Bones's limp body, riddled with bullet holes and arms wrapped around his brother, disappear down the well shaft, splashing a hundred feet below. I'd replayed those events ten thousand times, and no matter how often I reached out my hand, I could not catch him. Since that moment, I'd dealt with guilt, shame, anger, and a soul-piercing sadness I'd known only once before—when I lost Marie. One half of me could not shake knowing I was responsible for his death, while the other half knew I was not. I lived somewhere on that narrow ledge between what my head understood by reason and what my heart would never accept.

1

Bones knew the cost. He'd always known. His life for one chance to turn his brother. A gamble. Had he? Had he turned Frank? I don't know the answer to that. If I had it to do over again, I'd shoot his brother in the face and be done with it. But not Bones. Bones would not dismiss Frank. Never had. So, for the last time, he left the ninety-nine to attempt one more impossible rescue. In truth, it was a prisoner swap. His life for Frank's. In Bones's mind, it was the only way to bring Frank home. But that's the crazy thing about all this: Not every prisoner wants to be rescued. Some prefer chains to freedom, darkness to light. Bones knew this. He also knew there are no second chances in this business. Bones himself told me that. It's why he did what he did. Frank's attempted rescue was a one-way trip. Always had been. Despite the cost, Bones stuck with his brother. Let Frank pull him down that well shaft. Bones knew what darkness lay at the bottom, and my guess is that he didn't want his brother to face it alone.

When I close my eyes and relive those last few seconds, the image that returns is the look in Bones's eyes. It wasn't anger. Not sadness. Not fear. It was peace. Resolve. Bones had done what he came to do, and he'd calculated and committed to the cost long before he met me.

When I first met Bones, I'd discovered quickly he was something of a genius. Given his life's work, he'd been given broad latitude to hand-pick recruits and develop a program with a singular purpose: Find people. Specifically, lost people. One at a time.

When Bones first explained this to me, I had said, "So you work for the CIA."

He shook his head. "No, but they often work for me."

In my time at the academy, he'd routinely disappear for days at a time. No explanation. No goodbye. And then without notice, he'd return. When I started paying attention, I noticed that on several occasions, he was protecting some part of his body. Nursing an injury. One time he returned from a week's absence with an obvious problem in his shoulder.

"Cut yourself shaving?"

He didn't respond.

"You want to talk about it?"

I'll never forget his answer. He reached into his pocket and simply handed me a bullet. Not the cartridge that contained the shell casing plus the bullet. Just the bullet. The spent projectile. The copper thing had gone down the barrel at high speed and entered his body. When he dropped it in the palm of my hand, I picked up on the fact that Bones was playing for keeps, and this whole clandestine training thing ended somewhere other than a grammar school playground.

He stared at it. "Life is not a video game, and there is no do-over."

No do-over echoed through my mind as I stared through the snow. Down at the box. And when I closed my eyes, I saw Bones staring back at me.

Two weeks ago, we'd met as a group on the beach near Bones's childhood home and tried to say our goodbyes. I had lifted Shep onto my shoulders and waded out. Then, like now, we had nothing to bury. No ashes to scatter. So we buried his orange case at sea. Then, like now, I wanted to speak; I just couldn't. So Clay broke the silence and spoke beautiful words over the water, his deep baritone a balm to my soul. Then Eddie. Followed by Casey and Angel. Final words spoken at random. Our tears mingling with the ocean. I stood shattered. One breath. Two. In. Out. Repeat.

Finally, Summer had patted me. "Your turn."

I stared at the box. Scuffed. Scarred. One last voyage remaining. Solo. I tried to speak and could not. When I tried again, no words formed in my mouth. Then, on the wind, I heard his voice. There in that water, in that broken place of earth where the sand told the sea, "You will go no farther," Bones spoke to me. And when he did, I could hear him smiling. *Tell me what you know about sheep.*

I shook my head and spoke out loud. "No. I will tell you about the one who keeps them." Wanting to see him off, I had waded out past the breakers until the water rose above my chest and placed the orange box on the surface. There I let it go.

I let Bones go.

Staring through the snow at the flag-covered coffin, I knew I had not. I could not. As much as I knew I needed to, I was not able.

When we learned Bones would be buried with the highest of military honors, we scoured Freetown for mementos of Bones. Books, his Bible, a watch, a few nice bottles of wine, an old pair of boots, a pocketknife, his priestly vestments, a camera, a lens. I had deliberated adding the coin I carried in my pocket, but my hand wouldn't let go. As we scoured Freetown, returning with our offerings, Gunner appeared with an old wool sweater Bones wore when he sipped wine by the fire. Worn, tattered, a couple holes here and there, leather patches on the elbows, it smelled like Bones. When Gunner dropped it in the pile, I pretty much lost it.

A string of black SUVs and limos lined the road. Not a large crowd but a crowd nonetheless. As "family," Summer, Angel, Ellie, Casey, Shep, and I walked behind the horse-drawn caisson. Summer held one hand, Shep the other. Whether I held them or they held me, I could not say. We walked over two hills and down into a valley protected by giant sentinel trees. The caisson came to a stop and the casket team approached from the side, lifted the simple wooden box, and began stepping backward in perfect unison. In lockstep, they carried Bones's box to its final resting place, where one member spread a flag lengthwise.

I scanned the attendees and knew Bones would be uncomfortable with the attention. Platitudes were never the reason for the scars he carried. The directors of the CIA, FBI, and Homeland Security. The joint chiefs. Multiple members of the House and Senate. Speaker of the House. President pro tempore of the Senate. Secretaries of State, Treasury, and Defense. As well as the chief of staff to the president, who had been detained overseas. A bomb here could really mess up presidential succession. Most of these men and women had personal experience with Bones—he'd rescued someone they loved. Returned them to the dinner table.

Lastly, escorted by multiple Secret Service agents, the vice president exited a limo, refused an umbrella, and approached the coffin.

CHAPTER 2

Aaron Ashley was political royalty. The son of the former secretary of state and later vice president, Aaron was ruddy-faced, with tight-cropped red hair and a salt-and-pepper beard. He was also very physically fit. A stark contrast to his soft earlier life.

Having a father who held every significant political office save POTUS, Aaron spent his childhood in the lap of political protection and the privileged life of Riley. This childhood bosom led to an illusory superiority—not only did he think he was better than others, but he seldom thought of others. Having been raised under the watchful eye of the Secret Service, he never touched an elevator button. Never did his own laundry. Never cooked. Never did many things. In his youth, this made him a goldbrick who shirked any responsibility and stared down his nose with indifference at those who did shoulder it. Coddled as the vice president's son and strapped with a last name that sounded more female than male, Aaron made an unlikely cadet at the Air Force Academy. The laughingstock of the freshman class. His initials, along with the fact that he was rather scrawny and not overly coordinated, earned him the nickname Double-A. After the battery. As in small, containing little juice, and disposable. But then one day a bully on the playground—a fellow cadet jealous of Aaron's privileged existence—put two and two together, taking note of his reddish hair and ruddy complexion, and took it a step further. "Copper Top." Laughter ensued and the name stuck.

After a difficult freshman year, Aaron took a chance ride in a glider and, interestingly enough, found something he was good at. Really good at. Aaron took to flying like a fish to water and set his sights on pilot training. Something for which he had a knack. Turns out all that time spent playing video games had honed his eye-hand coordination, a talent that would one day make him one heck of a pilot. Graduating with honors, he was selected for United States Air Force Weapons School—the Air Force equivalent of the Navy's Top Gun school—where he excelled and graduated first in his class. Quickly assigned to foreign theaters, call sign Copper Top made a name as one of the military's best pilots. Shot down twice, he safely ejected and then found his way home. The first time, he hitchhiked back to base after spending a few days in a culvert pipe and an abandoned brothel. The second, he walked some forty miles across the mountains in freezing temperatures wearing what was left of his leather flight jacket. Upon his return, he climbed back into the cockpit and resumed duty. The same day.

Aaron didn't suffer fools, and getting shot down was all a part of flying. Not to mention payback was a . . . well, a real bummer. Copper Top had found his juice.

Following decorated service, he returned to the States. A no-nonsense, straight-shooting war hero with ice water coursing through his veins. For vacation, he took a few weeks off and drove cross-country in an old truck. Avoiding highways. Sleeping in RV parks. Something he'd always wanted to do. Somewhere in there, he stopped at a roadside produce stand in central Georgia. Squash. Carrots. Tomatoes. Turnips. And a pretty girl wearing a straw cowboy hat and jean overalls.

"Morning."

She nodded. A faint smile. The contrast between the two was striking. His shirt was tucked in. She'd been mucking the stalls. She noticed his flight jacket. "You a pilot?"

"Yes, ma'am."

He would soon learn she was spunkier than her attire suggested. "You any good?"

He nodded and said nothing, which was good because he couldn't take his eyes off her and any word coming out of his mouth would not help the situation.

"Can I help you with something?" Her South Georgia accent was intoxicating.

He held up the nearest vegetable and tried to speak but couldn't.

She laughed. "You like butternut squash?"

Another nod. More silence.

"Really?" One hand rested on her hip. "And just how do you cook it?"

He shrugged. "Soup."

The nearest RV park sat a few miles away, so he stayed a week. Returning each day. Finally, after a few days of beating around the bush, he asked, "Would you like to go flying sometime?"

She shook her head. "No."

"What?" He had not prepared for this contingency. "Why?"

Another half-smile. "I don't even know you."

"You ever been?"

She shook her head.

"You've never been in a plane?"

Another shake.

"Well . . ." He pointed. "I'm more comfortable up there than down here."

She laughed out loud. "I believe it."

"I could take you. Be no trouble."

She shaded her eyes with one hand and put her other hand on her hip. "You're not from 'round here, are you?"

He shook his head. "What gave it away?"

She laughed and glanced at a farmhouse set on the hill. A man standing on the porch. "You'd better talk to him first."

Fortunately for her, Ashley was not afraid of imposing men. "Take me to him?"

Turned out Esther loved flying.

Ten years and three kids later, Aaron hung up his flight suit and traded the military's most advanced fighter cockpit for farm life and then, when statewide conflict presented itself, the state legislature. Which led to the House. Then the Senate. Where he served several terms and worked tirelessly to protect Esther and the kids from the swamp in which he worked and the journalists who wanted access to his personal life. Remarkably, Esther made the transition from private farm to national platform and served with distinction both her husband and the country. And while she felt called to her role, her children were not. So she protected them like a hawk. Built a wall between them and the public. Three of the most beautiful children ever born on planet earth. Hair so blond it was almost white. Green eyes. Smiles that lit a room.

Following a distinguished Senate career, Aaron was tapped to serve as Secretary of Defense. Four years during which his popularity and name recognition grew and made him the first choice to be tapped to serve alongside the current president. America had fallen in love with Copper Top. Currently, Aaron was three years into his first term as vice president, and given that the current president had termed out, Aaron had thrown his hat in the ring, declared his candidacy, and received his party's nomination. Polls had him well ahead.

Placing both hands on the coffin, Aaron whispered words I could not hear, kissed the snow-covered flag, and took his place alongside Esther. Either unable or unwilling to sit, I stood behind Summer and the girls. As did Gunner, who stood alongside me and Clay. The rest of the team huddled closely.

While my body was here, my mind was not. The memories flashed like a slideshow across my mind's eye. I remembered lying in that cave. Having been shot with my crossbow days earlier. Infection had long since set in. My ship had sailed. I had an hour, maybe two at the most. Then Bones walked in. He'd found me. Saved me. He'd done what I had not.

The next slide showed me tending bar in Key West. Bones had found me at my lowest, put a pen and pad in front of me, and said, "Tell me what you know about sheep." Out of that rescue, David Bishop wrote books that caught fire, which funded Freetown, which gave Murphy Shepherd a reason for living. I'd found my place in this world because of Bones. Why?

One simple reason. I'd mattered more to Bones than Bones mattered to Bones.

The needs of the one . . .

My tutor still taking me to school.

The slide flipped again and I found myself in Bones's wine cellar, his orange box resting on a shelf. We had come to our wits' end. We couldn't find him. Had no clue. Then Shep pointed at the bird. The pelican. And the Pelican case. I remember spinning the box, clicking open the latches, lifting the lid, and staring wide eyed. Bones had left us, left me, several things: a bottle of wine, an opener, loaded spare magazines for his Sig, his satellite tracker, a first aid kit, a Williams pocketknife, a lighter, a pair of reading glasses, three canisters of unused Kodak film, a compass, paracord, a pair of Costa sunglasses, a small package of fishhooks with fishing line, a ballpoint pen, and a worn Bible. Taped to the underside of the lid was a picture of two suntanned, towheaded identical boys fishing out of a small johnboat. One standing in the front throwing a cast net. The other sitting in the rear with his hand on the tiller of the outboard. They might have been eight years old. And the bottom of the boat was piled three high with mullet. It was the same picture Frank had laid down before he died. Somehow, it held meaning for both of them.

Then I'd seen the letter. Lying folded across the middle. And across the envelope, Bones had written, "Murph." I remember everyone leaning in, focused on that envelope, and each one of us wondering, *Is that real? Is that what I think it is?*

While the snow dusted my shoulders, with Gunner pressed against my leg and Summer holding my hand, I recited the letter to myself. I didn't need to read it. I'd done that enough. I knew it by heart.

CHAPTER 3

Dear Murph,

Well, if you're reading this I'd bet Frank took me and you're fumbling around without a clue as to how to find me. Don't blame yourself. He's like that. Nobody thinks like him. It's evidence of his genius and his demented and evil nature, both of which he is, so don't be too tough on yourself. It's a good thing you don't think like him.

Let me help you out. Chances are near 100 percent that I'm in Majorca. I'd bet the bottle in this case, which is a good one by the way, that Frank has taken me back to where it all started, and he's stuck me down in my dungeon home. Years ago, he converted it into a home of sorts. It's one of the only places on earth where he can sleep, even if just a few hours. It's also where he can lock me up in the dark with my painful memories and leave me to rot. He will do all this because he knows he can't make me talk, so he'll use me as leverage to get you to bring him what he wants—probably his birth certificate. Which I don't have. Haven't for a long time. His obsession with that small piece of paper proves that identity precedes purpose. Whose you are matters more to the soul than who you are or what you are. I have my reasons for keeping it from him.

There is hope. The attached map should help. Follow the instructions. Closely. Don't deviate. See you soon.

Bones

Classic Bones. A simple here's-where-to-find-me letter. X marks the spot. It'd been there all along. And he wrote it in advance, which meant he knew we'd find ourselves in this position, which meant he didn't prevent it. Which meant he planned his own abduction.

Bones's hand-sketched map had ended with specific detail: "Once you reach the headwaters of the spring, look up."

Gunner and I had traveled up the underground river through caverns and caves, finally coming to a dead end. The headwaters. So I had done what he said. I looked up and started climbing.

Bones had added a PS to his map. "If you slip, don't worry—the water's deep beneath you. But it's also flowing with a force like you've never known, so hold your breath because it's about to take you on an underwater ride that not even Disney could imagine, and it will either drown you or save you." I remembered how Gunner whined as I climbed and how I could feel his heart pounding through both his and my vest in the same way I could feel it pounding against my leg now.

When the crowd was seated, the chaplain gestured to the vice president, who stood, removed prepared remarks from his coat pocket, and stepped to the end of the coffin. Above where Bones's head would have been. He opened the pages, stared at them, looked at all of us, then folded the sheets and placed them back inside his coat pocket.

Clearing his throat, he said, "They asked me to speak . . . I don't know why. We all know I'm a terrible speaker." A gentle laughter rippled through the crowd. A much-needed icebreaker. "I won't attempt to tell you what Bones meant. Or means. Your presence here is evidence of that." He shook his head.

"I met Ezekiel 'Bones' Walker when he rescued me. Literally. From a greasy fat man at a hotel in Idaho. Bones found me, little more than a kid, gagged and bound in the cab of a tractor trailer. I'd been taken eight days earlier. My father, who then held the office I now hold, had unleashed the entire intelligence community of the American government to find me—and they had not. No leads. Nothing. And then this random guy opens the cab door, smiles, lifts me out, and feeds me a burger while the blue lights flash. A few hours later, I was hugging my dad. Glad to be back in the arms of my mom. That day changed the trajectory of my life. It's why I'm standing here. It's no secret I grew up a privileged politician's son. My private school critics called me Riley. In turn, I hated the life. Wanted nothing to do with it. But something changed that day in Idaho. Bones took my indifference and gave me a reason. Gave me my 'why.' It is also no secret that, truth be told, my dad pulled some strings. While I was not cadet material, he secured me an appointment into the academy where Bones kept an eye on me. As a cadet, I tried to fit in. Tried to be one of the guys. But I was not. At all. Which was made all the more difficult when everyone around you worked so hard to earn a spot while you were given yours thanks to your daddy. A spot that rightly should have been given to someone else—a fact that only served to heighten my shame. With that as my backdrop, I didn't have many friends. In fact, I had none. Further, I had grown up lazy, so physical exercise was not my forte. The only thing I chased was the ice cream truck." More quiet laughter. "Again, no secret, I was more mush than not. One of the ways the academy whittles cadets is through this sadistic thing called an obstacle course. It separates the men from the boys. Those who want to be there from those who like the idea of being there. To be honest, it's a medieval torture device lifted from the catacombs of hell. I hated it. Hated every minute of it. But every freshman was required to complete the thing in thirty minutes or less. The first time I tried it, I ran, crawled, climbed, scurried, did everything I could in the earth-scorching time of forty-nine minutes and fifty-seven seconds. It wasn't difficult to read the writing on the wall." He paused, suggesting the next admission was painful. "Few knew this, but given my soup of circumstances, I was not in a good place." He shook his head once. "I'd written my letter. Had a gun. One bullet. My plan laid out. I even read medical textbooks and knew where to place the muzzle"—he pointed at his heart—"so that my mother could cry over my dead body and not have to close the casket because I'd blown my face off.

"While I was alone much of the time, I'd also noticed another ca-det with few friends. Unlike me, he was physically superior. One of those

Adonis-like miscreants who levitated when he ran." More laughter. "Made a mockery of most of the tests. Bones hovered in his orbit. I wasn't sure if he liked him or tolerated him, but as with me, he kept an eye on him. Late in our freshman year, prior to the final running of the obstacle course, we were all given strict instructions that while one day we would fight as a unit, this course was an individual accomplishment. We were not allowed, under any circumstance, to help another cadet. In fact, we were ordered not to. If we helped anyone at all, in any physical way, we'd be disqualified. Standing on the starting line, I knew this was the end of my tenure and I'd soon be the subject of more ridicule and shame and embarrassment to my family. I consoled myself, knowing the embarrassment would end that afternoon. I'd started the countdown. I'm not asking for your pity—I've lived and do live a blessed life—but I'm describing to you my experience at that time. When the starting gun went off, I watched as the entire company put distance between themselves and me. Twelve minutes in, breathing so hard I thought my heart would explode, that mysterious loner broke the academy record. That's right—twelve minutes. Basically, he lapped me and then some. Making him a shoo-in for pretty much any summer assignment he wanted. Military brass tend to applaud and reward physical prowess and mental toughness, both of which he had. Over the next several minutes, I clawed my way toward the finish line, which seemed no closer. As my fellow cadets crossed the line and rang the bell prior to the expiration of the time limit, shouting in joyful exultation, it became clear that—while I had improved a lot—I'd never make it. Then, about the time I lost all hope, I looked up and there's this guy. Running alongside me. With me. Step for step. And somewhere in my oxygen-starved brain, it struck me that he'd finished first only to immediately turn around and come back. Who does that?

"No one, myself included, thought I could make it. To make matters worse, by missing the cutoff deadline, I would cost my entire company a weekend pass. Making me that much less popular. Climbing a rope ladder, I slipped, my foot caught, and I found myself hanging upside down. Next thing I knew Spider-Man righted me and freed my foot. When I told him

I couldn't make it through the log maze, he told me I could and steadied me when I slipped. When I said I couldn't lift my arms for the final
pull-ups, he grabbed the bar and said, 'Just do what I do.' And I did. As
time dwindled and I snapped, telling him I couldn't make it, he leaned in,
pressed his shoulder to mine, and told me I could. We could. And for the
first time in my life, for reasons I will never understand, I believed him."

Ashley raised a finger and nodded. "Learned something else that day.
Two can do what one cannot. I've never forgotten that. With more ground
than clock, he told me he was staying with me. All the way. My time was
his time. We'd do it together. Him and me." A pause. "Since that time I've
flown over five hundred combat sorties, and in every single one of them, I
have heard his voice. 'We can.'" A nod. A quick glance at me. "I hear it still.
To this day I don't know how we did it, and to his great credit, I don't know
why. I just know he did. And because he did, we did. I rang that bell with
nine seconds to spare. Nine seconds. And when I did, I caught a glimpse
of Bones. Smiling."

CHAPTER 4

Aaron's voice shook the memory loose. What had been a difficult day for Aaron had turned out to be a very hard day for me. Turning around and disobeying a direct order did not make me many friends. None actually. My isolation continued.

One afternoon, after a rather difficult workout of flying 200s, the man in the priestly garb found me. Another bag of chips in his hand. I was standing at my locker, putting on dry clothes. The room was empty save us. He stepped closer. Within two feet. Emptying the bag of chips into his mouth.

"Tell me something"—he spoke around the crunch—"Why'd you turn around? Go back?"

"He wasn't going to make it."

"The obstacle course is, by design, a singular achievement. Start as a group. Get judged as individuals."

"And yet we suffer as a group if one person fails to make time."

"Orders are orders."

I looked right at him. "It's a bad order."

"That attitude'll get you thrown out of here."

"Sir"—I glanced at his robes—"or Father, or whatever it is you do around here. Do I look like I care?"

He raised his eyebrows. "You know, you're only the second one on record to do that."

"What? Disobey an order?"

"No." He laughed. "Go back. Help the stragglers."

"Maybe I was the only one who could, sir."

"Maybe."

"Permission to speak freely, Father sir?"

He smirked. "Granted."

I wasn't sure if I was in trouble or not. Would they discipline me? How? If so, I wanted to get it over with. "What is it that you do here? Why are we having this conversation? Why are you here?"

He considered this. "They tolerate me."

The dichotomy of "they" and "me" was not lost on me. Regardless, I'd had it with this man and his stupid riddles. "If you want to sift me, then do so. Be my guest." I gestured outside in the direction of the obstacle course. "I went back. I'd do it again."

He sat on a bench opposite me. "You don't fit in too well around here, do you?"

I wanted to say, "Thanks for the revelation, Captain Obvious," but did not. Instead, I said, "No, Father sir, not really."

"Not really or no?"

I pulled on a sweatshirt. "No."

"Why?"

"Well . . . we're busy during the day and there's not much time for social—"

"No, why'd you go back?"

I shrugged. For the first time I answered his question with a question. "Does it matter, sir?"

He wiped the corners of his mouth with a napkin, then pointed to Aaron's locker. "It did to him."

I shrugged it off and said nothing.

He rested his head on the lockers. "You know him?"

"Sir?"

He tapped Aaron's locker.

Given that my heart and mind were east with Marie, I had kept to myself and not embroiled myself in the who's who of my class. In truth, I didn't care. I shook my head. "Not really."

"So you really don't know who he is?"

Another shake of my head.

He raised an eyebrow but said nothing.

I pressed him. "What?"

"The fact that you don't know who he is, and more importantly whose he is, makes turning back that much more significant."

I was done with this strange man, this stupid conversation. And if I had my way, I would soon be done with the academy.

He was about to leave when he turned back. "You still haven't answered my question."

"Which one?"

His expression softened and his eyes focused on me. "Why'd you do it?"

"I don't think you'd understand."

"Try me."

It was no use. What would a priest know about that anyway? He was just a pansy, passivist has-been who couldn't hack it so he traded BDUs for white robes. I shook my head. "Just something somebody told me a long time ago."

He chuckled. "You mean after you climbed back onto Jack's boat a second time?"

That stopped me cold. How would he know about that? I didn't put that in my application, and I'd never told anyone else—save Marie. I stood there with my mouth open.

He leaned closer. "David, maybe we're not trying to get rid of you." He patted my shoulder. "Maybe I'm just trying to figure out why you're really here . . . and who you want to be when you grow up."

Aaron's voice brought me back to here. To now. To the snow, to Gunner whining and Bones's coffin stretched out before me.

Aaron continued, "I would later ask Bones, pointing to this mystery cadet who'd returned for me. 'You ordered us not to do that.' Bones had nodded. 'Did you know he would?' He nodded again. Knowingly. 'He can't not. It's just in him.' I remember studying that man. The quiet cadet who disobeyed a bad order to do what his heart told him he couldn't *not* do. I turned to Bones and asked the question that changed the trajectory of my life. 'You teach me how?' That night I burned my letter and later returned my dad's revolver to his safe." He reached in his pocket and removed a worn coin made from copper. "But I kept the bullet. Tried to give it to Bones as a thank-you. A memento of sorts. In typical Bones fashion, he had it melted down and turned into this medallion, engraved with eleven words that matter to him and me. They became my raison d'être. I've carried it every day since.

"In the years following, Bones became my tutor. In every area of my life. I am who I am because of"—he gestured—"this simple, towering man." Another pause. This one longer. "Because of my political connections, and because of the debt my dad felt to Bones, he helped create a way for Bones to do what he did with me on a broader level. To work with many of our agencies. Below the radar. Literally underground. With a singular mission: to rescue individuals. Lost. Taken. Stolen. Deceived. A decade in, and Bones had personally returned over five hundred sons and daughters to their parents." He eyed the crowd. "Many of them yours." He held up a small wooden box. "Because all of his work was classified, his medals were given, hung around his neck, and then taken back five minutes later. And stored in this cigar box in my dad's office. He later passed it on to me." He shook the box. "Colonel Ezekiel Bones was and is probably the most decorated government servant I've ever known, and yet he never said a word." He opened the box. "There are more Purple Hearts in here than places on your body to hang them. And . . ." He teared up. "I was invited into my father's office the day they hung the Congressional Medal around his neck." I shook my head. I never knew Bones had been awarded the Medal of Honor. He'd never mentioned it. "And then in classic Bones fashion, he thanked my dad, lifted it off, laid it in this box, and boarded a plane for some faraway country where some kid needed somebody to kick down the door.

"On the day I was elected vice president, some twenty years after my father held the post, I was sitting in his, now my, office, wondering just what in the world I'd gotten myself into. In walked Bones. He sat, put his feet up on my desk, lit a cigar, and said, 'Tell me what you know about sheep.'

"I knew the answer. 'They're completely lost without their shepherd.'

"Bones listened, considered my words, and nodded. 'Then be one,' he said. 'And be a good one.'"

CHAPTER 5

F or several minutes Aaron stared quietly at the coffin. Then he studied
the crowd, his eyes coming to rest on me. "If Bones and his mystery
protégé taught me anything, it's this . . ." It was here that, having been held
at bay this whole time, Ashley's emotions surfaced. "It takes a shepherd.
That uniquely gifted loner, maybe someone who doesn't play well with
others, who is willing to leave the safety and security of the flock to find
the one. To suffer cold. Hardship. Injury. Darkness. Even hell itself. To
track the one. Rescue them from harm. Lift them out of hell." As he spoke,
a tear cascaded down his face. "And this shepherd is the most unusual of
persons. He or she is willing, by some innate character trait and gift of
God, to pay a steep price. One that may include their own life. Theirs is a
selfless existence. It's a me-for-you life. And it makes no rational or logical
sense whatsoever. It"—he touched his stomach—"comes from down here.
Down where our love lives. Where our hope is birthed. And our courage
takes root. I can find no other explanation. These are the Keepers of us.
Bones was mine. And without them we are lost."

He shook his head. "That day in my office, amid a haze of cigar smoke
and Bones's muddy boots resting on my desk, I asked him, 'What about
you? What will you do?' Bones drew on his cigar and let it out slowly. 'Kill
the wolf.'"

A minute passed. Wind blew. Cold cut through me. Ashley continued, "And he did. Doing so cost him his life. A life he willingly gave."

Another moment. "Two weeks after Bones died, given the information he was able to obtain, our agencies around the world have freed and rescued over ten thousand trafficked boys, girls, men, and women." He shook his head. "Ten thousand. Kids who are home now. Back in the arms of their loved ones. And yet they'll never meet the one who freed them. Never know his name."

Having followed the GPS coordinates on the back of their childhood picture and found Frank's data vault, Eddie and the team had immediately begun unpacking it. When he called me, I could hear his excitement: "It's all there. Names. Numbers. Addresses. Accounts. Videos." He paused to catch his breath. "Frank gave you the truth."

From that moment, they had coordinated with Ashley and the people underground, who then coordinated with teams and agencies around the world. And ten thousand walked free.

Bones did that. Under the guise of capture, he'd gone back. For his brother. Something I'd never considered. Never contemplated. And I'm rather certain Frank hadn't either. My response to Frank was to crush his windpipe. Douse him with gasoline and set him on fire. Given the amount of evil he'd inflicted on planet earth, why not?

But not Bones.

Bones suffered beating after beating to reveal to his brother the singular fact that while he'd known a way out of that hell on earth, he'd come back. Every day. Including that final day. Bones was sending a signal to his brother: I will never leave you. No matter how guilty. Frank had no box for this. In the end, Bones's actions shook something loose in Frank. Something buried. Something maybe even good. One second before he died, Frank gave up the location and codes to the closet where he held his secrets. The second-to-last piece of the puzzle. And thanks to Guido and Bernie's help, who had sung like canaries, Eddie and the team unlocked all of it. The last piece was the evidence he held over his seven generals. What he used to blackmail them. But that undoubtedly died with Frank.

In the end, what we saw play out on the world's stage was a conflict of kingdoms.

In Frank's kingdom, one man—without feeling or empathy—enslaved the innocent and bled profit from their flesh. A world where the one dominated the many. Concealed in shadow and pungent with the smell of death.

A slave market.

In Bones's kingdom, one man walked into that same market and said, "I'll buy them all." And when the slave master scoffed, "With what?" Bones paid it. With his life. This exchange was inconceivable to me, and yet Bones had known it going in and walked in anyway. As he descended into that putrid darkness, he tore iron bars in two and ripped prison doors off their hinges. It's why Freetown is called Freetown.

I could understand running through hell to rescue the innocent. I'd done that and inked the record on my back. A record of those who felt undeserving. Of the betrayed, rejected, and abandoned. But Bones not only emptied the market; he ran back into that same hell—the hell of hell—a second time, to rescue the slave master. Why?

This was my problem.

As the days passed and the answer built, it weighed me down. Pressing on my soul. Then, unable to keep it at bay any longer, I felt it hit me all at once. A freight train. Because he, too, was enslaved. Unlike the masses, Bones found mercy for his executioner. Whereas, in my mind's eye, I'd killed him a thousand times over, cutting off his head and posting it on a stake outside the city walls.

Wanting justice, I'd kept a record of wrongs. Payment to be exacted from the guilty. On my terms. It fueled and justified my need for revenge. But not Bones. Bones had kept a record of hope, recorded on his heart.

There's a difference.

What had found me as a boy on a river troller had carried me through the academy. Through Roger's betrayal. Through Marie. Through Key West, tending bar, and Karen. Through more than a hundred countries and three times as many rescues. Through gunshots, knives, hospitals, and infections. Through Angel and Casey and Clay and Ellie and Summer and Shep. Through Freetown and Frank, the two words that would define my life.

Then Bones.

I stared at that coffin and wanted to scream at the top of my lungs. I did not understand. Why Bones? Why?

Had Bones's last selfless act had any effect on Frank? Did it change anything in him? If so, was the gain worth the purchase price, or was his sacrifice in vain? I couldn't say. In my mind's eye, I stared at the picture of the two boys. Suntanned skin. A contrast of sunlight and shadow. Ashley was right: thousands of prison doors had been flung wide. Ripped off the hinges. Shackles loosed. And slaves walked out of darkness. Out of one kingdom and into another. One life for the many—starting with the one I'd written off. Who wasn't worth the cost. In my life, I'd been loved and loved much, but I did not understand that kind of love.

Ashley glanced at me. "Bones used to come to our Georgia farm and spend a few hours. Swim in the spring. Ride the zip line into the pond. Mimic Mountain Dew commercials." Subtle laughter. "Every time he did, I was mesmerized by two things: eight-pack abs and the number of scars carved across his body. How many? I don't know. A hundred or more I should think. He earned twenty-seven from one shotgun blast. Eleven from a knife fight. Four from a grenade. A dozen or more from being tortured in a Russian gulag. And this says nothing of those that riddled his insides. Car wreck. Plane crash. Helicopter shot down—twice. During his last medical exam, I required a full-body scan. He pushed back. I ordered. We counted seven separate bullet fragments still in his body, and enough buckshot pellets to kill large farm animals by lead poisoning. His skin was a road map, a history of war. A record of rescue. Of ransom.

"When swimming in our pond, our kids would point and ask, 'What about this one?' He'd tell them about the dragon who blew fire or the knight with a flaming sword or the damsel in distress in the castle—something to feed their imagination and not their fear. Bones's scars told a story. Of blood shed on behalf of another. Of payment exacted. Of light shining in darkness."

Ashley studied the rows of white stones. "In a rare self-reflective moment, Bones once told me, 'We are but dwarfs perched atop the shoulders of giants.'" A nod. "Bones is my giant." Ashley cleared the snow off the flag and kissed the coffin. Then he turned to leave but thought better of it. When he spoke, his lip trembled, betraying what might be rage.

"Since I heard . . . of his death, I have wrestled with many thoughts, but one keeps returning. We live in an evil day. An evil age. Darkness is raging. The light is fading. As long as we live, there will be wolves. But here's the question facing me. Us. Do we still have the stomach to kill the wolf?" A tear leaked down his face. Ashley pointed. "He did. One life for ten thousand." His eyes scanned the crowd. "I pray to God we do, because"—he raised a finger—"wolves hunt in packs." He paused. Swallowing. A moment passed. Then two. "How do you measure a life?" A long pause. "I measure mine by his scars." Then he tapped the coffin, which sounded hollow and haunting. "Because without them, I'm not here and I'm not me."

When he finished speaking, a decorated marine to his left shouted orders. Startling me. In the distance, a line of seven marines raised their rifles and fired into the air, cracking the silence in half. Gunner leaned against my leg, whining. More orders followed. Another volley of fire. A final order. A final volley. Ordinarily, twenty-one-gun salutes were reserved for presidents. But the president had given an order. As the smell of gun smoke filtered through the air, two marines folded the flag and presented it to the OIC. Officer in charge. He smacked his heels, palms up, flag held aloft, and walked in straight lines and ninety-degree angles, coming to a stop in front of the family member Bones's will had designated. "On behalf of a grateful nation." I extended my arms and accepted the flag, which weighed ten million pounds. When I did, something deep inside me cracked down the middle.

Normally, the military honors service held at Arlington National Cemetery would close at that point, those in attendance would leave, and then a dedicated crew would actually bury the coffin. But Bones had made a final request in his will. "Ask my friends to lower me down."

The only thing heavier than that flag was that coffin. As the rope slid between my fingers, tears followed. When it came to rest on the frozen earth below, Gunner walked to the edge, whining. Sniffing. Then digging at the dirt. Pulling. Trying to will Bones back to the surface and the land of the living. But he could not. We could not. Bones was gone. I heard myself say that and shook my head. How could this be? As the snow fell heavier, blanketing the world in white and silence, a lone bugler played "Taps" and I lifted the handle. One shovelful. Then two.

The slideshow returned. I had found him. Majorca. Lying in a crypt. Face swollen shut. Bleeding out. Gurgling. Lungs filling. Somebody had really put the leather to him. The light from my headlamp bathed him as I laid my hand across his heart. Checking his pulse. Letting him know I was there. "Bones, I'm so sorry it took so . . ." My pitiful attempt at an apology.

He feigned a smile and shook his head. Mercy in his eyes. "There's . . . nothing to forgive." Then he had pressed my forehead to his and kissed my cheek. His final blessing. His last act as priest.

Spilling earth onto the lid of his coffin, I looked inside me and found much to forgive. Starting with me. I could not forgive me. Not now. Not ever. When he needed me most, I failed. I had one job. Get Bones. And I had not. When I looked down, I saw Shep had risen out of Summer's lap, walked to the ledge, and placed his hands on the handle. Helping me shovel dirt. His eyes were large, round, and glassy as he stared up at me. I gritted my teeth. Forcing the air in. Out. In. Out.

And buried my friend.

As the parade of black cars exited, Summer kissed my cheek and loaded into the Suburban with Shep, Clay, and the girls. Leaving Gunner and me alone with a mound of dirt that now shrouded memory in darkness. I don't know how long I stood there. Minutes. An hour. Two. I was trying to find words, but despite the fact that I, David Bishop, had published half a million words in some seventy-five countries and just as many languages around the world, I found none. Words failed me. I knew it was time to go but I didn't want to turn my back on him. Didn't want him to see me walking away so I bowed slightly, stepping backward. In reverence. In re-spect. For love of my friend. When I did turn, I found myself alone save one man. Camp. Standing quietly at my six. Dark glasses. Dusted in snow. A sentinel to my sadness.

CHAPTER 6

Unable to sleep, I tossed and turned, finally climbing out of bed at 2:00 a.m. Summer reached across, asking, "Where you going?"

"Not sure."

"Want me to go with you?"

"No, I'll be al—" She was asleep before I finished the sentence.

I turned to Gunner, who was sitting in the darkness staring at us. "You too, huh?"

I walked into the ginormous bathroom of our suite, dialed room service, and made my request to what sounded like a bleary-eyed chef. But given the constant flow of diplomats from around the world operating in multiple time zones, high-end hotels in the DC area are more than accustomed to middle-of-the-night requests. So twenty-four minutes later, room service appeared at our door with a twenty-two-ounce ribeye grilled Pittsburgh, medium rare, along with a twice-baked potato and a bowl of chocolate ice cream. I carried the tray back into the bathroom and sat alongside Gunner. I cut the enormous steak into bite-size pieces and held the first piece next to Gunner's muzzle. He sniffed it and turned away, laying his head flat on the floor. I offered it a second time. Same response. With him having refused beautifully marbled prime Angus steak, I cut up the potato, salted it, lathered it with a generous dose of butter, and made the same offer. This time he didn't even lift his head off the floor, so I sank the spoon in the ice cream and offered it, even dabbing his nose—which he didn't bother to lick off, proving I was not the only one with a broken heart. I pushed the food aside and Gunner slowly placed his paw on my thigh and let out a deep exhale. I rubbed his head and lay down alongside him.

"I know, pal. Me too."

As I scratched Gunner's ears, the slideshow returned. At the start of my spring semester at the academy, I had returned to Colorado to find my entire academic schedule changed. Completely. When I tried to contact my advisor, he had been replaced by some guy I'd never heard of in some building I'd never entered in a far corner of the campus to which I'd never ventured. A dungeon of sorts. Off by itself and connected to nothing.

My knock elicited a terse "Enter" from inside. When I did, I found the white-robed eater of potato chips. Feet on the desk. Pieces of Nikon cameras spread about the room. Black-and-white pictures on the wall. This time he was dressed in BDUs, his black boots were polished, and the look on his face a little less passive. More chiseled.

"You're late," he said without looking at me.

His BDUs were not standard issue for the academy. The color and pattern were different. The one thing that did stick out were the markings on his collar, which said he was a colonel. A full bird colonel. I wanted to throw up. Given the depth to which I'd disrespected him in our last conversation, I was certain I was either headed to a military prison or about to receive a level of discipline I would not enjoy. Either way, my weeding out was about to start.

I had just run a mile and a half through falling snow, which was now melting, producing a puddle around me. "Sir, I want to apolo—"

He tossed me a key and pointed to a room next to his office. "Three minutes."

I held up the key and glanced at the room.

"Two fifty."

I held up my class schedule. "Sir, I think I'm in the wrong . . . Um, I didn't—"

"Two forty-five."

I was not an extraordinary cadet, nor did I really want to be. I didn't know how to play or navigate the whole political-military-ladder thing. I also had a tendency to pick and choose which orders I obeyed and which I didn't, which made me rather unpopular with those who gave them. But to my credit, I'd learned when to shut up. I opened the door and found a locker with my name on it. Inside, I found several sets of clothes, fleece sweats, shoes, boots, and BDUs that matched his—all my size and bearing my name. "Bishop." Having not been told what to wear, I pulled on something similar to what he was wearing and returned to his office. He threw a small backpack at me and said, "Follow me."

"Sir, I'm going to be late for my next class."

He pushed open the door and stepped into the snow and cold, the temperature hovering at zero. "I am your next class."

We ran out of his office, through the campus, and immediately up one of the mountains that served as a rather picturesque backdrop for the academy. He took the lead, picking his way up a narrow track with the agility of a cat and strength of a bear. I followed, amazed at his conditioning and fitness. He hiked like a mountain goat; never once did he stumble or misstep. When we reached the peak some forty-five minutes later, he wasn't breathing much harder than I was.

He sat, motioned for me to do likewise, and pointed to the trail we'd just run up. "You like my trail?"

"Yes, sir."

"But you could have run it faster."

I could have. "Yes, sir."

"Why?"

"Why what, sir?"

"Why didn't you?"

I shrugged.

The look on his face suggested he was about to speak *with* me and not *at* me or *to* me. A first. "Lesson number two: No shrugging. Indifference is the twin sister to resignation, and both will kill you and/or your partner."

Evidently I'd missed lesson number one but decided I wouldn't mention that.

He emptied the contents of my pack onto the ground beneath a rock shelter and said, "How 'bout a fire." I acted quickly. Feeding wood as the flames grew. Ten minutes later, as we ate the lunch I'd hauled up the mountain, he said, "Tell me about Marie."

I swallowed hard. "Sir, can I ask you a question first?"

Before he answered, he pulled out a small bottle of wine and poured himself a few ounces. Then he crossed one leg over the other and sipped. "Sure."

"I'm pretty confused right now."

Another sip. "That's a statement. Not a question."

I went right at him. "Who are you?"

"My name is Ezekiel Walker. My friends call me Bones."

As he spoke, I noticed a cross dangling beneath his shirt. Which struck me as strange. "How do you know so much about me?"

He weighed his head side to side. "Might need more wood for that conversation."

I added more wood, and we watched in silence as a bald eagle floated effortlessly on the updrafts below us. A minute later, it disappeared over our heads. He continued, "I come up here sometimes. To make sense of what I can't make sense of."

"What doesn't make sense?"

He sipped, and when he spoke, he stared through me. "Love in an evil world."

He poked the fire and added wood. "I was once a lot like you." He waved his hand across the academy spread below us. "Didn't fit in." A chuckle. "At all." More poking. "But I was good at a few things, so they kept me around. One summer break, I was camping my way across the west. Just me, my truck, and a skinny dog I picked up on a beach in Louisiana. One night about 1:00 a.m. at a truck stop in Montana, I was putting gas in the tank when a greasy fat man backhanded a scared kid, sent him rolling head over butt, and then threw him into the cab of an eighteen-wheeler. Something in me didn't like it. So I started listening. And with nothing

29

better to do, I followed that truck. To a hotel in Idaho. When the driver disappeared into a back door of the hotel, I climbed into his cab where I found the kid had been tied up and gagged. I carried him to my truck. He had his share of bruises, but it was the fear in his eyes I couldn't shake. I fed that kid a burger and watched from across the parking lot as the driver returned. Finding his cab empty, he raged and screamed—but he couldn't go anywhere because of the flashing blue lights surrounding him.

"A few hours later that kid's mother hugged her son while the father cried so hard his shoulders shook. Eight days they'd been looking for him—from California to New York and Miami. Eight days of torment that had split their souls down the middle." He paused and sipped again. "That father is now one of the heads of our government. You've seen him on TV. And . . ." This time he turned, and when he looked at me, there was a tear in his eye. "That boy is a cadet in your class. You know him."

"I do?"

"You disobeyed my order. Turned around. Went back. Helped him cross the line. Something he could not have done without you."

"Sir, about that . . ."

"When I tell you I know people," he said with a chuckle, "I know people."

I swallowed, my confusion growing by the second. "But how'd you get from here to—" I pointed at his clothing. "The robes."

He poured more wine and stared across Colorado and maybe into Canada. When he spoke, his voice was a whisper. "I also priest."

CHAPTER 7

T he words echoed loudly as I stood in the shower, remembering yesterday and the image of that fresh mound of dirt. I toweled off and stood staring into the steam-filled mirror. Mouthing the words to myself. It was the first time I'd ever heard him—or anyone—use that word as a verb.

We sat in silence for several minutes, the fire warming our backs. The cold freezing the sweat on our backs. "Sir?"

"Yes."

"Who was the other one?"

"Other one?"

I pointed at the obstacle course winding through the hills below us. "To turn back."

"You're not going to let that go, are you?"

"In case you haven't noticed, I'm alone here."

"So what good is the answer to that question?"

I shrugged. "Might help me feel not so alone."

He sipped without looking at me. "You just shrugged again."

"You dragged me up this mountain and made me carry our lunch—not to mention your wine—without much explanation, so until you start answering my questions and stop speaking in riddles, you can get used to my shrugging." Then I said what I was really feeling. "And you're right: if I wanted to leave you on this trail coming up, I could have. But I didn't think then nor now that we were competing. I was running 'with' you. Not 'against' you."

My boldness surprised him. He nodded, followed by a long smile, and then he stared into what I can only guess was memory. "In answer to your question . . . me."

I had a feeling he was going to say that.

"That surprise you?"

I shook my head. Another academy no-no. "Can I ask you another question?"

"You do that a lot."

"What? Ask questions?"

"Well, that too, but you normally start by asking if you can ask another question first."

"Well, can I?"

"Sure."

"Why'd you do it?"

"I've already answered that."

"When?"

"That was lesson number one."

There it was again. The mention of lesson number one. "Must have missed that one."

"Nope." Another sip followed by a chuckle. "You didn't."

We were perched at about ten thousand feet where the air was a bit thin. "You mind telling me again?"

"No need to."

"Why's that?"

"You carry the answer in your pocket."

When he said that, a giant unseen hand lifted the veil that hung between us. The veil of mystery he had used to disguise himself. As it lifted, I saw the mysterious, riddle-speaking man who sat across from me at the Seagull Saloon. Then, to remove any doubt, he turned around and pointed to the granite wall behind us where someone—no doubt him years ago—had scratched into the stone the same eleven words that had echoed in my mind since he slid that coin across the table.

Staring into the mirror in our hotel room, the steam drying on my skin, I lifted the worn coin from the counter and turned it in my hand, whispering the memory: "Because the needs of the one outweigh those of the ninety-nine."

If it could talk, what stories would it tell?

Sitting on that rock shelf at ten thousand feet, as the snow and wind bit my nose, I heard his voice and the memory returned—an experience akin to driving eighty on the interstate and throwing the gear shift into Park. Stuff was exploding beneath the surface. The connection that Bones had been the man to rescue eleven-year-old me out of Jack's death grip, and then sit across from me at the Seagull Saloon, sparked more questions than it answered. Why? How?

I reached in my pocket and pulled out the hand-polished and well-worn coin. "You're him?"

He eyed it affectionately and nodded. Then he reached in my pack, pulled out his Nikon, and snapped a picture of me with that realization plastered across my face and all of Colorado behind me.

When Summer and I had married, she'd found the picture stuffed in a dresser drawer. When I explained its significance, she'd had it framed and put it in our bathroom. Something to greet me at 2:00 a.m. Unbeknownst to me, when we'd traveled to DC for the funeral, she'd packed it and set it on the bathroom counter, where it now stared back at me. I toweled the steam off the glass, and the knowledge that he'd taken that shot washed over me like a flood.

At the time, I had protested. I had ten thousand questions. "But—"

He held up a hand and nodded. "In time." Then he eyed his watch and the airport in the distance. "Right now, I've got to catch a plane." He threw snow on the fire and looked at me with a smile I would later come to love. "Race you down."

CHAPTER 8

While Frank was dead, our problem was not. Frank had built his empire on the backs of seven generals. Men, and possibly women, he'd blackmailed. As best as I could piece together, all seven were powerful people who had committed some illegal act of which they were ashamed. And had been caught. By Frank. If the act were made public, the consequences could ruin them, demanding both public shame and long prison stints. When alive, Frank had held whatever evidence he'd obtained— probably high-def video and sound—of their sadistic crimes as leverage, using it to get what he wanted. Everything he did was predicated on those seven people doing what he wanted when he wanted, however he wanted. But by killing Frank, we had opened Pandora's box.

And yet, in a weird twist, Frank used that same leverage to make those seven individuals very wealthy. So while they wanted freedom from Frank, they liked the money, which in turn made Frank otherworldly wealthy. The deckhands are less likely to mutiny when the hull is full of gold. This created an odd tension in the down line of his pyramid scheme. Each of the players wanted off the devil's ship—but what about the money?

Frank's death had temporarily "freed" those seven people from the shallow electronic grave in which Frank held them. Or had it? What if Frank had programmed an electronic timer to go off in the event of his death and populate the internet with video of their crimes? A data dump of the worst kind. Further, what if he'd told them that would happen to incentivize them to keep him around? To not kill him? The twists here were many.

The question that had kept me awake all night was simple: What would happen now? In my experience, evil people with power usually want more power, and they are willing to commit whatever evil is needed to get more of it. Evil is the currency. Power the prize.

For decades, Frank had kept seven identities a secret. From the world and one another. They were never in the same room. Never in the same state and probably not even in the same country. This blind separation strategy was key to Frank's evil genius. Keep the inmates in solitary. Lockdown. Don't give them windows. But now that he was gone, what would they do? Would they ride quietly off into the sunset with their billions and just hope the video evidence of their previous crimes stayed buried with Frank? Hope that while they'd done the crime, they'd also done the time Frank had demanded—and given this, maybe, just maybe, Frank had been kind enough, or maybe indifferent enough, to let it go.

I tended to doubt it. This was the same man who had kept a running list of all the priests who'd abused him and then returned to hurt them. One by one. Savoring each broken bone. No, Frank was not about to let it go.

But how do you prevent mutiny, or prison break? One answer quickly rose to the surface. Fear. Which brought me back to my internet explosion theory. If I were Frank, creating an empire based on blackmail, I would have programmed some ticking electronic time bomb hidden in cyberspace that was set to go off in the untimely event of my death. And I would have made sure the seven knew of its existence. Meaning, if Frank wasn't around to routinely reset the timer, let's say every few weeks or every couple of months, time would expire and an explosion would occur that would then populate the internet with high-res pics and video. Destroying all their lives. This, in turn, would pretty much guarantee none of the seven would attempt to off him. But what if someone else did? What then?

Further, what if any one of the seven had somehow discovered the identity of any of the others? Would they go to war or form an alliance? Seemed like an alliance came with certain risks but would serve them better, at least in the short term.

The more I thought, the more the questions mounted, and I had answers for none. All I knew for certain was that Frank had successfully blackmailed them and done so over a prolonged period of time, suggesting he had enough evidence to keep them submissive and under his thumb. But where was that evidence? It was not in his data vault. Eddie and the team had made sure of that. Which meant he had buried it someplace else. Someplace separate. And while I wanted to find it, I was pretty sure there were seven people who wanted it far more than me and were tripping over themselves to get it.

I walked back through the problem in my mind. Free from Frank's tyranny, what would the seven do? I felt safe in assuming they would want to keep the evidence a secret, which meant they'd fight to find and erase it. But how far would they go? What happens when the inmates run the asylum? My thoughts raced, answers eluded me, and Bones's absence weighed heavy on me. I needed Bones now more than ever. Everyone at Freetown was looking to me for answers. I had none. If I was honest, I wanted nothing to do with Freetown. Didn't want to return. Didn't want to walk the streets. And I certainly did not want to walk into Bones's Planetarium. Too many memories. Each one ripping the scab off the last.

When in DC, I liked to run the monuments. Washington. Lincoln. Jefferson. Early morning hours when I could watch the sun rise over the Mall. Doing so helped put things in perspective. At 4:00 a.m., I pulled on my sweats and turned left out of the hotel. I needed to clear my head, and doing so would require sweat and prolonged exertion. When I looked at Gunner sleeping on the end of the bed and motioned toward the door, he lifted his head, grunted, and laid his head back down on Summer's foot.

"Okay. Keep an eye out." He grunted again but didn't move.

A block from my hotel, I noticed company running in the shadows over my shoulder. Dark sweats. Hoodie. Thick shoulders. Ran like a cat. I smiled. I liked Camp.

Camp was ex-military. Navy SEAL. He was active duty until an IED detonated beneath the vehicle in which he was riding, detaching both retinas and rattling his noggin. Surgery repaired both retinas and his vision, but between that and the concussion, he had been medically discharged. Mind you, against his wishes. So he used the military's money, went back to school, and floundered in the business program until he took a basic computer class and discovered his second set of skills. From there he dove into computing languages and took to them like a fish to water. Ever since, he could get into and behind anyone's computer. Including the president's. Which he did. Leaving him an electronic yellow sticky plastered in the middle of his screen. The note read, "I'm keeping my promise. Your security needs some work. Almost as much as your golf game." Then he listed his name, rank, and phone number. Since the president had hung a few medals around his neck, they didn't bury him beneath the prison. Instead, after a rather lengthy interview, they thanked him for the heads-up and hired him to work in cybersecurity. After eight years and bored with the political arena, Camp aged into his late twenties and kept looking for the excitement he'd been robbed of when the bomb went off. He's unmarried, lives alone, and visits his grandmother on the weekends.

I hoped he'd stick around but I also knew it'd be tough to keep him. A guy with his gifts and pedigree could get hired anywhere or run his own show. I had a feeling he'd been wanting to talk to me about his departure since we accomplished the job for which he'd been hired—that is, killing Frank. Summer had cautioned me that this conversation was coming. I guessed this run was about to be that talk. I appreciated that he waited until after yesterday. It spoke volumes.

Three miles in, I spoke over my shoulder. "You gonna stay back there by yourself or come up here and keep me company?"

He trotted alongside. "Just giving you some space."

He was barely breathing. The presidential helicopter zoomed low overhead. Not an uncommon sight. It was headed in the general direction of the White House. I tried to break the ice. "You thought about what you might do?"

"What do you mean?"

"Well, you three—Jess, BP, and yourself—did what we hired you to do. Frank's gone. I'm sure each of you have offers. I just want you to know I really appreciate what you—"

"Are you firing me?"

This caught me off guard. "What? No, I just—"

He stopped. Faced me. Again, proving I was breathing harder than he was. His face took on an intensity I seldom saw. "Is there work yet to be done?"

"What?"

"Is everyone free?"

I shook my head. "No."

"Then, unless you're firing me, I'd like to stick around."

"You're not quitting?"

"No."

I was confused. "You're not running alongside me because you want to give me your two weeks' notice?"

He shook his head. The look on his face suggested that was a ridiculous notion. "No. Why on earth would you think I'd do that?"

"Well, I just thought . . ." A pause. "Honestly, Camp, I don't know what I thought. That's been one of the difficulties without Bones. Knowing what to think. And maybe even how to think."

He put his hand on my shoulder. "Murph, it's okay to not know. It's okay to hurt. We're all hurting. We'll figure it out. All of us. Together. We've got your back."

Man, I really liked this guy. "So you do want to stick around?"

He laughed. "Yes."

We started jogging again. "Good, because good help is tough to find these days."

He laughed again.

I tried to correct my word choice. "Sorry, that came out wrong. I don't look at you as 'help.'"

"No offense taken."

"You should probably know when I was at the academy my superiors wrote in my file that I didn't 'play well with others.'"

"Yeah, I read that."

"You did?"

An honest shrug. "I do have a top-secret security clearance."

"Oh, yeah."

"You learned to work alone. I learned to work with a team. Both have their place." A mile later, he cleared his throat. "There is one thing I'd like to talk to you abou—"

This time I stopped running. "You want more money?"

More laughter. "No."

I was so confused. "I'll pay more."

"Okay, great, but that's not what's got me—"

"Then what?"

"I wanted to ask your permission."

"Permission? Permission to do wha—?"

No sooner had the words exited my mouth than a black SUV pulled up sharply alongside us and a man in a dark suit exited, wearing an earpiece. He stood next to the door, his jacket bulging with the imprint of a submachine gun hanging from a single-point sling. He nodded at me. "Murph."

"Bill." Bill Stackhouse had worked the vice president's detail for over a decade. Ashley's top man. If Ashley had sent him, there was a problem.

"Copper Top requests your presence." The fact that he used the vice president's code name revealed this was not a personal call.

CHAPTER 9

Seven minutes later, the Escalade deposited us at the United States Naval Observatory, at Number One Observatory Circle in northwestern DC. They led us to Ashley's office where we found him seated at his desk, head in his hands. When he saw us, he stood, shook my hand, and hugged me. "Murph . . ." A knowing nod. "He was the best of us."

"Yes, sir."

He extended his hand to Camp. "Commander Camp, been a minute since Afghanistan. Good to see you."

"You too, sir. Although not under these conditions."

Camp talked very little about his time with the teams. That he was, continued to be, and always would be a Navy SEAL was obvious. I experienced the SEALs' effect on him most often in his decision making. Camp was able to assimilate large amounts of information, make a decision, and execute a plan. Without regret or navel-gazing in his rearview, wondering what he should have done differently. He also possessed an uncanny ability to pivot when needed. "Flexibly rigid," he liked to say. Camp exuded what I knew to be a battle-worn, quiet confidence devoid of arrogance, and despite the fact I knew he had, Camp felt no need to prove himself. He'd been proven. Leading men in battle had done that. Where I was a loner and worked mostly alone, Camp had learned to lead men. The more time I spent around him, the more I learned. Camp's "mission first, people always" mentality had become a comfort to me, and I'd learned to trust him.

Completely. I'd also learned that while he was calm and collected, there was a simmering volcano below. It lay dormant until triggered by a switch somewhere near his heart. If he cared about a thing or person, you didn't want to trigger the eruption.

I glanced at Camp and raised an eyebrow, curious as to why he'd failed to inform me of prior missions conducted under Ashley's tenure as Secretary of Defense. In typical Camp fashion, he shrugged. *No big deal.*

Ashley's office was full of pictures. Dignitaries. Fellow pilots. World leaders. A few celebrities. But none of his family. Not one. Not even Esther. The two had decided early on that while Aaron had chosen the public life, his family had not. Therefore, while photographs existed, they did so inside the Georgia farmhouse. Not out. Esther and Aaron had no desire to place their girls in the spotlight. Political life was complicated enough without adding paparazzi to the mix. Two decades earlier, Esther and Aaron had promised each other that no matter where his career took them, they would live simpler, less digitized lives. Doing so would protect them and their children. If, when they were older, their children chose public service, then so be it. But they'd choose it. Not have it forced upon them. This meant they kept the outside world outside. This meant their kids grew up free, as much as was possible, from the distractions of the world. This did not mean they were Luddites. They owned a TV. They just seldom watched it, choosing rather to read than melt in front of a screen.

As their girls grew in both beauty and maturity, and given the top-secret security clearance of Aaron's work with Bones, phones and social media naturally became an issue. One of the girls fought hard to override. When Miriam, the oldest, bought her own phone and created her own social media accounts, Aaron brought all three to DC down underground. He let them see firsthand how evil people used what most thought were innocent posts, and what happened to the innocent girls who made them. Instantly, social media became much less attractive. The girls never argued again.

The fact that they desired to live quiet, somewhat secluded lives just made the media outlets want to know more and pry deeper. While that created a feeding frenzy with the camera crews, it ingratiated the family to the Georgia locals, who voluntarily created a buffer, or hedge, insulating Aaron, Esther, and their girls. As his popularity grew, and both life and election took him to DC, greater and prolonged media presence became an issue. To say nothing of the 24/7/365 Secret Service protection for the girls. Without some sort of change in protocol, strangers with automatic weapons would stand out in a South Georgia town. Aaron's appointment to Secretary of Defense and his election to the office of vice president only made matters worse.

All of this was an uphill climb because all three girls took after their mother and drew attention without trying. Six feet. Blonde. Having grown up on a working farm, the girls were strong, fit, and used to long hours and hard work. Miriam, sixteen, liked horses, never met a cat she could turn away, and cared for all the farm animals. She had her sights set on becoming a vet. Ruth, fifteen, was the dramatic one and had played the lead in several local stage plays. She was trying to convince her dad to let her move to New York. Sadie was fourteen, sassy, entrepreneurial, and could probably run a Fortune 500 company by herself. All three liked boys. All three pushed against the boundaries of their protection detail. All three could drive both a tractor and a stick shift and had no problem baiting their own hook or swing dancing. And all three dearly loved their dad.

Sensitive to the disruption his life might bring to theirs, Aaron hand-picked the teams guarding his girls. Folks with accents. Who'd grown up hunting. Raised in small towns in the South. Kids who'd milked cows before daylight and knew how to drive a tractor. When he was accused of profiling in reverse, with not enough diversity among his staff, he nodded in agreement. "You're absolutely right." He chose people who would blend in with the locals. Become invisible while not sacrificing his girls' security. And as the pressure and threats grew from political opponents and enemies, and threats and attempts were made on his life, Aaron strengthened the circle around his girls while trying not to make them feel the pressure. The price of service.

By now, Ashley's three daughters, at least in their own minds, were grown. They each knew and loved Bones, but none attended the funeral.

Too public. Too risky. Bones would understand. Aaron Ashley didn't have skeletons in his closet. He had not bought or betrayed his way to the top, so the media and his political opponents had nothing they could use against him. No moral failure. No cover-up. No place where he had said one thing and done another. Sure, they liked to take potshots at his edges, but nothing stuck. Unlike many in DC, Ashley had kept his word. As a result, his political enemies could not stand in front of him and trade blows toe-to-toe. Ashley was too honest, too true, too strong, too well-liked. If his enemies were ever to inflict damage, they'd have to circumvent. Run an end-around. Aaron knew this, so he spent considerable time and energy protecting his flank.

There was a second reason. What the public did not know was the extent to which Aaron Ashley was personally involved with the day-to-day operations of Ezekiel Walker and Murphy Shepherd. Given his political position, Ashley served at the tip of the spear in the rescue and return of the stolen. Not even Esther knew the details, but what Bones and I needed, Ashley obtained. Whether through private Senate hearings, appropriations disguised as military defense, or trips across the aisle with a request for a closed-door meeting, Ashley did the dirty work in the swamp while Bones and I dirtied ourselves in the world. Truth is, Bones and I could not have functioned without Ashley. At least not effectively. Satellites, electronics, drones, computers, data retrieval, intelligence, state-of-the-art technology, all of it—much of which was top secret—was provided by and filtered through Ashley's hands. The digital access that Eddie, Camp, Jess, and BP used to help us take down Frank was afforded to us because Ashley opened the door. Without our silent partnership, we were dead in the water. Nonexistent. This was a well-kept, highly guarded secret, known by only a few, and those few guarded it. In a very true sense, Ashley was our lifeline. Hence, no daughters at the funeral.

Following our freshman year at the academy, Ashley had become a bit of a fitness nut. Once soft, now not. As he grew into one of the nation's best pilots, he became a functional exercise freak: a push-up, pull-up, plank fanatic. I guessed his body fat percentage in the 4 percent range. In his early fifties, Ashley walked around in the body of someone in their late twenties. Certainly no wimp.

I don't know what I expected to see when I walked in, but a weakened Aaron was not on my radar. When Ashley tried to speak a second time, his knees buckled, and he sank backward into his seat where he sank his head in his hands again and closed his eyes. For the first time I noticed the circles. Aaron had not slept. Palming his face, his composure broke. Unable to speak, he motioned to Stackhouse, who pressed a button on the remote control. As the screen flickered, I watched the footage, alternating between horror and rage.

CHAPTER 10

shley's South Georgia home encompassed several hundred acres and, since his election, had become more fortified compound than farmhouse. From infrared, motion-activated cameras to more than a dozen full-time agents to dogs to needing three different randomly generated codes to enter the compound to roaming patrols to a sniper team on the rooftop, wrongful or unsanctioned access was next to impossible.

Or had been.

The video was a minute and forty-seven seconds and had been spliced together from six separate chest-mounted NVD cameras and military-grade thermal imagers. The videos followed well-trained operatives, communicating via hand signals, as they bypassed one security protocol after another: stepping over or around alarms and avoiding the more than twenty security cameras.

The position of each personal camera was also purposeful. It allowed us, the viewer, to see the operatives' hands, which, when not communicating with the team, were "speaking" to us through sarcastic gestures. Someone was playing out a well-rehearsed script: "We're in control. You're not."

The video started with a team of six exiting an SUV and then walking single file through rows of pine trees to the edge of a field, where the team paused long enough for one member to range the distance to the rooftop observation post, which I guessed at close to nine hundred yards. In the next two and a half minutes, the team exercised practiced efficiency as they eliminated nine agents: the sniper-spotter team, two in a "secure" guardhouse on the border of the field, one at the gatehouse, two at a side entrance, and two in a golf cart, maintaining the perimeter and drinking fresh coffee. Save the first two, the remaining seven died from suppressed 9mm rounds that severed the brain stem.

When the team reached the porch, they pulled on gas masks and slipped some sort of outer sole over their boots, entering the house through the kitchen and climbing the carpeted back stairs. They first stopped at the master, sliding a tube beneath the door and releasing a gas into Esther's room, which put her into a deeper sleep and eliminated her as a threat. During this part of the video, one member of the team pointed at the door, then the tube, then gave the camera a thumbs-up. The hands then pointed to the door and then a thigh-holstered Glock, giving the camera a thumbs-down. This message was also clear. The decision not to shoot Esther was intentional. They let her live. Which means they wanted her to suffer, making them emotional terrorists.

Their next movements revealed the depth of their intel. Ashley had given each of his girls a well-trained Belgian Malinois, and that information had never been given to the press. No pictures existed. The video continued as the teams entered each room. No wasted movement. Nothing to chance. This included the dogs—more emotional terrorism. The video then recorded their silent retreat out of the house carrying three young women back across the field, where they intersected and eliminated an unaccounted-for agent exiting the bunkhouse. The video then cut to double-timing through pine trees, laying the girls in the back of an SUV, driving several minutes, then stripping them and scanning their bodies. After the scan, they were zip-tied, blindfolded, gagged, photographed, and placed into three separate, blurred-out planes resembling private jets. As the taillights of the departing planes disappeared down the runway, one set of gloved hands waved to the camera like Groucho Marx, and the video faded to black, ending with "That's all, folks."

The clock on the wall told me they had a five-hour head start, which meant we were looking for the proverbial needle in a hayfield with almost nothing to go on. Camp, having already clicked into operational mode, cleared his throat. "How'd they overcome the sniper and spotter atop the house?"

Stackhouse stepped forward and played the video a second time. "They looped the thermal feed."

Camp nodded. "Watching the same thirty seconds over and over without knowing it."

Stackhouse continued, "Rendering the team all but invisible."

Camp nodded then spoke, again demonstrating his ability to synthesize and summarize large amounts of information. "They had prepped ingress and egress routes based on location of alarms and cameras. They knew where Esther would be and yet they didn't kill her. And of the eight upstairs bedrooms, they knew exactly where the girls were sleeping, they knew about the dogs, and they had someone in their ear with a bird's-eye view because they knew when to walk and when not to."

Stackhouse spoke next. "There's nothing they didn't know."

Aaron nodded. "And nine agents gave their lives . . ."

I had two questions. "Any idea why or what they want?"

Aaron shook his head but Stackhouse spoke. "No communication other than the video."

Camp spoke up. "I can think of two reasons."

Aaron broke the silence. "Revenge for the ten thousand, or . . ."

I finished his sentence. "To cripple your candidacy."

Aaron nodded.

Camp again. "Or both."

I nodded. "If this is an attempt to deter you from running, they'll keep the girls alive. Send you five-second videos of blindfolded, emaciated, whimpering girls."

"Death by a thousand cuts," Aaron said.

"Which will give us time." I paused. "If revenge, they'll start an auction, post them on the black web, and sell them to the highest bidder."

"Giving us much less time," Camp said.

"And . . ." Aaron had seen enough of these situations to know what would happen next. His girls had no physical experience with men and . . .

they were his girls. His worst fears were materializing before his eyes. He finished my thought: "They'll bring a premium."

Helplessness began to set in. When Summer, Angel, and Ellie were taken, we had the hope of the GPS trackers I'd put into the jewelry I'd given them. Given that the batteries were so small, the signal would only last a week, but at least we had that. There was hope. But not here. When Aaron's girls were scanned at the SUV, their kidnappers had stripped them of their watches and any other jewelry. Proving they were pros who had done this before, they left nothing to chance. We watched the video a third time, but it was so well edited and produced that it revealed almost nothing.

Watching it brought to mind our IT team, which was second to none. Eddie had come to work with us after I'd rescued him as a kid with a debilitating stutter, which had disappeared not long after joining us. Since then, he'd graduated MIT and knew more about computers, what made them work, and how to break into them than most anyone on planet earth. Second to Eddie was Jessica Peterson. Jess grew up with brothers, possessed a short temper, liked to run ultra-marathons in her spare time, and had a beautiful knack for making room for herself in rooms where she was not wanted or allowed. She had been abused by an uncle as a kid, even being loaned out to his friends, and did not need to be convinced that trafficking was then and is now evil. She had unmatched loyalty, slept little, and had never met a puppy she didn't want to keep. Rounding out the team was Ben Potterfield, the youngest of the group. BP had graduated Harvard at sixteen, top of his class, and, after refusing offers from every major tech company in the world, went on to develop several multiplayer video games that he later used as a back door to gain access into the military installations, strategies, and plans of America's enemies, which he then emailed to the president's personal account, cc'ing the Sec-Def and joint chiefs. He was as uncoordinated a human being as I'd ever met, could not walk and chew gum, wore Coke-bottle glasses out of necessity, and had a nasty battle with acne as a kid. BP didn't need us and he didn't need a paycheck. When I asked him why he wanted to work with us, he just shook his head. "I've just seen men do stuff." I had no idea what that "stuff" was. I figured he'd tell me when he was ready. BP was tender, had a huge heart, and was known to cry during rom-com night at the Planetarium. One of his video games hosted a tournament every year. World championship. Teams of two. He won it the first two years running under an alias but figured it wasn't fair, so now he just monitored the players' actions and movements because he absolutely hated cheaters. Couldn't stand them. And he could spot a fake, or the fact that someone was trying to hide something, a mile away. Of great benefit to a code breaker. And a rescuer.

Maybe Eddie, Jess, and BP could pull something from the footage Aaron had received, but I had my doubts.

He glanced at his watch. "In three minutes, I'm going to walk out of this room and share this with my team, who are going to unleash the combined military, intelligence, and media capabilities of the United States government to find my girls."

Camp interrupted him. "There's just one problem with that."

Aaron nodded while Stackhouse spoke: "Whoever did this knows that."

"And will always be two steps ahead," Camp responded.

Aaron pointed at Bill. "Bill and I flew together. If I can't trust him, I can't trust anyone. Same with you two. But outside of you three, Esther and I have decided we can't trust anyone. Because we don't know who did this, and because I do know they did it from the inside, I have to assume everyone from our intelligence service to military to my own Secret Service to my staff is compromised. I can't trust any intel they give me. I have no way of knowing if whoever quarterbacked this is halfway around the world or sitting in an office down the hall. I have to suspect everyone." Aaron folded his hands and looked at me, and something akin to anger flashed across his face. Finally, he pointed at Stackhouse. "Anything you need, he'll get it for you. No questions." He palmed his face and I saw, maybe for the first time, the full effect of the kidnapping on him. Torment.

I was reeling. And I needed to prepare Aaron. We had so little to go on, and without communication, we were dead in the water. How did I tell him the chances of finding his girls were slim to very slim?

Aaron looked at me. "One more thing." A pause.

"Years ago, Bones came to me and Esther and painted a picture. Not a good one. One that included my election to higher office along with my continued behind-the-scenes work to support him and you . . . and the risk to my family. He told me if I did this long enough and well enough, somebody at some time would try to take my girls. At first, we put our foot down." A pause. "Then Summer and the girls were taken . . ."

"Right." I nodded. "The watches. The jewelry."

"Yes, but Bones said we had to think a step beyond that and assume whoever would come at me would know that and find them, along with any secondary trackers in earrings or a necklace."

Camp gestured to the video but said nothing. His point obvious. They had.

Aaron continued, "The question became what next? How do we protect them beyond level one? Bones presented us with a subdermal microchip . . ."

My heart leapt. If Aaron had microchipped his girls, there was a sliver of hope.

He continued, "But Esther put her foot down. 'Nobody is inserting anything into my girls.' Said it was the 'mark of the beast.'"

Silence fell across the room as hope faded. Then Aaron palmed his face and looked at me. "Which makes me a beast."

CHAPTER 11

"What?" My voice rising.

Aaron spoke with his eyes closed. "It's an RFID."

Camp nodded. "A radio-frequency identification device."

Aaron continued, "It's passive. About the size of a grain of rice. Has no battery. Doesn't transmit a signal. But, when 'read,' it triggers a response."

Camp again: "Like a chip on a credit card. Which means a typical scanner won't pick it up because it's looking for a transmitter. Or a battery."

Stackhouse this time. "Correct."

"Do the girls know?" I asked.

Aaron nodded.

"How's it work?"

Stackhouse explained, "Like a QR code. Pass it beneath a camera phone and it triggers a response. That phone begins pinging cell towers, transmitting location. Unbeknownst to the phone's owner."

Camp added, "Scanning more phones. More beacons."

Aaron sat back. "Bones explained it like a homing beacon. Or a sonar ping."

"Provided your girls can get access to a phone."

"Bones was certain that would not be a problem."

I voiced the thought. "Whoever took them would photograph them. Photographs equal leverage."

Aaron nodded.

"How close do they have to be?" I continued.

Camp this time. "Less than a foot."

"Where is it in their body?"

Aaron touched the base of his neck.

"Who knows this?" I asked.

Aaron waved his hand across the room. "Us and my girls."

"Anyone outside this room?"

"No."

"Esther?"

Aaron shook his head.

I sat back, knowing the answer but voicing the question nonetheless. "But she has one too?"

Aaron nodded. "I convinced our doctor to manipulate lab results from blood work. Order a colonoscopy. He inserted it while she was asleep."

"But never conducted the colonoscopy."

"Correct."

"Wouldn't she know that?"

He shook his head. "Too small. You can't feel it."

That's when I knew Aaron had one too.

The room was silent for almost a minute. Finally, I voiced the elephant in the room. "So we wait for one of the girls to get access to a phone?"

Camp answered me. "Check."

Stackhouse flipped open a laptop. "We know they're working because when they were photographed before being placed on the planes, their facial shots triggered the locator." He tapped the screen. "We know where that phone is but have no idea if the girls are still within the vicinity."

Aaron finally spoke. "Murph, we've known each other a long time. Traveled some road together. I realize what I'm asking you is next to impossible, but . . ." He closed his eyes. "You deal in impossible. Have been since we met. I'm trusting you and only you." A pause. "I need you . . . to do what you do." This time a tear spilled down his cheek, betraying both fear and rage. "Bring my girls home. Alive." He feigned a smile. "Please."

"What will you do now?"

He glanced at his phone. "Call Esther."

"And after that?"

He pointed behind him to what was about to become the war room. "Fake it." Then his composure changed, and when he spoke, he did so as a combat pilot. As a man who'd dropped bombs, shot down enemy planes, and been shot down. "And figure out who did this."

He reached across the table and handed me a small box. "Bones put you up. Congress approved it last week."

After Bones rescued Ashley from the trucker's cab, he was vetted, his background torn apart, every decision unpacked. They must have liked what they found, because he was invited to join, and eventually run, an elite and unnamed government agency created by executive order decades earlier. An agency with a singular task: to seek out and return the victims of high-profile abductions. Meaning, the children of powerful people.

Bound by no geographical lines, the only rule was secrecy, which explained why Bones spent years vetting me. He had to know if he could trust me. To the end. And not only could he trust me, but could he pass the baton? Could I run what he ran? Our work was so clandestine, so hidden, that by design only a handful of people knew about the agency's existence, which was both good and bad. It meant we could operate undetected without a lot of red tape and make situational decisions quickly on the fly. It also meant we didn't get a lot of help.

Bones had taken the reins from the previous leader, who'd served several presidencies and begun his own impressive record of rescue and recovery. By the time Bones tapped me at the academy, he held a storied position among the Washington elite, where the rumors surrounding his abilities and successes had reached mythical status. As time passed and those forever grateful children grew into powerful people in their own right—men and women who owned powerful companies and took powerful jobs around the world—the extent and influence of Bones's own reach exceeded the extent and influence of many of those who employed him.

In short, Bones could do whatever he wanted, whenever he wanted, however he wanted, wherever he wanted, and he asked no one's permission.

A pedestal that even Bones admitted tested the limits of absolute power and its effect on those who wielded it. But his challengers were few and no one opposed him to his face. Why? Because of the long line of people behind him who owed him their life. Simply put, it was difficult to argue with a saved life. Especially if the bullet scars on your body tied back to that rescue. Bloodshed made for an argument without rebuttal. The problem Bones's success created was that of a successor. Who would take up the mantle?

I was oblivious to all this.

For me, the question that nagged at me was what Bones had been doing on the banks of my island when he rescued me out of Jack's bear-paw death grip. Why was he there? When I asked Bones, he simply shook his head and shrugged. As if the memory were painful. The issue unresolved.

The address in the locker had led me to a church in South Carolina. Bones had taken up lodging in the attached pastoral retreat that served priests from around the country, allowing them to rest, pray, walk in the woods, and restore their weary souls. In the year prior, Bones had recovered the governor's niece, but the question of who had taken her remained a mystery. Someone was hiding at the top. A single clue surfaced in her retelling of the story. The clue was a name. Had it been Mark or Jim or Bill or Bob, it would have mattered none at all, but it wasn't.

The name was Genefrino. And Bones had sent me to tear his playhouse down.

Once I started digging, peeling back the layers, I learned quickly that power was not shared, there was always one person in charge, and he who had the money had the power. Most nights Bones and I would debrief at either his pastoral retreat or some prearranged diner. For my education on the sick and detestable world of human trafficking, it was immersion by fire. I soon found out Bones had forgotten more than I'd learn in a lifetime. In my seminary studies, Bones required that I read the collected works of St. Bernard of Clairvaux, who had championed the doctrine of Christian humility, in which he stated we are all but dwarfs perched atop the shoulders of giants.

It didn't take me long to learn Bones was my giant.

I accepted the box from Aaron and opened it. A silver bird stared back at me. I shook my head once. "Sir, I don't want to be a colonel."

"Tough. You are now."

"But—"

He raised a hand. "Bones is gone. It was his wish. Who else will take his seat before the committee?"

I wanted no part of this. I spoke more to myself than him: "He knew he wasn't coming back. So he put his affairs in order."

As we were speaking, someone knocked on the conference room door. Stackhouse opened it and whispered with a staff member. Closing the door, he looked to Aaron. "Sir, Senator Maynard is requesting five minutes."

Aaron nodded to Stackhouse.

CHAPTER 12

Waylon Maynard was a six-term senior senator from Oregon. During his tenure in DC, he'd been on every committee possible and was known affectionately as "the power behind the throne." Common knowledge was if you wanted to get elected, you should make sure Waylon was on your side. His nickname in the swamp was Oz, as he was thought to pull all the right levers. But to his credit, in over four decades of government service, he had not used those levers to enrich himself. Only others. It was why he was so endeared. Waylon didn't seek power for power's sake. He sought it on behalf of others to accomplish good. He'd been asked multiple times to run for president. To rescue both his party and the country. But he'd refused. Never accepted the nomination, choosing instead to put the full weight of his political currency behind candidates he believed in. Like Aaron. Which was good because Waylon had never lost. Widowed at a young age, he never remarried and had never been tainted by scandal.

Harvard undergrad, Yale law, Stanford MBA, he was one of those rare individuals who slept two to three hours a night. As senior member of the Senate, he currently served as president pro tempore but, after two terms, turned down his party's nomination to continue as majority leader, citing the need for younger blood with more energy. During his political career, Waylon had advocated for orphans in Kenya and, following civil war, built orphanages with his personal money in war-torn Sierra Leone. But it was his work to combat HIV/AIDS across Africa that crossed the aisle and earned him a Congressional Medal of Honor. During the ceremony, when the president asked why he spent so much of his personal time and money helping on the African continent, he responded, "Because they can't."

That three-word response became a mantra for the downtrodden, landed on the front page of every paper in the civilized world, and fast-tracked Waylon for a Nobel Peace Prize, which he won. Waylon had done more to bring nations together to combat poverty and disease than any other living member of the government. The only thing he had not done was ascend to the presidency, a role he said he did not want and would not accept. "I'm not right for the job. This country needs a leader who can make tough decisions in difficult moments, and I'm not him. I cry too easily." His response only endeared him more, and threatening to resign from the Senate was the only way he escaped the nomination.

Waylon Maynard was a rare bird. A man of his word. At seventy, he said he was aging out of politics but wanted to put his muscle behind one more horse. That horse being Ashley. He told the networks Ashley's candidacy would be his swan song, and he could think of no better candidate. Waylon had sat on or chaired every important committee and currently swayed influence in Armed Services, Banking, Finance, Foreign Relations, and Homeland Security.

In an attempt to summarize the giant who was Waylon Maynard, the *Post* said this prior to his last reelection, in which he ran unopposed: "Senator Maynard may not have his finger on the button, but he controls the power source that fuels it. Without Maynard, the United States government has no button." Two years ago, Waylon capped a seminal career with a number one *New York Times* bestselling memoir called *For God and Country*. The book sat atop the charts for twenty-two weeks, producing millions in royalties—all of which he donated.

I had little experience with Maynard. What I knew of him I drew primarily from news reports or interviews. He was rounded, a little portly, and reminded me of Edmund Gwenn, who played Kris Kringle in the 1947 production of *Miracle on 34th Street*. You couldn't not like him. There was nothing to dislike.

Aaron nodded, Stackhouse stepped aside, and Maynard entered the room. In a day sliced into three-minute segments, Waylon was not one to suffer fools or waste time. He was cordial but he didn't beat around the bush. Didn't waste either your time or his. And if Waylon Maynard had a gift, it was reading a room, which he did, causing him to swallow whatever he was about to say. Having been in enough top-secret conversations where difficult and painful decisions were being made, he clued into this one quickly. Waylon stopped in his tracks, studied our faces, then sat at the table and unwrapped a peppermint. Placing it in his mouth, he loosened his tie, motioned to his assistant to bring him a coffee, folded his hands, and said, "What can I do?"

Aaron turned to me. "Murph, you don't get to choose your promotions. Just whether you're in or out."

"I'm in, sir. You know that."

"And it is that singular fact that brings me any comfort right now."

I patted Aaron on the shoulder and Camp and I exited his office with far more questions than answers. Truth was, I had no answers at all. All our hope was predicated on Aaron's girls obtaining access to a phone. I agreed that chances were good they'd get photographed at some point, or have access to a phone where they could open the camera and "read" their own RFID. But what if that didn't happen? What if they were dead already? One phone was already pinging, but we'd seen the girls leave on three different planes. At least that was what they'd wanted us to see. Did the owner of that phone fly with one of the girls? Did the girls actually fly out, or was the video manipulated to make us think they did? Were they on one plane or three? Or two? Had the owner of the phone already passed the girls to someone else?

I worked to silence the hopelessness that simmered beneath the surface. I had to assume they were alive. And that they'd fight to stay that way. Until then, we were looking for a needle in a hayfield the size of planet earth. One thing I knew for certain was that whoever made this video was playing for keeps. Whoever did this wanted to wreck and destroy Aaron Ashley. I also knew one other thing. This would be the first time in my life

I'd attempted to find someone without Bones looking over my shoulder. No sounding board. No quarterback. No voice in my ear. And yet somehow Bones had known I'd be here, and he was here too, speaking. Or pinging. From the grave. Bones was dead and gone, literally washed out to sea, yet somehow his voice echoed from the deep. Giving us hope. Without him, where would we be in this moment? Camp saluted and extended his hand. "Congratulations, sir."

Lost in my thoughts, I stared at the eagle. "Thank you."

"Permission, sir?"

"To?"

"Speak freely."

"Please."

"You don't seem too excited." He pointed at the silver eagle. "Congressional approval and the president's signature. There are guys who work a lifetime and never get there."

"It's not why I do what I do."

Moments later, Camp asked me why I was shaking my head. I spoke the only answer I knew to give. "Then Bones."

CHAPTER 13

The black SUV passed beneath the streetlamps that shone down on us in DC's pre-dawn darkness. Maybe it was the intermittent flash. Maybe it was the headlamps of oncoming cars. Whatever it was started the slideshow of Bones's life and death across the back of my eyelids. Unwelcome and uninvited, it returned for the ten thousandth time, and I did not care to see it. But it didn't care what I thought, so it kept rolling. Wave after towering wave. Shattering me on the rocks.

This one started a little earlier. My junior year at the academy. About the time I'd started to find a rhythm. One night we were rappelling in a sideways snow, several hundred feet of darkness below us, temperatures below zero, eighty pounds on my back, couldn't feel my fingers, and he motioned to arrest my descent. Pointed to a ledge where I could rest my foot. Watching the stars above us, he wiped his forehead and waved his hand across Colorado spread out before us like a twinkling blanket. Tethered to the earth, suspended between heaven and hell, Bones spoke the words I'd never forgotten. I could recall them word for word.

In the years since, I'd come to look back on the "snow and granite speech" as one of the most important in my life. It was an inflection point. Something had changed in me. Bones had transferred something from his heart to mine. A knowingness. A grounding. Those words spoken would become my bedrock. My anchor. My tether to the universe. "People in darkness don't know they're in darkness because it's all they've ever known.

It's their world. They navigate by bumping off things that are stronger. Immovable. We, those of us who walk up here, have a tendency to look down our noses at them, but the truth is this: they don't know darkness is darkness until someone turns on a light . . ."

I shook my head and silenced the memory. I could not listen. As the city of DC passed beyond the windows of the SUV, I muted Bones's voice. Hearing it hurt too much. My world had grown darker and the light dim. And I had no answer for the question that hounded me. Who would keep mine lit?

I had no answer. I also had no answer for this growing agitation. This sense of vengeance. A volcano simmering beneath a thin mantle. We had lost Bones and evil had won. Evil had taken Bones. Because of this, my mind spun. Turning one question over and over: Was I bent on rescuing the innocent or making the evil pay?

I knew the answer and it wasn't good.

Bones's last act on this earth, the last lesson he'd taught me, had been to walk back across a scorched battlefield, descend into hell, and rescue the one I'd not thought worthy of rescue. Proving Bones was motivated by something I didn't possess. Didn't understand. The closest word I had was *love*. The real kind. The kind that says me for you. Even when you don't care. Don't love me back. When your every intent toward me is evil. I had no words for that kind of love. It was otherworldly. And if I'm honest, I didn't know it. Didn't have it. And I was pretty sure I didn't want it. Yet it was the very thing that had sent Bones back for Frank.

Camp touched my arm. "Hey, Boss. You in there?"

I nodded.

He tapped the flashing blue dot on his phone, indicating that he and Stackhouse had connected Camp's phone with the phone used to take the pics of the girls. "Thirty-seven thousand feet. Flying west." It made sense. Whoever it was would be moving. When Camp spoke next, he looked uncomfortable. "You want to sit this one out? Let me go it alone? I can recon, call you with updates. You can quarterback from here."

I just looked at him. I'd never said no.

He pressed me, saying, "It's just that I've been in some tight spots, and if your head's not right, you're a danger. Both to you . . . and to me."

He was right, but what was I going to do? Sit on a park bench and talk with him through an AirPod?

Camp's reaction told me he was picking up on body language I didn't know I was sending. In my pain, I was unable to hide my emotions. An occupational hazard. Doubt consumed me, rage simmered below the surface, and a part of me was screaming "No!" at the top of my lungs. Despite my friendship with Aaron and the brutal fact that his innocent girls were being tormented and held against their will, I wasn't sure I could handle what I might find. And I was pretty sure I didn't want to. What if they were all dead? Or worse, abused by a hundred sick reprobates and then dumped overboard, leaving us with the video evidence of their abuse and torture? How would I tell Aaron? Esther? Just how could I break that news?

There was a lot I didn't know, but I was pretty sure I didn't have the stomach to know it all. I closed my eyes to a slideshow on loop. It doubled down, pressed me to the seatback, and would not let me go. I simply could not shut it off. It had become a roller coaster with no stop, no exit, slowly click-clacking its way back to the top before it plunged again.

CHAPTER 14

At the academy, I had lived the life of a normal cadet. At least on the surface. Beneath the surface, I was anything but. Like Bones, I had learned to live a double life. When my class earned a forty-eight-hour pass, Bones would blindfold me, drive me hours into the mountains, drop me with what I carried in my pockets, and say, "Find your way home. And don't ask for help." Which of course I did. I'm no dummy.

Sometimes he'd wake me at 2:00 a.m., drive me to a truck stop, order eggs and coffee, and then ask me the color of the waitress's eyes and what the tattoo on her ankle said. Then there were afternoons when he'd take me far into the dungeon that comprised his world, and he'd teach me weapons systems. Loading. Unloading. Aiming. Trigger reset. Malfunctions and how to fix them. If it breathed fire and went "boom," he made me learn what allowed it to do that. Every piece. And how to make it work to my benefit.

One afternoon, he handed me a fifty-year-old rifle with ammunition that didn't come close to fitting it and shut me in a supply closet, telling me, "You can come out when you fire that thing." The lesson taught me to look outside the box and use what was available. Somewhere toward midnight, I shot a segment of copper tubing through the two-way glass through which he watched me.

And then in what was possibly the strangest turn of events, Bones walked into the weapons closet of the dungeon where I was cleaning a rifle and handed me a stack of strange-looking books. "Congratulations. You've been accepted. Class starts Monday. Tests every Friday. First two years are online. Get the requirements out of the way. Last two you attend on campus, which shouldn't be a problem."

I glanced at the titles. "What are you talking about?"

"Seminary."

"You must be joking."

Bones considered this. "I seldom joke and I never kid." Both of which were lies.

"But I don't want to—"

"And," he said, cutting me off, "you can't be enrolled there and here simultaneously, so I changed your name."

"What?"

"To God, you'll be known as Murphy Shepherd."

"Stupid name."

"Maybe, but it's yours, so get used to it."

"It's still stupid."

He didn't let me finish, which was his way of saying I had no say in this matter. "One day soon, you're going to encounter people in prison. Often the bars that hold them will be of their own making. It's one thing to unlock someone's prison door; it's another thing entirely to loose the chains that bind their heart." He tapped the barrel of the rifle. "To do that, you're going to need to know how to do more than just poke holes in them."

Thus began my first day of seminary.

Bones's seminary was as much a mystery as he was. When given the obscure Greek name, Google produced a website and pictures of a campus in Spain with satellites in Italy, Austria, France, South Africa, and, you guessed it, Colorado. Having been founded or chartered by the Catholic Church nearly a millennium ago, the college—if you could call it that—didn't follow standard academic protocol whatsoever. They had no desire at all to do anything that would keep or allow for accreditation of any kind. They couldn't care less. Also unique to the school was the one-to-one professor-to-student ratio. Throughout the course of his study, each student worked with one professor. A priest. Don't like your professor? Tough. Don't like your course of study? Too bad. And while administrative offices with a physical address did exist in Spain, Italy, and France, the institution had no formal classrooms. Class location was determined by the priest.

About three months in, having not slept for much of that time, I asked him, "Just when am I supposed to sleep?"

He shrugged. "Beats me."

"You do realize that the human body needs sleep."

He shook his head. "Overrated."

More often than not, our "classroom" was our lookout atop the mountain, which became a welcome break from the sterile mathematics of the academy. Strangely, and despite my initial protests, I enjoyed the seminary assignments and found myself engrossed in the writers, thinkers, and philosophers we read. What I noticed throughout my course of study was that, while the academy taught me to calculate—and to do so effectively, efficiently, and with relative speed—Bones was teaching me how to think outside that well-defined box. Both were needed but each was made stronger by the other. While my fellow cadets accepted deployments throughout their summers, I was attached at the hip to a riddle-speaking, wine-sipping, white-robed priest who was not so quietly disdained by his colleagues, more often rogue than team player, and—while older than me—the strongest human being I'd ever met.

The contradictions were glaring.

As was my continued lack of sleep. While my fellow classmates snored in their bunks up and down the hall, I slept, at best, one or two hours a night. Several nights a week I slept not at all. Meaning, I constantly bordered on sleep deprivation. Weeks felt like one long day. Much of my waking hours felt like an out-of-body experience and left me a little edgy.

A few months later, when the reality of my workload hit me, I threw one of the books at his head and asked him, "Why on earth do I need to know any of this?"

He looked at me as if the answer were self-explanatory. "Because you can't fake it."

"Fake what?"

"Priesting."

The fact that Bones used the word as a verb told me a lot about him. All told, 99 percent of my time and experience at the academy was dictated by Bones. When I asked him how he got away with such a singular existence amid such a military mindset, he just smiled. "I know people."

Years would pass before he made the introductions. Those "people" were Aaron Ashley, his father, Esther, and his three daughters. Who had just been snatched out of their beds in the middle of the night and were currently flying naked, blindfolded, gagged, and zip-tied across the United States. An unspeakable horror.

The last time my heart felt this helpless, I was mourning the loss of Marie. Which was when Bones showed up at a bar in Key West and said, "Tell me what you know about sheep."

So I had. I picked up my pen and vomited my pain across the page. Transforming pen to scalpel. Cutting out the gangrene. My own pen had probed the wound in me. But sitting in that SUV, having lost my captain, I doubted the power of that knife. And what was worse, I had no desire to pick it up. Why? Because I wasn't sure I could handle the pain of what it might find or remember. I wanted nothing to do with the written word, because to write it out meant I had to hear my inner self say what my inner self didn't want to hear. "I lost Bones."

There it was. I said it. I had lost Bones. And when I said it, a spear entered my chest and exited my spine.

Camp's phone flashed in front of me. I saw it. The flashing blue beacon. Indecision in these next few seconds could cost one of the girls her life. Time to make a decision. Made all the more difficult given Bones's burial yesterday. My own girls were hurting and I was not there to comfort them. Protect them. Another spear that pierced me. If we had any chance at all of finding Aaron's girls, we needed to move now. Not return to the hotel. Not detour for any reason. Nothing mattered more than that flashing beacon because it was all that connected us to the girls.

Bones echoed in my ear, *Bishop, this is what we signed up for. This is what we do. It's who we are. We go. We don't count the cost. We go no matter the cost. The question you need to answer is, "Why?"*

Bones had his answer. I was struggling with mine.

I spoke to the driver and sat back. Camp looked surprised. "What about the hotel? Summer? Don't we need to . . . ?"

I shook my head and didn't answer. I didn't have one.

Staring at my reflection in the glass, I could tell I was bleeding out and needed triage. I just didn't know what to do about it or how to stop and get it. Nor did I have time to figure it out. Three young women were in a bad way, and Camp and I were their only hope. I leaned my head against the glass and knew one thing for certain.

Those girls needed me. And I needed Bones.

CHAPTER 15

As a general rule of thumb, Bones was looked down upon by most everyone else at the academy. People thought of him as a token spiritual advisor who'd been given some plush, no-responsibility assignment because he knew somebody somewhere—although no one could say just who. Seldom seen without a Nikon camera around his neck, he wore nerdy glasses and occasionally taught a class when it didn't interfere with his schedule of torturing me.

Given the mystery, rumors swirled about his backstory. The most popular suggested that twenty-five years earlier he'd been a cadet who dropped out after his first love shunned him for another. Adding insult to injury, she accepted a career on the Vegas strip, which now explained his self-imposed life of celibacy. The second theory bubbled up from the "Coexist" bumper sticker on his Prius and centered on the idea that an undisclosed experience in the summer of his junior year caused him to dig into his soul. When he did, finally getting in touch with his real self, he discovered—to no one's surprise save his own—that he didn't believe in war and violence. Of any kind. True to his conviction, he quit wearing leather, refused to fire a weapon, and went completely vegan. The academy didn't know what to do with him, so they politely showed him the door.

Whatever the case, and however it had happened, he was dishonorably excused from the academy, whereupon he backpacked to Italy or Spain or some such place to study something other than war. Following his foreign education in all things pertaining to God, he responded to a "calling" and returned here by invitation to sway other misguided souls like his own from a wayward life of war-mongering because someone somewhere thought it a good idea that the cadets have a well-rounded academic education free from bias and bigotry. If nothing else, he would serve as the voice of the opposition.

In other words, the general consensus was that Bones was completely useless.

Which was exactly what he wanted.

Yet during my time in the academy, I knew of twenty-seven high-profile abductions and subsequent rescues that took place in more than sixteen countries—about which Bones never spoke a word, and yet for which I knew he was singularly responsible. Somehow he did all that with astounding secrecy. Everyone around me thought him the court jester while I knew him to be viceroy for the king.

Thanksgiving break of my senior year, I'd been granted a ninety-six-hour pass, and my only desire was to get home to Marie. Waiting at the gate for my plane to board, Bones sat down next to me and handed me a picture of a little girl. Pigtails. Not yet ten. "We have forty-eight hours before they transfer her across the border and she disappears."

I tried not to look at the picture. "Bones, not now . . ."

He waved the picture in front of me.

"What do you want me to do?"

"Bring her back."

"I'm . . . ," I stammered, "not you. I'm not qualified. I don't know anything about how to—"

"Experience is not transferrable."

Another riddle. The flight attendants were calling my seat. "What's that mean?"

"Some things I can't teach you in a classroom. Some things you have to learn on your own." He pointed through the huge glass windows of the terminal. "Out there."

"Why don't you go?"

He showed me a second picture. "Can't be in two places at once."

I held her picture in my hand.

Three days later, as I sat exhausted in the driver's seat of a cattle truck departing from a Mexico border town in Texas, having never seen Florida or Marie, I found I had learned a good deal. First, this line of work—if you could call it that—required not only the ability but also the willingness to pivot on a dime without thought. To change plans at the drop of a hat. No matter the emotional connection or damage. Second, this line of work cost far more than it paid.

But when I pulled into Dallas and the mother of that little girl who slept on the bench beside me lifted her off the seat and sobbed as she held her to her chest, I knew I'd pay that cost.

Ten thousand times over.

Bones was right. Experience was not transferrable.

Staring out the passenger side window as the overcast shadows of DC faded, I questioned, maybe for the first time, whether I would pay that cost now. Whether I wanted to. Then the girls' faces flashed across the back of my eyelids. I shook my head. Caught in a tension I didn't want and a war I was tired of fighting. If I'm honest, I was mad. Mad at Bones for leaving.

We pulled into the private airport where we were met by an Uber blocking access to the plane. Summer stood against it, arms crossed, hair blown across her face. Gunner leaning against one leg. Camp cut me off before I had a chance to ask. "Wasn't me."

That meant she was tracking my phone. I exited the SUV, and she walked toward me. Her body told me she was bracing for impact. It reminded me of the night I watched her steal a boat and head south down the Intracoastal when she didn't know where she was going and couldn't swim. Indomitable. Proving that in many ways, she was just tougher than me.

She placed her palms on my face. Her hands were warm, tender. As was the look in her tear-filled eyes. Trying to laugh, she said, "Gunner was tracking your phone."

"He's like that."

Her head tilted sideways. "I don't know why you've got to go; I just know you do."

I nodded as a tear trickled down my face. She swiped it with her thumb and kissed my cheek.

She paused and lay one hand flat across my heart. "I know you're hurting. Cracking down the middle. You feel as though part of you is dying and half the world is sitting on your chest. Every breath is an effort. Sailing on a ship with no captain. You don't know who you are or how to be who you once were or whoever you're supposed to be tomorrow." She nodded. "I get it. I do. But . . ." She pounded gently on my chest. "Let me tell you what's true." She inched closer, then motioned toward the plane. "At the end of that flight is someone. Or someones. And they're praying somebody will kick down the door and rescue them. Praying somebody will lift them out of the hell they're living in." She poked me gently in the chest. "You're the answer. So go do what you do and . . ." When she spoke, her lip trembled, revealing her inability to hide her own pain. "Remember Bones is always with you."

Oh, how I love this woman.

"Oh, and one more thing." She stood on her toes and made sure she had my eyes. This time when she spoke, she couldn't control the tears. "Murphy Shepherd . . ." She patted my chest with her palm. "I need you to bring David Bishop home. 'Cause I can't live without him."

I kissed her. Then kissed her again. Gunner and I boarded, where we found Camp madly typing on a laptop. Seated next to him was Clay, reading a newspaper. He glanced over the top of both his readers and his paper. "Murph."

I nodded.

He set the paper down. "I got the arthritis. Eyes ain't what they used to be. And I shuffle a little. But"—he held up his cane—"I'm pretty good with this, and"—he made a fist with the other hand—"I ain't afraid to use this." I smiled, cracked open a bottle of soda water, handed it to him, and motioned to the pilot, who began taxiing. Clay sat back and leaned his head against the rest. "Thought for sure you were going to tell me I couldn't go."

"Would it do any good?"

He shook his head. "No."

The pilot pushed the stick forward, and we shot heavenward. Turning to Camp, I eyed the flashing beacon. "Heading?"

"Generally? West. Eddie's tracking the plane. No destination yet. Want to follow it?"

"Yes, but we need to make a stop."

Camp spoke without looking up from his screen. "Check."

CHAPTER 16

Landing in Freetown, I exited the plane and was met by the muffled silence of fresh snow. Eddie met us and drove us back to the house where everything I needed sat waiting in the basement. I punched in my code, L-O-V-E-S-H-O-W-S-U-P, and only when my fingers had punched Enter and the door swung open did I listen to myself say the words. The reminders were everywhere. I couldn't escape them. I walked into my vault, my safe room, and sat at a table. Staring at the weapons of our warfare. Most everything in there breathed fire and rained down terror on those who would inflict horror. Because I didn't know what we'd need, I pulled NVDs, two thermal scopes and viewers, a Benelli M4, a suppressed 300 Blackout, and Jolene, my .300 Win Mag. I then grabbed enough magazines and ammunition to unload hell on whoever held Miriam, Ruth, and Sadie. Finally, I lifted my Sig 220. The last time I'd carried it had been in the tunnels with Bones. I closed my eyes, press-checked the muzzle, dropped the magazine, and allowed my index finger to tell me it was loaded to capacity, then reinserted it. But when I opened my eyes and stared down the sights, something caught my attention. Something I'd missed when I last cleaned it. Blood. I tried to rub it off with my thumb, but it had married to the metal. I held it in my hands, remembering. After I found Bones, I'd attempted to carry him. My shoulder under his. Arm around his waist, hand tugging on his belt. When I did, his blood had drained out his side and down mine, where it came to cover the rear sights.

I dropped the magazine, cycled the slide, and cleared the chamber. I'd never ventured out that door without the Sig Bones had given me, but I would tonight. I wasn't going to clean it, and because I wasn't going to clean it, the blood remained. That meant if I carried it with me, every time I stared down the sights, I'd see the reminder that I'd failed Bones. Which would not help me rescue Aaron's girls. I shook my head. I felt like more was being stripped away, and I didn't like it. I returned the battle-tested pistol to my safe when something else caught my eye that I'd not seen. Which was strange because it was orange.

Tucked in the back of my safe, hidden from view, sat a new orange Pelican case. One I'd not seen prior to my hasty departure to find Bones, so I lifted it out and set it on the table. Turning it in my hands, I saw the box was identical to Bones's iconic box he'd carried through all the years I'd known him. The box that had carried all he held dear: his personal Sig 220, flashlight, pocketknife, and various other odds and ends, not to mention the ever-present really good bottle of wine. Tied to the handle was a tag, written in Bones's nearly indecipherable handwriting: "Bishop." I sat back and stared. Bones used my real name when he wanted to get my attention. And he only used my last name when he really wanted to get my attention.

I clicked open the box and raised the lid, where I found a card sitting on top. It read:

Murph,

Merry Christmas. Before you open the contents of this box, the three gifts held within need explanation. First, when I first gave you the venerable Sig 220 now so many years ago, I did so for several reasons. I knew it would go "boom" when needed, which it has. It is supremely reliable and has certainly earned a place of honor. I also liked the .45 ACP as a cartridge and bullet with which to defend yourself and others. Both the pistol and its round are battle-tested and proven. And I certainly don't want to get hit with one again. But over the three decades we've been doing this thing called rescue, companies have made significant improvements to the 9mm, which has now been transformed into a formidable defensive and offensive cartridge. In many ways, superior to the venerable .45. You know this as well as I, as you've grown comfortable with the Glock universe. So with that in mind I've included the enclosed. It has been made for you by the custom shop of CZ USA. They wanted to express their gratitude for your work in bringing home one of their own. Now, before you ask, yes, I'm a fan. I have often carried one similar to this when in foreign theaters and .45 ammunition has been difficult to commandeer. I'm old school and an old dog, but having said that, if there's any handgun on planet earth that's been more battle-tested than our Sig, it may well be this one. You will find when you look below this card, there are two. Identical. Suggesting that the folks who sent them were doubly grateful. One carries your name, the other carries mine. I look forward to carrying mine alongside you. As with every weapon, I hope you never need it, but when you do, and my guess is that you will if you do this for more than about five minutes, I pray it does what it was designed to do—and does it every time.

Second, when you were young and I met you at the diner, I passed to you a coin. Something I'd carried in my pocket inscribed with eleven words as a constant reminder of why I do what I do. Since then, you've carried it in yours, but the years have worn the inscription and made it difficult to read. I guess that's what happens when you bump up against bullets. Maybe the same can be said of you and me. But if there's one thing you and I cannot suffer, it's blurred vision. We need to see clearly. Without obstruction. The moment we blur the lines, we lose. We lose our edge. Our conviction. And possibly even our life. So I submit this chain and freshly minted medallion as a concise refresher that will hang around your neck and dangle over your heart. Because it's our hearts that need to hear, that need to be reminded of what our minds take for granted.

Third, I submit this box. In Bones's world, everyone should have one. I don't know how people make it through this life without an indestructible, watertight box to keep stuff in. I mean, seriously. How do you protect what's dear? I've never figured that out. At any rate, here it is. Merry Christmas. Oh yeah, I almost forgot. The bottle. I guess that makes four. Take Summer on a date. Lord knows she's earned it. Enjoy.

> Your partner and brother in arms and in
> all things good,

> Bones

I set the card down and read it again. Then a third time. I needed to hear his voice. Dangling the chain over my hand, I read the inscription. Clear. Deep grooves. Made of bronze. Bones liked bronze because it could pass through fire and come out the other side refined. Which was how he looked at us. Passing through fire.

I lifted the bottle and set it on the table. A dusty bottle of Deerfield Ranch Cabernet. Next, I studied the two handguns. A matched pair of CZ 9mms from their custom shop. The word *Murph* had been laser cut into the slide of the first, and *Bones* into the second. Murph and Bones.

Never to work side by side again.

In all my life, all the rescues, all the confrontations with bad guys, in the thousands of places I'd carried a handgun, I wanted to think I'd never taken this thing for granted. It was a tool. That's all. A well-crafted tool that could blow fire and deal mayhem when needed. It wasn't a toy. Wasn't something to be romanced through video games or talked about ad nauseum via chat on some forum. It had one purpose. To stop bad men from hurting me or someone I loved. Period. If they died in the process, that was their problem. The old adage "God made all men, but Sam Colt made them equal" had merit. I'd known guys who were gun nerds, and I was not one of them. Guys who collected for the sake of how it looked on their wall. How it added to their collection. How it contributed to their cocktail conversation or how they thought it improved their status in others' eyes. I didn't view this thing as something to be collected. I viewed it like I would a spoon. Or a shovel. Or a hoe. A particular instrument designed for a particular purpose. I knew full well what it was capable of and what

I was capable of with it. I also knew that in the annals of handgun history, few were more storied than the CZ staring back at me. Maybe the 1911, and certainly my Sig 220, but while both had seen massive civilian and military adoption within the United States since their development, the CZ had seen much greater use worldwide.

I also knew that if Bones had given it to me, he'd had a reason.

As the pain of that realization kicked me in the gut, I hefted the new CZ, dropped the magazine, cycled the slide, press-checked it for confirmation that it was empty, then dug through Bones's holster bag where I found two thigh holsters custom fitted for the CZ. I ran my belt through the loops of the holster, strapped it to my thigh, and began loading magazines. I would not be wise to take an untested firearm into a situation where I needed it. In my experience, the two worst sounds in the world were "boom" when you were expecting "click" and "click" when you were expecting "boom." Walking into our underground range, I pulled on earmuffs and slowly emptied a magazine on paper targets seven yards downrange, focusing on my front sight and trigger reset. I was amazed at how well it cycled, recoiled into my hand, and grouped on paper. After the first magazine, I emptied a second. Then a third. And somewhere in between my eyes and the target, the slideshow continued.

CHAPTER 17

A week before graduation day at the academy, I submitted my final thesis required for Bones's self-imposed divinity degree. Forty pages on one verse in Scripture: Matthew 18:12. When Bones handed it back, he'd written one word on the last page. "Pass."

"That's all I get? Pass?"

He shrugged, wrote "Nice Job" next to it, and handed it back a second time.

I held up the pages. "I put a lot of work into this."

"I can tell. And . . ." He raised a finger. "Truth be told, you're not a bad writer."

I would remember this in the years to come. And the smirk he wore as he often reminded me how he recognized first what so many have since come to know.

As I worked to obtain my seminary degree, Bones had served as my only advisor and professor. When he handed me the diploma, true to his word, it had been made out to Murphy Shepherd. The fake me.

"What good is this if I can't take credit for it?"

He responded, "You didn't get it so you could hang it on the wall. You got it because you can't fake it."

I raised a finger. "Correction. I got it because you made me."

"You could have quit at any time."

"You picked a fine time to tell me."

He smiled.

That same day, he had handed me a box and said, "Inside are three things you might need. The first is something to help you arrive on time. Hopefully you'll use it because you're always late." Which was a lie. I'd never been late. But he knew this. "Second, there's a memento of our time together. Something to remember me by. On the other hand, you might need it. And third, a letter."

With that, Bones turned and walked away. No goodbye. No "Nice job the last four years." No "Have a nice life." No "Thanks for the memories." Just his backside walking away. To be honest, I had expected as much.

I opened the box and did in fact find three things. The first was a Rolex Submariner. The time had been set five minutes fast. A note attached to it read:

There are two reasons for this. You didn't quit when I gave you every reason. Your life would have been easier, but easy is overrated. You should get something for tolerating the hell you endured.

Bones's gift was exorbitant. I'd never owned a nice watch. Certainly nothing like this. And I'd worn it and carried it through a million miles with Bones, only taking it off when I gave it to Ellie, who'd worn it every day since as a reminder that her dad loved her and would come for her.

The second item was a Sig 220. Bones's letter had continued:

Do this long enough and you will find that the two worst sounds in the human ear are "boom" when you're expecting "click" and "click" when you're expecting "boom." This one has always gone "boom" when I needed it, which has been a comfort on more than one occasion.

The last was a key taped to the letter. It continued:

This fits two doors, both of which lead to the rest of your life. Unlock door number one and I'll give you a recommendation for any job anywhere or grant you any military assignment you desire. You pick. Walk through this door and I can guarantee you a fast track to advancement and compensation on Easy Street. The world at your feet. You've earned it, and I owe you this much. In the years I've been scouring talent for someone like you, you're the first not to quit. Congratulations. The previous thirteen bailed and told me where I could stick certain things. That makes you either crazy or just simply better. I'm still trying to decide which.

Door number two is a little different, and before you unlock it you need to know that, once you walk through, there's no turning back. No "Can I get off now?" No "This isn't what I signed up for." No "Oops, I changed my mind." You make up your mind here and now and you live with it. No matter the cost. For the rest of forever. That's the price you pay. If you don't like it or if this somehow offends your sensibilities or if it is hurtful to the child housed within you, then don't insert that key into this lock. Because wrong motives, malicious intent, or a half-baked, half-cocked, "Why not?" naivete only lead to a lifetime of regret. And probably you dead in some ditch or quarry or mine shaft on the back end of the earth with no one to hear your last breath.

Given that you're still reading, I gather I've piqued your interest. What then, you might ask, is the value of door number two? If door number one is cash, prizes, and life laid out on a silver platter, why would anyone in their right mind choose anything else? Why not just ride the gravy train into the sunset? Unfortunately, there's only one way to know. I will tell you this, and I'm qualified to speak because I walked through the door before you: there is something more valuable than money. Although you will have to dig deep to find it. I cannot promise you that door number two will lead to all your dreams coming true. In fact, a few will be shattered. But walk through it and I can promise you this: one day you'll look inside and amid the scars and the carnage and even the heartbreak, you'll find something only a few ever come to know.

CHAPTER 18

S tanding in our shooting range, where Bones and I had together put thousands of rounds downrange, I stared down at my feet where over two hundred spent shell casings lay. Bones had chosen well. The gun simply worked. I could trust it.

Returning to my safe room, I returned to the case and only then noticed the single key lying loose on the bottom. A nondescript key, tarnished by age and including no explanation. It didn't need one. I knew the key. I used it once and it had opened the door to my life. How could I forget?

I sat back. Staring. Bones was right. Shattered dreams, carnage, and heartbreak, mixed with something few ever came to know. The dichotomy of my life. If one thing represented all the emotions in my life, all the experiences I could not define in words, it would be the locker key staring back at me.

I shook my head, feeling the weight of it. Wanting to lift it but not wanting to. Finally, I unclasped the chain now hanging around my neck and threaded the chain through the hole, letting the key rest alongside the medallion, then let it fall, dangle, and rest over my heart. When finished, I policed my gear and turned for the door, where I bumped into Camp.

"You good?" he asked.

Uniformity was one of the first principles of a team. Written in stone. Bones and I had always carried the same weapons platforms in the event one of us ran empty. We could lean on our partner to get us what we needed and get us back in the fight—that is, a loaded magazine that fit the weapon in our hand. As a SEAL team member and later commander, Camp had carried primarily Glocks, although he'd trained with most everything. Including Sigs. But Glocks were what he'd trained with and learned, through experience, to trust with his life. Which he had done. He did not take the choice lightly. But personal choice always took a back seat to the needs of the team. Right now, I was his team lead. He knew as well as anyone that CZ magazines did not fit Glocks. I hefted Bones's CZ and asked, "You familiar with this?"

Camp nodded, feeling no need to explain.

I offered it along with Bones's holster.

He received both, dropped the magazine, and cycled the slide, eyeing the inscription. "You don't mind?"

I shook my head. "And I don't think he would either."

He studied it. "Seems like we should put this one up somewhere. Safekeeping."

"He was never one to just hang something shiny on a wall. He'd want it to be used. Not collect dust as a safe queen."

Camp nodded as he turned it in his hand. "Took one off a guy in Germany one time. Always wanted to carry it."

I pointed to the range. "Function-test it first."

"Check." Camp returned twenty minutes later having done so. He tapped his phone. "They're headed to Kahului."

I considered this. "R&R in Maui?"

"Maybe. Eddie's in his phone. It's a burner. Limited call log. Few contacts. He's looking into calls received but nothing so far. I imagine he'll ditch it once he lands."

We loaded up and were attempting to leave my safe room when Clay filled the doorway. Which he did by default. His voice was four octaves lower than that of any other man on earth. "Got something in there for me?"

I handed him the Benelli. He sized it up. "I was hoping for the wine."

I handed him the bottle and spoke to them both. "I'll meet you at the plane."

I exited the house with Gunner on my heels and pulled my hood over my head against the cold. The temperatures were in the teens and snow dusted the air. We set off down Main Street while Freetown stretched out before me. Sunset on the free. A sight I never tired of. Shops were closing. Restaurants were bustling. A local singer/songwriter named John T played live music on a stage to my left. Girls and their families were gathered on blankets or huddled around firepits while the young crooner wooed them with his vocals and a mesmerizing hand on what appeared to be an old Martin guitar. Some song about a cowboy's last ride. I liked it.

I stayed in the shadows. Back in the trees. Observing. Listening to the laughter. It was where this town got its name. The universal sound of freedom. I found myself in the Planetarium. Sitting in the corner. Leaning against the wall. Staring at the slideshow. Given the facial recognition installed by Eddie and requested by Bones, my face populated most of the pictures. Bones had asked Eddie to program the software to "read" the faces of the girls who walked in and then project a higher percentage of photos of them on the wall. He did that for several reasons, but maybe the biggest was this: The beauty of each one of us is matchless, and each one of us is worth celebrating. Most girls, boys, anyone who had been trafficked, got to a place where they no longer believed that. Where they doubted their own worth. Their value. This slideshow in the Planetarium reversed that. It put their fifteen-foot image on a pedestal and told all the world, "I am worth rescue."

Because each one was.

I sat along the wall, staring at the ceiling. Watching pictures of me. Holding hands with Summer. Running to the Eagle's Nest. Sitting in the beauty salon while Ellie and Angel laughed through my pedicure. Bones and me eating a sub at the deli. And then the town favorite, Gunner. Licking my face.

I'd known pain in this place and I'd known great joy. The real kind. Bones had been the spark. The reason this place existed. His absence was akin to a black hole in my universe. I honestly did not know how to walk out of here and go be the guy who kicked down doors without him. My internal voice of self-doubt was screaming at the top of its lungs. Gunner lay next to me. Whining. He hadn't been right since the burial. Since he tried to claw Bones's body back out of the dirt. I rubbed his ears. He opened his eyes and looked at me but didn't lift his head. He was hurting too. I knew nothing I could say would help, so I pulled him into my arms and just held him.

"Hey, pal."

He opened one eye.

"We got to go to work."

He stood up, then sat.

"But I need to ask you to do something."

Gunner tilted his head sideways.

I held out my hand, palm up, and he placed his paw in it. "I need you to be careful."

He half moaned and tilted his head the other way.

"No superhero stuff. We play this by the book. I don't want you getting hurt." A pause. "Not sure I could handle that."

He lay on his stomach, paws stretched forward, head high.

"No kidding. No funny stuff. I'm not in the best place right now, so I need you looking over my shoulder. I need your A-game. I'm not firing on all cylinders, not too sure about my ability to make good decisions, so if you see me doing something . . ." I scratched his ears. "I just don't want to get either you or Camp hurt."

He licked my face. Then he sat and barked once.

After takeoff, I thought of the single key now hanging around my neck and stared out across the sunset, wrestling with the memory of Bones's initial letter to me. Knowing what I knew now, would I have chosen what I chose then? Would I walk through door number two with the same idealistic naivete? Because now I stood on the other side of it. And on this side, I'd watched Bones die. Door number two led to the sound of a single gunshot followed by a splash as Bones's lifeless body slammed into the water a hundred feet below.

If I could go back to graduation day, what door would I step through? I closed my eyes and leaned back against the headrest. I had chosen door number two for reasons I couldn't even now qualify. I just had. I couldn't not. But now, three decades later, having watched Bones disappear, having inked the record of rescue on my back as the slaves had once done in the coquina of the chapel on my island, would I choose the same? Would I choose door number two?

For some reason, I glanced at the floor below Clay's seat where a stuffed tiger lay on its side. Left there by Shep after our trip to DC. I knew he'd be missing it about now. I placed it on the seat next to me, closed my eyes, and knew there had never really been two doors. There were not then and there were not now. No matter my pain. No matter my heartbreak. My life had one door. The question was not which door I would walk through, but would I walk through the single door staring at me now? I had a feeling the question would present itself about the time we found whoever was in possession of the phone producing the flashing beacon.

And my problem was not the question.

CHAPTER 19

We landed in Maui and navigated via a rented four-door Jeep with aggressive mud tires, making us look like surf bums in search of a rush. The warmth and gentle breezes were a stark contrast to the cutting winds in high-altitude Colorado. We landed ninety minutes after the beacon, which, according to Eddie, ventured to a barber shop, a liquor store, a grocery store, a tattoo parlor, and finally a cellular phone store before coming to a stop in the parking deck of a Marriott overlooking the water. It then wove a serpentine path through the grounds to the elevator of an eight-story timeshare, riding the elevator to the top-floor penthouse. Eddie was in his phone, so he'd been listening to the guy talk. American. Maybe Midwest accent. Tough to tell his age but probably midthirties. He did not invite conversation, didn't engage in it, and drew little attention to himself other than his stop at the tattoo parlor where he shared a beer with the owner and had some ink added to an area on his arm. Even then, his conversation was cryptic. The guy was good and had been living beneath the radar a long time.

We sat in the parking deck and Eddie piped in the guy's phone. The noise was muffled as the phone must have been in a pocket, but when he entered the penthouse, a female voice emerged. Enter character number two. They greeted each other, then it sounded like grocery bags were placed on a counter, along with some keys. Five more minutes passed while they greeted each other again, and then we heard what sounded like a pocketknife opening, followed by sounds we couldn't immediately make out until Clay said, "He's cutting open a box."

Thirty seconds later, the flashing beacon stopped flashing and the phone went dead. He'd just burned his burner. But he had one problem. Wi-Fi. His own. Everything from lights to thermostat to the coffee maker was controlled through some rather advanced smart technology with, sadly for him, a weak firewall that Eddie, Jess, and BP broke through in less time than it would take to pour a cup of coffee. Once inside, Eddie had access not only to the phone that had been there when the guy arrived but also the new one that just booted up, along with the cameras and the speakers attached to the cameras. In terms of technology, we owned him. The guy was toast. He just didn't know it yet.

The interior cameras proved that given both his build and his gait, he'd been one of the two snipers in the video as well as the one whose hands gave sarcastic signals to his chest-mounted cam. Whether or not that made him the commander of the unit I couldn't say, but it did make him somewhat cocky as well as really good at his job. He had just walked into the home of the vice president of the United States and walked out with Aaron's three daughters all while showing a level of black-gloved humor. His hands made light of a massively egregious crime. Which suggested to me that he'd done it before. Like he was numb to the depth of depravity of his own work. I knew very little, but I knew enough to know that he was comfortable being bad and this was not his first rodeo.

Fifteen minutes later, the duo rode the elevator down and exited toward the ocean. He was tanned, maybe even Hawaiian, long black hair pulled up in a bun, tattooed sleeves on both arms, muscled, zero body fat, and the aware-ness of a cat. His girlfriend, or the girl with him, looked like an Amazon and a former member of the Swedish Bikini Team. The two made quite a sight, which I tended to think he liked—attracting attention without attempting to attract attention.

They sat alongside the pool, and he ordered drinks from the cabana boy who delivered two umbrella drinks shortly thereafter. Clay, Camp, and I rented a room in the adjacent dog-friendly high-rise with views overlooking the ocean—and pool. Over the next two hours, the man ordered several more Mai Tais as well as a plate of nachos, all while appearing to read a novel.

Camp studied him through binoculars and shook his head. "You won't believe this."

I knew it before he said it.

I could tell he was smiling as he spoke. "You want me to tell you what novel he's reading?"

"No." I shook my head.

At sunset, the two meandered down the beach, and if the alcohol in his six Mai Tais had any effect on his cognitive or motor abilities, he didn't show it. They walked down to where a crowd of fifty had gathered and were boarding a large catamaran sailboat for what looked like a sunset cruise. Which it was. They boarded, were served more drinks with umbrellas, and then sailed along the shoreline under a picture-perfect sunset.

Knowing they were a captured audience gave Camp and me time to investigate their penthouse. Which turned up nothing of real value other than a prescription med bottle in his dope kit, which, after Eddie ran the name, proved not to belong to him. The owner had died six years earlier but was interestingly still collecting retirement. The search proved the guy was smart. As the sun faded and the boat returned to offload passengers onshore, Clay called and updated us, as did Eddie, who was watching in real time on satellite.

Camp and I exited, Eddie cleared the alarm history, and we waited as the duo returned, showered, and then once again descended the elevator, walking the short distance to the oceanfront steak house where the maître d' welcomed "Mr. Smith." To which Clay commented, "Well, he just lacks any creativity whatsoever."

After dinner, they stopped at the bar for a nightcap and then ascended the elevator to the penthouse. An hour later, the internal security camera system showed him brushing his teeth. Just before turning out the light, he reached into his medicine cabinet, lifted out a prescription bottle of pills, dropped one or two onto his tongue, and swallowed. Proving Camp's suspicion that he was nursing pain or an inability to sleep. Or both.

In studying people, if you are patient, sooner or later you can detect a chink in their armor. A weak spot. Evidently Mr. Mai Tai had been in this line of work a while and had the requisite injuries to go along with it. An hour later, he was snoring. As was she.

He was surprised when we turned on the light and doused him with cold water and a fan set on high. Even more surprised when he attempted to move and found himself naked, blindfolded, gagged, and zip-tied to a chair in the kitchen. After Eddie had disabled the alarm, we entered the penthouse and gave them both the same treatment they'd given Miriam, Ruth, and Sadie, aiding their ability to sleep deeply. So while Amazon Woman slept it off, Camp gave Mr. Mai Tai a second injection and woke him up for a little conversation. The clock was ticking, and if I'm honest, I was losing my patience. We'd sat around long enough. When I asked Camp where he learned these methods, he just shrugged it off. I was beginning to think I needed to get five or six beers in Camp and loosen his tongue. Get him talking. The problem was, he seldom drank.

I sat in front of Mr. Mai Tai and made sure I had his attention. How is not important. Only that I did. I then ripped off his blindfold, flipped his laptop around, and pushed Play so that his own recorded video began to play. His reaction convinced me he'd been down this road before. Even sat on my end of it. He relaxed. Completely. I watched his breathing return to normal. Amazing, really.

When I took the gag out of his mouth, he said nothing. Just stared at me. Waiting. So I stopped the video when it showed the three girls sprawled unconscious in the back of the SUV. "Where are they?"

He was trying to get the words "I don't know" out of his mouth but didn't. I lifted the syringe from the table, pressed out any air in the needle, and slammed the eighteen-gauge, two-inch needle into his thigh muscle. Having emptied the syringe, I laid it on the table. "That's enough fentanyl to kill a horse."

I then laid a Narcan inhaler on the table. "You have about six minutes." A pause. "Give or take."

CHAPTER 20

I tapped the screen a second time and waited.

He chose his words carefully. "It's obvious you've done this before. And it should be obvious to you that I've done this before. Can we skip to the end?"

"Love to."

"I have a team. Six members." He nodded to the video. "We're expensive. We work word-of-mouth only. I never know my employer." This much was probably true. He continued, "We got a phone call some thirty-six hours ago."

"How'd they find you?"

"Initially?"

I nodded.

"Word-of-mouth, which led them to an address."

"Where?"

"Black web."

"What's the address?"

He answered out loud, which gave Eddie a chance to run it from his desk in Colorado.

"Why initially?"

"Last night was not our first job for them."

"How many?"

He calculated. "Two dozen."

"How do they pay?"

"Transfer. Same as everyone else."

"Did you know who you took last night?"

"Intel provided the details, yes."

"How'd you get behind their walls? How'd you know their routes?"

"The voice in my ear provided all that. We were simply meat and labor. Breach. Eliminate. Extract. Video. Wash our hands."

"Where are they now?"

"Team or girls?"

"Either, but I'd prefer the girls."

While I'd been speaking, Camp had taken a close-up pic of his face and identifying tattoos, scanned his fingerprints, and sent all of that to Eddie, Jess, and BP, who I imagined were rapidly running all that information through secret government databases. Mr. Mai Tai shook his head. "Can't tell you. And before you start ripping out fingernails, cutting off parts of me that I'd rather keep, and pouring water up my nose, I've done all that too. Chances are good I'll last a while. Time you can't afford." I tended to believe him. He eyed the syringe. "And time I don't have."

"Your employer?"

He shook his head. "Don't know. Don't care. Don't want to. Occupational hazard. I know they're serious when they wire the retainer. Then we go to work."

"What's your retainer?"

"Hundred grand."

"These folks pay it?"

"Times five." He nodded. "Then again when completed. Which explains why I'm on vacation in Maui . . ." He looked toward the bed. "With her."

If this guy wasn't such an evil turd, I might have liked him.

"Girls." I inched closer, my breath washing his face. "Location."

"Delivered to a runway. Extract was handled by a team I didn't know. Didn't know the pilots or the teams. They separate cells on purpose. We only know so much. Can't trace it back to them."

"What can you tell me?"

Camp flashed his phone in front of me, showing brief details about Steve Plexis. Former special operator, three tours, decorated, served with distinction, did not reassimilate well after leaving the military. Got sideways with the VA hospital over surgery and meds. Later, spent time in three federal prisons on drug and laundering charges. Camp adjusted the screen to show me a picture of two girls. One little. One trying not to be. The first was eight. Pigtails and a dress. Laughter. Innocence. Too young to know any better. The second maybe eighteen. Purple hair. Not happy. Beauty behind her eyes but definitely some daddy issues.

I turned my attention back to him. "What do you care about?"

About now, I had a feeling he was telling the truth. His eyes shot to my phone, to the empty syringe, then back to me. "Iris and Rose."

Flower names. Interesting. "And they are?"

"My daughters."

This struck me. "And yet you took three of someone else's, stripped them, gagged them, bound them, photographed them, and delivered them to the highest bidder."

He nodded, studying us. As I was formulating the next question, a flash occurred in front of my eyes, followed by a nasty, bone-cracking sound and a scream. Steve's forearm had been snapped in two by Clay's cane, and one end of the bone now protruded through the skin. Steve's eyes rolled back and forth in his head as he fought to shed the pain. He tried to gather the words. Finally, he spoke. "I do see the hypocrisy."

I held up the picture. "Which one's Iris?"

He began sweating profusely and I began to smell urine. "Younger."

I sat back and turned the Narcan inhaler in my hands. "Steve . . . help me help you."

CHAPTER 21

The look on Steve's face said the pain was excruciating and the fentanyl was starting to mess with his head. I held up the picture of Miriam, Ruth, and Sadie. "Steve. They matter. You don't."

"And my girls?"

I shook my head. "I'm not like you."

The relief on his face was palatable.

I glanced at my watch. "You might have sixty seconds."

I placed a phone in front of him.

I knew he could easily call someone and use predetermined words to signal that he was under duress. Need help. Come heavy. I'd done it with Summer. "Midnight ballet." I also knew that he probably knew that I knew.

He eyed the phone. "If I initiate contact in the next seven days, they'll know I'm in a bad way. You won't have much time."

"I expected as much. I'd feel let down if you didn't have protocols. Who else can you call?"

He spoke the number from memory. I dialed. It rang twice when somebody with a thick New York accent picked up. "What!"

Steve attempted to sound like he was not in pain. "Problem with the transfer."

The man cussed and responded, "No. You're milking me." Followed with more cuss words mixed in for color.

"Follow the money. Where'd it come from?"

"An offshore account. Transferred in from another offshore account that came from a third and so on."

Steve tried to sound tough but his resolve was waning. "Do you make money off me?"

"Don't start that. I perform a service."

"Do I have friends?"

The vulgar, accented voice on the other end didn't sound so certain at the mention of "friends." "Hey, I don't rat on you. And I don't rat on your customers."

Steve's eyes rolled back in his head and stayed there for several seconds before he shook it off. "Not asking you to rat. Asking you to text me the trail of transfers."

A pause. I heard keystrokes in the background. By now, I was pretty sure Eddie had discovered the identity of the mysterious voice on the other end. Anything more out of him was gravy. "Check your phone."

Steve motioned to me to hang up, which I did.

"That will buy you a little time, but not much. When . . ." Steve eyed the phone. "He gets to drinking tonight, he'll get mad, rerun this conversation in his mind out loud, at the bar, and then he'll start dialing for sympathy. Eventually he'll dial one of the guys on my team. In a few hours, they'll figure it out." He looked around the room, then at me. "Then we'll start hunting you."

"I'd be disappointed if you didn't."

What Steve didn't know was that as soon as we left this room, Stackhouse and a few of his government buddies were going to enter this room like cats and silently remove Steve to a room that doesn't exist in a military prison—a room from which he would not soon see the light of day. And his friends wouldn't be as kind as me. I stared at him a minute. Studying his tattoos. His left, unbroken, forearm contained a US flag. Stars and stripes. The ink on the flag was older. The ink on the flames surrounding and now consuming the flag was not.

My observation brought a realization to mind. Steve was fit. Cool under pressure. Calculating. At one time, Steve had been idealistic. Probably a gifted soldier. Fought for a cause. Then something happened and he became disillusioned. Something doused his passion. Steve sold out. And burned his flag. I leaned in close. I eyed the ink. Then him. "What happened to you?"

He paused. My question seemed to make him more uncomfortable than Clay's cane. He squirmed. "The money."

I shook my head. "No. Before that. Before the money bought you."

More squirming. "That's classified."

Camp handed me his phone. Eddie had uncovered it. Steve was telling the truth. I sat back. "Steve, did people betray you, or did your country?"

"What's the difference?"

"I'm your country. Aaron Ashley is your country. His daughters are your country. You took an oath."

"They left us, sir."

I don't know if it was the pain or my words, but Steve's eyes became glassy. I paused. "Was it worth it?"

He studied the girl. The penthouse. His broken arm.

So I asked again, "What have you gained?"

Steve shook his head. "Can't seem to find my way back, sir."

Staring at Steve, I knew one thing beyond a shadow of a doubt: Without Bones, that could have been me. I could be Steve. Disillusioned. Sold out. A broken man filled with regret. But Steve didn't have my commanding officer. He didn't have Ezekiel Walker. Bones had walked down into my disillusion and turned on a light. He'd rescued me before I walked into the darkness. Before I ended up right here. A singular thought echoed through my mind: *Then Bones . . .*

I injected the Narcan into Steve's nose. The effect was immediate.

I stood, studied Steve, and felt the pain of Bones's absence. Camp studied Steve's burner phone and the text received from the vulgar voice in New York. Camp read the text, then nodded. I turned to Clay, who was still standing within a cane's reach of Steve. "You have anything you want to say?"

He shook his head once. "Already said it."

Steve knew his die was cast. "Sir?"

Halfway out the door, I turned.

He swallowed, and judging from the look on his face, the truth was not sitting well. "Any possible way for a return?"

I knew what he was asking. "To what?"

He shook his head. "Just lost my way, sir."

Eddie spoke in my ear. "Stackhouse is three minutes out."

I turned back to Steve. "That's up to you. But if Aaron Ashley's daughters don't make it out alive, unmolested, and soon, then the answer is not just 'no' but 'no forever.'"

Steve hung his head and didn't plead. Didn't beg me to give him one more chance. He'd had too many already. He knew that. Steve was surrendering. He knew it was time.

As I pulled out of the parking lot, my phone rang. Caller ID read "Stackhouse."

"Yes."

Stackhouse sounded amused. "Somebody wants to talk with you."

Steve did not sound good, suggesting that whoever Stackhouse had brought had put the leather to him. Steve sounded as though he was speaking through a mouthful of marbles. "Check your phone. He's not one of my team, but he will know who hired us."

"How do you know him?"

"We worked together." A prolonged pause. "Before."

I knew what he was saying, but I wanted to hear him say it. I wanted the reality to set in, and I knew it would if it came out of his mouth. "Before?"

"Before I lost my way." A pause. "Sir?"

I waited.

"If I could ever help you . . ."

"Help me what?"

"Just trying to get back to good, sir."

I hung up rather certain I'd not seen the last of Steve Plexis.

CHAPTER 22

The contact lived in Israel. Outside Jerusalem. A fifteen-hour flight. I knew flying that far risked keeping us from a quick response to anything inside the US, but what else did we have to go on? Ashley's people had turned up nothing. Steve's interrogation had turned up very little.

Camp again found me shaking my head. "You good, sir?"

The extent to which I'd become unaware of my own actions was concerning. "Thinking about the girls."

"Yes, sir."

"Camp?"

"Sir?"

"We're level on the playing field. You don't have to call me sir."

He tilted his head from side to side. "Colonel, sir. I was standing there when the vice president promoted you."

"And the people we're chasing couldn't care less."

"You called Bones 'sir.'"

"That's different."

"How so?"

"He's my mentor."

"And you're not?"

I hadn't really considered that. "But he's . . . Bones."

"And you're . . . Murph."

"Camp, I'm just a guy who kicks down doors."

"Sir, among us—guys that care, guys that still believe—you're . . . storied. You're who we're hoping to be. I've worked with other governments and their operators talk about you. They whisper your name." He waved his hand across me. "Your tattoos, the whole back thing, it's . . . Sir, you just need to know, you're the pinnacle."

I tried to drill it down. Get at the root of what was bothering me. And what was bothering me was the sense that Camp felt about me the way I felt about Bones. Which meant if something happened to me, Camp would hurt the way I was hurting. And I couldn't prevent that. Couldn't make that hurt any less. I knew what he was saying was true. I also knew that to love is to be vulnerable. To risk. When in pain, we adopt the lie that to protect our hearts, we must put them away. Lock them in a vault. Suck the air out. The problem we encounter is that when we open that chamber and try to use this once-fleshy thing we call a heart, we find it hard. Impenetrable. Icy. Unbreakable. Unfeeling. That's what I was asking Camp. In saying, "Don't call me sir," I was asking Camp to become unfeeling. To lock his heart away in a place where my absence or death couldn't hurt it. In pain, I had wrapped myself in self-protection, demanding he do the same. For him to do what I wanted him to do, to wipe "sir" out of his mouth, he'd have to become unfeeling. Pulse-less. But to do this work, to endure, to get off this plane when it landed, you had to be able to bleed. Which immediately presented a problem. How did you stop it? And if the wound was too deep, could you stop it at all? My experience proved not.

This was the worst type of rescue. The waiting kind. With nothing to go on. No lead. Languishing in earsplitting silence. All we could do was try not to think about what was happening to the girls. Their fear. Their pain. Their disbelief and horror. I sat in the plane and tried not to think about them, which only made it worse.

Camp put his hand on my shoulder. "Sir, we'll find 'em."

I remembered when I allowed my hope to speak. Before my pain choked it out. I nodded and stared out across the shimmering blue below.

Five minutes later, Eddie called.

CHAPTER 23

Years ago, I tracked a kid to Stuttgart. Found him in a warehouse awaiting transfer. It was early. Before dawn. His exploiters were still jacked up from the night before. Extraction was cut and dry. I walked in, lifted his emaciated body off the floor, and asked him, "What's your name?"

"E-E-Eddie."

"How old are you?" I knew these answers but I was trying to get his mind off the hell he'd endured.

"Tw-tw-twelve."

"How long have you had a stutter?"

"S-s-s-since I was a k-k-k . . ." He swallowed, closed his eyes, and started over. "Kid."

From his file, I knew his birth father had abused him and left him, leaving a hole. Into that void, the stutter stepped. The mom remarried, a good man who adopted the boy, but the stutter remained. No amount of love could root it out. Six months earlier, while playing video games at a movie arcade, he was lifted, sold, and shipped overseas—all in less than a day. When the exploiters discovered they'd lifted the son of the CEO of a solar company worth a couple hundred million, the first ransom note came in. Five million dollars. Which the parents quickly paid. That was followed by a second note asking for more, which they also paid. "Transaction complete." But still no boy.

When the third demand came in, Bones got a call, and I got on a plane. "Don't pay it."

As I walked out of that warehouse, he put his head on my shoulder, his breathing labored. But he wasn't crying. His shock wouldn't allow it. Not a single tear. We flew overnight and landed in DC, and I returned him to his mom and stepdad, who had been inconsolable. It was weeks before he started to cry. Once he did, they couldn't get him to stop. He didn't eat, didn't sleep, didn't speak, didn't hug them back. He had been muted, save the tears.

So I went to see him.

He sat up when he saw me, tears streaming down his face. I sat down, took off my coat, and unbuttoned my shirt, which made him flinch. Then I turned slightly. I said, "Can you read?"

He nodded.

"Can you read the last one?"

He studied the names on my back, finally reading the last installment. "E-E-Eddie F-Fisher."

He read it without inflection. "Can you read it again?"

"E-ddie Fisher." The second time he read it, his eyes widened and he whispered, "Eddie Fisher." It was his name.

I faced him, buttoning my shirt. "Wherever I go, I carry you with me."

At the sound of this, he almost smiled. "F-f-forever?" The side of his mouth turned up.

"Can you count to a hundred?"

"Y-yes."

"Two hundred?"

He nodded.

"If you were to count all the names before yours, you'd find 173. That means there are 173 kids like you. Many of whom now live at a place called Freetown."

"Wh-where's th-that?"

"The mountains of Colorado. Would you like to go there?"

He looked at his parents, who nodded, smiling. He said, "Are you there?"

I weighed my head side to side. "Sometimes."

"Wh-wh-where do you g-go?"

"To find kids like you."

"Do you c-c-come back?"

I laughed out loud. "Yes."

"Always?"

"Up to now, yes."

"Ca-can I h-h-help you?"

"What do you mean?"

"F-f-find k-k-kids like m-m-me."

It was the first time the rescued had ever asked to rescue. I glanced at his folks, who quickly said, "Anything you need."

Which explained why much of Freetown ran on solar power, and why Eddie ran our comms department along with Jess, BP, and Camp.

Seeing "Eddie" flash across my caller ID reminded me of that first glimpse in Stuttgart. He was helpless back then. As was I in this moment. And I did not like it.

I put him on speakerphone. "What do you got?"

"Ariel Underwood. Former Mossad. Although, once Mossad, I'm pretty sure you're always Mossad."

Camp nodded.

Eddie continued, "Decorated military and intelligence career. Retired as brigadier general. Now runs his own shop. Works in the shadows. Good with a knife, and don't let him get you on the ground. He's something of a Krav Maga master, known to his team as 'The Cat.' Picks and chooses what he wants to do while also doing whatever is required. Money's not really an issue. Lives along the wall in the Old City." Eddie paused. "When they need somebody got, they send him. When they need to know for sure, they send him. And the prime minister trusts no one more."

Clay chuckled. "He's the Israeli version of you."

"How'd he get hooked up with Steve?"

"Joint operations. Back when Steve was true."

"He expecting us?"

"Evidently."

I knew he, Jess, and BP were working round the clock, but I couldn't help myself. "Any sign of the—?"

Eddie cut me off, suggesting his own frustration. "Crickets." A pause. "But you should know, the story is public. Along with edited parts of the video. And more pictures. Not the kind you want to see. Every network is running wild with the story. Don't know who leaked it. All the talking heads are asking, How'd it happen? How could Ashley let it? How could a war hawk let his guard down? If he can't protect his family, how will he ever protect us? It's more feeding frenzy than sympathy-fest. And . . . there's a demand letter. Just in."

"Who got it?"

"Media outlets."

"Of course they did."

"It's simple. 'Start raising the money. If you can buy the presidency, you can buy your girls.'"

"So is it about money?"

Camp considered this. "Or is it about power?"

His question was insightful.

Eddie again. "Murph, the pundits are saying that Ashley's façade is cracking. He's fumbled a few questions. It's only been seventy-two hours, and it's not looking good. Actually, it looks really bad."

"Thanks, Eddie."

CHAPTER 24

I called Ashley from the plane. He picked up after the third ring. His voice sounded tired. "Hey, Murph." He tried to sound strong. "How about some good news."

"Sir, we followed a lead to Maui. Now Jerusalem. We are en route."

"Anything solid?"

I chose my words. "Not yet."

I could hear him rubbing a stubbled face.

I pressed him. "Sir, how's Esther?"

"Um . . ." A long pause followed by an honest admission. "She's . . . not good."

I could hear people in the background, so I said the only thing I could. "Hang in there, Ash."

When he finally spoke, his voice cracked. "Murph?"

I knew what was coming. "Yes, sir."

"Find my girls. Please find my girls."

We were met by Customs in Tel Aviv, who seemed to be expecting us. They also told us we could keep our sidearms and they said nothing about Clay's cane. Indicating that Ariel felt safe enough in his own security protocol and setting to allow armed strangers to enter. This told me a good bit about him. Against his protests, we left Gunner on the plane. Not because I didn't need him. We did. But he draws attention like a magnet, which we did not need. We needed to get in, get out, and leave no impression in the process. We took a private car inside Jerusalem and stopped at a nondescript gated home on the outskirts of the northern end of the old city walls.

We walked through the Damascus Gate at sunset, turned left, and wound down a tight alley hugging the ancient wall. Left. Right. Up a small ramp. Another left. Down several steps. Up another ramp. A left. Followed by twenty long steps that covered more distance than height. The stones were smooth, worn, and spoke history. We stopped at several large buildings that grew out of the wall's interior where a gate led into a courtyard.

I knocked and a kid opened the door. Maybe twelve. A soccer ball under one arm. He half bowed, then pulled the door open and gestured to the stairs. "Dad's up there." The smell emanating from the house was almost intoxicating enough to cause me to miss the more than twenty cameras capturing our arrival and the four men staring down on us from elevated positions. I liked this guy already.

We climbed the stairs, wondering what on earth was cooking in the kitchen and who we had to pay to get some. The stairs ended on a landing that bled into a library. Several thousand books. Mostly history. Some fiction. He had three of those cool ladders that slide on wheels along the shelves. We found him atop the third, a book in hand.

He descended and extended a hand. "Murphy Shepherd."

He was smaller than me. Sinewy. Dark eyes. Wisps of gray showing in his beard. Little to no wasted movement. "Ariel Underwood." I shook his hand. "You can call me Murph."

He raised an eyebrow. "Or maybe Colonel."

"News travels quickly."

"I was and am sorry to hear about Bones. I knew him to be a man who did what he said he was going to do. Rare these days."

"You worked together?"

"Many times." A nod. "He got me out of a few tight spots. And . . ." He covered his heart with one hand, suggesting either an honest admission or failure. Or both. "When my niece ran away with a young man with bad intentions, Bones found her and brought her back. I owe him much."

Despite all the miles and all the time spent in his presence, I never cease to be amazed how little I actually knew Bones. Underwood's present-tense use of the word *owe* was not lost on me. Ariel motioned for us to sit. A lady, presumably his wife, entered carrying hot tea. "Since you are working . . ."

I accepted the tea. "I didn't realize it had been made public."

"You have your secrets. We have ours. Sometimes we are able to keep them."

Clay's bear-paw hands had a difficult time grasping the dainty teacup. After several unsuccessful attempts to bring it to his mouth without spilling it, he just set it down.

Ariel turned to Camp. "Commander, we've never actually met."

"No, sir. But we've shared the same geography for a time."

Ariel smiled and nodded. Then he turned to me. "You managed to do what no one else has."

"Which is?"

"Get the better of Steve Plexis."

"What can you tell me about him?"

"Teams guy. Good at his job." He weighed his head side to side. "Used to love his country. Sold his soul when his CO left him someplace he shouldn't have been. Lost a few buddies."

"Why'd he send me to you?"

Ariel rubbed his chin. "Francis Walker."

The image of Frank falling backward down the well and taking Bones with him flashed before my mind's eye. I waited.

Ariel continued, "When you did the world a favor and sent Frank to his watery grave, you, in a very real sense, opened the gates of hell."

I was pretty sure I knew this answer, but I asked anyway. "How so?"

"Frank had seven generals. All either wanting out or vying for Frank's seat. No lost love between any of them. Steve knew we had special interest in the identity of those men. Those people."

"We?"

He tapped a star of David hanging around his neck. "Us."

"What does that have to do with Steve and the vice president's daughters?"

"Maybe nothing." A pause. "Maybe something."

"Why do I get the feeling there's something you're not telling me?"

He looked to each of us. "Gentlemen." He stood and beckoned. "Please."

We followed him downstairs and through two keypad-controlled security doors. The second of which included face recognition technology. The door opened to reveal a network of tunnels. He spoke as he walked. "Much of the stone Herod used to build his magnificent city above us came from these underground quarries. During the multiple times the city has been overrun, my people have hidden down here." We came to the end of a long tunnel, turned right, and continued straight. As best I could tell, we were either beneath the ancient wall of the city or just beyond it.

Finally, the tunnel led us to a third keypad. Underwood typed in his code and presented his face to the scanner, and the door unlocked itself and swung open, breaking the air lock. Underwood smiled at me. "I'll show you mine if you show me yours." The room was large and filled with several people staring at screens, typing on keyboards, and speaking quietly into ear-mounted microphones. He stood aside, allowing us to take in the room. "From here we monitor what concerns us." Israel's satellite and drone technology was second to none, and the high-def resolution of the screens in front of me proved that.

"Let me back up," said Ariel. "Frank controlled an empire by controlling seven generals, for lack of a better term."

"Correct."

"Until now, the identity of the seven was closely guarded by Frank. Only he knew. We've tried for years to discover just one, but each ended in a dead end. Frank enjoyed sending us on, how do you say, wild-goose chases." A pause. "He controlled these seven evil people by leveraging their deviant sexual sins against them. Evidently in the form of extensive video footage, which, if exposed, would lead to only one place."

"Prison."

"Correct. And we assume these people don't want that footage seen to the extent that they were willing to do what Frank commanded, which was to manage one-seventh of a sex-trafficking empire."

"Correct."

"But to Frank's credit, he knew that sooner or later they'd tire from being led around by that ring in their nose, so he sweetened the deal by paying them otherworldly amounts of money, making them worth hundreds of millions, if not a few billion. Proving the age-old adage 'How do you prevent mutiny?'"

"Give the crew a piece of the gold."

"Exactly."

Camp spoke next. "An interesting mousetrap."

Then Clay. "Nothing like money to keep the family close."

Ariel raised a finger as if asking a question. "But how long can money, mixed with the not-so-unspoken threat of prison, keep them compliant?"

"I think Frank was assuming the rest of their natural born lives."

"Agreed." Ariel continued, "But if you're paranoid on a level not easily measured . . ."

"Which Frank was," I added.

"Then you have to assume that at some point one or all of these people will discover they are rich enough to disappear. Buy an island. Plastic surgery. Whatever. At some point their money can grant them freedom."

"If"—I raised a finger—"they're willing to leave the life they currently lead."

He nodded. "So, given this possibility, and knowing that at any moment any one of them could give you the finger, what would you do to keep track of these seven people upon whom you've built your empire? To what extent would you go? Let me ask it this way: What would you not do?"

These were good questions, and I found myself liking Ariel and his process. "You have a theory?"

He nodded. "It's thin. Not a lot to go on. More of a hunch really. But I want to show you something." He motioned to a woman sitting at a terminal who punched several keys on her keyboard, which powered on a screen above a large table. The screen showed a shimmering blue ocean with astounding clarity. More key clicks caused the perspective to zoom in on a land mass. An island. And an airstrip on the southeast coast of that land mass.

He turned to me. "Look familiar?"

It did. Also familiar was the pain it produced in my stomach. I nodded.

CHAPTER 25

A riel continued, "Stop me if you've heard this. Fifteen hundred years ago a Franciscan monk followed a vision that ended here, and he and his brothers built what, five hundred years later, would become a thriving monastery where they would live in peace until the Crusaders adopted it as one of their outposts around AD 1000. This attracted the attention of the Moors, who then drove out the Crusaders, whereupon the grounds fell into disrepair and became the home of an eventual hermit. Around 1500, the Christians retook the citadel, refortifying it, and discovered that the rocky and fertile soil, along with the requisite sunshine, grew desirable grapes. A thriving church soon followed. Along with 'entertainment' for the priests seeking respite from the rigors of celibate life. Monastery, vineyards, retreat, and private conference center—priests from around the world would trek here, often walking the last fifty to hundred miles, making the destination a pilgrimage of sorts. Then they would spend weeks or months, each day confessing the sins that occurred in the dark world below."

The satellite picture followed the narrow road that led from the mainland into the peninsula, traveling along the mile-wide plateau that fell off like a table to rocky, goat-strewn cliffs that descended a couple hundred feet into the turquoise waters of the Balearic Sea. Ariel shone a laser on the screen, circling the structures with its red light. "From a defensive standpoint, it's easy to see why Frank liked it." More laser. "One road in and surrounded by water on three sides. An inhospitable terrain inhabited by goats, burros, and short, stubby trees that look to be constantly bracing against the wind." More keystrokes from the woman at the console and the picture zoomed in on a small resort village a few miles away, revealing bleached white sands and gin-clear water.

The pain in my stomach was piercing. The slideshow fast-forwarded itself across the back of my eyelids.

Ariel nodded to the woman.

More keystrokes. A prerecorded video began playing. We watched from an aerial view as a small Zodiac left a crowded marina, captained by a single man and a dog, and navigated the waters to the island's edge. There the two disappeared underwater.

Ariel nodded again to the woman, who fast-forwarded several hours to when the man and his dog returned, climbed into the craft, and motored back to the marina, leaving a red trail along the gunnel of the boat.

Ariel nodded again to the woman and then looked at me. "Here's what you didn't know." The video rewound to one hour prior to my leaving the marina. The perspective changed to a different satellite angle, moving to the northeastern corner of the island. It passed over an elegant sailboat under way to a moored megayacht in a protected cove. Maybe two hundred feet in length. The woman at the terminal split the screen; one half showed the sailboat sailing out of the screen, leaving only the megayacht sitting idly, while the other half showed me in the Zodiac leaving the marina. As I idled in from one side of the island, the yacht cranked her engines and began easing out into deeper water. More laser. "The *Dark Profit*—and don't let the double entendre escape you—was rented to a shell company owned by a shell company tied to a parent shell company. Which is not unusual."

I stepped closer. "Any idea who was aboard?"

"That's the ten-million-dollar question." Ariel moved closer to the TV. More laser. "Watch this tender. It leaves the island, approaches the *Profit*, those four men disembark, and then two of them return and hold umbrellas while this man walks beneath."

Clay lifted his cane and motioned to the absence of clouds in the sky. "Only one problem. No rain."

Ariel studied the screen. "Exactly."

I spoke next. "So mystery man knows somebody is staring down at him from fifty-five miles above the earth."

Ariel nodded.

"Can you estimate the size of the man?"

The woman typed a few lines of code into the keyboard. Ariel again. "Maybe five feet eight to five feet ten. One-eighty to two hundred."

"So he's either jacked or portly."

"Correct." Ariel moved his laser. "His heat signature shows him entering here, and what's worse, he never exits in port. Which means he got off somewhere en route and we missed him."

"That means he was certain you were watching."

Ariel nodded.

Me again. "So somebody, and not just Frank, hacked not only our system but yours."

"Correct," Camp chimed in. "And of the eight billion or so people on planet earth, it could be any one of them."

Ariel acknowledged this. "Yes, except . . ." Ariel circled the man with his red laser. "Heat signature shows this man wearing a watch." The video zoomed in with incredible clarity on what looked like an Apple watch. "We know it is transmitting on both cellular and satellite signals, but it's not captured by any of them. It's 'piggybacking.' Stealing bandwidth from whatever is available. But here's the kicker: We've never seen it before. It's not commercial. Not Apple. Not Google. Not Garmin. And it's not military. Rather sophisticated stuff."

I was pretty sure I knew where this was going. "Frank used the same thing with his bookkeeper, a guy named Bernie, and a runner named Guido we intercepted in New York City. Frank used it to keep close rein on those two. With it, he knew their location and eavesdropped."

Ariel seemed surprised by this. "He could listen in?"

I nodded. "And he knew if and when they took it off."

He pressed me. "And you know this how?"

"I took it off them."

CHAPTER 26

I nteresting." Ariel nodded. "Now fast-forward through time-lapse and watch what mystery man does. By the time you exit in the Zodiac, only you knew Frank was dead. News had not reached the outside world. Or had it?" The perspective switched from me in the Zodiac back to the megayacht, which had motored south, while the beautiful sailboat had tacked, turned, and now paralleled the island. "Here he is, sitting in the lounge, one leg crossed over the other. Judging from the angle of his arms, he's reading documents. He's calm, controlled. Anything but animated. Then his phone rings. He answers, stands up, paces, and his arm movement suggests he grows excited. After thirty-seven seconds, he ends the call, walks to the handrail, and what's the first thing he does? He slings that very phone like a Frisbee out across the water. But he's not finished. This man, who again won't come out from underneath the canopy because he knows some eye in the sky is watching him, can't get the watch off fast enough and, without a second's hesitation, ceremoniously pitches it in the water. See that splash? Then, as if he's made a game-winning three-pointer at the buzzer, he raises his hands in exuberance. In freedom. Frank hasn't been dead ten minutes and this guy rids all technology that could tether him to his master. But wait, he's not done. He's so elated that he walks to the bar, the bartender pours a glass, and then the man raises the glass and downs it." A pause. "He's toasting Frank's death. Good riddance." Ariel paused for effect.

"At this point, he thinks he's free of Frank." Ariel looked at me. "Given what you know of Frank, do you think he's free?"

I shook my head. "Not a chance. Frank allowed no room for error. Too paranoid."

Ariel nodded. "That's our theory as well."

He looked at me. "Let me ask another theoretical. Do you think it's possible for Frank to command permanent absolute allegiance in his generals with only video evidence of their crimes?"

"Depends on the graphic nature of the evidence and the amount of it."

"But would you chance that?"

I shook my head. "No, I would not."

He returned to the video. "Who would so quickly toast Frank's demise?"

"You mean other than me?"

Ariel bowed slightly, acknowledging and paying silent respect to what the video did not show—my and Bones's struggle with Frank in the tunnels. And the fact that Bones had just died.

I tried not to think about it, and Ariel was making logical sense. I continued, "Someone controlled by Frank."

Camp pointed at the man. "So how did he know? Who called?"

Ariel lasered the monastery. "We think he had someone inside."

Camp again. "Somebody who worked for Frank?"

I nodded. "Somebody playing both sides. Hedging their bets."

"Why do you say that?" Camp asked.

"Frank would anticipate this. He would never limit himself to one failsafe." The conversation with Ashley replayed in my mind, along with the thought: If Ashley inserted a passive chip into his girls to protect them from bad guys who wished them harm, then why wouldn't Frank insert one in his henchmen to protect and ensure him against their escape?

Ariel continued, "There is a technology today. A passive chip. Contains no batteries. No need to recharge. It's invisible to scanners. You'd need an X-ray or CT scan to see it. It's similar to the chip on your debit or credit card, and it triggers a reaction when swiped. When 'read.' The civilian version, made popular in Sweden and now spreading across Europe, is something about the size of a grain of rice. Inserted primarily into the hand. Those who have it claim you can't feel it. Most commonly it contains personal and financial data, but it can contain whatever you want. Including location."

Clay spoke to himself but loud enough to be heard. "The mark of the beast."

"Possibly," Ariel admitted. "It's triggered whenever they swipe their hand. What most don't know is that it can also trigger a 'reading' when they're within a certain distance. Give or take five feet."

I picked up on his thoughts. "For instance, someone with this grain of rice in their body can drive out of a parking deck with a rental car and get scanned without knowing it."

Ariel added, "Or a hotel elevator or room requiring a key card."

Camp chimed in, "Or a gym membership."

Ariel nodded. "The possibilities are endless."

Clay was nodding his head. "So if this thing is in you, you can trigger fifteen different scanners just going to the grocery store, gas station, and ATM."

Ariel nodded. "More advanced military chips trigger multiple reactions—including a phone's camera. When the camera takes a picture it triggers a signal, or something like a homing beacon, indicating the location of the person scanned by the camera. Some of them even send the picture."

Camp nodded. "You could unknowingly give away your location and send a picture of yourself at that location—"

I finished his sentence for him. "Every time you take a selfie." I didn't voice it, but I wondered if Underwood knew about Ashley's daughters' chips.

Ariel continued, "The problem is simple. Each chip contains an encrypted identification number. Hard-coded into the chip. Know the number, track the chip. Don't know the number, you might as well be spitting into the wind in the middle of a hurricane. The chip doesn't tell you who's carrying it. Only that they are."

Clay again. "So theoretically, you can follow someone anywhere in the world."

Ariel considered this. "All of our financial, cellular, and social media companies do it now. They keep track of us. Much closer than we think. As long as we're buying, calling, or posting, they can pinpoint us within a few feet."

Camp spoke next. "The difference here is these chips trigger any scanner within a certain physical distance, and yet the person carrying the chip has no idea."

"Exactly," Ariel said.

I added my two cents based on what I knew of Frank. "This would fit Frank's MO. He would have had insurance in the event one of his generals thumbed his nose and trashed the watch. Possibly more than one."

Ariel circled the guy on the screen with his laser. "Which he just did."

Clay stood there shaking his head. "But he don't know that Frank, or somebody, can still track him 'cause he don't know the thing is inside him."

"*If* it's in him." Ariel emphasized the word *if*. "Again, it's a theory."

Camp chimed in, the sarcasm thick. "And here I was thinking all of our personal financial data was safe."

Clay pointed his cane at the guy on the screen. "But if it's in there, how'd Frank get it in there?"

"Yeah, how do you insert something like that, subcutaneous, without them knowing it?" Camp asked.

Ariel explained, "We've been amazed at what otherwise law-abiding doctors will do for a couple million dollars. Not to mention the fact that inserting the chip is harmless to the person."

"So," I said, finishing Ariel's thought, "they can insert the chip and theoretically continue to 'do no harm.'"

CHAPTER 27

T he four of us stood considering the ramifications. I broke the silence. "So if Frank inserted something like this into any one or all of his generals without their knowledge, even though he's dead, their chips are still signaling their location."

"And will be for the next decade."

Camp asked the next obvious question. "But who's listening?"

"If Frank was the only one who knew, then no one," Ariel admitted, "but that doesn't stop them from signaling." He smiled. "The chip doesn't know no one is listening."

I tried to bring the conversation back around to next steps. "Then to track his generals and tear down his playground, we need the encrypted IDs."

"Known only by dead Frank," Camp said.

"Correct," I muttered. "Except that he willingly gave me the GPS co-ordinates to his data vault. If he knew he was about to die, why give me the keys to his kingdom but deny me these encrypted numbers identify-ing the very people who make the kingdom possible? There was no love lost between these people and Frank. He held no loyalty to them. At all. They were disposable. Slaves. They performed a service like the people he trafficked. That's all." I paused, letting this reality sink in, then turned to Ariel and voiced the question I couldn't answer. "Why share this with us? Your intelligence is as good as if not better than ours. You don't need us."

Ariel nodded. "We think Frank might have given them to you and—"

Camp cut him off. "We don't know it because we don't know what to look for."

Ariel nodded.

I dialed Eddie, put him on speakerphone, and asked Ariel to explain what they wanted and what they wanted access to.

Eddie listened, then considered the ramifications of letting foreign intelligence rummage through the data vault. "Murph, I'm good, but it's your call."

I wasn't too worried about Ariel. He was knocking on the front door. Laying his cards on the table. Or at least some of them. If he wanted to sneak in a back door to the vault, his people could find it. "The more eyes the better. But now we're splitting our focus. Diverting time and energy away from Ashley's daughters. And the clock is not working in our favor. Going on four days."

"Correct," Ariel admitted. "But it might help you find who took them. Or find the one who paid someone to take them." A pause. "And if it helps us discover the identities of the seven, or even just one of the seven, what will that do? How many will that free?"

I liked this guy.

Eddie spoke over the speaker. "May I throw you a curve?"

We waited.

"The data we're looking for doesn't make sense without knowing the identities of the people carrying the passive chips. Essentially, we're looking for a spreadsheet of data that is meaningless without that connection. It's simply transactions. Mostly small dollar amounts. Coffee. Gas. Parking. Lunch. It also contains no account numbers. These are not bank transfers. We're looking at what happened in the past with little to no connection to the future. It's simply a record of what happened."

Ariel nodded. "Correct."

"So if you were Frank, and you already had your hands full trying to keep valuable data protected, which is what we found in his vault, then why would you bother hiding a spreadsheet of transaction data inside your vault?

Why not hide it in plain sight? In fact, it would make much more sense to keep them separate at all costs."

Camp was nodding now as well.

I wasn't quite sure where he was going. "So what are you suggesting?"

"When I was a kid, one of my favorite things was to buy cereal with secret decoder rings. Lucky Charms. Frosted Flakes. Cap'n Crunch. Healthy stuff like that. Then I'd spread the secret message out across the kitchen table and 'decode' the message. "'Drink your Ovaltine.'"

I doubted anyone but me got the *Christmas Story* reference.

Eddie continued, "If we know anything about Frank, he probably kept the identities in his head. He knew the identification numbers by heart. So if he was the only one who knew the decoder ring, why try to keep secret the passive or active transactions? They are meaningless without the data in Frank's head. If that's me, I'm going to hide it in a Google spreadsheet with an address known only to me. You might stumble upon it, but if you did, all you'd find are receipts. Nothing of real value."

"Why would he do that?" I asked.

"Because he could keep it separate from his data, outside his vault, and access it from anywhere. And he wouldn't have to worry about someone hacking in. It would be 'hidden' among a trillion other documents and make sense to no one but him. It'd be like discovering an ancient language with no way to translate. Without something telling you what the symbols mean, it's just scratches on stone."

Ariel picked up on the idea. "And if he was worried about it somehow getting corrupted or deleted in some massive Google accident, he could duplicate it with some simple code."

I nodded again. "Create a redundancy."

"Yep. Have three to five of the same document floating in the ether."

Ariel looked at me, nodding. "You have a good team." He looked at the speaker. "Eddie, if you ever tire of Murph, I'll hire you. And double whatever he's paying you."

Eddie laughed.

Jess had yet to make her presence known, although I knew she'd be sitting there with Eddie and BP. At a break, she said, "So . . ." She paused for effect. "*If* the chips exist, and *if* Frank bribed the doctors, and *if* they've been inserted into Frank's generals without their knowledge, and *if* they are passing within a few feet of a scanner, and *if* the chips actually do what you say and trigger a passive scan, and *if* Frank wrote the code to gather that data—then those scans are registered as receipts or transactions, something insignificant to anyone but Frank, and are then gathered automatically and updated every second or so to a spreadsheet housed somewhere in the inter-web."

Ariel laughed out loud. "Please tell me your name."

"Jess."

"I'd like to hire you as well. Are you available?"

Jess's no-nonsense pragmatism was a real plus to the team. She didn't beat around many bushes.

Camp continued Eddie's line of thinking. "So we could be sifting the data vault for something that's not there when in reality we need to be sifting Google for a single spreadsheet that only makes sense to a dead man."

I tried to bring us back to square one. To remind us of the main thing. "Frank built an empire on the backs of people who did not want to be controlled, and yet he did it by blackmailing them with evidence of their sins. While Frank was evil, he wasn't dumb. He knew, sooner or later, they'd tire of the forced servitude and escape the cage. Undetected, passive chips ensured they could not and did not. To Frank, knowing the location of the chip at any moment in time was priceless. And it's brilliant because it's only priceless to him. Everything he did hinged on this." I paused to let the totality sink in. "Knowing Frank, he probably inserted more than one chip."

Camp paused. "So this spreadsheet . . . in a sense, we're not looking for a needle in a haystack, and we're not looking for a single grain of sand on the beach, or a grain of sand on planet earth. We're looking for a single grain of sand somewhere in the Milky Way."

"That pretty much sums it up. But . . ." When I spoke again, I made sure I had everyone's attention. "We are still no closer to finding Miriam,

Ruth, and Sadie. And right about now, they need us to find them. Not to mention Aaron and Esther."

Silence weighed heavy across the room.

I turned to Ariel. "This still doesn't explain why Steve sent me to you when he had just kidnapped the vice president's daughters."

Ariel shrugged. "It's an olive branch. Steve is playing this card because he's looking at the strong possibility he never walks out of a military prison. Never sees the light of day unobstructed. And . . ." Ariel paused. "He was once one of the good guys."

I nodded. "You mean before he shot and killed a dozen men on the vice president's detail?"

Ariel nodded.

"Steve sold out. He's lucky to be breathing. He doesn't have many cards."

Ariel nodded again and motioned, saying, "Follow me."

CHAPTER 28

We climbed several flights of stairs, exiting onto the top of the ancient city wall surrounding the north end of Jerusalem. The lights of the city flickered warm amid the cold air. Ariel walked to the edge, leaning against a stone once guarded by Crusaders and Moors and many others. After a minute, he pointed across the street. "Some say that is your Golgotha." He paused, gesturing to the line of city buses. "Today it is the busiest bus station in all of Jerusalem." The air smelled of diesel, burnt trash, and hot asphalt. He looked at me. "Does that offend you?"

I shook my head. "I tend to find it rather fitting."

He studied the wall. The Mount of Olives and Garden of Gethsemane to the east. City of David to the south. Temple Mount between.

I waved my hand across the stony earth before us. "Lot of war here."

He nodded, not feeling the need to speak.

"Why live here? Wouldn't you be safer somewhere else?"

"Safety is an illusion." He stared out across the ancient mountain, finally shaking his head. "I am a watchman on the wall."

When I spoke, I did so with intention. "A repairer of the breach?"

He raised an eyebrow, surprised I knew the context. "Given my history, the world is not safe for me. So we live here."

He pointed again. To quiet lights on a stone wall just beyond the building to the left of the bus station. "Your garden tomb."

I knew the place. I'd been there. I turned. Made eye contact. "Is it mine . . . or ours?"

He nodded and smiled. "One day soon, we will know."

I shook his hand and was certain I'd not seen the last of Ariel Underwood. "Until then."

"Until then."

Camp, Clay, and I returned through the Old City. After a few minutes, I paused to window-shop. Camp idled up alongside me. "You see him?"

"Yep."

"Ariel's men?"

"Doubtful." I dialed Ariel. He answered on the first ring. I heard his son in the background. He spoke first. "No, they are not mine. If I wanted to follow you, you wouldn't know it."

"I believe you. You able to detect any communication from them?"

"No, but when we do, I'll let you know."

"My thanks to you."

"Oh, and, Murph?"

"Yeah."

"There are two of them."

The second I had not seen. "Check."

I hung up and Camp, Clay, and I continued to meander. Taking our time. We bought shawarma, then a coffee, then Camp slipped into a store and appeared to shop before slipping out the back, leaving Clay and I as bait. A few moments later, I heard a crack followed by a muffled scream followed by another crack and a not-so-muffled scream.

Clay and I rounded a corner and turned into an alley. Camp was standing over two men dressed in black. Both disarmed and staring in disbelief at the unnatural bend in their knees. "I don't suppose these dummies know anything either."

Camp shook his head. "We can try to massage it out of them, but they're no different than Steve. Just a two-man cell with a for-hire sign that answered a call an hour ago and then took some fast money to follow us."

I knelt, took pictures of the guys' faces, and scanned their prints with my phone. "Just two guys minding their own business." I was growing tired of idiots for hire with no moral compass. The man closest to me was hardened. Box chin. Curved nose. Seen his share of fights and, judging by the muffled obscenities coming out his mouth, not used to losing. I didn't have time to get the information I needed. Nor would we get very far in the streets of Jerusalem. But I knew someone who could.

Ariel answered on the first ring. I could tell he was smiling when he spoke. "I'd like to hire Camp as well. He's good."

"If I leave these guys, can your men sweep them off the street and ask them a few questions?"

"What do you want to know?"

"I want to know how they were contacted. Where they hung their mercenary-for-hire sign."

"Shouldn't be too hard."

"My thanks."

CHAPTER 29

W e left the two idiots hobbled, gagged, and tied back-to-back, which they did not appreciate—and they were quite adept at expressing their dis-appreciation. As I boarded the plane, my phone rang. I did not recognize the number. I sat, answered the call, and pressed Speaker, allowing Camp and Clay to listen in.

"Murph?"

I recognized the voice. "Speaking."

"It's Waylon Maynard. Is this a bad time?"

It did not escape me that I was receiving a phone call from maybe the most powerful man in DC. A man with no enemies. "Hello, sir. How's the vice president?"

"Not good." Maynard cleared his throat. "He's a good man. Maybe the best. But this might be more than he can handle. And Esther . . ." A pause. "Aaron filled me in on your and his conversation. What can I do to help? Any resource you need."

I wasn't sure how to take that. To be honest, something in me did not trust it. "Sir?"

I heard a chair squeak. "When we spoke, I knew he had shared with you what he would not share with either his team or certainly the press. So I pressed him. Told him I would exhaust myself to help. We need him. The country needs him."

I looked at Camp. Then Clay. Clay shook his head. Prison had hard-wired into Clay an ability to read people. And Clay's face told me he did not like what he was reading in Maynard's voice. He kept shaking his head slowly side to side. I'd never had any reason to suspect Maynard, but staring at that phone, I discovered that my distrust-meter was dinging loudly. I just didn't want Maynard to know that. I wanted to keep him on the line and make him feel invited into my confidence. Make him feel that he was a needed part of the team. The solution. I needed to make him feel like I had no reason not to tell him everything. I also knew I had to be careful. If he was in any way not what or who he pretended to be, then we were about to play a game of chess—and he'd been playing it a lot longer. He could detect a fraud a mile away. I also didn't need him to feel baited. I needed him to feel brought into the fold. I decided I had to give him something small but realistic. Something that might trigger a reaction. "Sir, the thermals in the hallway only gave us facial recognition on three of the men. One led us to Maui. The second, here to Jerusalem. We're tracking the third down now, but no leads."

"Did you learn anything in Maui?"

"Only that they're well financed, professional, and arm's length. Totally clean. They were hired for a job, did it, and now they're probably on to the next." Then I threw this in there and I can't really tell you why. More of a hunch. "Sir, I know the media pushed the 'bow out now and we let them go' demand letter, but I think that's disingenuous. I think it's a head fake to spend resources. Aaron has no competitor. No one to fill the void. This isn't about the presidency."

"I follow, and the team here tends to agree. But what are you suggesting?"

"Ultimately, this comes down to money. Whoever hired them wants more. A lot more. And, given his position and favorable ratings, they know they can put the screws to Aaron and get it. He'll have donors flocking, falling all over themselves to fund the ransom, get the girls back, and make him look like a loving dad caught in an impossible crossfire—which will only make him look more human. More likable. I'm anticipating a second demand letter soon, which will also stipulate that if he makes it or the dollar amount of the demand public, he'll never see the girls again. He'll need you to help rally the donors. Dial for dollars."

"I agree. How much are you anticipating?"

"Sir, even his critics believe he'll win in a landslide, which means he'll have people coming out of the woodwork to support him. You would know far better than I, but if a presidential race today costs near a billion, I think we could be looking at half that."

"Murph, you're spot-on. I'm on it. I'll do what I can."

"Thank you, sir." While I knew the answer to the next question, I asked it because if Maynard was in any way untrue, or not who we all believed him to be, I didn't want him to think Ashley and I were in as close communication as we were. I wanted him to think I was an officer following orders, not a friend helping a close friend at any cost. To help with this, I referred to Ashley by his position, not his name, giving the impression that Ashley kept me at arm's length. "Sir, where's the vice president now?"

"Georgia."

"He's with Esther?"

"Yes, and his team is scouring the ground."

"Sir, I want to be careful not to unduly burden the vice president. I would feel better if I could communicate details with you and your team."

"This is my personal cell. Use it anytime."

"Thank you, sir."

I hung up, and Camp shook his head. "What was all that about?"

"I don't know, but—"

Clay cut me off. "Something stinks."

I nodded.

Camp closed the airplane door. "Where to?"

"Georgia. We need a face-to-face with Aaron."

Camp picked up on the meaning behind my assertion. "You concerned?"

"I'm concerned Aaron's compromised."

He agreed. "If they can circumvent the Secret Service detail and his security system and disappear without a trace, then you can pretty much bet the farm they're in his phone."

CHAPTER 30

We landed in Georgia twelve hours later. Day five and counting. I'd slept on the plane for the first time in days, which was good because I'd been running on fumes and my ability to make quick and intelligent decisions was becoming compromised. But the sleep was fitful and there was little peace in it. Every time I closed my eyes, I saw either Miriam, Ruth, or Sadie lying helpless and abused. Once I was able to shake those images, I saw Bones, lifeless and riddled with holes.

When we approached the gate, a new security detail met us. Four guys dressed in tactical gear surrounded the vehicle while two more covered us with rifles from an elevated position. They waved us through, we drove the half mile to the house, and Aaron walked out the door when we pulled up the drive. He was dressed in jeans, a sweatshirt, and boots and carried a pistol. Oddly, Esther did not appear.

Aaron led us through the house, retracing the steps of the six abductors. Through a side door. Up a carpeted stairwell. We stopped at Esther's room, and he explained how they put her into a deeper sleep. Then the girls' rooms where he detailed the death of the dogs and how the girls were taken. Then we retraced our steps, exiting the house, walking through the pasture, stopping to understand where the snipers had lain prior to entry, and then slipping through the pines to where the SUVs had been parked. It was simple. It was also unbelievable that they'd gotten away with it.

Aaron was quiet. And his strength was waning. What man could endure this torture? The not knowing. It was horror defined. When we returned to the house, I wrote on a piece of paper and showed it to Aaron. It read, "Can we talk?"

He gestured to his office but I pointed to the pecan grove and pressed my finger to my lips. I also pointed to his phone and shook my head. Aaron understood and left it in his office. We walked into the grove beneath the sweeping arms of old pecan trees. Free of the house, he turned to me. "Anything?"

I shook my head. "No."

He instantly deflated. If a chair had been present, he'd have sat down. Without too much detail, I briefed him on our conversation with Ariel Underwood and how that might lead us to the source who funded his girls' abduction. Then I relayed my conversation with Waylon Maynard, ending with, "Sir, something's off. He was fishing. And I don't trust him."

Aaron was not convinced. "Yet everyone in DC does." Then he shook his head. "I've known him a long time. He's good people."

"I realize that, but he had a sense that you told me something you didn't tell anyone else. That's why he called. He thinks there's something he doesn't know. So I want to ask you to do two things."

Aaron waited.

"I need you to confer exclusively with Maynard. Bring him into your confidence. Tell him things you don't tell your team. I'm not saying it has to be true, but let him think he's your primary confidant. I'll do the same on my end. We'll make him think he's the center."

"I can do that, but why?"

"I don't exactly know, but my hunch is that he knows more than he's saying. If I'm wrong, then you've just confided in the most trusted man in politics who alone can help you get elected more than any other."

"And if you're right?"

"That brings me to the second thing." Aaron waited. "I need you to begin talking about suspending your campaign."

"Why?" He waved his hand across the exit route of the abductors. "So these miscreants win?"

"No, sir. I don't want you to actually do it. I just want you to begin talking about it, privately. With me."

"What does this accomplish?"

"I want to see what he does. Bear with me . . . I want you and I to walk back into your office where you shut the door, sit me down, and begin talking with me, and only me, in hushed tones, about suspending. I need for you to have given it some thought. The weight of all this is too much."

In a rare show of emotion, Aaron broke, snapping, "It is too much."

"I'm sorry, sir." A pause. "I don't mean to be so insensitive."

He shook his head. "It's not you. It's just . . ." His eyes wandered to the covered dock at the pond. Esther sat alone, staring out across the water. "She's inconsolable."

"We'll find them, sir."

"And if you don't?"

I had no response, because there wasn't one.

He gathered himself. "Continue."

"I'll object to the suggestion, but after you convince me otherwise, I'll float the idea that you need to run it by Maynard."

"What will that accomplish?"

"Two things. It will make him think we think this entire thing is about money."

"Well, isn't it?"

"No, sir."

"What, then?"

"It's about the presidency. Your job. It's about power."

"Continue."

"I told Maynard that if a presidential campaign could cost a billion, the ransom could be half that."

"You believe that?"

"Doesn't matter what I believe. What matters is what he does with it. You get a ransom note anywhere near that, and my suspicions are founded."

"I'm listening."

"I want you to bemoan raising the money. Talk about your personal finances, how everything you have is invested in the campaign, how even selling the farm is not a drop in the bucket. How you would need help from donors."

"I follow you."

"If sometime in the next few days, you and Esther get a ransom note that first demands you not make it public, and second demands several hundred million dollars wired to an offshore account, then I think you're not far from a phone call from Maynard. And I'll bet once you"—I held quotation fingers in the air—"'reveal' the ransom letter to him, even slide it across the desk, he'll offer to rally the troops."

"But he'd offer to do that anyway."

"Yes. Which will not make him suspicious of us. This is about timing. Sir, we are fishing. We need to know if he's listening to you."

"You think my office is bugged?"

"Sir, I think your life is bugged."

He waited, considering this.

"But I'm the vice president of the United States."

"And someone just abducted your three daughters while your wife slept down the hall. No way that happens without someone or someones on the inside."

Aaron's face told me his mind was traveling down all the rabbit trails created by this revelation. "I'm listening."

"If he's listening, then I want to see how long it takes him to contact you and how he approaches you in that contact. What's his posture? His suggestion?"

"You think there's a connection between Maynard and my girls?"

"I don't know if there's a connection or he's capitalizing on it."

Aaron nodded.

"There's a lot we don't know. I also want to give you a phone. It's been cleaned and encrypted by Eddie. I don't want anyone to know about it and I only want you to communicate with me on it. Don't let anyone, not even Esther, know of its presence."

"You realize this is against the law."

"I do. But honestly, sir, I don't care. And neither do Miriam, Ruth, and Sadie."

"Okay, let's say he takes the bait. What then?"

"Play along."

"You want me to actually begin the process of suspending my campaign?"

"No, sir. I want you to begin talking about it."

Aaron's eyes wandered to Esther. "For this to work, we need Esther. She can spot a fake a mile away. She'll never go for it if she's not in on it."

"I'll talk to her."

Aaron continued, "And if you're right, and Waylon is as conniving as you say—which flies in the face of about four decades of selfless work in Washington—then he won't trust your and my private conversation. He'll test Esther. See what she knows. If she's in, he'll believe. If she's not, he won't."

"Agreed."

"In the meantime, what will you do?"

"Return to Freetown, gather my team. Ariel's idea about Frank's generals and how he might have inserted this chip without their knowing has merit. We need to follow up on it. If, by some chance, we uncover something, I'll text you on the new phone. You can call me when you're clear."

"Clear?"

"This plan involves you, me, and Esther."

"Stackhouse?"

I shook my head.

"You think he's compromised?"

"No, sir, I don't. But we have to reduce the variables. Control what we can. And the fewer people that know, the more we can control."

He paused. "Maynard's been playing this chess game a lot longer than us."

"I realize that. Which is why I think he'll wait a few days between sending the note and calling."

"How many?"

131

"Three. Maybe four. He would want you in pain."

"I'm already there."

I said nothing.

He continued, "Let's say you're right. What does Maynard want? The presidency? He's turned that down. Multiple times. So what's his endgame?"

"I don't know, sir."

"And if you're wrong? We're spending energy and resources that we need elsewhere. And you're gambling with my girls' lives. The consequences of that"—he shook his head—"are more than I can fathom."

When Bones first took me under his wing, he often separated me from my fellow cadets. I trained alone. Learned to work alone. To make difficult decisions alone and then act on them. Quickly. And without deliberation. I alone bore the weight and consequences of right and wrong decisions. When I asked him why, he said, "It's easier to turn a johnboat than an aircraft carrier." For years I didn't understand. What we do is a combination of defense and offense. Rescuing the taken requires both. And we need to be able to pivot on a dime if the strategy demands it. Staring at Aaron Ashley, I was reminded of why. Because convincing a team to do hard things, in the middle of a hard thing, is wasted energy. That training must happen before the war. Not during. I had bounced Miriam and Ruth on my knee and was at the hospital when Sadie was born. I had birthday cards in my dresser drawer at Freetown addressed to "Uncle Murph." There was nothing I wouldn't do, and Ashley knew that. And I knew he knew that. I also knew the pain was talking. And when it came to pain, none was deeper than what Ashley was currently living.

"Sir . . . this is not a job. I don't clock out."

He palmed his face. "I'm sorry, Murph. It's just that—"

"Sir, we'll get them back."

CHAPTER 31

A week passed at Freetown. Then two. For Miriam, Ruth, and Sadie, the clock had ticked through nineteen days. The team and I had nothing. No hint. Ashley's girls had disappeared literally without a trace. I had seldom felt so helpless. Eddie, Jess, BP, and Camp, with input from Ariel's team, had scoured the data vault and come up empty-handed. Zilch. We were no closer. We didn't disagree with Ariel's theory, but the data he suggested we'd find was not in Frank's servers. If his theory was true, the data existed someplace else, and it began to look like Eddie might be right. If the data existed, Frank hid it in plain sight somewhere in one of ten trillion possible addresses on the internet.

In the meantime, Ashley moved a piece across the board and began living the drama. His public appearances were uncharacteristically not good. People in his own party began to not so subtly suggest he rescind the nomination. Step aside. Some even suggested he step down. During this time, who was his sole ally? Who stood by his side, making the prime-time rounds, arguing with the talking heads and prognosticators? Who was the singular voice speaking contrary to the critics? To the party?

Maynard was a rock.

The waiting was always the hardest part. It could be excruciating. I tried not to listen to the whispers of what could be happening to the girls in that very moment, because there was nothing I could do about it. I tried to remind myself that if there was, I'd be doing it, but that was little consolation. Without more to go on, finding Miriam, Ruth, and Sadie was like finding a needle in the Milky Way. We were in a holding pattern until something happened. And we were useless until that something happened. Well, maybe that wasn't entirely true. Eddie, Jess, BP, and Camp were scouring the black web. Combing the internet. Burning the candle, looking for anything. I, on the other hand, because I did not possess their tech-savvy computer skills, was the one who was currently useless. I could have stood around in command central, but I'd only be in the way.

With more going on in my head than I knew how to process, I had to give my hands something to do. Busy hands freed up a tangled mind. So when Ellie pushed open the door at 5:00 a.m., she found me cleaning guns in the basement. They weren't dirty, but that wasn't the point. Bed head, pajamas, blanket in tow, slits for eyes, she sat next to me and dug her shoulder beneath mine without saying anything. Evidently her mind needed unwinding too.

Ellie had taken to life in Freetown with all she had. She was all in. She worked with Summer in the dance academy during the day, had been learning photography from Bones in the evenings, and tended the ice cream parlor on weekends. She was always busy. Always cheering somebody up. But every once in a while over the last few months, she'd ask me a question about Marie. "Dad, tell me about Mom." At first, she wouldn't ask me in front of Summer. Felt it was some sort of betrayal of Summer. Felt like she had to sneak around and find me alone. Then Summer overheard her one day, walked in, sat behind her, and began brushing her hair while I told her stories about her mom. When I finished, Ellie was leaning against Summer's chest, and Summer had both arms wrapped around Ellie's waist. That was the end of the shame.

Despite my best attempts, I felt like no matter how hard I tried or what I told her, I always left her wanting more. Answering nothing. Or very little. I tried to give her something to hold on to, but it was difficult to touch a memory. But oddly, when she walked in the basement, I heard myself ask myself, "Or is it?"

She leaned against me, just content to be in my presence. Finally, she wrapped an arm around me and said, "Tell me about Mom?"

That was when it hit me. Maybe it wasn't impossible to touch a memory. I nodded. "Yes. But not here. Get dressed first. We're going on a trip."

Thirty minutes later, as the first rays of sunlight were cracking the skyline, we were buckled into our seats and climbing to our cruising altitude of forty thousand feet. Three hours later, we touched down at Craig Field in Jacksonville. We taxied to my hangar, and the pilots shut her down just a few feet from the door. I brushed the cobwebs off the keypad and pulled back on the doors, shedding light on one of several gear rooms I had stashed around the country. Ellie loved going with me into my gear rooms. Said she always learned something new about me. I handed her a helmet, pulled on my own, cranked the BMW GS1200, and she climbed on the back. I pulled out of Craig, turned west on Monument, and headed north on I-295, exiting at Heckscher Drive. She loved riding a bike with me but not as much as I loved riding one with her. She'd wrap her arms around me and cling tighter every time I accelerated. So I accelerated a lot.

We wound north up Heckscher Drive and finally turned left onto a dirt road that led onto my island.

The coastal islands of North Florida are not Hawaii or the Bahamas. And they're not something you'd see on *Gilligan's Island* or read about in *Robinson Crusoe*—which, by the way, is possibly my all-time favorite book. The coastal islands along Northeast Florida and Southeast Georgia sat within eyesight of the mainland, separated by patches of marsh, tidal creeks, or the Intracoastal Waterway. The ICW. Some were connected by short bridges, and we called them islands because "marshy extensions" didn't sound as romantic and didn't help sell. Most all of them were inhabited by Native Americans at some point due to an ample food source such as fish or oysters, and at the turn of the twentieth century, many of them were turned into wealthy country clubs for the uber elite such as the Morgans and Rockefellers—Sea Island and Jekyll were two notable examples. My island was a small pitch of land just across the creek from Fort George Island. It was there, during one idyllic summer of my childhood, that I'd met Marie and shown her my secret world beneath these majestic oaks.

I parked the bike, Ellie slipped her hand inside mine, and we walked through the shade and back into my memories. I had not rebuilt since Frank blew up my boat and set my entire world on fire, so I pointed as we walked through the charred remains. "That's the old slave chapel." The two-foot-thick tabby walls were impervious to fire, meaning what was left of the roof just leaned against it.

"Does it make you sad?" Ellie asked.

I nodded. It did. We walked the exterior of the chapel. "This is where I first met Angel." She liked the thought of that. Her eyes lit. "Really?"

So I told her the story.

"So this is where she first started calling you Padre?"

I laughed. "Yep. Right here."

I pushed away some burnt timbers and we walked inside where the pews used to line the floor in front of the altar. I showed her the wall. This intrigued her. She pointed. "What's that?"

"This chapel was once part of the Underground Railroad. It was more of a destination than a stop on the way. Once here, they were free. So they carved their names along with the date as best they knew it. It's a record of who they are. And that they matter. It's as if they stood here and said to the world, 'God made me. I matter. What you see when you see me started in the mind of God. He actually took the time to think me up.'"

Ellie traced her fingers through the grooves. "Is that what led to the tattoos on your back?"

"I think so."

I watched her run her fingers through each of the letters. "Your mother used to do that very thing."

"Really?" She smiled.

"She'd trace every one. Tell them they weren't forgotten." I studied the fallen world around me. "This island was a declaration. A stake driven into the surface of the earth. Both an ending and a beginning." Above the names, someone had carved, "Even the Rocks Cry Out." Ellie traced this too.

"What does this mean?"

"I think it means that no matter how dark the darkness, light pierces it. That no darkness can keep out the light. Darkness is powerless against light."

"Did Bones teach you that?"

I nodded. "Yes." A smile. "He did." Another pause. "And your mom did too."

We walked down what was once a well-worn trail now overgrown and green. I pointed to the mounds we'd made as kids. "We'd dig here. Hours at a time. All the way to China. That hole used to be above my head."

She giggled, knelt, and ran her fingers through the dirt.

"Found several megalodon sharks' teeth in here." I circled one of the mounds. "Your mom and I planted those citrus trees."

She reached up, pulled a green lemon from a tree, and smelled it, saying nothing.

"One afternoon, I uncovered this grave of what I had to assume was a Native American. Slowly, we removed the dirt, trying not to disturb anything. We couldn't tell how he died. All his bones were intact and he'd been buried wearing something on his head, a fishhook in one hand, a small knife in the other, and a rather primitive bow and arrows lying across his chest."

She sat on the mound and pulled her knees to her chest.

"The bow was worn, maybe three feet long, and the string must have been something like catgut. The arrows were surprisingly straight and flint-tipped. Sharp enough to penetrate hide. The feather fletching was long since gone. Your mom was amazed at him. Just lying there. We must have sat right about where you're sitting and stared at him for hours. Wondering what his life was like. Making up stories about him and that bow." I sat next to her. Shoulder to shoulder. "I don't know if I've ever made this connection, but it was probably right here that your mom taught me to daydream. To wonder. To tell a story."

Ellie stared up at me. "Mom taught you that?"

"Yeah. I think so. I remember the feeling of standing in that hole, staring at those bones lying beneath these trees, and just letting my imagination run free. Your mom used to love to listen to me spin a story about 'the old man,' as I called him."

She giggled again.

"I know, not very original, but it's all I could think of at the time." I pressed into the memory. "During that summer, your mom would sit and listen to me for hours as one story led to another. About the pirates who stored gold beneath the old man's bones. About the girl who escaped the ship and swam ashore here." I shook my head in wonder. "I guess if I had to say, this is where it happened. This is where I learned to make story."

She was shaking her head and smiling. "Mom did that?"

"She was the catalyst."

"What'd she do?"

"She gave me the freedom to think outside the box—to dream and then put words to the dream without worry of criticism. Without causing a knee-jerk in me that it might not be good enough. That it might be stupid." A longer pause. "Your mom was never a critic. I never knew that from her. So, much later in life, when I found myself in a rough spot, tending bar in Key West, I found an outlet for my pain. My pen."

"So all these books that you've written, they all started here?"

"The process did." I stared at the mound. "As the sun was setting, we knew we needed to return him to the ground, so we slowly and quietly covered him back up. Returning the stones as best we knew how. Then, to make sure the dirt held in place and wouldn't erode too quickly, we transplanted several ferns and two lemon and two lime trees to mark the four corners." I pointed. "And from the looks of things, they did just that."

I lifted her by the hand and we continued walking the path. "This is also where I learned to hunt. Killed my first pig over there. It was trying to dig up the old man."

She wrinkled her nose. "Oooh."

I pointed at the recent signs. "Feral hogs have been here since the Spanish landed on that beach over there. They'd brought them with them in the hull of the ships as a food source. Once here, they domesticated them, but some got loose. They populate fast, so it didn't take long for them to take over. They can pretty well annihilate a patch of ground rooting for worms and grubs."

A pause. "In the summer of my junior year, we had our own archaeological dig in here, and it was your mom who discovered a large collection of shells. Kind of a three-hundred-year-old trash heap. We spent the summer digging right there. This mound became the mother lode of pottery shards, arrowheads, shark's teeth. Even glass beads."

She looked up at me. A sly smile. "You kiss Mom here?"

I laughed and shook my head. "No. Too afraid. I wanted to, but we were just two kids, nothing but sweat, dreams, and innocence. Plus, I didn't know anything about how to kiss a girl. The thought of that scared me half to death. I was much more comfortable with a fishing pole or a cast net."

This time Ellie laughed out loud. "I see little has changed."

I studied her. The image of her mother. I could even hear it in her tone of voice. Looking at her was like looking into the eyes of Marie. "When did you ever get so grown up?"

"Dad." She put one hand on her hip to emphasize her point. "I'm not a little girl anymore."

"Yeah, I'm seeing that." And she wasn't. Ellie was becoming a woman.

We spent the afternoon beneath the shade on the beach. I fished or threw the cast net while Gunner terrorized the mullet. Ellie lay in the sun, her face hidden beneath a straw hat and sunglasses, and held a paperback in her hands. Her voice brought me out of my memories. "What're you looking at?"

"Huh?"

"You've been sitting there staring at me for five minutes. What're you looking at?"

"Sorry." I shook my head. "If I squint my eyes, I see your mom."

She liked the thought of that. "You think Summer is jealous of Mom? Of the memory of her?"

"No." Another shake. "Summer knows who she is. She walks in no woman's shadow. She also knows that love is not something you have to cut in half when you meet another. Love is not like a bucket and that's all you got. Use sparingly. It's more like a well. Or a river. The more you draw from it, the more water it pours out. Love doesn't halve—it doubles. Triples. It's an exponential thing."

I didn't know the full effect of my words on Ellie. If I'm honest, while one half of me was here on the island with her, the other half of my mind was worrying about Ruth, Miriam, and Sadie. Would they ever get to walk in the woods again with their dad? To just spend a lazy day in each other's presence? I did my best to hide that from Ellie, to be present here with her in this moment, because the longer we stayed on my island, the more her demeanor changed. She was "becoming" before my very eyes. Becoming what, I wasn't sure. But her posture was changing. I was watching a shift in the tectonic plates that made up her soul. As if her shoulders were rolling back and this connection to Marie, to her beginnings, was birthing something in her that I could only relate to something Bones once told me: "Identity precedes purpose. You can't know who you are until you know whose you are. Belongingness matters."

Here, for some reason, Ellie was learning whose she was. Who she belonged to. Here beneath these trees, her heart was learning that she was ours. Mine and Marie's. Together. Standing on this island, she had placed her finger on that pulse and knew that the beautiful thing that had happened between Marie and me, the love we shared, had grown and become her. That love made her. And I think the impact of that was more than I had anticipated. As the sun set and the shadows stretched across the beach, I found myself stalling. I knew we needed to get back, but I was waiting. Waiting for one thing. One sound.

Then, as if on cue, it cracked through the stratosphere. There it was. I might have left. Traveled the globe. But it never had. It had remained. If heaven has a frequency, it must be this one. It is both a lonely echo and a magnificent cry. Made by a singular creature. While I don't pretend to understand sound waves, this one travels. I don't mean it's loud. It's not. It's actually quite quiet. More like a whisper. Something you have to train your ear to hear, and if you're not careful, you'll miss it. It's the song of the mourning dove. One dove calling to its mate. Cooing. For me it has long been the cry of heaven, and I've wondered, more than once, if it's the sound of angels. The truest cry of the human heart. One lover calling to another. I waited and there it was again.

This time she heard it. She pointed. "Is that . . . ?" She fell silent and there it was again. Off to our left, a second dove answered. I nodded and said nothing.

We sat there as the two lovers called back and forth. She whispered, "They really do call to each other."

"They really do."

Moments passed. "I think that may be one of my favorite sounds. Ever."

There it was again. "Me too."

"Dad?"

We returned up the trail, her hand in mine. I looked at her but said nothing.

"Thanks for bringing me. I know it's been difficult."

"Being with you is never difficult. It's one of my favorite things."

"I mean, being here while Ruth, Miriam, and Sadie are out there and you can't help them."

I had kept the wave of urgency at bay, away from my mind and heart. But when she said that, I could hold it back no longer. It came crashing down with a vengeance. "That's the other thing your mom gave me."

She waited.

I pointed out across the water that led into the Atlantic. Then I pointed at the single ring she wore that had belonged to her mom.

CHAPTER 32

Y ou remember when I gave that to you?"

She nodded.

"Want to hear the whole story?"

Another nod.

We'd made it back to the slave chapel, and she sat on what had been a pew, the burnt sticks of what remained of my barn just over her shoulder. I did not hurry. Didn't rush the story. I had a feeling this was why we'd come.

"I worked at a tire store. Got off at nine. Your mom was a bit of a partier. I was not. She had this crazy group of friends. Actually, they weren't friends. Friends don't do what they did, but anyway, they hung out. I owned a Gheenoe. Sort of a canoe with a motor. I knew she was at this party, and I had no interest in the party but I wanted to see if she was okay. Just hear her voice. So I cranked the engine under a full moon and a flood tide. Which meant there was a lot of water everywhere. The marsh was flooded. The big reds love it in there, so I was casting beneath the moonlight, wishing I could pull her away from that party to be with me." I smiled. "Maybe I was having a little pity party."

She smirked. "Seems like I've heard a version of this before."

"You have. Want me to stop?"

"No way." She tucked her knees back into her chest as if she were hugging herself.

"Midnight found me toward the mouth of the river, where the IC meets the St. Johns. It's big water and no place for a Gheenoe, but the reds were there, so . . . About 12:30, I heard a helicopter. Then I saw a boat motoring slowly downriver. Two large spotlights searching the surface. Never a good sign. Then the helicopter passed overhead, a larger searchlight, and then the boat. I heard loud, frantic voices. I flagged them down. Several guys from school, the guys with letterman jackets and college offers. They told me they'd gone night tubing and one of the girls had been thrown off. They couldn't find her. 'What's her name?' I asked. One of the guys flippantly waved his beer through the air. 'Starts with an *M*. Mary. Marcia. Something.' Three Coast Guard boats appeared soon after. Flashing lights. Sirens. Followed by two helicopters. The water became a choppy mess and no place for my boat. That flood tide was about to turn and head out, and I knew it'd be moving fast. Which meant whoever they were looking for would be moving fast too. 'What time this happen?' I asked. The guy swigged his beer and threw the can in the river. ''Bout 8:30.' Four hours had passed. I looked at those idiots like they'd lost their ever-loving minds. They were all looking in the wrong place."

When I had first told this story to Ellie, I'd just found Casey in the shower and taken her to the hospital. She was touch and go. Summer was looking for Angel, and we weren't sure if she had been sold or not. Add to that Ellie's granite exterior, and we were swimming in uncertainty. Back then Ellie wasn't sure she liked me, and she certainly didn't trust me. If her life had taught her anything up to that moment, it was to never trust men.

Here in this moment, sitting on that charred pew, wrapped in the arms of my island, her castle walls had crumbled, granting me unfettered access to her heart. Proving that love is and always has been the most powerful weapon in this universe or any other.

I continued, "I cranked the engine and made my way by moonlight about three miles toward the inlet where the St. Johns River meets the Atlantic Ocean."

She interrupted me, nodding. "'The Jetties."

"Correct. When I got there, the waves were over my head. Even if I was able to navigate out of the channel, against the waves, when I returned, the force and height of the waves would nosedive my boat and sink it like a torpedo. I had cut the engine, felt the pull of the current taking me at six to seven knots, and knew your mom had already passed through. She was floating in the Atlantic. Out to sea. So I cranked the engine and pointed the nose through the waves. Once I broke free of the Jetties, the waves calmed and I could make out the surface of the water in the moonlight. I cut the engine, let the current pull me, and listened. I did this every couple of minutes as the lights of the shoreline grew farther and farther distant. Finally, with land six or seven miles to my west and a whole lot of really big water to my east, I just sat there floating. Listening. Letting the current pull me. Somewhere in there, I heard a voice rise up out of the water. In the middle of that really big dark ocean, I heard my name. Faint. Then louder. I searched frantically but couldn't make it out. So . . ."

I clasped my hands together and acted like that was the end of the story. She knew better, as I'd done the exact same thing the first time I'd told it to her. She smiled and rolled her eyes exactly as she had before. "Hey." She tapped the ring. "At least I didn't throw it in the water."

I continued, both of us wrapped in the warmth of memory. "Couple hundred yards south, I saw a disturbance. Could have been anything. But I aimed for it and held the throttle wide open until I reached where I thought it had been, then I cut the engine, coasted, and listened. Your mom was screaming at me off my starboard side. That's the—"

She raised an eyebrow. "Dad. I know it's the right side."

"Just making sure."

She laughed.

"I pulled hard on the tiller and found her clutching a piece of driftwood and wearing a life jacket, which probably saved her life. She was cold, in shock, her head barely above water. I knew I'd never make it back through the Jetties, and I wasn't sure if I had enough fuel to make it back to land, so I pointed the nose at the lights onshore and hoped. We ran out of gas a couple hundred yards from shore. I paddled the rest. When we pulled the Gheenoe up on the beach, I built a fire, and we sat there holding each other until the sun rose. We never told anyone what happened. When they asked her at school, she told everyone she'd hit her head on a dock piling and was only able to climb up before she passed out. When she woke up, she walked home."

I paused, letting the images settle. "But that night on the beach, after she'd finished shivering, she held up a single finger, touching mine with the tip of hers. She said, 'You could've died out there tonight.' She was right. I could have. Shaking her head, she asked me, 'Why'd you do it? Why'd you leave everyone to find me?' I'm not sure why I said what I did, but whatever my reason, I told her the truth."

I pulled the worn coin out of my pocket and turned it. "Bones gave me this as a kid, not far from here in a diner. He'd had it inscribed with the eleven words that had become the window through which I saw the world."

Ellie thumbed a tear, smiling. Even nodding. And spoke them from memory. "Because the needs of the one outweigh those of the ninety-nine."

CHAPTER 33

W hen I said that to your mom . . ." I sat on the bench, facing Ellie, and held out my index finger just like I had with her mom. She reached up, touched mine with hers, and I spread my fingers and intertwined hers with mine. "This silly hand gesture started on that beach that night. It became the fabric of us. Our thing. It was how we remembered the moment. We could be in a crowd of people, loud music, chatter, and all she had to do was touch my fingertip with hers, and immediately we were back in that water. Sitting on that beach. Her and me. Us against the world. Then it wasn't so silly anymore."

Ellie waited for me to tell the rest of the story. "That morning as the sun rose, we walked the beach. Hand in hand. Maybe the most perfect sunrise in the history of the sun rising. With the water foaming over our ankles, the sun hit the beach and shone on something at the water's edge. I lifted it. A silver cross. Washed up by the same flood tide that had ripped her seven miles out to sea. It was hanging from a leather lace. I tied the lace in a square knot and hung it around her neck. It came to rest flat across her heart. She leaned against me, pressing her ear to my heart. Beneath the waves rolling gently next to us, she had whispered to me, 'If I ever find myself lost, will you come find me?'"

By now, Ellie was full-on crying, so I just wrapped an arm around her. Whatever had been hurting her was leaving. Purged. Taking the pain with it. "And"—I smiled—"that was the first night I kissed your mom."

She smiled. She liked that thought.

"Although to be honest, she kissed me. I was too afraid."

Ellie laughed and wiped her nose on her shirtsleeve.

I continued, "I told you then, and I'm telling you now, finding people is what I do. I found your mom. And we will find Ruth, Miriam, and Sadie. I don't know how, but we will."

She leaned into me.

"I didn't know what to do with all that hurt, so I began writing and didn't stop until I'd emptied myself." I pulled her closer. Up underneath my shoulder. "I don't know if you know this, but I wrote a novel about a character named Fingers."

Ellie laughed and smeared her tears on my sleeve. "Yeah. I know. I've read it like a dozen times."

"Well, maybe you'll remember the letter my protagonist wrote to the female love interest?"

She stiletto-poked me in the rib cage. "You mean Marie."

A laugh. "The very same." Ellie was laughing, and the breath coming out of her was healing.

"Well, anyway, I—I mean, my protagonist—wrote a letter."

She nodded. "Dad, I feel like we're in some sort of wrinkle-in-time thing here."

"Me too. Anyway, it was a letter I—I mean, he—wrote to her when he couldn't find her. It was everything he wanted to tell her and never got the chance. I think it goes something like . . ." I spoke the letter from memory:

My love, I know this letter will hit you hard.

You remember that night I found you out here? Everybody was look-ing for you, but nobody thought to look that far out. But there you were. Floating six or seven miles out. You were so cold. Shaking. Then we ran out of gas a mile from shore, and I paddled us in. You were worried we wouldn't make it. But I had found you. I could have paddled the coast of Florida if it meant we could stay in that boat. Then we built a fire and you leaned into me. I remember feeling the breeze on my face. The fire on my legs and the smell of you washing over me. All I wanted to do was sit and breathe. Stop the sun. Tell it to wait a few more hours. "Please, can't you just hold off a while?" Then you placed your hand on mine and kissed my cheek. You whispered, "Thank you," and I felt your breath on my ear.

I was nobody. A sixteen-year-old shadow walking the halls. A kid with a stupid little boat, but you made me somebody. That night was our secret, and seldom did a day pass that we didn't see each other. Somehow, you always found a way to get to me. Then my senior year came, and you were the only one who thought I could break the record. Forty-eight seconds. I crossed the line and the watch showed forty-seven-point-something, and I collapsed. We did it. I remember the gun going off but I don't remember running. I just remember flying. Floating. A thousand people screaming and all I heard was your voice. It's all I've ever heard.

I don't know how to climb off this beach. I don't know how to walk out of here. I don't know who I am without you. Fingers said to forgive you, but I can't. There's nothing to forgive. Nothing at all. Not even the . . . I want you to know I'm sorry I didn't find you earlier. I'm real sorry. I tried so hard. But evil is real and sometimes it's hard to hear. I wish you could have heard me. So before you go, before . . . I just want you to know that I've loved you from the moment I met you, and you never did anything—not one thing, ever—to make me love you less.

My heart hurts. A lot. It's cracking down the middle, and it's going to hurt even more when I go to stand up and carry you out of here. But no matter where I go, I'm carrying you with me. I'll keep you inside me. And every time I bathe or swim or drink or walk through the waves or pilot a boat or just stand in the rain, I'll let the water keep you in me. Marie, as long as there's water, there's you in me.

When I finished, Ellie was pressing her face to my chest. Sobbing. She was crying so hard her shoulders were shaking, so I just held her. I just wrapped my arms around her and tried to shield her from the pain. Truth was, I couldn't and I knew that, so I just held her while the aftershocks shook her. I kissed her forehead and waited for the tremor to pass. When it did, I brushed her tearstained hair out of her face.

She shook her head in disbelief. "You know it by heart?"

"Of course. That's where it came from. So it stays in there. Here's what I want you to know. Your mom did a thing in me. She made me who I am. I'm not me without her."

"What about Bones?"

"Of course. Bones too. But without your mom, we're not having this conversation. She's the epicenter. She also gave me a gift. A priceless gift. And this magnificent gift has her mom's eyes. Her mom's laugh. Her mom's grit. She's crazy beautiful and she's amazing. I can't wait to see what and who she becomes."

We walked, her arm locked inside mine, back to the bike. Sitting behind me, the engine idling, she took one last look across the world where she'd started. She spoke in my ear. "Dad?"

"Yeah."

"Is it okay if I come back here to your island from time to time? Just to remember this?"

"Yes, but . . ." I shook my head. "It's not my island anymore. It's ours. Yours, mine, and your mom's."

CHAPTER 34

By day twenty-six, I was pacing. Coming out of my skin. But not as much as Aaron and Esther.

I was sipping coffee just prior to 5:00 a.m. when Stackhouse texted me, *You're gonna want to see this.* I clicked on the news to see Ashley standing at a podium. Jeans. Hadn't slept. Haggard. Three-day stubble. No notes. Cameras clicked at fifteen frames per second, attempting to memorialize his pain-riddled face. For the last four weeks, the news had covered his girls' disappearance. Weeks one and two were rather kind. Empathetic even. By week three the tone started to change. Questions surfaced. "Our investigators have uncovered surprising evidence of lax security measures." Now they blamed him. Personally. One outlet asked, "How could he fail his daughters? He had one job."

Ashley cleared his throat and stared into and beyond the cameras. The room fell eerily silent as even the cameras quit clicking. After a long pause, Ashley spoke. "Twenty-six days, eleven hours, and thirteen minutes ago, six deviant reprobates entered my house and took Miriam, Ruth, and Sadie." Aaron held up a family picture with his and Esther's arms wrapped around their laughing daughters. A beautiful family moment. "Now, some four weeks later, I am not able to perform the job for which I have been elected— which is not good for this country. When I was first elected to the House, I made a promise to help keep you safe. You and your kids. Throughout my career, I've worked hard to do just that. But when it mattered most, I failed to keep that promise. And as much as I love this country, I love my daughters more. They are my country. When they needed me, I wasn't there. I cannot—"

Ashley broke off. While he was in excruciating pain, there was an undercurrent I'd not seen coming. Ashley was using this press conference to stoke the fire. He was picking a fight. Taking it to the enemy. Up to now, the ransom note had not come, but I wondered what effect this would have. He cleared his throat. "I am considering not seeking or accepting my party's nomination for president." Ashley's voice cracked as he fought to maintain his composure. A vein popped on his right temple. "To my girls, I love you and . . . I'm coming." Another pause. His eyes were steel. Locked. Cold. And penetrating. "And to the men who hold them . . . this earth is not big enough."

With that, Ashley turned and walked away as reporters shouted questions, which I doubt he heard.

I wanted to call him. Offer some encouraging word, but I had none. In terms of a percentage, our chances of recovery were low. Single digits. Feeling helpless, I did the only thing I knew to do. I laced on my boots, and Gunner and I walked into the basement. I opened the safe intending to grab Jolene—my Bergara .300 Win Mag with which Bones and I dispatched the barge captain at a little over a mile—but for some reason I felt the tug to go old school. So I slung Maggie over my shoulder, and Gunner and I began climbing to the Eagle's Nest, setting out in the snow under the fading moonlight. I ran hard, pulling with my arms as much as my legs. Willing my lungs to eat more and more air. I had grown angry and exasperated and needed to cleanse my body of the emotional toxins that simmering rage had produced so that my mind, and heart, could think clearly. Every time I closed my eyes, I saw two images I could not process. Three abducted girls and one dead man.

One of my favorite ways to clear the fog was to give my mind something else to think about. A problem to solve. Climbing hard and then shooting long range did that. Hitting a target at a thousand yards, or maybe two, could be a rather complicated math equation. In a relatively short amount of time, the shooter would have to take into account distance, wind, speed and weight of projectile, ballistic coefficient, stationary or moving target, elevation, suppression or lack thereof. If the target was far enough away, you even had to account for the Coriolis effect—the effect of the earth's rotation on the flight of the bullet.

Summer told me that my habit of naming my guns with feminine names was weird and I should rethink it. She said it was like I was cheating on her. I told her they weren't all female. I had a shotgun named Bruce Lee because every time I pulled the trigger, he thumped me in the face. She laughed. Really, though, naming the weapon came from long hours spent behind it. Staring through the optics, I'd begin to view life through that lens. Those of us who hunted wolves often found ourselves clinging to our weapon when hunted by the pack, because what we did, we often did alone, and a companion was a comfort. Especially when we knew our weapon by name, because it meant we'd been here before. So . . . we named them.

Bones and I had placed steel targets throughout the mountains at distances from a few hundred yards to well over a mile. Actually, I carried them, some as heavy as a hundred pounds, while Bones pointed. "Put it there." He was management. I was labor. Steel targets were helpful because they gave the shooter an auditory response. A sound. Paper targets couldn't do that for obvious reasons. Paper targets often required up-close inspection because they didn't show holes well, but up-close inspection could be difficult when they were a mile and a half away. Getting to the target and back could take an hour, maybe more, depending on the terrain. So steel let me know whether I'd hit it or not. The gong told me.

Maggie was a Ruger 1 chambered in .30–06. That description alone should give you some history. It was a single shot rifle. Meaning, I loaded one round at a time through the breach. It was an extremely strong receiver, a design initially used in tanks and larger weapons, then downsized for human hands and designed to hunt elephants and dangerous game in Africa because of the mechanism's ability to withstand extreme pressure. Given its rock-solid success and reliable track record of going "boom" when called upon, it was brought back to the States a hundred years ago and chambered in smaller calibers. The venerable .30–06 (thirty-aught-six) was maybe the most storied cartridge in the history of the world. Some gun pundits argued this, but they were simply wrong. Given more modern technology and a growing population of shooters who pushed the limits looking for bigger, stronger, faster, quieter, and with less recoil, the .30–06 had grown out of fashion in recent years, but it was quite possible more animals and people had been killed with it than any other caliber. Created in 1906, it cut its teeth in two world wars and served faithfully in Vietnam and Korea. It was highly probable the .30–06 was the most tried and true cartridge ever placed in a chamber. As a cartridge, a .30-caliber projectile sat atop fifty-five to fifty-seven grains of powder, which produced an average muzzle velocity of 2,700 to 2,800 feet per second when pushing a 165- to 180-grain bullet. These were averages, as the case would hold sixty-seven grains of powder, but as I'd aged, I'd come to appreciate a rifle whose recoil didn't bruise my shoulder. And Maggie did not. Not to mention, with the right optics, barrel, and trigger—which she had—she was good out past a mile.

CHAPTER 35

Maggie was a gift. My first from Bones. During my time at the academy, Bones taught me to shoot longer distances. A learned skill. His purpose was simple. Most movies glorified rapid rainstorms of lead. Someone shooting thousands of rounds a second, most of which never hit their intended target, while someone hid behind a couch or a bush or something totally incapable of providing cover. The Ruger 1 receiver was unlike most other modern sporting rifles. It was sleek while also tough as nails. Matter of fact, the first gunsmiths to test it commented that they simply could not blow it up. It was reminiscent of John Browning's 1885 Winchester and the venerable Sharps and Remington rolling blocks made famous during the eradication of sixty million buffalo. But unlike most of those single-shot breach-loaders with exposed hammers, the kind you cocked with your thumb, the Ruger 1 didn't work that way. It featured the patented function of a Scot named John Farquharson. A lever below the receiver dropped the breach, exposing the chamber, where a round was loaded before the lever was brought upward again, closing the breach and cocking the action. The "Farquharson action" was later refined by Swedish, German, and Finnish gunmakers, eventually coming to rest in the hands of Sturm, Ruger & Company, which began producing the Ruger 1 in the late 1960s.

By any description, it was a simple weapon. No frills. It was not sexy in the current tactical world of high speed, low drag, and increased magazine capacity. Its weakness, if it had one, was that it could shoot only one round at a time. Which was exactly why Bones gave her to me. The lesson was simple. Whether your weapon was belt fed, magazine fed, or hand fed, you still had only one round in the chamber. So you should make that one count. Maggie, more than any other rifle, taught me that I only needed one round. And given that I had only one, I needed to focus all my energy on it. Not the next one. Not the one after that. Only the one in the chamber. Because it was the only one that mattered. Shooting Maggie required me to slow down. Focus. Unlike the tactical precision rifles used these days, which were mostly all black, comprised of a combination of aluminum, carbon fiber, and other space-age technology, Maggie was old-school hand-oiled mahogany and blued steel.

I spread my shooter's mat on the snow, laid Maggie across a sandbag, opened the breach, loaded a single cartridge, and rested my cheek on the stock, allowing my eyes to settle through the scope and the sight picture to materialize. Gunner nuzzled in next to me, eyes staring downrange.

The inclusion of a spotter, or a dog to keep you company, meant you had to consider their ears. Guns make loud noises. As a result, metal tubes filled with sound-muffling baffles, called suppressors, or what the media mistakenly calls silencers, can be affixed to the end of the barrel. Contrary to Hollywood myth, they don't silence the percussion. They simply mute it slightly to make it bearable to human ears, reducing the sound by almost thirty decibels. In short, suppressors reduce recoil slightly and make the shooting more comfortable by preventing the loud bang from blowing out your eardrums. Knowledge that wasn't too helpful when a dog didn't understand why you were trying to put earmuffs on his head. Which Gunner didn't tolerate. He wasn't having it.

The target was an eight-inch round plate at 1,842 yards. In shooter's lingo, that meant I'd have to shoot a half minute of angle or better to hit it.

The wind was at my back, 1 or 2 mph slight left to right. Chances were good it changed somewhere in the mile between me and the target, but if I missed, the rock face behind the target would indicate point of impact and I'd adjust.

With a target sitting at over a mile away, one last hurdle had to be considered. The Coriolis effect. In summary, when shooting longer distances, say anything over a thousand yards, I had to account for the effect of the earth's rotational spin on the flight of the bullet. The bullet could be in the air for several seconds, during which the earth would continue to spin. Which meant the target that was at one spot when the trigger was pulled would not be at that same spot when the bullet arrived. This is a gross oversimplification, but let's say you were shooting at a horse on a merry-go-round. When you pulled the trigger, the horse would be frozen in time at a given place, but three seconds later, the horse obviously would have moved given the rotation of the ride. So the bullet would hit behind the horse. Or off target. Coriolis is something like that. Or at least that was the way Bones first explained it to me. To make matters even more complicated, the earth rotates at different speeds. Faster at the poles and slower at the equator. In the northern hemisphere, when firing north or south, the bullet sways to the right. To the left in the southern. Its effect is less when firing east to west or west to east.

I let the crosshairs settle in the middle of the plate and dialed up 105 MOA, or "minutes of angle." Most of my optics were calibrated in milliradians. Maggie was not. Maggie had been given to me before MILs became popular. Bones had spent a month's paycheck to purchase the best Schmidt & Bender glass he could afford, and I never replaced it. Why dial in 105 MOA? Because I had zeroed my rifle at two hundred yards. Anything beyond that and the bullet would drop gradually, then severely, because bullets don't fly in a straight line. It's more of an arc. Think of a football in flight. If your favorite quarterback throws a ball sixty yards in the air, he can't throw it straight. He's not strong enough. So he arcs it a bit. Gets some air under it. Same with bullets. In aiming at a target 1,842 yards away, I couldn't just aim straight at it. I had to compensate for the distance. In reality, given so great a distance—longer than a mile—I had to aim 2,001 inches above it. That's 166.75 feet above the target. More than sixteen and a half stories. The only way to do that is with a scope that allows you to "dial distance." Hence the 105 MOA.

Why travel this rabbit trail? Why all this rumination on the physics of the flight of a piece of copper? Because I needed to take my mind off what I couldn't take my mind off. And I needed to remember that what was in me had been put there by another. Poured in. I could not take credit. Nor did I intend to.

I focused the diopter, pushed the safety to off, and slowed my breathing, watching the crosshairs steady. As I did, Bones appeared in my mind's eye.

CHAPTER 36

He was sitting cross-legged with his shirt off. Mind you, the temperature was near zero. I rubbed my eyes and tried to sit up. Only then did I notice his bandage. Right shoulder. Just below his collarbone. He was in the process of peeling off the bloody one and replacing it with a clean one. His skin had been sutured. Front and back.

"What happened?"

My question caused him to pause. He raised an eyebrow, applied the dressing, and chuckled. Finally, he pulled on his shirt, fleece, and down vest and puffer, then a Gore-Tex shell. He leaned back against the stone wall, crossed his legs, and sipped his wine as a crimson sun spilled off the side of the planet. "Shoulders don't react well to bullets."

I guess that was when it hit me. He'd returned a week ago from Central America and we'd not talked about his trip. Since then, we'd climbed this stupid mountain three times and finally, tonight, or rather early this morning, as I'd slipped and started falling, he'd mustered the strength and gumption to reach out with his right arm—the one that had been shot—and not only pull me back but place me safely on the rock. To this day, I had no idea how he did that. Anytime I'd been shot, I'd turned into a boy with a man-cold and started crying like a teenage girl watching *The Notebook*. You can ask Summer. It's ugly. But not Bones. He was on the mountain with me. Who did that? I knew of only one man.

The insanity of it struck me. So I asked him, "You mind telling me what we're doing up here?"

He stared into his wine as a cold wind washed across us. When he spoke, he did so from both memory and experience. "People who steal people, and then line up a train of miscreants and perverts deserving only of a single bullet, don't think like you and me. Their business model is rape for profit. Twenty times a day. They open the door—'Please. Come in.' Then they sit at the table and count the dollars or smoke a Marlboro as some little girl or little boy's spirit slowly exits their body beneath a blanket or another's sweat or bodily fluid. The only way you and I ever catch those people, the only way they ever pay for their sin, is if we learn to think more like them and less like us." He held up a finger. "Notice I did not say 'become like.' I said 'think like.' There's a difference. And one way we force ourselves to do that is to override what our body is telling us. Pain is a signal. That's all. The body's response to discomfort. We are here learning to mute it. Because if we don't . . ." He waved his hand across Colorado and the earth beyond. "We can't hear the cries of the dying and those who wish they were dead."

While he was sitting there with his legs crossed, I could see the bottom of his right boot. Into the Vibram sole he'd used something like a knife tip to carve two bones between the flat space of the arch and the heel. Normally, that area of the sole wouldn't touch hard-packed ground, but in snow and soft sand it would, leaving an imprint. As I studied the snow around me, I realized I was surrounded by bone-imprinted footsteps. And as I stared back down the path I'd ascended, I saw even more.

"What's with the bones?"

He nodded, leaned his head back, and closed his eyes. For the last two years I'd asked him the same question. Each time, he'd shaken his head. "You haven't earned that."

By that time, I'd broken every known record he held at the academy. "When will I?"

"If you have to ask when, then you haven't."

159

Lying on the side of that mountain, face blistered, having worn the skin off my fingertips, "when" had come. I simply pointed at his boot.

He stared into his wine and then at me. "Majorca. The dungeon. I'd lost count of the months, had named all the rats, and was pretty sure I'd die in that grave." A pause. "Whenever the priests"—he made quotation marks with his fingers—"'visited,' they'd bring a lantern. But I was too busy fighting for my life to see my surroundings. Plus, a lantern shoots light downward. It doesn't shine up, so I never really got a good look with my eyes. I'd walked around feeling the walls, but that only allowed me to 'see' what I could reach. It wasn't until Frank smuggled in a flashlight that I saw what I'd been missing. And it was a lot." He sipped his wine. "I knew my ceilings were taller than I could reach, and based on the echo, they were a good bit taller. But how much, I couldn't guess. Enter the flashlight, and I could not believe my eyes. Frank slipped that thing in my hand and I began scouring the world around me. It nearly took my breath away. I wasn't in a dungeon and the bars weren't prison bars. The entire cavern was an underground chapel, and I was living in a crypt whose bars separated it from the altar. It blew my mind. This entire time I thought I was just in some dank cell, but in reality, I'd been living in a thousand-year-old tomb. Prior to the flashlight, my hands told me there were these holes in the stone. I thought people had put candles in there. But the flashlight allowed me to see they were a ladder cut into the rock that led up to where the body had been laid. The entire time, some old guy had been lying in a tomb. Shield. Sword. The works. The story etched into the wall said he'd saved more than a thousand people after the Moors invaded. Lived underground for a couple of years but somehow managed topside raids at night. No one could ever discover how he got out. Night after night. He rescued countless people from untold horror, getting them out of the city. Yet when I studied the walls, no one had written his name. The only inscription I found was a single word." He paused. "Study Scripture and the word *bones* is equated with the person. There's no difference between this hard thing"—he tapped his leg—"and me. I am that. That is me. So there I was, stuck down in that hole in the earth with this pile of bones, and that's when it hit me. I am—"

I finished his sentence. "Bones."

A nod. "I've always liked the name. Just seemed to fit. Maybe I was half crazy, but I felt like that old guy spoke it over me. So that night I took my knife and carved a set of bones into my shoe. I would have carved it into me like a tattoo or brand, but I was tired of people hurting me and didn't want to add to my pain. Something about putting my mark on the sole of my shoe meant I left an imprint wherever I went. Like, 'This is me. I was here.' Which, as a boy living in that dungeon, I thought impossible. In the years following, wherever I traveled, I took that old guy with me. And maybe what he did for me, in some small way, I've done for others."

He sipped. Nodded. "Least I'd like to think I have." He studied his boot. "Frank saw the crude carving and the name stuck. Which was helpful because neither of us knew our real names, so one was as good as any other." He paused. "Maybe it was my way of telling the world, 'You may stick me down here in the bowels of this earth, abuse me, forget me, treat me like an animal, and strip me of my hopes and dreams, but you can't take my name." He tapped himself in the chest. "I'm Bones. That's me. You can take everything else, but not that. And I'll be here long after you"—he waved his hand above him in the air, signifying the priests who lived in the world above him—"sick miscreants are gone and burning in hell."

The falling snow muted the world around us. "My name became a knowingness. An understanding. I knew that I knew that I knew that a reckoning was coming. That's what it was. My name was a reckoning. There in that hell, all I had were my words. And there and then I gave myself one. A name. It was the only thing I could give me. Because I had nothing else." He raised a finger. "In the years since, I've come to understand—no, to know—through the hundreds of people I've rescued, that nothing matters more than a name. It's why it's always been the first thing I've asked them. Because no matter what hell they've endured, a name can call them back out. A name establishes a record. Drives a stake in the ground. Shouts across the stratosphere, 'I'm here! I matter! I'm not invisible! And while you may think very little of me, God Himself actually thought me up. What you see in the lens of your eye, this thing we call me started in His mind. He actually took the time to think me up.' Imagine." Another leg tap. "God thought of me. Molded my bones like a potter. And if that's true, and He thought of me, and then made me, and then named me, then there's a record of my existence. Evidence that I'm real." He was quiet a moment, slowly swirling his wine. After several minutes, he said, "When you're in hell, slavery, nothing matters more than a name. Because with it, someone can walk up to the bars that shackle you, point at you among the many, and call you out—by name. A name is the singular thing that separates us from the ninety-nine. A name makes us the one." The look in Bones's eyes was one of longing. Of remembrance. And of pain. "Without a name . . . there is no record."

As the snow dusted our shoulders, he stood, walked inside the cave to his left, and pulled out a rectangular padded canvas case. About four and a half feet in length. He carried it around the fire and laid it at my feet. Then he turned and spoke out across the earth, his words blanketing me. "Never doubt the power of a single bullet."

Enter Maggie.

The memory stung and the longing returned. As did the questions. The shame. And the doubt. I missed him. I missed Bones more than I could say.

I focused through the diopter and the target came into view. I slowed my breathing, allowing the crosshairs to settle, and placed my finger gently on the trigger.

CHAPTER 37

"Hey, Boss . . ."

Camp's voice echoed over me. Only then did I notice the half inch of snow covering my body. "You've been staring through that thing for over an hour and it's getting cold out here. You okay?"

While I had lost all track of time, Gunner had burrowed into a ball next to me and snored quietly. Did he say an hour? I straightened my finger and pulled the safety to the on position. "Yeah."

Camp knelt, laying his pack alongside him. "You see the news?"

I nodded.

Camp rolled out his shooter's mat, lay beside me, and stared through Swarovski range-finding binoculars in the same direction of my barrel. Took him a few seconds to find it. "You sure you don't want to get a little closer? You're gonna have a tough time hitting that mountainside, much less an eight-inch piece of steel."

"I'm good."

Doubtful, he studied me. "What're you doing up here staring through that thing?"

"Sometimes I see more clearly through it."

"I don't doubt that, but isn't the point to pull the trigger?"

"Not always. Sometimes I just need help seeing through the fog."

He studied me. "You okay? You want to sit this one out?"

I turned my head slightly.

"Permission to speak freely?"

"Yes, but you don't need to ask. You can just go ahead."

"If you're distracted, not a hundred percent, you're a hindrance. A liability. Worse, a danger to us and those girls."

"I know that."

"So do you make the call . . . or do I?"

"I'm in pain. So I'm up here staring through this thing, processing it. Trying to make sense of what doesn't make sense. You're catching me in the middle of that. So how about maybe you cut me a little slack while I stumble through being human."

"Wow. That was really well said. I'm gonna write that down. 'Stumble through'—did you say 'being human'?"

I turned my head even more and raised an eyebrow.

He stared back through his binoculars. "Well, since I got you talking and you obviously have doubt about your ability to hit that target, can I ask you something?"

"Well, since you just hiked uphill over two thousand feet of elevation through the snow, I'd feel disappointed if you didn't."

"Yeah, about that . . . what is it with you and impossible hikes in treacherous situations?"

I considered this. "Bones."

"He was one tough dude."

The weight and pain of the word *was* did not escape me. "That he was."

Camp paused. Looked like he was remembering something he'd rehearsed. "Murph . . ."

I waited. When he didn't speak again, I said, "Yes?"

"Um . . . well, you see . . ."

"Is this about the money thing again?"

He shook his head, "No. Just let me get this out." Then he spoke almost as if to himself. "Why can't I put together a coherent question when it comes to this?"

I turned completely and stared at him. "What's 'this'?"

He took a deep breath, closed his eyes, then opened them and locked on to me. "I want to ask your permission to marry Casey."

The words rattled around my brain, finally settling somewhere in the middle. I said the words out loud to myself. "Marry Casey."

He nodded. "Yes." A pause. "I've been trying to ask you, but . . ."

The question caught me out of left field. "Marry?"

"Check."

"As in walk down the aisle, 'I do,' 'I do'?"

"That's what I've been trying to ask you."

"When?"

"DC. When we ran the mall."

"Why're you asking me?"

"You're her dad."

"Yeah, but she's a grown—"

"Doesn't matter. You hold that place in her heart. And rightly so, but to get to her, I've got to go through you, and I don't want a marriage with you in the middle of it."

This guy was much smarter than I gave him credit for. I sat up, leaned against a boulder, took my hat off, and shook the snow off my face. It was time I taught this young whippersnapper a lesson. I pressed him. "Only been a couple months. Sure you're not moving a little fast?"

"I agree." He nodded. "I didn't see this coming either, and I wasn't looking for it. But it was obviously looking for us and here we are."

Needing more to be convinced, I decided to figure out if he was really serious. "How's she like her ice cream?"

"Two scoops chocolate, two scoops raspberry sorbet, gummy bears sprinkled on top. Sometimes chocolate sprinkles. Whipped cream always."

"What about Fridays?"

"Break a Kit Kat bar and sprinkle it on top. Add chocolate syrup."

"Man, you're good."

"I've been paying attention."

My head was spinning. "I'd always hoped a guy would come along for her. She deserves someone to—"

"I love her."

More confusion. "You do?"

"Yes."

"When did this happen?"

"The moment I first laid eyes on her."

"Really?"

He nodded.

His assurance made me wonder what planet I'd been living on. "Well, have you taken her out on a date?"

He laughed. "Yes."

My voice rose. "When?"

"Lots."

"What's her favorite movie?"

"*Wizard of Oz*. The Judy Garland one."

"What size shoe does she wear?"

"Nine. Sometimes eight and a half. Depends on the shoe."

"What's she allergic to?"

"Needles."

"Favorite color?"

"Moonlight."

This guy was good. "What's she afraid of?"

"Being alone. And Gremlins."

"Which leg is shorter?"

"No idea."

I didn't either, but he didn't know that. "You know, marriage is a big deal, not to be taken lightly." Listening to myself, even I thought I sounded strange.

Another smile. "I've commanded men in combat in more than twenty countries around the world while receiving heavy incoming fire. I don't take life lightly. And certainly not this."

CHAPTER 38

I kept pressing. Making sure he was true. Not yanking my chain. "What's your favorite thing about her?"

He spoke without having to think about it. "Her hope. Which is second only to her love. To have suffered what she suffered, and yet still wake up hopeful, smiling, and not bitter and angry at the world. That's some crazy kind of love."

I scratched my head. "You really love her?"

"With all of me."

"She love you?"

He nodded. "Think so."

In the last few months, with all the pressure to find Frank and then Bones, I'd been singularly focused and known little life outside that cauldron. While I'd been away from Freetown for weeks at a time, Camp had been there. Standing on the wall. But that stance also placed him in close proximity to Casey. "So you've actually been on a date with her?"

"Lots. Although it's not like I've picked her up in my dad's Mustang and taken her to a nice restaurant or anything. Given everything, we've been forced to get to know each other inside a pressure cooker. First her book. Then Frank. Now Bones." A pause. "Life hasn't been exactly normal. We fell in love in the middle of a war."

I knew the answer, but I was goading him. "You sure you don't just want her money? 'Cause she has a lot of it."

"I'll sign anything you or her want me to sign."

"You've only known her a couple months. You sure?"

"When you know, you know."

The more I hung around this guy, the more I liked him. "You asked her yet?"

"No." A chuckle. "Which explains why I'm kneeling in the snow after hiking up Everest. I been needing to talk to you first."

"When were you thinking you might do that?"

"I'm doing it right now."

"No, I mean ask her."

"Oh." A shrug. "Tonight."

"Really? Working kinda fast, aren't you?"

"Maybe. I don't know." He pointed down the mountain, toward Freetown. "There's that crab boil tonight, so I thought we'd do that and then maybe ride the lift up to the Eagle's Nest. If that's okay with you?"

The day had the looks of a clear night, which would make for a romantic ride up and back. Not to mention the view from the porch. His thought process made me feel a bit guilty. I hadn't thought much about Summer lately. I certainly hadn't taken her on a date. The ache in the pit of my stomach told me it was probably worse than I thought, and Summer hadn't said anything. "Where'd you get that idea?"

"Afghanistan."

"What?"

"We were in the mountains. Ten thousand feet. Colder than I'd ever been in my life. Took shelter in a mosque only because we'd saved the imam's kids. I remember standing on that ledge, overlooking a bunch of hardship below and promising myself that if I ever got the chance to ask a girl to marry me, I was going to do it from a place like that. Someplace high up where what hurts below can't get to you."

"Did you seriously think of that all by yourself?"

"Well . . . sort of. I been reading these novels, and they got me to thinking."

"Novels?"

"Yeah."

"Which ones?"

He shrugged.

The thought that my own words had anything to do with this was a strange comfort. But it also picked at the scab. The ache grew, proving that maybe I'd been more in touch with the tender part of me at one time.

"You nervous?"

A pause. "Just a bit."

"You getting down on one knee?"

"Of course."

"Good, she deserves that."

He nodded. "She deserves the fairy tale."

Told you I liked this guy. He continued, "If it's okay with you, I worked it out with Summer to have a little get-together afterward down in the Planetarium. Thought we'd play a bunch of pictures of Casey."

"You really thought this out."

"You learn that in the Teams."

"Evidently. You got a ring?"

A single nod. "Clay put me in touch with your friend Mr. Harby. He made one custom with my mom's stone."

"Just checking. Us guys can sometimes miss the things that matter."

CHAPTER 39

I sat there shaking my head. Amazed at how I'd missed an entire courtship.

He spoke as much to himself as me. "Haven't eaten in three days. Can't keep it in. Coming out both ends. My palms are sweating. I can't put together a coherent sentence. If I don't ask her soon, I'll be in trouble."

I laughed. He really did love her.

He prompted me again: "But you still haven't answered me."

I knew what he wanted. Truth was, he didn't need it. But I loved him for asking. I also knew he was true. Clear through. "I don't really think you need my permission, but since you're asking . . ." I paused, the memory returning. "When I picked her up off the shower floor, about three heart-beats from dead, she reached up and hung her limp arms around my neck. Holding fast with what little strength remained. In that moment, the tether that held her on this side of the grave attached to me. And what I'm about to say, I'm not saying because she's weak. Casey's one of the toughest people I've ever known. I'm saying this because of what she suffered. The depth of her horror. Casey doesn't know how to live without that tether. It's a lifeline. Maybe one day she'll wake up and recognize it's gone. Until then, she needs to know that somebody will walk back into a burning house and lift her out. No matter what. You've got to be willing—"

"Murph." He put a hand on my shoulder. Then he tapped his heart. "I'm willing." A pause. "I'll walk through fire."

170

I didn't know what to do, so I just hugged him. Two grown men standing for a long, odd minute while the snow dusted our shoulders and Gunner stared at us. When I finally let him go, I said, "I thought you were giving me your two weeks'."

He stared off toward the target. A single shake of his head. "Not if you'll let me stick around. I feel like I finally found my place in the world."

It was time to bring him in. All the way. I held up a finger. "One condition."

He did not seem to be expecting this. I caught him off guard, which was unusual. "Which is?"

How many times had Bones asked me this question? I could not count. I stared at Camp's eyes. Bright. Piercing. Focused. Genuine and true. The first time I tried to say it, the words didn't come, so I swallowed and tried a second time. That didn't work either. Finally, on the third try, I squeaked it out. "Tell me what you know about sheep."

He never hesitated. "They need a shepherd."

I pressed him. "What kind?"

"The kind that will spend his life for the sheep."

I nodded and heard Bones's echo. "Then be that kind."

"Yes, sir." This time he raised a finger.

I waited.

"If you teach me."

I shook my head in wonder, not disagreement. "I'm still learning. There's a lot I don't know. The moment you stop, or the moment you think, *I got this*, something bad happens. Truth is, we don't got this. Never have. Never will. Evil is good at being evil. Odds are always stacked against us. How 'bout we just keep learning it together?"

He smiled. "Yes, sir."

We stood there shuffling, neither sure what to say. Finally, Camp broke the silence. "Oh, and there's one more thing."

"I'm listening."

"In my past life, I may have made some people mad."

"May have or did?"

"Did."

"Why're you telling me? Everybody's mad at us."

"Because they might come for me. And for those I love."

"Who are they?"

He told me.

"Okay."

"That's it?"

I shrugged.

"These are not good people. They have power. Political power. And money."

"Great. Let's go see them."

"Go see them? Have you lost your mind?"

I laughed. "Look around you."

"Good point."

"Why are you telling me?"

"I just want you to know what you . . . what Casey is getting."

I put my hand on his shoulder, the same way he had mine. "Camp . . . I know who we're getting, and I know who she's getting. And I'm good with him." I paused. Stared out across the mountain. Then I lay back down, settled my cheek on the stock, and stared through the diopter, focusing on the target. I pushed the safety off, touched my finger to the trigger, and settled my breathing. Then I looked at him. "You're one of us. You are us. If they come, they've got to go through me." Returning to my sight, I confirmed the location of the crosshairs and gently pressed the trigger.

Two seconds later, the gong sounded.

We returned to Freetown and found Clay waiting for us on a bench. Readers on the end of his nose. Cup of coffee in one hand, newspaper in the other. He noticed the two of us, then raised his coffee cup to Camp and sort of nodded. Suggesting a secret shared between the two. Camp smiled and nodded back. Then we descended to my safe room, cleaned and stowed the guns, and climbed the stairs into the kitchen where Summer, Angel, and Ellie were all sitting cross-legged on the floor before the fireplace. Hot chocolate. Eyes wide. Giddy with expectation.

Summer spoke first. "So . . ." Her tone of voice betrayed far more than her words. "How was your time on the mountain?"

The collective look on their faces suggested they were in a lather. I shook my head and headed for the shower.

Evidently the Camp-Casey thing had been a thing for a while. Like from the moment they met. Which I missed entirely, causing me to wonder what planet I'd been living on. Where did I miss the signals other than everywhere? Finding Frank and then Bones had been all-consuming, and I'd known little life outside that. Somehow in that mess, they'd fallen in love, a thought that produced in me a feeling akin to joy. A strange emotion amid grief. I almost felt guilty for feeling it. But the hope of that joy was one of the reasons we did what we did. To watch the free live in freedom.

Bones taught me that.

CHAPTER 40

The afternoon was a bit of a flurry. I checked in with Eddie and the team, but we still had nothing. No signal. I tried not to think about Aaron's girls, but it was tough not to. The crab boil ended and Camp and Casey disappeared, walking toward the chairlift, at which point Summer grabbed my hand. "Come on, Romeo, we've got about thirty minutes to get the room decorated."

"What?"

She looked at me like it was self-explanatory. "The biggest moment in Casey's life." A single shake of her head. "No way we're missing this."

Clay chimed in, "I been blowing up balloons all afternoon. 'Bout to pass out I'm so dizzy."

I shook my head. "Shouldn't they have the privacy of the moment?"

She nodded. "Yep. That's why we're watching it from a distance. Sort of. Come on."

I shook my head. "One of these days, I need to take a class on people. Relationships. And how to navigate them. I feel like I'm living on Mars."

"That's because you are. Which is one of the reasons you have me. I keep you grounded."

Didn't take long to decorate as all of Freetown pitched in. Then at precisely 8:00 p.m., Eddie broadcast a live picture of the porch of the Eagle's Nest on the ceiling of the Planetarium. Another plan Summer and Camp had hatched. Camp wanted the girls to be able to see it. Live it with Casey.

He thought it'd feed their hope for the fairy tale. And he was right. There was not a dry eye anywhere. The picture was not so close up that we felt like we were intruding, and we certainly couldn't hear anything, but we were spectators with permission. Sort of like watching people at the park. Or a game on the field. They exited the chairlift, then stood wrapped in a blanket and huddled together against the cold. A good picture. They laughed. Pointed out across the earth. Then Camp turned, took her hands, and knelt. At which point the estrogen in the room broke loose and all the females screamed at the top of their lungs. And when Camp and Casey hugged and he kissed her, something good happened in Freetown.

Hope returned. We needed it.

When he kissed her again, the screen switched back to a slideshow, allowing them some privacy in the moment. While the slideshow ran inside the Planetarium, and Clay entertained in his tuxedo, top hat, penguin wing tips, and cane, I stood off in the shadows, watching everyone watch the show. The delight on their faces was a welcome reprieve. I almost forgot about the ticking clock.

Casey stood next to Camp. Alongside. With. They made a great pair. Seeing them together did my heart good. I wished . . well, I wished he was here to see it. As I watched her, I remembered when we met. After she was airlifted to the hospital. We had found her in bed, the drugs wearing off. Reality returning. Clarity settling. Summer had climbed into bed with her and just cradled her. A safe pair of arms that wanted nothing from her. Then she had kissed Casey's forehead.

For the first time, Casey had spoken. She spoke without looking at me. "The men were . . ." She turned her head further. The shame fell like a shadow. "One after another. I lost count. Weeks." She swallowed. "Then they injected me."

The men had injected her with enough narcotic to kill a horse. Two maybe. How she survived only God knew. She looked up at me. "Is my life over?"

I remembered looking at her and thinking that this right here, this beautiful soul, this once-indomitable spirit, this magnificent child of God, was what those men had spit out. The residue. When they were finished, this was what was left over. My anger roared. Countless times I'd knelt by similar bedsides and been asked similar questions. I shook my head. "I think you're only just beginning."

"Feels over."

"You have any family?"

"No."

"You up for a little travel?"

She nodded. "Anywhere but here."

"I'm going to talk to these doctors, and when you get well enough to travel, I'm going to request they release you into my custody. Or at least some folks who work with me. They're going to come get you and fly you on a private plane to Colorado, where they'll nurse you back to health, give you a place to live, and get you in school. You'll meet other girls like you."

"Total losers."

I laughed. "Don't kid yourself. We all lose our way. Sometimes it just takes somebody else to find us and bring us back. Remind us."

She laughed almost derisively. "Of what?"

I leaned in close and spoke slowly so my words would register. "That we were made to want and give love. That no matter how dark the night, midnight will pass. No darkness, no matter how dark, can hold back the second hand. Whether you like it or not, whether you want it or not, whether you hope it or not, whether you build a wall around your soul and cut out your eyes, wait a few hours and the sun will crack the skyline and the darkness will roll back like a scroll."

The tears drained. "This place . . . is it really real?"

"Yes."

"Will you be there?"

"I'll come check on you."

"You promise?"

"I do. But first I've got to go find someone."

She glanced at the cross. Then back at me. She was shaking her head. "They won't let her leave." She was talking about Angel.

"I know."

"They're saving her. Taking bids. Her and a couple others. An online auction. They take pictures of her. Some when she's passed out. Then they post them. Bids get higher. They're bad men. Guns and . . ."

I nodded. "Any idea where they're going?"

"They're hush-hush. But I heard them say Cuba. They're excited because they're getting a lot of money for her and they don't want to end the auction." She squeezed my hand. Tears rolled down her cheeks. "I'm sorry."

"Shhh." I stood. "Breathe. In. Out. Then"—I smiled—"do it again. Wash. Rinse. Repeat. You'll like Colorado this time of year."

She stared at the window. "I've never flown on a plane."

"Well, this will ruin you for ordinary travel, but it's a great way to start."

She was crying now. A fetal ball. Sobbing silently. Holding in her grief. Summer cradled her. For a moment, Casey wouldn't let it out, but after it built and she couldn't hold back anymore, it burst forth. I'd heard the same noises before, which made it all the more painful. The deputy poked his head in, but when he saw what was happening, he nodded, backed out, and stood guard.

I knelt next to her bed, my face inches from hers. When she opened her eyes, she was looking beyond me. Into the past. All the ugly stuff. The memories the darkness painted. She tried to form the words, but they wouldn't come. Finally, she whispered, "Who will ever love me after . . . ?" She motioned to herself.

I cradled her hand in mine. Waited until her eyes locked on mine. "Right now, there is a man walking this earth who can't wait to meet you. He's been waiting his whole life."

She chuckled. "I thought I was the one on drugs."

"When he meets you, his heart will flutter. His palms will sweat. He'll think somebody stuffed a bag of cotton in his mouth. He won't know what to say, but he'll want to."

"How do you know?"

"It's how we're made."

"You've seen this?"

"I've married these people."

"Are you a priest?"

I shifted my head from side to side. Paused. Then nodded once. "I also priest."

"But—"

"Love is an amazing thing. It takes the brokenness, the scars, the pain, the darkness, everything, and makes it all new."

"You've really seen this?"

"I've lived this. Known it. Know it."

"And all this is in Colorado?"

"Yes." I considered my next question carefully. "You like to read?"

She nodded.

"Okay, I'm going to send you some books. Something to pass the time. Mostly they're just check-your-brain-at-the-door romance novels, but they're entertaining. They might take your mind off things and maybe we can talk about them next time I see you."

She nodded, wanting to believe me but afraid nonetheless. When I turned to leave, she wouldn't let go of my hand.

CHAPTER 41

I stood in the Planetarium and watched the two of them. Two kids in love. Their entire lives before them. Nothing but hope and possibility. I guess I was lost in the memory longer than I thought, because an arm slid inside mine. When I turned, Casey stood beaming. Locked arm in arm with me, she whispered, "You were right." When I looked at her, I noticed for the first time that Casey was behind her eyes. Completely. She was home. "There is a man on planet earth who could marry someone like me."

"Yes, there is. And he's a good man. Even the best of men."

"You approve?"

"A hundred percent."

"And you're doing the ceremony, right?"

"If you wish."

"I wish."

"Done."

She chuckled. "You gonna be able to get through it?"

I smiled. "I make no promises."

"You gonna cry?"

"Definitely."

A beautiful laugh. "It's one of the reasons we all love you." She held both my hands, stalling. Finally, she said, "I have a favor to ask of you."

"Anything."

She pointed. "You see that man over there?"

Camp had been invited to the front of the room by Clay, who was now
pretending to be a sports announcer interviewing a player after the game.
Holding his cane like a microphone, he was asking for the blow-by-blow.
"Son, were you nervous?"

"Yes."

"How much the ring set you back?"

"Pretty much everything I had."

"Did you plan on getting down on one knee, or did you just fall over?"

"Both."

"Where are you two going on your honeymoon?"

"Wherever she tells me."

"Are we invited?"

"Not a chance."

Laughter rippled throughout the room. If hope fed the fairy tale, then
every girl in the room was eating at a lavish banquet tonight. No eye was
dry. It was the most fun we'd had since the wedding.

I nodded.

Casey continued, "He's my whole world. And I want to try to be a wife
and a mom and a friend and all the things, but I can only do that . . ." She
paused long enough for the worry to creep up into her voice. "If he comes
home every time he leaves with you."

I saw where this was going.

She locked arms with me again while we watched Clay embarrass
Camp. "So I'm sorry to do this to you, but I need you to watch over him.
He still thinks he can leap tall buildings in a single bound."

"I've spent some time with him, and I'm pretty sure he can."

"Until he can't."

I nodded.

She pressed me. "No kidding. Straight up. I want your word."

I didn't have the heart to tell her it was my job to watch over Bones. I
faced her. "I'll watch him the way Bones watched me."

"Thank you."

"Can I say one more thing?"

She nodded.

The two of us stared across the room. The countless smiles. "Sometimes things work out. Sometimes the good guys win. Sometimes love is easy. It's okay to be excited."

"That's an upstream swim for me."

"I know. And the two of you get to love your way through it. But remember this . . ."

She was smiling and crying at the same time. Reality setting in. He'd asked her. She'd said yes. Her dreams were coming true, but she had two emotions yet to bury. "You are priceless. Magnificent beyond measure. And you are worthy of your dreams—so let them come true." She was really crying now. "And fear is a liar. Tell him to take a hike. And don't let him steal tonight, or tomorrow."

She hugged me and kissed my cheek, slobbering snot all over my face, but it was a beautiful slobber. Years in the making.

CHAPTER 42

After the party, I slipped off by myself because I admitted to myself that I'd grown worried about Gunner. He was not at the party tonight, which was unlike him. As I thought about it, I realized he'd been keeping to himself a lot and was not so animated. I couldn't figure it out. I still owed him a steak as he'd refused the one in DC, so I poured charcoal in the Big Green Egg and lit it, knowing the smell would draw him out of hiding, which it did. When the charcoal was hot, I grilled a ginormous piece of meat while he watched. Four minutes in and he was drooling, which I took as a good sign. Somewhere between medium rare and medium, I pulled it and set it on a plate at about eye level with Gunner while it cooled. He sat ramrod straight, tail occasionally moving left to right. It was not so much a wag as an indication that he was watching me. Alert. After six excruciating minutes, I sat on the floor and cut the steak into small pieces. He slid into something of a sphinx position and then crawled toward me, finally bringing his muzzle within inches of my hands. I set the plate on my lap and stared at him. He stared at the plate, me, then the plate, then rubbed his muzzle with his front paw and looked back up at me. "Last time I did this you didn't want it."

He whined quietly.

"Hundred-dollar steak down the drain."

He made no response.

"I think this one might be cooked a little better, but I'm pretty much a steak snob and particular to my own cooking."

He licked the saliva off his muzzle, which at this point was pouring out of his mouth like someone had turned on a spigot inside his throat.

I lifted a piece and held it between index finger and thumb. "Now I need to tell you something."

He inched forward.

"I know I've been a little out of it lately. Not myself. 'Distant' is probably a better word. But I just want you to know that it's not your fault. I've just got some stuff I'm trying to work out . . . and I don't really know how to work it out."

He sniffed the meat, then licked his face again.

"See, it's . . ."

He whined.

I touched the meat to the front of his nose. He opened his mouth and inhaled it. Then swallowed. Didn't chew once.

I held up a second bite and did the same. Same response. Then a third. No change. Evidently he was feeling better.

After I fed the steak to him, I let him lick the plate, then he lay on his back and turned his stomach toward me, paws in the air. Which was Gunner-speak for "Here, scratch my belly while you're jabbering on." A minute later, he was snoring.

"Glad we had this talk."

As I said that, a warm hand touched my shoulder and Summer sat alongside me, wrapping a fleece blanket around my shoulders. "Me too," she said.

"You heard all that?"

She nodded. Then turned toward me, sitting cross-legged. "Want to talk about it?"

"Not really."

"How about I take a shot?"

I waited.

"You have a problem."

I didn't see this coming. "I do?"

"Yes. Stop interrupting." She sat up straight, bringing her eye level with me. "You don't know how to be . . . who you need to be . . . because you don't know who you are . . . now."

I tried to process this, waiting for the pieces to align. When they did, I realized she was spot-on. Arguing with her would get me nowhere, nor did I have the bandwidth. "Pretty much."

She continued, "So the question is, what do we do about it?"

"I don't have an answer for that."

"I wasn't expecting one. It was rhetorical. I know you well enough to know that if you could have done something, you would have."

I tried to follow her logic but could not. "I'm not quite sure where this is going or how to engage in this."

She scooted closer. Slipped her shoulder under mine. Partially sitting on my lap, placing her palm flat across my heart. "One of the reasons I fell in love with you was your ability to love deeply when others could not or would not. The thing that drove you then and drives you now . . . is your love." She waved her hand across Freetown below us. "Ask anyone. It's the thing that sets you apart."

I still wasn't quite sure what to do with this. "Okay."

"But you have a problem."

This I agreed with. "Yes."

"Your heart is broken."

I didn't see that coming either. And I'd never considered it. "What?"

"You watched your best friend and mentor get shot and die in front of you, and you could do nothing about it. Shattering your heart. So now you're trying to do what you've always done, including carrying all of us and all of our pain, but you have a problem." I waited. "Your heart lies in pieces and it's struggling to beat."

Her words made sense.

"I can't help you find Miriam, Ruth, and Sadie. And I can't bring Bones back."

I was lost again. But I knew better than to admit that, so I didn't speak.

She turned my face toward hers, where I noticed, for the first time, tears. "So, my love . . . you face a decision."

CHAPTER 43

Summer is not a drama queen. Tears, when they fall from her eyes, start in her heart. They tell the truth. I waited. "David Bishop is only Murphy Shepherd when he risks everything. To love deeply, you must be willing to risk a broken heart. Again. It's the price that you alone pay. The unspoken cost of the love you give. If you're not willing to love all out, at all times, then Bones taught you nothing. His life with you was for naught. All in vain. Bones went back for Frank because his love was deeper than his hate. Deeper than his pain. And, as a result, stronger. So here it is, Bishop." This time when she pounded my chest, the tears broke loose. "Will you risk your love? One more time? All or nothing? Take all these cracked and shattered pieces lying around you on the floor and sweep them up into your chest where only one thing can put you back together? It's not anger and it's not cold, callous indifference. The love you have is the only thing that will get you—and me—through the battle for you."

There it was. In a nutshell. The battle for me.

She turned and sat up on her heels, nudging her knees against my thigh. "You taught me this. Love is the only thing in this universe or any other that will cause you to leave the safety, comfort, and security of the ninety-nine to set out in the dark and cold with all the odds stacked against you to find the one. No other power can do that. Only love walks down into the prison, amid the shackles and the bars and the stench, and says to the slave master, 'I'll buy them all.' And when he balks and scoffs, 'What will you pay with?' if you're serious, and if you really want to free them, and if, in the end, you want to live free, then there's only one answer."

I waited, but I knew it before she said it.

The tears trickled off her chin when she whispered, "With every last piece of me."

When she voiced it, the echo sounded within my chest. Faint at first, then louder. And when I closed my eyes and looked again, I did not see Bones lying dead. He was gone. While that was painful, it wasn't piercing. I couldn't bring him back; I had to begin to let him go. And I needed someone to tell me that it was not a betrayal of my love for him to do so.

When I looked again, the only image I saw was three scared girls praying for someone to kick down the door.

And for the first time in a long time, I wanted to.

Summer continued, "So here's the thing . . ."

Uh-oh. That tone sounded bad.

I opened my mouth to say something stupid when she held up a hand, then pressed a finger to my lips. "Don't interrupt."

"Yes—" I tried to say "ma'am," but she kept pressure on my lips.

With her other hand, she placed one of my hands on her leg, which was warm. Like she'd just exited the tub. It was also smooth. Shaven. Waiting until I'd made eye contact, she continued, "It's true, you've been in a bit of a funk. But"—she tapped her heart—"Murph, I get it. You're allowed to hurt. You're allowed to not be at your A-game when it comes to you and me. You're allowed to miss Camp and Casey entirely. It's okay. We've got time. But here's the thing, and I need you"—she poked me in the chest—"David Bishop, to clue into what I'm saying. You have loved well, and deeply, and yet Bones is gone. He's not coming back. That's life. Welcome to planet earth. You loved him. He loved you. But if you're going to do this, to be you, you've got to be willing to risk everything all the time. Nothing held back. You can't do this in second gear. It's all or nothing. And right now, you're holding back. One of the things I love most about you is that you love really well, even when it hurts. Your heart is bigger than you, and you make room for everyone, but it's time for you to pull your head out of your A-double-crooked-letter."

Sweat dotted her top lip. And the veins in her neck were thick as rose vines.

"There are three girls out there right now praying that you'll kick down the door, and if you're not up for that, if you're just gonna lie here in this little pity party you've cooked up amid your pain and misery, then you're worse than the men who are holding them, 'cause you're giving those girls false hope. And false hope . . . well . . ." She shook her head, blinked, and a tear broke loose. She took my hand and laid it flat across her heart. "You taught me that this thing in us is the most powerful weapon in the world. Nothing, not one thing, ever, can stand against it. In all of human history, the heart is undefeated. There's just one catch. The best of them are tender and they wound easily." She pounded her chest gently with my hand. "And when it does, you have a decision to make, so listen up and put on your big boy pants. You can stuff it in some box where it lies pale and lifeless, where all the blood runs out, where you can protect it, where no one can ever hurt it again. And you can leave it there. Cold, dark, and dead. And safe from any pain. And for a little while maybe no one would blame you. 'Cause we know how deeply you loved Bones. But you just need to know that if you do that, if you bury this thing in a box along with Bones's memories, and then try one day to resurrect it and shove it back in your chest, it won't fit. Not like it did before. 'Cause then, when you unearth it, dust it off, and try to love again, you'll find that it won't. Dead hearts don't love. They only hate. Doubt. And cower. Because down there in the darkness, they've become a collection of scars. Little more than rocks in our chest. Weighing us down. Carrying us to the bottom of the ocean. So, David Bishop, you have a choice to make. And it's really simple. Here it is. In three words."

I waited.

She leaned close, her breath on my face, and whispered, "Live or die."

Oh, how I loved this woman.

I held her flushed face in my hands, my own tears pouring down. Grief and maybe shame exiting my body.

She kissed me and whispered again, "You taught me there are two rescues. First is this thing you're holding. The body. Then"—she tapped her own chest—"this. Right now, I'm snatching back your heart." She straddled me, squeezing me between her knees and pushing my shoulders against the wall. Her posture was that of a triage medic, waking someone who was fading in and out of consciousness. "I'm not going down without a fight. I'm not letting you stay here." Her face steadied just inches from mine. And every ounce of energy in her body was trained on me. "I'm not giving you up. I'm not yielding to the pain and the hurt and the grief. Yes, they are real. Yes, I know it hurts like nothing has ever hurt. But if the darkness comes for you, it's got to go through me first."

"I love you, Summer Shepherd."

She shook her head. And then did the windshield-wiper thing with her finger, her body still taut, pinning me to the wall. "Bishop. Summer Bishop. It's on my marriage license."

I smiled.

She sat back on her heels and held up both hands. "I'm not finished. So stop trying to kiss me."

I did as ordered.

"When this is over, when you find these three girls and bring them back safe to their mom and dad . . ." She paused to let that possibility sink in. "You're taking some time off. I'm taking your phone and I'm putting you and Gunner on a plane and we're going fishing."

"I didn't know you like to fish."

"I don't. I want to watch you do it."

"But I don't really like to fish."

"Tough. You'd better start."

"So you're just gonna sit there and watch me fish."

"Nope. I'm gonna soak up the sunshine, the salt water, bathe my body in coconut oil, drink little drinks with umbrellas, and if you stop testing me, I'll bring my bikini and all the cellulite that comes with it."

"We've been through this. You don't have any."

"Yeah, I do. Look."

"Oh, trust me. I'm looking."

She slapped my arm affectionately, then pointed a crooked and double-jointed finger in my face. "I'm not kidding." She turned and pointed to the back of her thigh.

I shook my head. "Not seeing it."

"You're supposed to say that, so thank you, but you need to get your vision checked."

"Summer, when I think of beautiful legs, yours come to mind."

She raised an eyebrow. Suspicion growing. "What do you want?"

"Nothing. Well, maybe that's not entirely true. But I'm just not agreeing with this whole cellulite thing."

Gunner rolled over and moaned, asleep under the haze of twenty ounces of nicely marbled ribeye. "What about Gunner?"

"What about him?"

"I mean, he's been working hard too."

"Yes. Gunner can tag along. Maybe we can find him a girlfriend." With that, Gunner sat up sphynx-like and tilted his head, whining. She paused, returning to me. "So?"

I nodded. "I can do that."

"Can or will?"

"Yes."

"So you're not fighting me on this?"

I shook my head. "Would it do any good?"

"Absolutely not."

"I gathered that."

Having made her point, she turned, settled her back against my chest, and nestled in between my arms. We sat there several minutes. I felt her heart pounding strong, rapid, and fierce inside her chest. A drumbeat.

After her breathing slowed, she spoke. The cooling sweat brought goose bumps on her skin. "I want one more thing."

"Just one?"

"I'm serious."

I waited.

CHAPTER 44

She pointed at the chairlift leading up to the Eagle's Nest, which hung suspended several thousand feet above us. "You owe me. Clear night. Blanket. Wine. Cheese and crackers. Crackling fire. The whole thing. And I'm not talking about some Two-Buck Chuck red blend. I mean I want you to rob Bones's cellar and get the good stuff. A dusty cabernet. Old and expensive. He's not gonna miss it."

I actually laughed. It was the first time I'd done that since he'd been gone. While I felt slightly guilty for doing so, it also felt good.

She continued, "He left it all for you anyway."

I nodded.

She stared up, then placed her hand on her hip, raised both eyebrows, and tilted her head slightly. "So what's the holdup?"

"I thought you meant in a few weeks or something."

"What gave you that impression?"

This entire conversation was going completely over my head. "I think I need a manual for the female specie—"

She snapped her fingers.

"You mean right now?"

"You got something better to do?"

"Well, no, but it seems selfish when Ruth, Miriam, and—"

"Murph." She kissed my nose. "You can bring that stupid phone. You're not a robot. I know Bones trained you to act like one, and sometimes it

190

can be a good thing, but remember, you're a human being. You're also my husband. And right now I need you to act like it."

"Well, I can steal the wine, but I don't know where I'm going to find crackers this time of night. Maybe down in the—"

"Oh my goodness. Sweet eight-pound baby . . ." She bit her lip. "Then get saltines. Get Wheat Thins. Get Cap'n Crunch. I don't care. It's not about the blasted crackers."

I knew this, but I just liked to see her get excited. "But I thought you said—"

"I'll get the crackers."

When she said this, she stood and took the blanket with her, but in doing so she revealed the short gown she was wearing. Which was all she was wearing. And which I, like an idiot, had not noticed. I would describe it but I'd just mess up the moment and you probably get the picture. "You going dressed like that?"

"Maybe. Why? You don't like it? I bought this for you and I've been waiting for a chance to show you. Now, are you saying—"

"Hold it, hold it. Easy there, killer. I like it. I like it a lot. I'm just saying it's probably hovering around zero up there and you might get a little cold."

She evidently hadn't really considered this because she stopped and chewed on her lip, which meant she was calculating. "Well then, I'm going to need a sleeping bag. A warm one. One of those feathery fluffy things, keeps you warm in a blizzard."

"Check."

"What?"

"Nothing. I'll get the bag."

"You got any more stupid questions?"

I laughed. For the second time. For which I was grateful. "No. Well, maybe. What if I can't find any cheese?"

She pointed that same crooked finger at me, then fussed with the gown, bringing attention to both it and her. "Murphy Shepherd, I'm through playing. I'm a married woman. You're a married man. And just so you don't miss the obvious, we . . . are married to each other. This"—she motioned to herself—"is what we get to do. I won't tell if you don't." She raised an eye-brow. "Now, you've got about thirty seconds to figure out how to live with me"—she paused for effect—"not only as my protector and my husband, but as my lover." Evidently my eyes had wandered, so she lifted my chin and redirected me. "You picking up what I'm putting down?"

I think I nodded.

I'd first met Summer when she stole a runabout and headed off alone down the Intracoastal at night in search of Angel. She didn't know where she was going and she didn't know how to swim. To say she was tough or tenacious was a massive understatement. She had no quit. Summer fought for those she loved, and in this moment, she was fighting—with all she had—for me, and I loved her all the more for it.

On our wedding night, walking from the ceremony to the reception, she directed Angel to lead me to a small room. I pushed open the door and found Summer standing in front of a mirror. Fussing with her hair. A second dress hanging beside her. The intoxicating residue of her perfume hanging in the air. I stood nervously looking over my shoulder, not quite sure what to do with my hands. She read me and pointed toward the room full of people. "They can wait. It's our reception." She handed me a slender box about the size of a sheet of paper, covered in gift wrap and tied with a ribbon. "Open it."

"I thought we agreed not to exchange gifts."

She nodded. "We did."

"Can't believe I fell for that."

While I fumbled with the ribbon, she lifted her hair off her shoulders and said, "Unzip me." Then pointed at her wedding dress. "Can't dance in this thing."

I did as instructed and then returned to the gift. Inside the box, I found an 8½" x 11" ebony picture frame. No picture. No glass. Simply a smooth, see-through wooden frame. I studied it like a monkey staring at a Rubik's cube.

Laughing, she said, "Hold it up."

When I did, my eyes focused on the image through the frame.

She smiled. "Stop moving it around."

Centered in the frame stood Summer. Her dancer's body laid bare. Onstage yet shared with a singular audience—me. The only thing she wore was the cross I'd bought her. Both my jaw and my arms dropped, which brought another giggle out of her. She shook her head, saying, "Nope," then reached forward and lifted my arms. "Keep 'em up."

I tried.

She walked closer. Then she just stood. Unashamed. Unafraid. Unfiltered.

She whispered, "You're blushing."

I nodded and swallowed. "Yes, I am."

She placed her thumbs on both of my temples. "Before we go any further . . . in that room . . . with those people . . . in our life . . . I want to replace the pictures"—she tapped both sides of my head and tilted hers just slightly—"rolling around in here. I want to give myself to you, before I give myself to you."

Her skin was warm and soft. Another swallow. I managed, "Mission accomplished."

She lifted the ebony frame, focusing my eyes through it once again, and then stepped back and twirled. Once. Then twice. She half turned. "You good?"

I shook my head. "Not really."

Sweat misted on her temple and across the top of her breast. I handed her my folded handkerchief, which she used to dab the sides of her face and top lip. She eyed the unwrinkled and spotless white cloth, reading the date and our names. "You do this all by yourself?"

I shook my head. "Clay."

She laughed. "Love that man." Another twirl as she clutched my handkerchief. "You starting to get the picture?"

Music and laughter from the reception spilled through the walls. "You don't actually expect me to eat dinner with these people now, do you?"

"And dance."

She turned, pressed her body to mine, and kissed me, her hands hanging behind my head. "I can't compete with your past. No woman can. It's been there too long, and to make matters worse, you immortalized it in books that are now in every civilized country in the world. In maybe the most beautiful way imaginable—of which I'm your biggest fan—you idealized a painful reality. And because of your magnificent words, and a heart that is bigger than this body, we all love Marie, and I love you all the more for it. But . . ." She laid her hand flat across my heart. "We cannot start the rest of our lives staring through the rearview mirror. So rightly or wrongly, I brought you here to push pause for just a moment and give you a glimpse of me with"—a laugh—"all my cellulite and wrinkles, and my dancer's body, which lacks some things men find attractive, before we walk in there." She held my face in her hands. "I brought you here to give you an unedited image into our future that, I hope, drowns out the written, rewritten, and edited echo of the past."

"There's that word again."

She closed her eyes. "Which one?"

"Hope."

She nodded. Waiting.

I stood in wonder. "I don't see any cellulite."

She pointed above us. "It's the lighting."

Now, she pressed her forehead to mine. Exposing the risk she was taking in this moment. When Summer had stolen the boat and set off down the Intracoastal, full throttle, in search of her runaway daughter, she'd done so while unable to swim. Driven by love, she risked the consequences. Even death. Here and now, she was risking her heart to rescue another.

Me.

Summer had rescued me. Both in that moment and in this.

I pointed. "Chairlift. Twenty minutes."

She shook her head matter-of-factly. "Eight."

"Yes, ma'am."

She smiled, revealing that she'd gotten what she wanted. "Thank you."

While she had my undivided attention, one thing caught my eye. It was her most beautiful feature. Her heart.

It was one of the best moments ever.

No sooner had the words exited my mouth than my phone rang. Caller ID read "MIT." She turned, suspicious. Then a wrinkle appeared between her eyes, which she rolled. "You've got to be kidding me. What could he possibly want this time of . . ." About then, she answered her own question, the color drained out of her face, and reality set in.

I accepted the call, but before I had a chance to say anything, Eddie erupted, "We got something."

CHAPTER 45

I flung open the IT door, where I was met by Eddie, Jess, BP, Camp, and Casey all staring at a wall of screens. Clay stood behind them, studying the same screens and trying to make sense of the data. Eddie spoke first, and he was thoughtful when he did so. "We might have something."

I waited.

"When they were taken, their phones were not. On purpose. To prevent us from tracking them. On a hunch, Jess cleaned them, and while none of the three had social media accounts, all three did have one peculiar thing in common. They all played the same game: Words with Friends. They played exclusively with each other. No outsiders." Eddie paused. "You familiar with how it works?"

"Vaguely."

"The computer generates a random rack of seven letters at the bottom of your screen. From those letters, the first player tries to form a word and places that word on the center square. Points are assigned to letters. The next player gets his or her own random rack of letters and uses them to construct a word that connects to either end of the first word or some letter in the middle."

"I get the general idea."

"Each of the girls has their own player identity, but for security reasons, they didn't use their real names so, they used something random. Something that didn't stick out. Miriam's is 'MAabc123.' Ruth's is 'RA123xyz,' and Sadie's is 'SA789def.'"

I was struggling to see where this led. "So?"

"Nobody else on planet earth would know who they are unless they told them. And again, for security reasons, they only played each other, or the computer."

"Okay."

Eddie smiled. "They also played their dad."

I waited.

Eddie continued, "Three days ago, his staff reported his phone received an invite to play a game with a random person. The staff member declined. Then today, a second invite appeared."

"Why is this important?"

"Because Aaron Ashley's player name is 'AAzyx321.'"

I was starting to put two and two together. "And why would you ask that player name to play unless you knew who was behind it?"

Jess nodded. "Correct."

"Who's asking him to play?"

This time it was BP. "Random player. 'Scooteriq172.'"

"Any way to unpack who that is?"

"Not yet."

"Has the vice president responded?"

As soon as the question left my mouth, the speakerphone on the table sounded. "No." It was Aaron's voice. "I have not. I wanted your input." His voice sounded weak but stronger.

"Hello, sir."

Eddie again. "We think it's possible that one of the girls has access to a phone with this game, and she's invited her dad to play."

"Why doesn't she just take a picture of herself?"

"We don't know the answer to that. We do know that an invitation has been received, and she might use that interaction to send some sort of signal. Location. Anything."

The speakerphone barked again, followed by muffled whispers in the background, interrupted by the signature voice of Senator Maynard. I couldn't make out what he said, but his presence was noted. Aaron broke the silence. "Murph, unless someone on your end can recommend other-wise, I'm going to accept the invitation."

Everyone in the room nodded at me. At the same time, it struck me as odd that we were discussing a game app on the phone of the vice president of the United States of America and whether he should accept the invitation to play the game. "Good call, sir."

A member of the team had rigged it so we could see Ashley's phone. In order to accept the invitation, he would click "Accept Challenge." Which he did, causing five letters to spill off the top of the screen and line up in the center row, meaning whoever had invited him to play had created their first word. "ROLES."

Eddie again. "Sir, this may be impossible, but we need to try to con-struct words where possible that ask for information."

Ashley responded, "Affirmative." A pause.

Jess this time. "Um, sir, no offense, but may I suggest that we cheat at this game?"

"You mean use AI to create words for us that do just that?"

"Yes, sir. But there's actually an app that does it just for this game."

Ashley again. "Apparently, a couple members of my staff are way ahead of you."

The rack of letters was EIASOTS. My team began typing and waited for the results.

Ashley again. "'Siesta' or 'oasis'?"

The team talked among themselves. "Sir, we vote 'oasis.'"

"We do too." Ashley entered the letters coming down from the O in "ROLES." Six points were added to his score.

We waited, but nothing happened. Sixty seconds elapsed, which felt like an hour. "Sir, we have to wait until the other player responds. She might not have access to the phone right now."

As he said that, the word "COLD" appeared next to the last S in "OASIS" to form "SCOLD." Ashley's new rack of letters was EOTENWP.

The team began speaking the possibilities. "'Townee,' 'tween,' 'weep,' 'wept . . .'"

Ashley typed without asking for consensus. "WEPT." After he entered the word, the game automatically advertised three other games, each with ten-second commercials, which offered no way to skip the ad. This obviously aggravated the vice president. "Anybody got a workaround for these ads?"

One of his staff members must have asked for his phone, because a drop-down menu appeared and a $9.99 button was selected, which blocked ads for thirty days. Ashley again: "Ten bucks, thirty days?"

"Yes, sir."

"I'm in the wrong business."

With the ads blocked, the assumption was that we could respond to moves more quickly, which might be helpful if the person on the other end was under duress or had a tight window. Both of which proved true.

Ashley asked, "Is it possible to crack the back door of this thing and determine where that game is being played?"

BP spoke this time. "Mr. Vice President, sir . . ." BP's fingers were typing at warp speed. "Game companies, like social media companies, profess not to track that information, but they know where that phone is within about three feet."

"Can you tell them that the vice president of the United States needs the information?"

"No disrespect, sir, but that would only make it worse."

"And a warrant would take too long?"

"And probably get bottled up in the courts."

"So our only hope is that you can break the encryption?"

"Yes, sir, but don't worry, I broke into DOD and the White House and the CIA, and, well . . ."

"You did?"

"Yes, sir, it's one of the reasons I have this job."

"Son, I don't care what you do or how you do it so long as it leads us to my daughters."

"Yes, sir."

CHAPTER 46

Eddie waited until Ashley had finished speaking. "Sir, one problem we might encounter is something akin to a scrambler. Something programmed to bounce the phone's Wi-Fi or cell connection off other servers around the world, thereby—"

"Not letting us confirm the location?"

"Yes, sir. Most hackers do this for obvious reasons."

"What makes you think this person is?"

"Well, sir, we don't know what we don't know, but if they are holding your daughter, and if they are smart, and if they don't want to be found, they'd scramble the signal simply as a precaution."

"Which begs the question why they would allow my daughter to play in the first place."

"They probably don't know she's playing you. If it is, in fact, your daughter."

"Explain."

"Sir, the fact that she's not sending you a direct message could very well mean someone is looking over her shoulder and she doesn't want to tip them off. The game is designed to encourage interaction between players. Direct messaging is built into the platform."

Jess this time. "Could it be they're using one phone?"

Eddie considered this. "It could mean exactly that. If someone is holding her, and that person is, let's say, bored, or passing the time, he or she could use their phone and pass it back and forth."

"But wouldn't that person know she could simply turn on the Wi-Fi, play the next move, as well as play you, then turn it off and pass the phone back?"

Ashley again. "Any other possibilities?"

"Her holder could be asleep."

Ashley considered this. "I like option one better."

"We do too, sir."

"But why would he risk giving her the phone?"

Ashley spoke up. "Because, if he did his homework, he'd know she had no social media accounts, didn't watch TV, and didn't play electronic games. None of our girls have an electronic footprint."

Eddie looked confused. "May I ask why, sir?"

"Because Esther and I felt that my job and their innocent beauty would make them a target. So we worked hard to invite our girls into an adventure outside the world of the screen. Rather than scroll and post, they read. Our library has over five thousand books. If this person came into our house, he'd have noticed we don't have a TV. It's difficult to miss."

"What about her phone on a bedside table?"

He shook his head. "Our girls charge their phones in the pantry."

I spoke next. "May I ask why, sir?"

Ashley paused. "We had a little incident with a boy and climbing out a window at night."

A few smiles cracked around the room. "Yes, sir."

Eddie offered his next thought. "If her holder thinks she's just some innocent homeschooler whose folks have shielded her from the world, he might be inclined to pass the time with a 'harmless' word game, having convinced himself that she has no experience with it."

"Any one of my three daughters could convince someone of that. They can be persuasive when they want to."

Another word appeared. "SIS."

Silence blanketed both the room and the speakerphone. Other more obvious words would have produced two to three times the points, so someone playing to win this game would not have chosen "SIS."

Ashley again. "I don't know if it's anything, but when Sadie was little, she called Ruth 'Sister.'"

Ashley's new rack of letters appeared: EOENYSP.

We each read the words the app produced. Someone on the other end suggested, "SEE."

Ashley again. "Murph?"

"Sir, I don't think what you say here is as important as what returns."

"Agreed."

Ashley tried to attach "SEE" anywhere on one of the other words but there was no fit. "Option B?"

I said, "How about 'COP' starting from the C in 'CASE'?"

"That works." Ashley dragged the two letters and constructed the word. The word fell into place, and we waited.

Ten excruciating minutes passed. Camp, who'd been quiet the entire time, hovered over a laptop. He spoke next. "The signal's coming from Alaska."

Jess was quick to follow with a nod while staring at her screen. "Anchorage."

"How do you know that?"

Camp looked at me. "We need to get on a plane."

"You sure?"

He closed his laptop. "Positive."

Jess clarified, "I doubt they're in Anchorage, but the extent to which that server is receiving and transmitting suggests they're within a few hundred miles."

I spoke to the speakerphone. "Mr. Vice President, I'll call you from the air."

I tore out of the command-and-control center, ran through Freetown, descended into my safe room, grabbed three rifle bags and two duffels, threw them over my shoulder, and began bounding back up the stairs, Gunner at my heels. Clay slid to a stop in the truck out in front of the house. I climbed in, Gunner jumped into the back, and we sped to the runway. Seven minutes later, we were shutting the cabin door when the end of a cane prevented me from doing so.

"Mr. Murphy?"

I pushed open the door, pulled him in, and shut it. Sixty seconds later, we were on our way to breaking the sound barrier. I turned to Camp. "You do realize the state of Alaska is twice the size of Texas and much of it is not populated."

"Yes."

CHAPTER 47

I called Ashley en route. Another hour passed while one of the leaders of the free world, along with my team and at least one of his staff members, constructed five more words on an app on his phone. The five words in return were "BOON," "NICK," "DARK," "SLOB," and "SAME." We weren't quite sure what to make of the words, and any rabbit trail we traveled led to some rather dismal thoughts, so we encouraged Ashley to keep playing. Keep her in the game. An hour into our flight, the words stopped populating. Suggesting that her holder had paused the game or she had been caught—an idea we didn't want to entertain.

The last word to appear was "HURT." When the word dropped, nobody spoke. A minute passed. Then another. While we wrestled with the deeper meaning and its implications for the girls, one of Ashley's aides spoke in a hushed tone in the background. "Um . . . Mr. Vice President?" A pause. "You need to see this."

Another voice, knowing we could not see what had been handed to Ashley, answered the question on all of our minds. "It's a ransom note."

Several seconds of silence passed as Ashely gave his attention to something other than Words with Friends. The aide spoke again. "Sir, they also sent a picture." Another pause. And then somewhere in there I heard a man's emotions crack and then a failure to control them.

Five minutes would pass before Ashley was able to speak again. When he did, he spoke as few words as possible. "We need to begin the process of sus . . . suspending my camp—" Ashley trailed off.

No one spoke. No one challenged him. They had broken him.

Several minutes later, the vice president managed, "Murph."

It wasn't a question. It was a commanding statement. And a weak, broken, and breaking plea. Rolled into one giant mess. Ashley was riding the edge, and I heard it in the tone of his voice. He was cracking. His one word to me was all he could muster while he tried not to reveal it to those surrounding him in the room. That was all he said. Spoken once. Nothing more. One of the most powerful men in the world was powerless to save those he loved most.

"Yes, sir," I said.

When we first met, I'd disobeyed direct orders and run back through the crowd, locking my arm beneath his, and the two of us had run together to the finish line at the end of the obstacle course. Classmates yet strangers, running with fear, with anger, and with desperation. In the end, we beat the clock. Crossing the line with seconds to spare. Actually, he didn't so much cross it as collapse over it. He lay there gorging on air, his stomach rising and falling several inches with each breath. Saliva, sweat, and vomit frozen to his face. He told me later it was the first time he'd "emptied" himself. And he had. After several minutes, he crawled to his knees and took notice of what we'd done. What he'd done. No longer could they harass and look down their noses with disdain.

Then I watched Aaron Ashley do something. He laughed. Disbelief exiting his body. It was as if he'd broken free from the chains he'd wrapped himself in due to privilege and entitlement. There in that moment, he shed them. Left them right there at the finish line. And maybe in some way, Aaron Ashley was born in that moment. Seconds later, he looked at me. Whether with tears or pain I knew not, but his eyes were glassy. He crawled to his feet and extended his hand, gratitude painting his face. "Aaron."

It was the first of many times we would extend hands to each other. "Bishop."

Staring at my phone, listening to his voice, I didn't hear the vice president. I heard my friend Aaron. Husband and father who played word games with his girls. As his voice had betrayed his emotion at the finish line, so it did now. How could it not? What father could bear up under this? In several hundred rescues, I had yet to meet him. The continuous and tormenting thought of what his girls might be enduring and under what conditions was a horror no father should ever live through. A thousand times worse than death. I understood. So I said it again just to let him know I heard him. "Yes, sir."

The line clicked dead, and I sat staring out the window, studying the white earth beneath while Camp worked on his laptop. His understanding of all things computer dwarfed mine, so I double-checked my gear bags. Having left in a hurry, I wanted to make sure I had what I needed. What I discovered surprised me.

Months ago, when I'd shot the captain of a barge on the Intracoastal at nearly a mile away, I'd done so with my preferred long-distance precision rifle. A Bergara .300 Win Mag I'd named Jolene. I'd carried her on maybe fifty rescues and would tell you I felt naked without her. She was a comfort and faithful companion. But as I opened my padded canvas rifle bag, I saw I'd not brought Jolene. I zipped open the case, laid the rifle out, and lowered the lever, confirming an empty chamber. Then I opened the box of 178-grain ELD-X Match bullets and loaded twenty into a carrier on my vest. I sat staring at the worn mahogany, blued steel, and Schmidt & Bender optics. Maybe in that moment, I had some inkling, some realization, that while Bones was gone, a part of him was always with me. I spoke to myself. *You and me? One more time?*

In response, I heard him say what he had told me several dozen times. *You only need one. So focus on that one.*

Over my shoulder, Camp spoke. "You say something?"

"No. I'm good."

As I said that, the intercom crackled. "Twenty minutes out."

I sat, buckled up, and found myself tapping my fingers. Two minutes later, my phone rang. "Murph?"

"Yes, sir, Senator."

"Wanted you to be the first to know, his people just called me. Ashley is suspending his campaign."

I stared at the phone. The word *fork-tongued* came to mind. "Thank you, sir. I'm sorry, sir."

"Me too. We all are. I can get on the phone. Gather some good people around him. Half the government would have his back. But before I spend that political currency, I need to know . . . can he rally? You know him as well as anyone. Can he come back from this and be the man and leader we know him to be?" Another pause. "Sometimes in politics, you have to know when your horse has run its last race. There ain't no shame in a last race, but everybody has one."

I considered his words. "Sir, I don't know what Aaron Ashley will or won't do. The Aaron I know is a strong man. Even the strongest of men. That said, I don't know how much more he can take. In the short run, I think it's unfair to him and unwise for any of us to ask him to be anything other than a father."

He didn't fight me, and I could hear him nodding in agreement. "The nation is losing one of its best." A practiced pause. "But who can blame him? What father could stand under this pressure?" Another pause, and while this one was also practiced, it was a little too short. "If we could just catch a break. Find his girls"—it sounded like he slapped the desk or table in front of him—"we could put an end to all this foolishness and put a good man back in the White House."

I'd said enough, so I said little else as I wanted to give him as much rope as possible to hang himself. "Yes, sir."

"He says you've got a lead."

"Yes, sir. Albeit small."

"You need any assets on the ground?"

"Not yet, but with permission, please keep your phone on."

"You got it." A chair squeaked, which suggested he had left Ashley's war room and returned to his office. Or someplace without Ashley, which told me he'd made this call in private. As he signed off, his voice took on a familiarity I'd not heard before. "Bring 'em home, son." His tone suggested we were now on the same side. Teammates, even.

"Yes, sir."

The line clicked dead and I had that same feeling in my stomach. While the world loved Waylon Maynard, I didn't trust him as far as I could throw him.

Approaching a frigid landscape, I took account of what I knew for sure: somebody was playing a game with Aaron. An invite-only game. So either somebody had lucked into a randomly generated player name and thrown it on the wall like spaghetti until someone responded, or . . . one of his daughters had sent a cryptic cry for help. According to Ashley, not only did his staff not know his player name, but they didn't even know he played the game. For the first time since I'd watched Bones disappear down the well shaft, his eyes closing as life faded out of them, my hands unable to reach him, I felt an old and familiar ache rising from the pit of my stomach. Something I'd missed and yet something I wasn't sure I wanted back. Because while the payoff could be rescue and return, the flip side of that possibility was a soul-piercing pain that I couldn't endure. And if I'm honest, I wasn't sure I wanted to.

Love like that is a risk. It's vulnerable. To risk the breaking so that another might become unbroken.

There in that moment, the memories returned, and I remembered. I remembered what I'd tried to forget.

No matter how much it hurts, no matter the cost, love doesn't die. Not ever.

It may sleep awhile, lying dormant in memory. But no matter what you do, or how hard you try to silence it, you can't kill it. You can drown it with drink, stupefy it with drugs, or placate it with indifference or idols or lovers, which are just different words for the same thing. But when you exit the boat, run up the beach, round the corner spitting sand, and kick down the door, you will find yourself, in that millisecond, confronted by one in-controvertible and inescapable truth: love is stronger than you. Always has been. Always will be. You can hate it until the hate sours you, eating you from the inside out; you can deny it, muting its voice and its tug on your soul; or you can assemble the angry masses, accuse it, and attempt to drive a stake through its chest. But in the battle of the ages, only love still stands. Love is the only thing in this universe or any other to run back across a minefield-littered landscape and lift the wounded off the battlefield while taking shrapnel en route to triage. And when love drops you on the table, bleeding from multiple holes, love smiles, kisses your forehead, and then turns, smiling, even a wink, only to tear off once again into the darkness that shrouds the field. That love has a name. And a reason. And the reason is rescue. The reason is return. The reason is freedom. And from the first day to this day, that love had been unwavering, undefeated, and undeterred. The mushroom cloud rising out of the darkness was caused when love, riddled with slivers of metal, deep scars, and third-degree burns, flung the doors off their hinges, snapped locks, and broke chains for one singular purpose.

Bones taught me that.

And from the grave, he was teaching me again. I had not wanted to learn it the first time. I did not want to learn it now. But I had. And I owed him everything for that.

CHAPTER 48

No sooner had the call with Maynard clicked dead than Camp jolted and sat ramrod straight. "We got a pic."

He turned his screen to me.

The picture populated. Sadie sat on the floor of a cabin, fireplace behind her, leather furniture around her, bear rug on the wall, another on the floor. She was not clothed. The coffee table in front of her had a mirror top. The corner was fogged. As if she'd breathed on it. Looking closer, I saw she'd hastily scribbled a word. Camp turned the screen and read the three upside-down letters. "HRY."

"Hurry."

Looking closer into the mirror on the wall, we saw the reflection of Miriam and Ruth sitting across from her, huddled close to the fire, knees pulled to their chests. Neither clothed.

Camp shook his head in disgust.

"If you wanted to deter them from escaping and it was minus ten outside, what would you do?"

He still didn't like it.

"Got a location?"

He waited as the pilot crackled over the speaker. "Runway in sight."

Approaching landing, with the wheels a few feet off the tarmac at Ted Stevens International, Camp nodded. "Yes. Yes, I do."

"How far?"

"Maybe two hundred miles as a crow flies."

"Can we get there?"

He studied the landscape, "Not easily. It's nothing but frozen tundra, a collage of lakes and rivers and small islands." Then a pause. "Wait a minute. I got a town. Something that looks like a runway. Ten miles northeast."

I turned to the pilot. "Can we land there?"

The wheels touched down, and the pilot pushed the stick forward, rocketing the G6 skyward and pinning me into my seat. Ascending what felt like a vertical climb, he cautioned over the intercom, "Hold on, boys. Gonna get a little bumpy."

Three minutes later, having leveled and returned to our cruising speed of 594 mph, I asked him, "Can this thing go any faster?"

"Not if you want enough fuel for a return trip."

I didn't hesitate. "Burn it."

He nodded and inched the stick forward. When it passed 700 mph, I quit looking.

CHAPTER 49

We landed at Iliamna airfield. The plane came to a stop and Clay, Camp, Gunner, and I exited into a world covered in ice. It was possibly the most brutal, cutting landscape I'd ever seen. We walked to a hangar where a young guy huddled beside a wood-burning stove. Any closer and he'd have been inside it. He spoke over his shoulder. "Morning, fellas. Great day for a flight."

"Morning." I pointed to the screen of my phone. "Can you get us here?"

He shook his head. "Sir"—he held out greasy hands—"I just work on 'em. Don't fly 'em. Least not yet." He was young, midtwenties. "This time of year, there's nothing there but a few hungry wolves and a lot of cold." He studied my clothes with a doubtful look on his face. "You ever been out there?"

I pointed again to my phone and to the lake next to the cabin. "Is that frozen?"

He nodded. "Solid. Two feet or better."

"If someone were inside that cabin, would they hear that plane land?"

"Chances are about a hundred percent." Another nod. "That's a Beaver. The best bush plane to ever fly Alaska, and given a 450-horse, nine-cylinder, air-cooled, radial Pratt & Whitney Wasp engine, the loudest."

I pointed to another lake, one mountain pass away. "How about here?"

He shook his head. "Maybe, maybe not. But are you trying to get to that cabin?"

"Yes."

"How?"

I traced a path across the screen of my phone. "Walk."

Another shake. "Never happen." Then he paused and added, "No disrespect. Snow is above your head. And the forest you're walking through is not flat. It's up and down, and any path you choose is blocked by a thousand downed trees. You'd die in the trying. Bears would feed on you the next day or so." He paused. "I take it this is important?"

I nodded.

"And you're trying to get in there quiet like?"

"Undetected."

"I guess you could parachute, but you'd be a Popsicle by the time you touched down." He stared at the fire, then back at me. "Sir, forgive me for asking, and you look like a man not to be trifled with, but is this on the up-and-up?"

"Some bad men are holding three young girls against their will. We think they're in this cabin. Time is short."

He nodded toward the plane. "The pilot is currently three days drunk down at the pub. He does that come winter. Don't touch it during the season, but come cold he falls off the wagon." He paused. "Sir, again no disrespect, but this time of year, nobody flies. So if this plane is within three to five miles of that cabin, they'll hear it and they'll know you're coming. Might as well blow a trumpet." He pointed to several pairs of earmuffs hanging on the seat back. "There's a reason we give 'em to the passengers."

"Snowmobiles?"

"Even if you could get 'em in there, which you can't, you've still got the same problem."

I looked to George and Mike, the two pilots who'd just flown us in here. "Either of you fly this thing?"

George, early sixties with ten thousand hours in the air, said, "An hour with the manual and I can get you in there, but you've still got the noise problem."

Frustrated, I pointed again to the Beaver. "Any way to quiet this thing? Put a muffler on it?"

He was about to answer when a voice sounded over my shoulder. "I can."

A team of twelve Secret Service agents, led by Stackhouse and wielding automatic weapons and earpieces, entered the hangar, followed by the vice president. Ashley was wearing a weathered lambskin flight jacket and insulated pants. He walked up to the kid, extended his hand, and said, "Aaron Ashley. I can fly anything with a stick."

The young man swallowed and turned back to me. "Um, sir, am I in trouble?"

"No. But we need to land on that lake, and we needed to do it an hour ago."

The young man zipped up his down coat, pulled on his gloves, and snugged a beanie down over his ears. "Sirs . . . follow me."

Gunner looked up at me and whined. "Come on, boy."

Bill Stackhouse whispered, "Murph."

"Bill." I nodded to the vice president. "Sir."

Aaron nodded but said nothing.

We walked to a van, loaded our gear, and climbed in, most of the Secret Service following in a second van save Bill, who rode shotgun alongside Aaron.

We drove six minutes down gravel roads to Pike Lake, which, like everything else around here, was frozen solid. We exited next to the lake and a plane sitting on what looked like huge skis. The plane looked old, or at least older. The large, wide wing sat on top of the cockpit and the fuselage looked large enough to carry six to eight people and some gear, provided they didn't mind sitting on top of one another.

The young man gestured to the plane. "Sir, this is a—"

Aaron spoke over him. "De Havilland DHC-2 Beaver. Single engine, high wing, propeller driven, short takeoff and landing aircraft. The best bush plane ever built."

The young man nodded. "Yes, sir." He admired his plane. "History books will tell you they started making 'em in '47, but this one served in

World War 2, although we've never been able to find out exactly what she did. The records are classified."

Aaron looked at him. "I can help you with those records."

We still had not addressed the problem of noise, so I turned to Aaron. "Sir, if they hear us . . ."

He shook his head confidently. "They won't." He pointed to the young man. "Crank her up. In this temp, it'll take thirty minutes to bring the oil temp up for takeoff."

In the meantime, Camp and I rummaged through the hangar for anything that would help keep us warm during the flight, where the outside temperature was twenty-five or thirty below. We were also thinking about the girls and how to cover them up. We found a few blankets, a greasy sleeping bag, and one insulated snowmobile suit. Ashley ordered Bill to put it on, which he did, making him look like the Michelin Man. Once he got zipped up, he said, "I can't move in this thing."

To which Aaron responded, "Bill, you're no good to my girls if you're dead."

Clay stood by the fire and raised his cane. "I'll keep the fire stoked."

"Good call."

CHAPTER 50

Ashley sat in the pilot's seat, Bill to his right. Camp, Gunner, and I filled the middle seat, and three agents filled the rear. When I told Gunner to "load up," he looked at me like I was crazy. The look on his face said, "You don't really expect me to get in that thing, do you?"

"Yes, I do." I knelt down. "I know it's cold, but so are Miriam, Ruth, and Sadie. Come on. Time to go to work."

Gunner bounced inside and sat in the middle seat where I gently put earmuffs over his ears. He didn't like them but didn't shake them off, either. Looking dubious, Camp pulled me aside. "I know he's your friend, I know he's a pilot, and I know he's the vice president, but has the power gone to his head? I mean, do you hear this thing? It's earsplitting."

Ashley turned and tapped his headset. The rest of us reached above our heads, pulled down our headsets, and adjusted the volume. Ashley spoke calmly as he manipulated the stick and watched the mechanic standing off to one side give him a thumbs-up indicator when the rear flaps responded. "I want to thank you all for going." A pause while he collected himself. "Esther and I . . ." He didn't finish. He just stared out the windshield and shook his head. Ashley pushed the stick forward, sliding us along the snow toward what looked like a runway. As he pushed the throttle forward to max power, he spoke calmly. "I know you all have questions about our approach." A pause. "Fear not. I'm going to turn this thing into a whisper."

Our takeoff was short, so Ashley gave it full power, what he would call a maximum performance takeoff given the short field. The conditions were less than desirable—icy lake with blowing snow. He set the flaps to extra lift in an effort to force us airborne in as little distance as possible. Knowing our payload was maxing the capabilities of the plane, and that conditions were going to make lift a little more difficult than usual, he pointed the nose into the wind, ran the engine up to max power, released the brakes, spun the airplane 180 degrees left into the wind, and took that momentum to launch us forward, slingshotting the plane.

As we rocketed forward, my phone rang. It was Steve. Calling from prison. I had no idea how he'd obtained a phone. All I heard him say before the line went dead was, "Be careful." Then I thought I heard him say the word *trap*. I pocketed the phone, knowing full well what we could be walking into. I also knew that meant somebody had either eyes or ears on us, or possibly both, but we'd have to tackle that when we returned. While I wasn't all that worried about me, I was worried about the man flying the plane. And if I'm honest, I was worried about Camp. Had his whole life in front of him. A life with Casey. Which I very much wanted the two of them to live and live happily.

As the bumps increased, I spoke what we were all thinking. "You sure you can fly this thing?"

"Like riding a bike." Aaron paused then spoke to all of us. "Men?"

Camp answered for the group. "Sir."

A pause. "Thank you."

The sound of his voice told me more than his words.

Camp nodded. "We'll bring 'em home, sir."

We were heavy and Ashley was fighting sink, which is pilot-lingo for sinking air complicated by competing downdrafts. Not the best conditions. Rather than fight it, Ashley continued to accelerate, hovering five to ten feet off the ground. An inexperienced pilot would have tried to climb prematurely, but not Aaron. He buried the nose, filled the front window with the horizon, allowing the tree line to get closer and closer. Then, just as we thought we were about to plow into the trees, Aaron pulled back on the stick, leaving earth behind.

Had it been anyone else but Ashley, I'd have been suspicious. Given our history, I knew what probably no one else did. Ashley had learned to fly at the academy late in his freshman year. His first planes? Gliders. He spent two years in gliders before ever touching a single engine, eventually becoming an instructor before his senior year. We would have been hard-pressed to find a better glider pilot anywhere on the North American continent. I didn't know how that experience translated into our present flight plan, but I trusted Aaron. I spoke loud enough for everyone to hear. "Just get us on the ground, sir, and we'll take care of the rest."

The ground distance was twelve miles from takeoff to cabin. The first five were rather delightful minus the cold. When we reached the seven-mile barrier, Ashley climbed to eight thousand feet and crackled over the headset again. The temperature had dropped considerably, and I was starting to shiver. Our breath was freezing on the inside of the windows.

Ashley spoke while studying the landscape below him and the instruments before him. "Gentlemen, I don't want you to be alarmed by what you're about to experience." A pause. "The only way to silence this bird is to shut her down. Which I'm about twenty-two seconds from doing. When I do, we're going to drop, and you're going to think I'm not in control." He shook his head. "Don't think that. I am. I'm generating energy." He began flipping switches. "Any plane can become a glider if you have enough elevation and someone who knows how to ride the updrafts." A nod. "Which I do. I once turned Air Force Two into a glider, although you never heard about it."

Stackhouse nodded in affirmation.

Ashley paused thoughtfully while he pointed to mountains in the distance. "On the upwind side of that ridgeline is an updraft. We're gonna hitch a ride down into the valley."

Camp leaned forward. "No offense, sir, but how do you know the updraft will be there?"

Ashley continued his shutdown and smiled. "God put it there."

Camp nodded. "Yes, sir."

Ashley again. "That said, the problem is not getting her safely on the ground; it's stopping her once we do. So buckle in."

Without another word, he completed the shutdown, bringing the propeller to an awkward stop in front of us. This caused the propeller to windmill, or slowly spin as air flowed over it, which increased our drag. Something Aaron didn't want, so he pulled back on the stick slightly, trading current airspeed to stop the propeller from spinning, which it did. Creating a strange emotion. Sitting in a plane several thousand feet in the air and staring at an unmoving propeller. My brain couldn't make sense of it.

Then Aaron did something he'd not communicated, which was probably a good idea on his part.

CHAPTER 51

Aaron turned the plane sideways, basically eliminating our forward flight and turning the plane into a midair barn door. That door caught the wind in the face, and Aaron used it to his advantage. He brought the plane nearly to a stop, then pushed the stick forward, slipping us inside the wind and causing us to drop.

Like a rock.

As my stomach jumped into my throat, Camp—apparently unfazed by the sudden loss of altitude—tapped me on the shoulder. "You going in the front door?"

I nodded.

"Don't you think that's a bit rash?"

I shook my head. "Nope."

Camp nodded. "And if it's a trap?"

"I'm not in the mood to be trapped right now."

Camp nodded and didn't argue with me.

I had flown inside a glider many times with Ashley, and I knew the tension for any good glider pilot was the seesaw between carrying too much energy or not enough airspeed. Without power, having shut down the engines, Ashley was maximizing the invisible. Harnessing what he could feel with his fingertips and trusting in what he knew the plane would do when put in certain situations. The point, as in any flight, was to make it to the runway and land. And do so without the aid of a motor. A glider pilot is

220

constantly riding energy and storing energy for what comes next. Spend the energy too soon and come up short. Don't spend it and overshoot the runway or worse, shoot through the end of it. Which is why glider pilots are possibly the most exceptional pilots bar none. They fly on feel. Period. It's all they have. Along with a good amount of faith.

I also knew from flying with Ashley that he'd taken into account the glide ratio of the Beaver, and given the seven-mile distance to the cabin, I guessed the glide ratio of the Beaver at seven to one or better. Meaning, with the power shut down, and our current glide speed of 92 mph, we'd glide, in theory, seven feet for every one foot we descended. That, of course, would be with perfect conditions, which we did not have. The feeling in my stomach told me we were dropping like a lead weight.

Once he spotted the lake, he then had to determine wind speed and direction. Again, by feel. What his fingers told him. Ashley said almost as if to himself, "Crosswind and ten-mile-per-hour tailwind." I had no idea how he knew that, but he seemed confident in it.

I also knew from flying gliders with Aaron that a tailwind was the kiss of death. You did not want that. Why? Because you couldn't stop the plane.

Ashley had another problem. Skis. Once we hit the ice, he had zero control over stopping, and the lake didn't look long enough to allow us to slide to a stop.

At fifteen hundred feet and still a mile out, Aaron harnessed the energy he needed, shoved the stick forward, dropped the nose, and sent us earthward. A sensation akin to falling off a ten-story building. My stomach jumped back into my throat, and Gunner whined as both our heads hit the top of the fuselage. We descended almost a thousand feet before Aaron pulled back on the stick, leveling us just briefly before he caught one more updraft along the ridgeline rising up along the lake. Less than a half mile from the lake, he gave it a full boot of rudder, dipped the wing, and basically turned sideways. Again. Barn door number two. He stopped our forward progress so fast, I thought Gunner would fly out of my arms. The slip once again forced our accelerated descent. I knew that at some point we had to come out of the slip and land. Come out too high and carry too much speed. That would be bad. Come out too low and carry too little. That would be bad too. Aaron came out of the slip, centered the stick, skimming treetops, centered the rudders, and then used back stick to level off. Clearing the edge of the lake, he glided out across the snow-covered landscape, hovering five to ten feet off the ice. Having leveled but still carrying too much speed, he once again pulled back on the stick, releasing energy, or airspeed, and set the plane gently on the ice.

Ashley had just put on a clinic, known only by us.

While it was a comfort to be on the ground, or at least on the frozen water beneath us, the tree line was rapidly growing larger in the windshield, and our ability to avoid it was zero. Realizing his ability to control the plane was limited to minor steering adjustments, giving him the choice of hitting either the massive pine on the left or the massive pine on the right, Ashley aimed for a small window between the two and spoke calmly. "Crack the doors open. Brace for impact."

I wanted to ask him what he meant by "crack," as in how far, but figured now was not the time to address that. So while Camp flung open the port side door, I opened the starboard, catching brutal cold in the face. I knew enough to know that the fuselage could crinkle, and no doubt would upon impact with something harder than itself, which was pretty much everything out here. When it did, we did not want to get trapped inside where we would freeze to death within the hour. Cracked doors offered us hope of a way out, so at least we could freeze on the outside of the plane rather than in.

In the glider world, "speed is life." And Ashley had used it to textbook perfection flying us in undetected and safely. But now, on the ground, speed was not our friend, and neither was the ice. Matter of fact, the present combination of the two could well prove fatal. The tree line loomed large, and while my inclination was to duck, I couldn't. Neither could Bill, who lurched left, throwing his body in front of the vice president as the tree limbs tore off the propeller and blew out the windshield. Calmly, as if driving through a car wash, Ashley threaded the needle and steered the plane between the pines, which ripped both wings off the 1947 fuselage and sent us careening into a snowbank.

Which brought us to an abrupt stop.

When the snow cleared, Gunner licked my face. His way of asking me if I was okay and telling me he never wanted to do that again. "Me neither," I said. Then he licked me again. "I'm good, boy. Come on." We dug ourselves out only to find that Bill had already pulled Ashley out the windshield. Ashley stood, teetering a bit, a gash on his forehead. Blood spilling down his face. Bill was mopping it up as I spoke. "You good, sir?" Any idiot could tell he wasn't, but I also knew no power on earth was going to keep him out of that cabin.

He blinked to clear the blood from one eye. "Never better."

Camp walked up alongside and put his hand on the vice president's shoulder. "You really stuck that landing, sir. Almost perfect, 'cept I had to deduct two-tenths for ripping off both wings. Nine-eight is the best I can do."

Aaron half smiled and Bill chuckled.

CHAPTER 52

B ill and his three agents took a satellite reading and found we were four hundred yards from the cabin, which Camp confirmed. "Three ninety-seven."

I pulled my suppressed AR from its soft scabbard, cycled the bolt, and loaded a 220-grain hollow-point .300 Blackout into the chamber. For close quarters, which this was, I wanted something relatively quiet that would thump them. Which this would. I then handed the thermals to Camp as we inserted comms into our ears. I passed Maggie to him too. "You quarterback. I need you on overwatch. I need the location of cameras and trip wires. Not to mention people."

He stopped me. "What're we calling the bad guys?"

I considered this. We needed a word that stood out and could be discerned above the wind noise. "Popsicles."

He nodded.

I pointed at the three agents. "I want you three around the back. But don't get caught in the line of fire. Take cover. There's gonna be a lot of lead headed your way, and I don't want to accidentally shoot you. I doubt the girls are in the main cabin. Probably an outlier. Whatever degenerates are holding them will no doubt feel comfortable near the fire and insulated below these low clouds and snow. Not to mention the cold. They're feeling safe in these conditions, even cocky, which is to our benefit. If they haven't heard us, and don't see us, we'll catch them off guard."

Camp interrupted me. "And if they have and do?"

I pointed to Maggie. "Then you'd better get skippy."

I turned to Ashley. "I don't suppose there's any chance you're gonna sit right here and let us go in without you?"

He spat blood and wiped his face with his sleeve. "None whatsoever."

I was about to offer an objection when he said, "My girls need to see their dad walking into that hell. Not the vice president sitting out here worried about his life."

He had a point. I motioned behind me. "Then you're on my six. And you don't move until I tell you." He was about to speak when I held up a hand. "That is not open for discussion."

Ashley had been powerful long enough that he didn't like being told what to do. But he also knew I was right and that he was no good to his girls or the country if he was dead. He nodded.

I looked at Bill. "You don't need me to tell you what to do."

He stepped in front of Ashley. "I got him."

I turned one last time to Ashley. "You bring anything that belongs to the girls? Maybe smells like them?"

He opened his flight jacket and pulled out a small stuffed tiger, about the size of my hand. Most of the hair was worn off, one eye was missing, and one ear had been chewed off. The tail had been sewed back together in three places. It was a beautiful tiger.

"It's Sadie's."

"Thank you, sir."

I skirted the lake as the ice cracked beneath me. I'd never been colder in my entire life. Gunner circled my legs, sniffing the air. When the cabin came into view, I studied it. Whoever had chosen this location had done so after some forethought. Dense forest surrounded the cabin on three sides. Each side was an organic mess. It looked like God had played pick-up sticks with the earth, leaving snow-covered mounds in an indiscernible and certainly impassable pile, making a natural fortification. The thought occurred to me that an underground bunker was more than likely. Something to remember once we got inside.

I knelt, Gunner alongside me, and studied the door and windows. Some two hundred yards. No movement but I could see the glow of a fire inside and a shadow passing by one window. I crept through the trees, Camp in my ear telling me I was clear of cameras and wires. In my mind, I heard Steve's voice warning me of a trap.

Gunner was the first to hear it. Followed by Camp. "You hear that?"

Come to think of it, I did. "Yes."

We studied the air above us. A hundred feet off the deck a drone appeared, making a programmed grid search of the island. We froze. I whispered, "You got it?"

Camp whispered, "Hold."

A suppressed rifle has a distinct sound. Sort of a crack followed by a prolonged whistle that fizzles out. The wind was constant at ten miles per hour with gusts to fifteen, both of which wreak havoc on a bullet. A second passed as Camp adjusted his windage, then pressed the trigger. The wind muffled the percussion crack of the projectile and most of the whistle. The bullet struck the drone, flipped it, and blew it into several pieces that fell quickly all around us.

Camp muttered, "Shoots a half minute right."

I smiled. Camp's description of Maggie's point of impact relative to her point of aim was a sarcastic and degrading comment on my ability to zero a rifle. I let it slip, but what I did not let slip was how calmly Camp performed under pressure—after having survived a plane wreck. "Keep an eye on the cabins. I imagine someone is about to come looking for their fifteen-thousand-dollar drone."

Thirty seconds later, Camp whispered, "Contact nine o'clock."

Gunner had already seen them and was trained on the sound of boots on snow. Through the trees, I spotted two scouts carrying SBRs patrolling the perimeter. Based on the language coming out their mouths, they were neither focused on the perimeter nor happy about searching for a drone. They didn't like the cold any more than I did.

"Murph?"

Camp's question was a tough one. Did we shoot two men walking around a remote island in Alaska when we didn't know for sure the girls were here? What if we discovered they were not? Given the conditions, my ability to surprise, overwhelm, and eliminate a threat using my hands was next to zero. They'd hear me crunching through the snow, not to mention the fact that my movements and reactions wouldn't be all that fast given the cold.

"Hold."

"You sure?"

"Check."

The two passed, not finding the drone, said something about the wind gusts, and returned to the cabin. Camp crackled, "Clear."

No sooner had he said that than he whispered again, "Contact three o'clock. Danger close."

CHAPTER 53

A single sentinel had obviously been sent in the opposite direction and had come to investigate. This guy had no neck, the biggest muscles I'd ever seen, and looked like a caricature out of a movie. His rifle was pointed in our direction, and based on his projected path, we were not going to be able to miss him. He was coming right at us; he'd just not seen us. Stackhouse painted his red laser on the guy's forehead, which was a comfort as I came out of the trees, my sound camouflaged by a wind gust. I caught him from behind and thought I'd wrapped him up pretty good, sinking my arm around his throat in a rear naked choke, when he reached behind himself and literally plucked me off his back. I'd seen the Incredible Hulk do the same thing in movies. He threw me off him, spinning me through the air like a Frisbee, and was in the process of drawing a pistol when I heard the crack of both Camp's and Bill's suppressors. Camp's 178-grain bullet was traveling at 2,800 feet per second, while Bill's 220-grain moved more slowly, around 950. Despite the difference in speed, both bullets hit their intended target within the same millisecond and rendered the ginormous man unable to think. Or live. Threat eliminated.

Camp was the first to speak. "You through messing around?"

I dusted off the snow, pulled my beanie up off my eyes, picked up my rifle, and slung it back around my neck. "Cold out here."

"I'm sitting in the same cold you are."

Gunner looked at me, tilted his head, and seemed to narrow his eyes.

"Now don't you start too."

Just then my sat phone rang. Camp heard it. "You gonna answer that?"

I accepted the call. Ariel Underwood spoke before I had a chance. "You busy?"

I was still trying to catch my breath. "You might say that."

"We picked up some chatter. You made the wrong people mad. I don't know what they're doing, but whatever it is, they're doing it now. Something about transporting three out of the ice. That make any sense to you?"

"Starting to."

"Just thought you'd want to know."

"Appreciate the heads-up." Another breath. "Hope I can return the favor one day."

"Oh, and one more thing: you got five bad men exiting the house from the rear, three west, two east, intent on flanking your position. You got about eight seconds."

That was information I did not have. "Thanks again."

"Don't mention it."

The line clicked dead. "Camp?"

"On it. Two Popsicles. Four o'clock. Coming in hot."

About the time he said that, I heard bullets whizzing by my head. The three of us dove for cover and Camp and I began returning fire. Which, based on the fact that they were running in the open, they were not anticipating. So much for a surprise entry. Bill and his men concentrated their fire east, while Camp and I focused west. When I looked down ninety seconds later, two empty magazines lay at my feet and Gunner's muzzle was covered in blood not his own. Three dead guys lay around us. One at my feet. The vice president stood protected behind Bill, who was standing alongside me. I placed my hand on Gunner's shoulder. "Easy, boy."

I could feel his heart racing above the pounding of my own.

Camp spoke first. "Clear."

I looked at Bill. "We missed our window. Stay on my six."

We ran for the door. I reached it first and skipped the subtle tactic. The frame splintered, the door flew open, and gunshots rang out from the inside. I rolled, came to a knee, and found a man standing in the center of the room, one arm around Sadie's neck, a Glock to her head and a bad look on his face. I steadied both my red dot and my laser on the man's forehead, considering my options, when a blur broke through the door, rolled, and came up firing. One shot. The round from Ashley's SBR surprised the man and caught him squarely in the nose, rocking his head backward and laying him out flat. Sadie, both angry and scared, turned, picked up the man's Glock, and emptied it into his chest cavity. When finished, the naked girl stood over her abductor, threw the empty pistol at the man's head, and screamed just inches from his face, "I gave you a chance! Told you he was coming! You didn't listen. Who's the idiot now!"

The man lay dead on the floor, bleeding from multiple holes.

Aaron wrapped his arms around his daughter while Bill wrapped them both in a blanket. I spoke next. "Camp, we need you."

When he responded, I could tell he was running and out of breath. "Three seconds out."

Camp entered the door as the vice president's three agents entered the back. Aaron quietly asked Sadie, "Where're your sisters?"

Sadie pointed to the cameras in the corner near the ceiling and shook her head. I was afraid of that. Without hesitation, Ashley's agents shot the cameras, rendering operational blindness to whoever was watching us. I knelt, slid the worn tiger from inside my vest, and let Gunner sniff it. "Find 'em, boy. Find the girls."

Gunner began sniffing every corner of the room, then the attached kitchen, followed by an attached game room. He then crept down a short hallway. A door on the left exited outside into freezing temperatures. No way they did that. The girls' skin would freeze in minutes. A door on the right led into a library of sorts. Gunner circled the room, then the wood-burning stove, finally sitting next to the stove.

Smart. Very smart.

CHAPTER 54

All eyes on me, I walked to the stove and slid the carpet away from one side, revealing circular scratch marks on the wood floor. Scratch marks caused when the stove was moved on its axis and slid out of place to expose the stairwell beneath. I pointed to the marks, then made a rather crude attempt to show a man walking downstairs with my fingers, which evidently worked. We circled the stove, which, unfortunately for us, someone had recently stoked and to which they'd added several pieces of wood. Another very smart move. I grabbed the poker, hooked it around the base of the stove, and pulled it in the direction of the scratch marks. As if sitting on ball bearings, the stove slid in a tight circle, turning inside its chimney pipe, suggesting a sophisticated and well-thought-out design.

To my right, Bill was talking on the phone. Nodding. When he hung up, he turned to Aaron, "The cavalry'll be here in seven minutes. They've got sat view of the island. Anybody tries to leave, we're on 'em."

Aaron nodded.

Once the stove was moved, a basement stairwell revealed itself. If Ariel was correct, whoever we were fighting could have moved Miriam and Ruth out this tunnel long before we got here. We had no way of knowing, and standing there deliberating about whether to descend into a dark basement was not helping. I had two options. I could send Gunner, risking his life, which I wasn't about to do, or skip the steps and jump. Complicating matters was the nagging thought that had it been my basement, I'd have wired it with explosives. Which reminded me of Steve's call. But we'd already lost a lot of time, and time is life.

I turned to Ashley. "Sir, I need you to back against that wall."

He knew his presence in the tunnel would require us to fight in two directions—the bad guys in front of us and protecting him behind us. He nodded.

I grabbed the truss, which would have been above my head had I descended the stairs, swung myself in, and jumped. My feet hit the ground about the time the explosion threw me against the far wall. Fortunately for me, jumping into the basement rather than running down the stairs meant I wasn't standing where the explosion would have done the most damage. Other than being unable to hear, and having suffered what was probably a pretty good concussion, I fared pretty well.

Also fortunately for me, the explosion was more disorienting than maiming or flesh-tearing, which I saw as a real plus. I lay there, my bell rung, and kept thinking to myself, *These guys are good and they are well financed.* I almost felt like I was fighting Frank. If I hadn't seen him shoot himself in the head, and the resulting damage of that bullet as it passed through, I very well could have been.

I woke to find Gunner licking my face. He was glad I hadn't sent him down the stairs, and this was his way of both waking me and thanking me. "Hey, boy. Love you too."

Camp knelt over me, and while I couldn't hear what he said, I could read his lips. "You 'bout done?"

"Well, now that you're asking, I'm tired of being shot and blown up."

He ran his light across my pupils. "You still with me?"

I nodded. "I'm in here. Head hurts."

"I'll say."

He helped me to my feet as the ringing in my ears subsided just enough for me to make out faint sounds. He pointed to the tunnel. "Mind if I lead?"

"Not at all."

Clarity returned as we followed Camp down the dank corridor. Watching him move, I realized how catlike he was in these situations.

While I had become a rescuer and had learned to make war in order to do so, Camp was a warrior who had turned to rescue. He'd become a true partner, and I felt much safer with him by my side. A brother in whose hands I'd willingly put my life. In addition, I'd grown to like his battle-earned humor. Walking behind him, watching his senses and skill function at an extremely high level, I experienced a strange and surreal emotion: Camp reminded me of Bones more than I liked to admit, and his presence made Bones's absence that much more painful.

The tunnel wound through the hillside, coming to a large steel door several hundred feet from the entrance. Our lights reflected off the steel and we stopped. I tapped him on the shoulder. "Not to be Captain Obvious, but you do realize that's locked from the outside."

He nodded and began pulling C-4 from his vest, which he gently attached and molded to the back side of the door, eventually inserting the blasting cap, or ignitor, and then walking backward while he unrolled the trigger wire. "Excuse me." C-4 is a plastic explosive that looks like modeling clay. It's relatively stable until detonated via a trigger mounted to a cord attached to the blasting cap, at which point it produces a lot of gas and heat in a short period of time. When ignited, the resultant gases expand at 26,400 feet per second. So all those movies we've seen of people running away from a C-4 explosion are ridiculous. One minute everything is calm. The next it's destroyed. How far the blast spreads depends on the amount of C-4 used. In Camp's case, he used enough to blow the door off its hinges.

Having backed around the first turn, out of sight of the door, he glanced behind us. "All clear?"

I double-checked our six. "We're clear."

Camp triggered the detonator, igniting the C-4, and blew the massive door off its hinges, giving way to daylight, snow, and splintered evergreens. Camp was walking carefully to the door when I tugged on his vest and handed him a small mirror on a telescoping wand. He extended it, and we studied the picture. He shook his head. "Man, these guys are not messing around."

"Nope." I reached into my soft case, which Camp carried over his shoulder, and lifted Maggie. I extended the bipod and lay prone on the gravel, slowly inching my way forward. I was still several feet within the door but was trying to get a view of the cabin on the opposite hillside. If I could stay hidden inside the shadow of the doorway, maybe we could remain unseen.

The bullet whizzing into the tunnel told me we had not.

I'm right eye and hand dominant, so I normally shoot right-handed, but the configuration of the tunnel made that difficult, so I rolled, repositioned the rifle, and switched eyes and hands. This meant I was now shooting left-handed but doing so from a much more natural point of aim. In short, that meant my body tension wasn't fighting my attempt to aim. Relaxed body equals relaxed aim. Camp knelt over me, studying the cabin porch through range-finding binoculars. He said, "That's 2246 to the angry man with a rifle."

Given that I'd zeroed Maggie at 200 yards, I came up 160 MOA, which meant I was now aiming more than 3,560 inches above the man. This bullet was more akin to lobbing in a mortar round than rifle cartridge. "Any guess on the wind?"

"At the door, maybe ten, right to left. Out there . . ." He shook his head. "No idea."

CHAPTER 55

I dialed sixteen minutes of windage into the scope and let the crosshairs settle on the man who, lucky for us, was standing exposed behind a tripod-mounted rifle. I didn't know for sure the caliber of his rifle, but judging by the sound of the projectiles pinballing off the rock walls around us, it was either a .338 Lapua or .50 cal. The distance between us, one and a quarter miles, gave him the confidence to stand out in the open because he thought no one was capable of shooting back.

Camp, still staring through binoculars, said, "Hundred bucks says you don't even hit the house. Much less the man." I closed my eyes, measured my breathing, slowed my heart rate, then opened my eyes and placed my finger on the trigger. The trigger was a Kepplinger. Its normal pull was two pounds, but if you "set it," or pushed it forward the opposite direction you would normally pull it, it became a hair trigger with a six-ounce pull. I took a breath, set the trigger, let it out slowly, and was in the process of applying pressure when two more rounds whizzed above us. Followed by three more, this time closer. The presence of so much lead inside the tunnel confirmed for me that making a run for it was out of the question. Camp was still looking through his binoculars. "He's getting that thing dialed in. If you're gonna—"

I pressed the trigger and Camp and I watched—him through binoculars, me through my Schmidt & Bender—as 5.3 long seconds elapsed while the bullet crossed the distance between us. When the bullet made contact with his chest, it flipped him backward, tearing him away from the rifle and sending him through the window behind him. A surprise offensive attack that brought three angry men out of the house. One of whom righted the tripod and began staring through the scope. It would only take him a few seconds to find us. "Time to go," I said.

We exited the door at a full run, following footsteps in the snow. Or rather, two sets of footprints and what looked like two drag marks where Miriam and Ruth had been unwilling to walk.

We wound through the woods as the new shooter at the cabin peppered the trees around us. With Gunner in the lead, we ran nearly a quarter mile down a well-beaten snowmobile path until we heard what sounded like the engine of either a dirt bike or a snowmobile. Given our surroundings, it wasn't tough to guess.

We crept through the trees to see two snowmobiles at less than two hundred yards and two bad men trying to wrangle two unwilling girls atop them with little success. To the girls' credit, they were fighting for all they were worth. While I was glad they weren't going down without a fight, their movements made it impossible for us to shoot. I hit the path at a dead run, where I was nearly overrun by a man running next to me. Stride for stride. This time he wasn't telling me how he couldn't make the line before time expired. Aaron Ashley was barely breathing. The look on his face told me he wasn't running alongside me as vice president, and he wasn't even running as a father. The only word that came to mind was "reckoning."

We closed the distance to 150, 100, then 50 about the time one of them threw a vicious right at Ruth's chin and knocked her naked body unconscious. With 40 to go, I unholstered my CZ and handed it to Ashley. "Sir—"

Ashley palmed the grip, cycled the slide in midstride, making certain it was loaded, and launched himself at the man on the right when still five or six yards distant. He caught the man in the chest, toppling him and separating him from Ruth and sending him sliding out across the ice, pawing for purchase with little effect. Ashley grabbed Ruth with one arm, cradling her and protecting her from return fire, then, leveling the pistol, he fired five rounds. None missed.

I'm not quite sure why, but I have an uncanny ability to pick fights with people who are stronger and faster than me. Silverbacks disguised as professional MMA fighters. Somewhere prior to our arrival, he had managed to bind Miriam and throw her sideways across the seat. He was in the process of throttling up and exiting at a high rate of speed when I launched myself at his head. My forward momentum pulled him off the snowmobile, and we flew spinning out across the ice. The only thing that saved me was hooking my arm around his neck before he got his bear paws on me.

As we rolled across the ice, I knew rather quickly that I couldn't out-muscle him, given his size and strength. So, thinking maybe I could out-quick him, I attempted to put him to sleep via rear naked choke. I only had one problem. He didn't want to be choked, so he stood up, wearing me like a backpack, and then jumped, arching backward and slamming us both onto the ice where I and my rib cage served as his cushion. The blow knocked all the air I'd ever breathed not only out of me but out of my memories. I tried to maintain my grip, but he was twice as strong and three times as mad and was in the process of ripping my right arm out of its socket when, thanks to the force of our impact when he slammed us earthward, the ice broke and we fell through.

The shock was paralyzing. Not to mention that between the two-hundred-yard run, the body slam, and my futile attempt to wrestle this behemoth to the ground, I was out of breath. He must have had lungs the size of a zeppelin because despite the amount of sheer strength he was using to unhitch me from his back, he didn't seem to be breathing hard at all. Quickly I thought through my two options: hold on or let go. Neither was all that appealing. I didn't know what would happen if I held my grip, but I was pretty sure what would happen if I let go. So I decided to hang on for all I was worth, which seemed dumber and dumber as he fought frantically and we sank deeper into the icy darkness. Everything in me wanted to let go and fight for the surface now, but I knew if I gave him an inch, he'd crush me with his bare hands and bury me at the bottom of this lake. I squeezed my forearm and biceps as tight as my fleeting life would allow, placing pressure on his carotid. Seven good seconds was all I needed. I just doubted I had seven seconds left. They ticked by slowly. Each one taking a year as he thrashed and pulled and we somersaulted in the icy water.

The walls were closing in and I was close to blacking out myself when I felt a flash of weakness, followed by a sound and a few kicks, and then he went limp. Knowing I had but a half second to get topside, and knowing he might well be playing possum, I pushed him down as violently as I could, kicking him farther with my feet on his shoulders and willing myself to the surface. Out of air, I pulled and kicked and pulled and kicked again, but we'd descended farther than I thought. I was waterlogged and my vest now served as an anchor. I could see the light of the surface, but the distance was too far. The walls closed in. I pulled one last time and the world went black. Save one image.

Bones.

Dressed in flowing white robes. Holding a glass of wine. A cat-eating grin. Waving. He was mouthing something, but I couldn't make it out. He was fit. Tanned. And his eyes were bright. Looked like he'd been eating healthy. Oddly, he danced a little jig when I waved, which was strange because I'd read one time that the dead don't dance, but at the moment I couldn't remember where I'd read it.

If I'm honest, I wanted to go to him. I wanted to be finished with the pain. The pain in my lungs. The ache in my heart. And now a stinging pain in my leg caused somewhere in the last three minutes. Evidently someone had shot me. If the cold didn't kill me, and the water didn't drown me, then surely I'd bleed out through the hole. Things were not looking good.

When I was about to cross the chasm between Bones and me, a hand grabbed my vest and rocketed me out of the water. When he found me unresponsive, he blew air into my lungs and began chest compressions, which hurt a lot. Coughing up half the lake, I pushed Camp's hands away and told him if he kept doing that he was going to break a rib.

As I lay there, gorging on air, allowing the light back into my eyes, the man in the water reemerged.

CHAPTER 56

Wielding a pistol, the man rose from the water like a torpedo, turned toward me, and was in the process of pulling the trigger when my CZ rang out. I didn't count the percussions, as they were rapid, but when I looked up, Ashley was kneeling over me and the barrel of my CZ was smoking, the slide locked back. Meaning, he'd emptied nineteen rounds. Without taking his eyes off the red spot in the water, he dropped the magazine with his right thumb while reaching into my vest with his left and removing a loaded magazine, which he then inserted into the CZ, dropping the slide. Camp, Ashley, and I sat staring several seconds, wondering if Aquaman was going to reemerge. When he did not, we began belly-crawling off the ice where Bill and some other agents had already wrapped Ruth and Miriam in blankets and were carrying them back to the cabin, warm clothes, and the fireplace.

I made it to solid ground and rolled over on my back, still enjoying the amount of air filling my lungs, then tapped Camp on the shoulder. He, too, was struggling to breathe. "You got a tourniquet?"

He slid the tourniquet from the back of his vest and then knelt to determine why I would ask. Evidently he'd not seen the tomato puree I was spreading across the snow. Examining my wound, he nodded while tightening the tourniquet. "Pass-through. No bones. No femoral contact." He smiled while also trying to catch his breath. "You'll live to drown another day."

I laughed. It was all I could do. Being wet, we had about three minutes before I froze to death, so the three of us stood and limped back to the cabin. Camp on my left, Ashley on my right. When we climbed the stairs leading into the great room, the girls, now clothed, ran to their dad.

I sat there watching them cry on his shoulder and him, one of the most powerful men in the world, cry on theirs. It was a beautiful moment. One I needed to see. A reminder of why we do what we do. Because in my pain I had forgotten. Grief and loss had clouded my purpose. And maybe that was Bones's last lesson. Maybe that was why he showed up in the water. Pain is a thief and fear a liar. Always have been.

The room was buzzing with Secret Service personnel wanting to check the vice president, but he wasn't having it. He just pointed to his girls. "Not me. Them." In the distance, I heard the sound of a large helicopter growing closer. The cavalry no doubt. With the shivers growing almost uncontrollable, I knelt in front of the fire and pulled off my wet clothes down to my shorts. Someone wrapped an emergency blanket around my shoulders, and I inched as close as I could without actually getting inside the stove. The heat felt better than good.

Interestingly, while my head still pounded from the percussion, the ringing in my ears had almost totally subsided. No idea how. Maybe the cold. Camp knelt next to me, hovering over two mugs of hot chocolate. "I wasn't sure if you liked marshmallows."

My mug was spilling over. A half bag at least. It was the best hot chocolate I'd ever drunk in my life. Then, in one of the most heart-satisfying moments I'd known in a long time, I got to watch as Aaron called Esther. He was seated in a chair. Phone in one hand. Head in the other. When she picked up after half a ring, he tried to speak and couldn't. Then tried again. "We got 'em."

I wouldn't soon forget the sound she made in response.

As the cabin filled with more Secret Service and law enforcement personnel, the truth of their abduction became clearer. Despite our hopes, the girls had not escaped unscathed. Not only had their captors been given free rein over hour-long intervals, but the three separate rooms in which they were held all contained a series of ropes and pulleys controlled by small, powerful motors mounted along the walls. Each room also contained eight cameras controlled by precision, medical-grade motors that could extend into any area of the room. From one millimeter to ten meters. At any angle. Someone else had violated the girls from a distance.

I wanted to throw up.

We returned to Anchorage aboard a massive helicopter rented by the US government and flanked by three others spilling over with agents along with several F-35s offering cover from 43,000 feet. I'd never felt safer in my entire life. As we hovered over the hangar, I could see that a media circus had preceded us. Maybe a hundred reporters and camera operators were running toward the landing pad. They looked like ants en route to a snow-covered food source.

Ashley spoke through the headset. "Murph?"

"Sir."

One arm around Sadie, the other around both Ruth and Miriam, he shot a glance at me. "Find 'em."

I stared out across the earth's white face, knowing that evil lurked just beneath the surface. And the only way to find it was to shine a light in dark places. "Yes, sir."

CHAPTER 57

We touched down amid the media frenzy. News outlets across the West Coast and all of Alaska had sent their people, intent on feeding on what remained of Aaron Ashley. Ashley led his girls aboard Air Force Two, where doctors began seeing to each of them. Each wanted their mother, who was currently in a jet traveling almost twice the speed of sound. Once the girls were settled with medical personnel, Ashley exited the plane and walked inside the hangar to an eerie hush and standing room only. He approached the microphone and stood a moment, gathering either his thoughts or the words he would use to communicate them. But rather than speak, he pointed to a reporter on the front row. "Yes, ma'am?"

Ordinarily, reporters shouted over one another to be heard. Not today. She stood and said, "Sir, how are the girls?"

Ashley nodded. "They're safe. Long road ahead."

The reporter again. "And you, sir?"

Ashley considered this. "Better."

Ashley pointed to a man to his right. The man stepped forward to be heard. "What will you do now?"

"Tell my girls I'm sorry."

The reporter was quick to respond. "For?"

"Not doing my most important job."

"Which was?"

Ashley was slow to respond. "Protecting those I love."

"Sir, with all due respect, I didn't vote for you, but no one here would accuse you of that."

Ashley's pain had surfaced. His face was riddled with it. No one pressed him on this.

Despite several hundred people being crowded into the space, the only noise was the wind outside. Ashley pointed again. The woman motioned to the swelling on his face along with the bandage that now covered stitches. "Unconfirmed reports state you cut the engines at seven thousand feet and glided to a hard landing. Is that true?"

"No. The landing was soft. The impact with the tree line was hard."

While Ashley was not attempting to be funny, a slight chuckle rippled across the room, allowing some much-needed oxygen to enter.

Ashley pointed again. The reporter seemed hesitant to ask. "Any chance you'd reconsider and accept your party's nomination?"

Ashley didn't hesitate. "No."

A final point. "Sir, do you know who did this?"

"Not yet."

"Chances are they're watching this. Any words for them?"

Aaron looked into the camera and paused. Then he spoke one word. "Yes." With that, he returned to Air Force Two.

Clay stood next to me shaking his head. "That's a tough man."

"Yes, he is. And he's about to get tougher."

Three seconds later, my phone rang. I stepped into the hallway and accepted the call. "Senator?"

"Are they safe?"

"Yes, sir."

"All of them?"

"Yes, sir."

"Do they need medical attention?"

"The doctors are treating them now aboard Air Force Two."

"Was it bad?"

"Their bodies will heal. Their hearts might take some time."

He paused, and I could hear his chair squeak. "How's he doing?"

"Managing, sir."

"And Esther?"

"She's en route."

Another pause. I offered nothing. Letting him drive the conversation. "I know it's too soon, but any chance you can get him to push pause on his plans? Maybe agree to a sit-down with me and some other senators? He's now political royalty. Lightning in a bottle. He'd win in a landslide."

"I don't think so, sir. He's pretty rattled."

"Looked like the impact was severe."

How would he know what it looked like? "Yes, sir. It was. He threaded a needle."

"Nice job, son."

"We caught a break."

"Murph?"

"Yes, sir."

"Bones'd be proud."

I stared at the phone, considering this. Interesting that he would play the emotional card. "Thank you, sir."

"I'm putting you up for the Congressional Medal."

"That's not necessary, sir."

"But much deserved. Get 'em home. And if you need anything, you let me know. I'll move heaven and earth."

"Yes, sir. Thank you, sir."

I hung up and stared at the windstorm outside. Was Maynard genuine? Or brazen? What was my deal with Maynard? Was I making this up? Paranoid? Finding fault under every rock or phone call due to my own wounds?

While my mind couldn't tell, my gut had no doubt.

CHAPTER 58

Esther landed, ran through the snow and ice, and boarded Air Force Two. Camp, Clay, and Gunner, along with all of Ashley's staff, stood outside where we listened to the soul-gutting wails coming from inside the plane. Miriam, Ruth, and Sadie had been rescued, and they were safe, and they were headed home where these bad men could not hurt them anymore, but there was a second rescue yet to come. And it would take some time.

An hour after takeoff, Stackhouse walked to the rear of the plane and sat alongside me. He was sipping bourbon. Which surprised me because I knew he didn't drink. "Aaron asked me to . . ." He cut himself short and then just said, "He can't."

I waited.

"Seven-man teams alternated every five days." Stackhouse sipped. "They were allowed to do whatever they wanted, so long as they maintained the perimeter and patrol schedule. They thought their security was pretty good. Aaron saved his girls when he turned that Beaver into a glider." Bill stared into his bourbon. "In between the rotation of men . . . the girls were secured hand, foot, and head to a series of highly sophisticated ropes and pulleys. Robotic arms controlled several cameras and . . ." Bill swallowed.

"A sadistic puppeteer and his marionettes."

Bill nodded and finished off his bourbon. "All while a computer-altered voice came from the surround sound."

"A voyeur outside the cabin not only financed the abduction but participated in it from a distance."

Bill nodded, then stood and returned to Aaron's office, where he closed the door. As he did, I glimpsed Aaron crumpled on the floor, arms around Esther and his girls, his shoulders shaking. Aaron was breaking. Cracking down the middle.

Studying the pieces, trying to make sense of the picture, I dialed the number. He answered on the first ring. "Yeah."

"How'd you know?"

"Prison grapevine."

"Gotta give me more than that."

"Couple operators I used to work with came to see me. Fed me a line. Asked me indirectly about you. I didn't know where or when, only that they'd be waiting." A pause. "Are they safe?"

"They're alive."

His silence told me he could read between the lines. "You good?"

"I'll live." As my anger bubbled, my tone changed. "If I find out that you know more than you're telling me . . . your prison experience will not be a peaceful one."

"I don't expect you to believe me, but our orders were to deliver the girls to a private airport in rural Virginia. They'd be held a few days and released. Unharmed."

"Do you hear yourself?"

"Yes, sir. I know what it sounds like."

"You sure? Let me break it down for you. Somebody instructed you to enter the home of the vice president of the United States, kill all the members of his security detail along with his dogs, and then abduct his three daughters using pharmaceutical-grade drugs. You then haul them out of the house, drag them across their yard, strip them, shove them in the back of a vehicle, photograph them, and then jet them out of the state. Does that strike you as unharmed?"

"No, sir."

"You want me to believe it was a harmless snatch and grab, no harm, no foul. That right?"

"Yes, sir."

I walked to Aaron's office door and held the phone up, capturing the wails emanating from the other side of the closed door. I let him listen for several seconds. "Does that sound unharmed?"

His voice dropped. "No, sir." A pause. "It does not."

I made sure. "That sound? That's on you. You did that."

A long pause. "Yes, sir. I did." I could hear the tension in his voice. "I have no excuse. They trained me well. I followed orders."

That didn't sit well. I could have ripped his throat out. "Steve, some orders you don't follow."

His response was slow and weak. "They never taught me that, sir."

"Nope. You don't get to play that card. You're not a victim of your training. You're a product of who you chose to be on this side of it."

CHAPTER 59

The words exited my mouth, and the memory returned. We were in Spain. I was still green. Finding my way. Only a few names inked on my back. And I carried the pain of Marie daily. She was ever with me.

We were staring through binoculars from a twenty-story balcony at another balcony two stories below just across the street. A man and his wife sipping coffee. Reading the paper. Their feet were touching. They were playful. A couple of kids wearing footie pajamas played with a train set just inside the glass door. Oddly, the kids were held within a ten-by-ten net. A square prison. Something they couldn't get out of.

Bones got a call, said, "Yes, sir," then said it again, followed by, "I understand." He hung up and said, "Let's go."

We descended the elevator, crossed under the street using the parking tunnels, rode the elevator up, and exited at the eighteenth floor. Bones was quiet. Troubled. Normally, he'd tell me the plan before it was time to execute it. This time, he said nothing. The closer we got to the door, the more defined the wrinkle between his eyes. Standing outside the door, Bones shook his head, said, "Nope. Not doing it," and then picked the lock of the empty apartment next door to the happy couple. We wound our way to the balcony, and Bones snaked a camera around the corner. Focusing the image, we watched as the happy couple entered back into the apartment and started fixing pancakes. The kids had spread syrup and powdered sugar everywhere.

Bones studied the video for almost five minutes. Just watching. Then without explanation, he looked at me and said, "Some orders you don't follow." Then he held up a finger, which was shaking in anger. "No matter what."

Twelve minutes after we'd left our balcony perch across the street, Bones dialed the number from his last call. The voice on the other end answered and Bones simply said, "Target extracted. En route to rendezvous."

The voice said, "Check," and hung up.

Bones pointed at the elevator. "In about ninety seconds, bad men are going to exit that elevator and enter next door. I'm not quite sure what they want, but they wanted us to do their dirty work."

Seventy-eight seconds later, I discovered he was right. Three men exited the elevator and approached the door. Bones met them in the hall. One guy got tough; Bones let him know he wasn't. The other two were turned back toward the elevator when I met the first one with a fire extinguisher in the face. The third put his hands up and began backpedaling.

Interrogation a few hours later uncovered what Bones had suspected. Someone had electronically copied one of his contacts in government and used that voice to communicate to Bones that our loving couple had kidnapped the two kids and were putting on a ruse. The net was confirmation.

In fact, our happy couple was actually a happy couple. One of their kids was on the spectrum and had a tendency to run around a bit. Oh, and the net was, in fact, an indoor batting cage.

With the three goons singing like canaries, we arrested the voice a week later—in California. A billionaire investor who owned businesses around the globe, including some very fast cars. The husband of our happy couple happened to be an engineer for a Formula 1 team and had developed an algorithm that somehow improved the performance of the car. The voice owned a rival team.

Bones and I spent the evening on the balcony back across the street. As the couple returned to their porch, wineglasses having replaced coffee mugs, kids watching a movie on the couch inside, Bones sat quietly a long time. When the sun fell behind the other end of the earth, Bones sipped an old Spanish red and then sat up, placing his elbows on his knees, swirling the wine, watching as the legs formed. "I can't train you this. Either you have it or you don't."

"What's that?"

"Which orders to obey and which . . . not to."

"How will I know?"

He tapped the side of his head. "You won't always." Then he poked himself in the gut. "You have to know."

"That's not much help."

He touched his heart. "There is a voice inside each of us that knows what is true and what is not. You have to learn to listen to it."

"What if it's not speaking?"

"It's always speaking. The question is whether we're listening."

"What if I can't hear it?"

He stood, stared down, then out, then at me. "You will. It's out there, out beyond the noise. But don't expect it to rattle you and demand your attention. It won't. Won't shout over competing voices. Won't make a power play to be heard. The truth is a whisper. Usually spoken amid storms. And that whisper lies at the heart of what we do and who we are. It's the plumb line. If we ever lose it, we would do well to find another line of work."

"What if stuff is coming at me fast and I don't have time?"

He shook his head. "No excuses. What we do is life and death. We have to hear. Have to know. Every time."

"But that's impossible."

The memory of Bones's face lingered. I could still see it. And I could hear his echo. "So is what we do."

CHAPTER 60

I sat at the window staring out. Vesuvius bubbling inside me. Threatening to crack the mantle. I didn't know anything about Steve's training. Even now, I didn't know much about Steve other than he stopped listening to the whisper somewhere prior to the night he took Aaron's girls. What I did know was this: I had Bones. He did not. And the difference in our lives' paths was profound. While I was a cauldron of anger, I also felt a ripple of immense gratitude. Of pride in another. The question was quick in surfacing: Without Bones, where would I be? The names on my back might argue otherwise, but the hard truth was that I could easily be sitting alongside Steve. Bitter, deaf, and misguided.

As both the image of Bones and his echo faded, I felt the now-familiar tug. The ache. And yes, I missed him. Missed him more with each passing day. Especially now. These moments—having rescued, now flying home—were never free of pain. The girls had suffered greatly. They were suffering still. And in my experience, they would continue to suffer for some time. Trauma and grief are real. The body keeps the score. But they were on this plane, their parents' arms around them. They had a chance. I knew there'd be a struggle to come and a pain cave to walk out of, but they would live to fight another day. The sun would rise tomorrow. And in these moments, when Bones and I had walked into the darkness and pressed it back, we would, for just a handful of moments, sit quietly in the present. Not racing the clock. Not regretting, not rehashing, not calculating, not strategizing, and not preparing. We were just being. And we did that together.

Camp sat across the aisle. Staring at me. "Want to talk about it?"

I shook my head.

"This partnership isn't going to work if you don't let me in on what I'm not in on."

I made no response.

"If Bones were sitting here, would you tell him?"

"Wouldn't have to."

"Why?"

"'Cause he could read my mind."

He chuckled. A minute passed. "So?"

"Maynard called."

He chewed on a toothpick for about half a second. "I'm in."

"You don't know the plan."

"Yes, I do."

"What is it?"

"You're gonna bring his playhouse down."

Maybe he did know the plan. "Pretty much."

"And if you're caught?"

"It'd be the end of me and probably the end of Freetown."

"Is it worth it?"

I made eye contact for the first time. "What is one life worth?" I paused. Watched the world spin beneath us. "I think Maynard is more than we think."

"More what?"

"That's what I intend to find out."

"How?"

"Telling you that will make you an accessory."

"You think I actually care?"

He pointed to his earpiece, connected to the comms worn by myself and the entire team that breached the cabin. I'd taken mine off in the cabin.

Stackhouse had not. Camp raised an eyebrow. "I heard it from the doctors. You got the G-rated version."

"I don't have much to go on."

"What do you need?"

"Highly sensitive, super-high-def, invisible viewing and recording equipment. And I need a lot of it. And I need it put someplace it's not supposed to be and won't ever be found."

"No problem." He nodded matter-of-factly. "When?"

I glanced at my watch. "Couple of hours."

"Done."

Moments passed as my thoughts raced. When I dialed the number, he answered on the second ring. "Looks like you had fun."

"You have an interesting definition of fun."

Ariel laughed. "You sound like my wife."

"Got a question for you."

"Can't promise you an answer."

"You heard any rumblings about a high-ranking US government official working with Frank?"

"How high?"

"At or near the top."

He was quiet a minute. "Let me do some digging."

I dialed a second number and Eddie answered before it had a chance to ring. "Hey, Boss."

"Eddie, I need you to determine where Waylon Maynard lives. Not his listed address but where he sleeps."

"And then?"

"Breach his system. Give me an hour on the inside. Then wash the data so not even the programmer would know I was there."

"Check."

Eddie hung up, Camp smiled, and I closed my eyes. Which wasn't difficult.

The news on the screen above us switched to News Flash and a live shot outside the Lincoln Memorial. Waylon Maynard walked to the podium.

"First, I've just spoken with Vice President Ashley. His girls are safe. I told him they have the prayers and the resources of an entire nation. Second, he informed me he would not be pursuing further office. Honestly, I tried to get him to take some time. Think it through. Let things settle. He would not. But he knows, even in his pain, that a leadership vacuum is bad for the country. In his absence, the party has asked me to carry the banner. To accept the nomination." A practiced pause. "I have never sought the presidency, and I do not seek it now. But if it seeks me and the American people need me, I will consider. I do so reluctantly, understanding the great weight and responsibility that come with it." While I listened to him, I couldn't help but think he'd written that speech maybe two decades earlier and dusted it off sometime in the last few months. My question was, Why now? Of course he wanted the office. Always had. That was clear. But what was below that? He could have had the nomination ten times over in the past but always refused. Why now? What had changed?

We huddled around the screen aboard Air Force Two as Maynard tearfully prepped the country. This was a setup. A masterfully planned and thoughtfully worded setup. "I cannot in good conscience think of myself today. This is a day of great and profound sadness, and I have too much respect for an American hero like Aaron Ashley . . ." Then, after another practiced and almost perfect pause, Maynard stared into the camera as his eyes became glassy. "Aaron, the prayers of an entire nation are with you."

CHAPTER 61

Maynard was widowed. They'd never had kids and he'd had no steady girlfriend. In the decades since his wife died, he'd gone to dinner a few times, but nothing serious. Photo ops mostly. He was a devoted public servant who had given his life to his country. From what we could uncover, he owned three residences. A condo near the capital. A respectable log cabin in Oregon along a storied salmon river where he entertained other high-level officials while they scared the fish and sipped expensive Scotch. And a rural western Virginia farmhouse. Cell phone data suggested he spent a lot of weekend time there, but we found no evidence that Maynard ever entertained there. This was a very private residence. In fact, we found nothing to suggest he had ever received visitors at the farmhouse. If that didn't set our alarm bells dinging, it got worse.

As Eddie peeled back the layers, he found that not even the United States government possessed such an impenetrable firewall. Eddie said he'd only seen its equal once. When I asked, "Who?" he raised an eyebrow and half shrugged, which could only mean one person. Frank. What surprised us most were the drones. Sixteen of them. They flew in pairs, thirty-minute shifts, making random thermal scans across the property while the others docked in their charging stations. This meant Maynard had drones in the air 24/7/365. Which begged the question, Why? And if that wasn't enough, Jess and BP discovered that Maynard had patched into several private satellites that gave him next-gen military-grade accuracy at the touch of a button.

After Eddie relayed the near impossibility of my undetected entrance, he shook his head. "Dicey."

"Can you do it?"

"Maybe."

"What's the worst that can happen?"

"He watches you bug his house on some video monitor we don't know he possesses. And if he is who you suspect he is, and if he had anything to do with the disappearance of Ashley's girls and the trap you walked into, then chances are really good that he's not going to get caught watching the paint dry."

"Meaning?"

"He'll be waiting for you."

He was right. "That would not be good."

Somewhere in here I clued into the fact that Waylon Maynard was paranoid.

So how did you spy on someone who couldn't be spied on? And how did you trap someone who'd already set a trap for you?

I turned to Camp. "When you were a kid, you ever play dress-up?"

"What, you mean like women's clothes, high heels, wigs?"

"No."

"Good, 'cause I was about to tender my resignation."

"I mean like cowboys and Indians."

"We played Dukes of Hazzard all the time."

I nodded. "Perfect."

We landed in middle Georgia to a media frenzy. The sharks were circling. Ashley gathered Bill, Camp, and me. His face was granite. He pointed to the sea of cameras nearly a mile in the distance. "Esther and I would like to get the girls off—"

Bill cut him off. "Taken care of, sir."

Aaron nodded.

Because we had made what looked like an unscheduled stop in the middle of nowhere, we had no hangar to hide in while the girls descended the steps in private. So, bravely, they exited the plane and walked across the tarmac while cameras appeared out of nowhere and snapped their pictures from a distance. His staff had suggested Walter Reed, but Ashley shook his head. "Bring them to us. My girls need familiar right now." Miriam, Ruth, and Sadie disappeared behind tinted windows and the seven-car caravan disappeared down quiet country roads en route to home.

I watched them drive off, wondering what memories awaited. Fear or peace. As I thought about it, red taillights appeared and the third vehicle swung a U-turn. Returning to me. They pulled up alongside and when the door opened, Sadie stepped out. Wrapped in a blanket that did not look to be keeping her warm. An odd mixture of pain, peace, and simmering strength. She looked up.

"Uncle Murph?"

I knelt. "Yeah, sweetheart."

She swallowed and a tear broke loose. Thumbing it away, she stared off toward the circus and the flashing cameras. A question rested on the tip of her tongue.

I held out my hand and she took it, studying it. As if she was trying to remember how she once saw it. Finally, she held it with both hands. "Does the good stuff ever come back?"

The words left her mouth and something in me cracked down the middle. Pieces spilling around my soul like jacks on granite. I tried to maintain my composure, but I could not. In that moment I made a promise that I would not speak. And only Waylon Maynard would know when I kept it.

"Yes."

"You've seen it?"

"I have."

She launched herself forward, wrapping arms and legs around neck and waist. Clinging. Burying her face in my neck. Moments passed as her body convulsed, every muscle screaming in revulsion at the top of its lungs. Trying to rid her heart of the memories. When the tremor passed, she spoke without lifting her head. Holding on had taken all she had. Her voice was little more than a hoarse whisper. "Do you know when?"

Bones had taught me all he knew, but there was one thing he could not teach me—and he knew that too. He could arrange the intersection of the experience with my heart, but he could not cause me to know that experience. To live in it and through it. To identify with it in such a way that the truth of that moment became my plumb line. My reason. In my mind's eye, I saw the dungeon at the academy. Bones handing me the letter. Two lockers. My life laid out before me. Wrapped in her shaking arms, I heard the echo of his words plain as day.

What, then, you might ask, is the value of door number two? If door number one is cash, prizes, and life laid out on a silver platter, why would anyone in their right mind choose anything else? Why not just ride the gravy train into the sunset? Unfortunately, there's only one way to know. I will tell you this, and I'm qualified to speak because I walked through the door before you: There is something more valuable than money. Although you will have to dig deep to find it. I cannot promise you that door number two will lead to all your dreams coming true. In fact, a few will be shattered. But walk through it and I can promise you this: One day you'll look inside, and amid the scars and the carnage and even the heartbreak, you'll find something only a few ever come to know.

Kneeling, sitting on my heels, cradling her, I heard the echo again. And there in that moment, I came to know it again. For the ten thousandth time. Something I'd promised myself never to forget . . . but then the pain came. And the memory faded. And I wanted to forget. Something else Bones knew but could not teach me. Pain will cause you to want to forget what you know to be true. It's a lie, and in my pain I'd agreed with it. But her grip on me, the shaking and the wailing, reminded me. I was so sorry I had forgotten. There is a truth in this universe: Evil is real and it's playing for keeps. It wants to kill us. Rip off our heads and post them on stakes outside the city walls. Because it can't be appeased, can't be negotiated with, and there's no such thing as land for peace. That's a crock. Always has been.

The solution is not popular. Not easy. In fact, it's next to impossible. What is required is one who leaves the ninety-nine to rescue the one. With no promise that he'll ever return to those he loves. That's the price. The inescapable cost. Bones had paid it. Cradling Sadie, thinking of all that was stolen and lost, but knowing it would return and she'd once again dance and laugh and bathe in the sun, I remembered the price. The price was me. Bones, dead and gone, was still teaching me. Continuing my schooling. And I loved him all the more for it. Now, as then, I stared at the locker in my mind, the letter, and walked once more through door number two. Willing to pay all that I had. Freely. Again and again. Why? I held the answer in my arms. Of the several billion people on the planet, she had a name. One that set her apart from all others. As unique as her fingerprint. Sadie. Sadie was lost. Taken. Abducted. Then somehow, despite incredible odds, found. Rescued. Snatched back. Names matter. Early in my career, I'd tried to remember them, so I forced myself to carry them. Inked them onto my back. A permanent record. Starting with Marie, every name written and yet to be written on my back, including Ruth, Miriam, and Sadie, reminded me. But one name had not been etched into my back. It had been written deeper. Seared into my soul. Why? Because it was the most important. Because of his name, all the other names mattered; without his, none mattered. I loved and was able to love because he loved me. Period. I could take credit for nothing. Bones had made me and he was making me still.

Sadie lay limp in my arms. Despite the cold, she was soaked in sweat. I wanted so badly to gather up all the evil and take it away. To take it on myself. I wasn't immune, but I was willing. If I could have saved her the pain crumpling her face, I would have.

But I knew better. I could not.

I shook my head. "I don't know when. But . . ." When I pressed my forehead to hers, she closed her eyes and breathed. "I know that you are loved and that you are beautiful beyond measure."

When I said that, Gunner, who had been sitting obediently by my side, couldn't take it any longer and started licking the tears and snot off her face. Too tired to wiggle and too hurt to giggle, she lay limp in my arms, so I carried her to the car, set her in her mom's lap, and closed the door quietly.

When the taillights disappeared, I press-checked my CZ and said, "Time to clock in."

Camp watched the caravan. "Never clocked out."

Clay pointed his cane at me. "I'm in and don't give me no back talk. I been schooling whippersnappers like you since before you were a gleam in your daddy's eye."

CHAPTER 62

The flight from Georgia to Virginia was short. When we landed, Clay bought an old Suburban. Four-wheel drive. Lifted a foot. Ginormous tires. Steel bumpers fore and aft. Somebody had gotten ahold of the engine and made a few modifications to the horsepower. Not to mention the muffler. If we wanted to announce our arrival, we were doing a pretty good job. Think the *General Lee* meets monster trucks.

While we were still a mile out, the first drone locked on to our approach. Eddie was speaking into our ears. "Second drone locked on."

"Check."

Clay drove erratically. Swerving. Trying his best to appear inebriated. Unintelligible rap music blared through the speakers. When he crashed through the gate, even I was convinced he'd been drinking. The gate wasn't so much a deterrent to keep people out as something to set off alarm bells for whoever was watching it electronically. And based on the addition of two more drones, it did.

At a rather rapid yet erratic rate of speed, we drove the half mile to the house, winding a circuitous and serpentine path through the woods. Approaching the home, Clay floored the accelerator, and the monster truck ran up the front steps and through the front door. Our lame attempt at shock and awe. But the smile on Clay's face told me it was worth it. Maynard had two backup power systems. One diesel, one solar. Which meant we couldn't just cut the city power to the security system and sneak in through a back door while he panicked trying to get power turned back on. Maynard had been in the game a long time. No one accused him of being born yesterday. Hence, Eddie suggested the drive-through-the-front-door technique. He said if we could distract some unsuspecting person watching some computer terminal, who was not expecting a truck to drive through the front door, he maybe could catch them napping, electronically speaking, and then quickly program some code that might give us five minutes of blackout before they knew what hit them. The trick would be getting us out of the house and Eddie out of the mainframe without them ever knowing Eddie was there.

The Suburban came to rest in what looked like a living room. While Waylon had beefed up his intel and security protocols, he'd done very little to the house. Which meant old wood gave way quickly to steel bumpers and 600-plus horsepower. Clay played the drunk, unable to shift gears, all while berating me and Camp as we spilled out of the truck, along with a case of empty PBR cans, and began pushing on the front of the truck—as if we could extract the nearly two-ton vehicle from the house. Camp then walked into the kitchen and appeared to relieve himself in the sink. Genius really. We looked like a couple of drunk thugs looking for a concert. Jess had added one addition to our Trojan Horse that helped as much as any: a fog machine. Like those things used at concerts by rock stars. We had placed the outlet of the tube near the muffler, making it look like smoke from the engine. To the natural eye watching this scene unfold on some terminal, no one could tell the difference. To us, the benefit was enormous. It helped mask us. A camouflage of sorts.

True to his word, Eddie, with help from Jess and BP, managed a backdoor end-around of Maynard's system. Total blackout. T-minus five and counting. I could only imagine that got someone's attention at a terminal somewhere. With the clock ticking, Camp quickly began placing cameras. With a few minutes to myself, I did what I was so good at doing. I snooped around.

The bedroom was plain, sparsely decorated, and seemed staged. As if not actually lived in. Same with almost every other room. I felt like I was looking at a childhood time warp from the fifties. There was nothing modern. Nothing electronic. No color pictures. Even the sinks and toilets were from the fifties. Yet nothing seemed original to the house. Everything was too perfect. Like a movie set. Or like someone had brought in a designer and retro-fit the entire interior to make it look like a memory.

Sixty seconds in, I cracked a doorway to find a stairwell leading down. Most homes like this had cellars, so it wasn't out of the ordinary. But what I found was. I descended the steps, cognizant that the last time I did that somebody tried to blow me up, and landed in what looked like a normal farmhouse basement. Again, nothing strange. Save one thing.

Carpet. Who carpeted the floor of a cellar? Cement walls, cement floor, shelves for canned vegetables. Usually, an underground room like this had the feel of moisture. I doubted it would flood, but we were belowground. The air down here was New Mexico dry. As if someone had sucked it out.

The carpet was pseudo-shag. Dark brown. And it had been thrown down. Not fixed. I pulled up a corner and smiled. A circular groove. A perfect arc. Half-inch deep. Leading from the wall to the floor beneath me.

Before me stood a plain concrete wall. Four feet wide, eight feet tall. But judging from the groove beneath my feet, that wall wasn't a wall. It was a door. So, because there was no handle, I pushed on it. To my surprise, it clicked. And swung open. Thinking he was busy upstairs, I spoke into my comms. "Camp?"

He tapped me on the shoulder. I studied him. He must be half cat. I never heard him.

We clicked on headlamps and began walking the corridor. Twenty-three steps to a right turn. Then fourteen to a left. Finally, twelve more to another door. This one steel. I turned the knob and pushed it open.

What I found did not please me.

The room was paneled. Airtight. Servers stacked along one wall. Housed in neat racks, which produced substantial heat counteracted by the HVAC currently circulating. A desk of sorts sat along one wall. A dozen screens. A keyboard. And something else. I pointed. Camp shrugged. It looked like a joystick, but what did it control?

The room held no decoration. No paper. No pens. No other chairs. No nothing. The singular item sat on a shelf just above the computers. Worn. Tattered. It, too, looked straight out of the fifties. It sat limp, one leg folded beneath the other, one eye having come unsewn. Strings dangling.

It took me a minute. Then I saw it for what it was. A puppet.

A marionette.

Camp busied himself with planting cameras in what we knew was the mother lode for sick and sadistic activity for whoever sat in that chair and manipulated that controller. This room was an epicenter for evil.

Eddie crackled. "Thirty seconds."

If we took anything, like say a drive, he'd know it. And we didn't have time to copy any data. We had to leave it.

So we backed out, shut the door, and retraced our steps, climbing out of the basement and then sprawling ourselves back across the foyer floor in front of the Suburban just as Eddie reported, "You're live." Camp and I did our best to stumble and laugh and act too drunk to walk, finally making our way back to the Suburban where a belligerent Clay sat waiting, revving the engine. Which I thought was a nice touch. Not to mention, the fog machine had been set on max and had filled the entire house with enough smoke to bring visibility to zero.

We backed out and drove six miles down the road. Then, having exited the Suburban and removed the fog machine, we dropped the stick into Drive and allowed the truck to drive itself off the side of the road, where it tumbled down a hillside and into the base of some trees. Totaling the old Chevrolet but not mangling it so bad that its drunk passengers couldn't rally, climb out, and stumble toward whatever concert they'd been searching for.

Ruse complete, we drove an hour to an airfield and were airborne seventy-two minutes after leaving Maynard's den of iniquity. In flight, Camp began populating his screen with the twenty-seven cameras he'd planted in the house while Clay sat smiling like a Cheshire cat and sipped orange juice.

One image stuck with me. One image I couldn't shake. The mario-nette. And when the pieces came together, Camp must have seen the horror on my face. "What?"

"Maynard."

"What about him?"

"He's the puppeteer."

CHAPTER 63

Summer and I loaded onto the gondola and rode the chairlift up to the Eagle's Nest under a clear and cold starlit sky. Which was much better than climbing up by foot. Required much less work. Gunner thought so too. We stepped off, I opened Bones's wine and uncovered the little cheese plate that Angel and Casey had helped me decorate—complete with parsley—and we slid into the hot tub. She eyed the tray and raised an eyebrow. "Well played."

"I had some help."

She ate an olive. "No. Really?" The sarcasm was thick. She slipped her shoulder beneath mine. We could see eighty miles in any direction. "But you get an A-plus for effort."

Three silent days had passed at Freetown. The cameras showed police arriving at Maynard's house along with an assistant of sorts, but Maynard never surfaced. Nothing changed, save one thing. Maynard was now actively campaigning. Filling the networks with sound bites. And judging by the look on his face, he'd dreamed of this moment for years. He looked ten years younger.

We soaked. Sipped. Laughed. Ate cheeses with names I couldn't pronounce. Talked about the future. Talked a little about the past. Summer had become my safe place. No pretending. No lies. No façade. Half a bottle in, I had the nerve to say what was on my mind.

"So, I've been thinking."

She stared up at me.

"I know I promised to take you fishing. But I want to ask your permission to do one thing first."

She sat waiting, holding her glass in both hands, sweat sliding off her temples.

"I realized something in Alaska."

She sipped.

"I never got to say goodbye."

Another sip.

"To Bones, I mean."

She waited.

"I want to go back. To Majorca. Just me and Gunner. And I want to tell him goodbye. I need to do this because—"

She held up a finger and pressed it to my lips. Then she pointed to our airport. Oddly, our largest jet, a Falcon with transatlantic range, sat lit on the tarmac. Rather than housed in its hangar where it should've been. Then she lifted my wrist and checked my watch. A cheap field watch I'd ordered off the internet. Having given Ellie my Rolex and Shep my Omega, I was down a timepiece and couldn't stomach the thought of several thousand dollars for something when that same something could cost me a hundred. "You leave in fifty-seven minutes."

"What?"

She pointed again. "Fueled. Camp and I made the arrangements."

"You know all this?"

She nodded.

"But how? I haven't told anyone. Not even Camp."

"I'm a woman. We know things."

"So, you don't mind?"

She shook her head.

I tried to speak and she cut me off. "I get it. I understand. Go. You need it. It'll be healing. You need to close this door so you can open the next one."

"Which one is that?"

"The one Bones left in front of you. The one where you become who he made you to be in his absence."

She moved closer. "I know it will be difficult, and I've thought about going with you 'cause I don't like the thought of you hurting alone. But I think this is something you and Gunner need to do. Just the two of you."

I thought that too, but I was glad I didn't have to convince her. "Might be a few days."

"I'll be here."

That had gone easier than I imagined. I double-checked. "You sure there's no 'but'? No condition?"

"Every time you leave, there's one condition."

I knew it but I loved to hear her say it.

She kissed me once. "David Bishop." Then a second time. "I need you to bring my man, Murphy Shepherd, home because I can't live without him."

At that second, my phone dinged. It was Camp. "We got something."

"Maynard?"

"At his Virginia farm."

"And?"

"His computers are active."

"Meaning?"

"I'd have to show you, sir." He sounded hesitant.

"But what?"

"You're not going to want to see it."

I turned to Summer. "Hold the plane. I gotta do something first."

We cleaned up our mess and rode the gondola down. When we arrived at the comms center, Camp stood between us and the screens where Eddie sat flittering around the keyboard like a hummingbird. He looked at Summer. "Ma'am. You're not going to want to—"

Summer peered around his shoulder, recognized the image, covered her mouth, closed her eyes, then bent over a trash can and vomited.

He was right. We did not.

CHAPTER 64

Formulating a plan was difficult. We'd never get back into his farm-house undetected. We'd managed once because we'd played the fool. It wouldn't work again. He'd spot us a mile away. We couldn't very well shock and awe him by running in guns a-blazing. If he was in his dungeon, he'd close down his computers, burn his drives, and escape through some secret tunnel out the back. He'd planned well. We'd never cover all the exits. We had to catch him someplace else.

I spoke first. "We need a trap. That doesn't feel like a trap."

Camp offered the obvious next question. "How do you trap a man who has everything and who is well aware of what a trap looks and feels like because he's set most of them himself?"

Clay, ever the wise one, supplied the answer. "Offer him what he doesn't have."

This time Jess spoke. "Which is?"

I broke in. "The freedom to do what he wants, when he wants, with whom-ever he wants, wherever he wants. Right now he's hiding in a dungeon where he controls all the variables. Guaranteeing his continued freedom. But he's an arm's-length voyeur, and every voyeur I've ever encountered, at some point, likes to get their hands dirty. They can only look for so long because look-ing doesn't satisfy what touching does. Offer him a hands-on experience with the added excitement of different surroundings and the promise that he can't get caught. But it can't smell like a trap and can't feel like an offer. You can't sidle up next to him at the bar and drop a business card. 'Yo, bro, room 202.' He has to stumble upon the opportunity. Overhear what he shouldn't. He'll refuse a direct offer a thousand times over. He didn't get this far by being stupid. But he might seize on a one-off if he thinks he can get away with it, especially if he believes he overheard you and you don't know it. Remember, it's got to feel like a shadow because he's comfortable in darkness."

I turned to Eddie and the A-Team. "I know you've been following and backtracking his phone. Any patterns?"

Eddie nodded. "The Gilded Kilt."

I waited for an explanation. "While Maynard comes from Oregon, his people did not. They came from a bit farther east. Across the pond. Turns out he shares their taste in beer. Stouts, specifically. Couple nights a week, he tosses one or two back at the Gilded Kilt with like-minded beer drinkers who grant the esteemed senator a little slack. Even protecting him from outsiders. The locals have been known to toss a nosy journalist. It's a family of sorts. A rather insulated crowd. Live music couple nights a week. But what happens street-side holds little comparison to life below street level. Have to be a member. There's a bit of a wait list. As in a couple of years, unless you know somebody who can move you to the front of the line."

"Which, I imagine, Maynard can do."

Eddie nodded. "Only members can nominate future members, and any one member can blackball any nomination. No questions asked."

I interrupted him. "This is good intel. You come by this alone?"

He shook his head. "Stackhouse."

"Really?"

"Maynard nominated Ashley twenty-plus years ago. Ashley makes an appearance once or twice a year to rally the troops." Eddie continued, "The underground space stretches a block or two. They have a couple of speak-easies, which are rooms for move private conversations. A basement card game frequented by DC elite. Maynard's no good, loses constantly, but I doubt he's as bad as he makes out to be."

"What makes you say that?"

He handed me a slip of paper. "The other names at the tables."

I scanned it. "Lot of 'Honorables' on here."

He nodded. "Federal too."

"So you think maybe Maynard is playing the fool so he can keep his ear to the track?"

"If Maynard is the power behind the throne, the Oz of DC, he's only as good as his information, and that doesn't just fall from the sky. He gets it from somewhere, and I tend to think the blackjack table isn't the only place he's spending money."

"You think he's paying people off?"

"Wouldn't you?"

"If I put myself in Maynard's shoes, I guess that depends on the information and what I intended to do with it."

Eddie again. "We know he's a regular two to four nights a week depending on activity on the hill. We also know he's been a member there for about as long as he's been in the Senate. If he lets his guard down anywhere, it might be there."

Jess and BP searched the other names. "Lot of chiefs of staff, too." A quick count. "Over thirty."

I shook my head. "We don't have time to plan an op like that. Too many contingencies. Too many unknowns."

"Maybe not." Eddie raised a finger. "Since that time you and Ellie flew to your island, Camp's been schooling us on how we might trap Maynard at his own game. It's risky, but if it works, it's ironclad."

I glanced at Camp, who shrugged. "Somebody's got to catch the bad guys."

"So you've done this before?"

"I told you that not long ago I made some guys mad."

"Same guys?"

"Different guys. Same kind of power."

"You should probably fill me in on that sometime."

He nodded. "Probably."

"So what's the plan?"

They told me. And while the plan was solid, it had one glaring problem.

"All of this is predicated on getting into the club and downstairs where the secret members meet. Which we can't do."

Eddie again. "Upon acceptance into what for all intents and purposes is a secret society, members are given an engraved key. No two are alike. It's not high-tech. It's old school. A physical silver key. Big thing, too. Like something used on a ship's locker. Anyone with that key is granted access and all the benefits of the member. No questions asked. It's viewed like a signet ring. Whoever holds the key holds the senator's power. The theory is that much of the business of the Senate is conducted underground, outside the capital, between staffers."

"Any idea who nominated Maynard for membership?"

"No. But every key is engraved with the member's name and their sponsor's. And their sponsor's. And so on. It's a bit of an honor thing."

"How old is the club?"

Eddie shrugged. "Rumor on the street says it predates the Civil War and that the keys were minted from Union silver, although later members sympathized with both sides. It is also believed, though undocumented, that Booth left from there en route to the theater. True members are tight-lipped, but the keys don't lie when it comes to lineage."

"Interesting." I paused. "I'm assuming Ashley has such a key."

Camp nodded. "Stackhouse offered it."

"Looks like we need it. So who's going down underground?"

Jess poked her head up. "I love stout beer."

I smiled. "Why does that not surprise me? But to pull it off, we need two in on the ruse."

Clay, who had been listening quietly, spoke next. "You know, present company excluded, for most of my life, I haven't been allowed in places like that." He tipped his imaginary hat to me. "I'd be honored, if'n you don't mind . . ."

He was perfect. "Done." I spoke to the group. "But everything rests on timing. Down to the minute. The second even. If we miss it, Maynard will sniff a fake, and we won't ever get it back. Remember, offer him darkness. Shadow. Meet him where he lives."

And so the waiting began.

PART II

"Tell me what you know about sheep."

CHAPTER 65

I spent the flight thinking about what faced me when we touched down. The hurt. I couldn't deny it. I saw the slideshow in my mind. In the days following the last time I made this flight and everything that happened here, we went to the beach where I mainly sat in the sand and drank Bones's wine. We did our best to tell him goodbye, even pushing his iconic orange box out to sea. A soldier's burial. Then I'd sat while the tide returned and washed over my toes. Somewhere in that twilight I'd seen boot prints in the sand. Followed by smaller feet with a high arch. They looked real to me. But maybe that was just because I couldn't deal with what was really real.

All I knew then and all I knew now was that Bones had saved me. Again and again and again. Ever since that moment, I'd been struggling with how to tell his story. Could I? How did I talk about the man who defined *man* for me? I could tell all the stories, relive all the inconceivable things he did, but one moment stood alone. And that moment started here. On this island. Why? Because it was here that he taught me the one lesson I'd yet to learn. A lesson I didn't want to learn. That lesson was this: it had never crossed my mind to save Frank. I just wanted to shoot him in the face. Several times. Then rip off his head and post it on a stake outside the city walls as a deterrent to his generals. *I'm coming for you.*

But not Bones. Bones had other ideas. Bones was trying to save Frank. How far was he willing to go? All the way. And he did. Bones died trying to save his brother. He gave his life. Did Frank know that? I tended to think so. Bones demonstrated to Frank that there is something greater than hate. More powerful than evil. It's love. The kind of love that walks down into a dungeon, breaks chains, rips prison doors off their hinges, and says, "Me for you." I stared out the window, wiping tears that were flowing freely. I didn't try to stop them. Chances were good that over the next few hours I'd cry my face off, and I was okay with that. I loved him that much and I missed him that much.

Every hour of the flight, Gunner sniffed my face, then licked the dried salt off my skin and lay back down. His way of saying, *Worried about you, old man.* I'd brought Bones's letter. It was soiled. Bloodied. And torn. But still served its purpose, which was to guide us back. Truth be told, I didn't need it. I knew it by heart. But it was a comfort nonetheless, so I stuffed it next to my heart.

The pilot touched down on a private airstrip on the southeast coast of Majorca. Gunner and I walked to the hangar where Bones had leased space, I punched in the combination, and the lock clicked open, revealing Bones's old Toyota truck. We loaded up and skirted the coastline. Driving slowly. Tasting the air. Sipping the sunshine. The road narrowed to one lane and routed through small coastal towns, leading to a rocky peninsula a mile wide and several miles long on the northeast corner of Majorca.

The narrow road led from the mainland into the peninsula, traveling along the mile-wide plateau that fell off like a table to rocky cliffs that descended a couple hundred feet into the turquoise waters of the Balearic Sea.

From a defensive standpoint, I saw why Frank liked it—one road in and surrounded by water on three sides. The inhospitable terrain was inhabited only by goats, burros, and short, stubby trees that looked to be constantly bracing against the wind. Bones's map led me to a small resort village a few miles away, where oiled beachgoers lounged on bleached white sands, snorkeling lovers frolicked in crystal-clear water, and kayakers and paddleboarders crisscrossed the glassy surface. It was a vacationer's paradise. It was also a strategic place to store a small boat with which to navigate the coastline.

The marina was small and home to more than a hundred small yachts, center consoles, and sport fishers. I parked, and it wasn't hard to find the slip a second time. I pulled off the cover and found the same well-used Zodiac. Gunner jumped in and began sniffing around as if he, too, recognized the craft. As the sun dropped below the horizon, I turned on the Garmin and entered the coordinates. Not that I needed them. I could return by heart, but I wanted to walk the same steps. Something about that was healing. I dropped the boat in the water and cranked the twin Yamahas. Gunner assumed his *Titanic* ear-flapping position on the bow, reminding me he felt as at home on the bow of a boat as he did the hearth of a fireplace in Colorado. I eased out of the marina, brought the Zodiac up on plane, and Gunner and I began skirting the shoreline, being careful to steer clear of the massive rock formations that lay just below the surface.

Bones's letter gave specific coordinates and a detailed description of our destination. A small cove on the northern side protected by a curved elbow of steep rock. If not careful, I'd miss the entrance, which was only ten to twelve feet wide, bordered by steep cliffs. I throttled down, bringing the Zodiac off plane, trimmed the engine as far as I could while keeping the propeller in the water, and steered into the smooth rock entrance. It felt good to be back on the water. I'd missed it. And I'd missed my boat, *Gone Fiction*, ever since Frank blew it up. The opening of the cave was S-shaped, meaning no vessel longer than thirty feet could navigate in, and the smooth, tide-worn walls meant no purchase. No place to hold on.

We navigated the serpentine entrance and found ourselves in a hidden pool of water larger than several Olympic swimming pools. According to the Garmin, it was thirty and forty feet deep. The first time we'd made this trip, we'd hoped dearly that we'd been undetected. If anyone had known, we'd have been sitting ducks. Like shooting fish in a barrel. For the second time, we idled to the far end where a rock shelf sat just a foot below the water's surface. The water here was glass. Not a ripple other than those we made. I cut the engines and sat on the rubber gunwale while Gunner whined.

"You gotta stay here this time. I need to go do this alone. I don't expect you to understand, but this is just something I got to go do." Gunner did not like either what I'd said or my tone of voice, because he returned to the bow and lay down. Facing away.

I located the same crack in the rock, marked by a tree growing out of the crack, stepped into the water, and tied off to the tree. This next section was a bit tricky and the reason I was leaving Gunner. I had to swim underwater for a good distance, and I was worried about him making it through this pitch-black world again. No one was in danger, so why take the risk? I slipped into the water, and Gunner stuck his head over the gunnel. Looking down at me.

I pulled up by the ropes and rubbed behind his ears. "You're still the best partner I've got. But I need you to stay here." Gunner walked to the stern, then returned to me, where he hung his face over the side and licked me. I rubbed his head again. "I know. I love you too." As he had done the first time, he jerked his head sideways and made that one little Scooby-Doo sound he makes when he's hungry. "Yes, stay here. Watch the boat. And when I get back, I'll grill you a ribeye."

Excited by my promise, he made the sound again.

"Yes, a big one."

Another whine.

"Of course I'll cut it up for you."

Gunner's tail was wagging, so I told him to go lie down, which he did. Keeping his eyes trained on me. "I'll be back."

CHAPTER 66

I pulled my mask down, turned on my headlamp, and, for the second time in my life, fell into the bosom of a beautiful Spanish afternoon. I swam down only two feet, then horizontal some eight feet, then up. Easy peasy. I poked my head into the dark cavern and found myself again in an underground lake of sorts. Roughly the size of an Olympic pool. The cavern roof hung some twenty feet above my head. I swam to a smooth rock that led up out of the water and climbed out. Last time I was here, I'd buckled Gunner into his vest and then attached to it various supplies that either Bones or I would need once we found him. This time, I had no vest because I had no Gunner. I had a backpack, and rather than carry my CZ 75, which I'd come to like, I'd brought the Sig Bones had given me. The venerable 220. Was I going to need it? Probably not. But it was a comfort. And sometimes comfort is hard to come by.

In ancient days long ago, an underground river cut these tunnels. Tall enough for a man to stand in and level enough for walking. Modern machinery could not have done better. Bones's map had given detailed, step-by-step instructions. Twenty-seven steps to a Y-intersection. Don't take the left. Turn right. Take 214 steps to a T. Turn left. Then take 407 steps up the serpentine path, which exited to another lake.

I knew the words by heart, so I walked them by memory. Then, as now, the fact that Bones had discovered this as a boy, and in the dark, was the eighth wonder of the world and final proof that he was and always had been tougher than me. Distance underground was difficult to measure, but my best guess was that I'd wound nearly a quarter mile into the heart of this rock when the tunnel emptied into a second lake. This one bigger. The ceiling was covered in stalactites that hovered some forty feet above my head. There was one difference between this water and the water I just swam through: This was fresh. That was salt. I swam the long lake, about a hundred yards, exiting the water into another tunnel, this one narrower. Just wide enough for my shoulders but requiring me to stand in knee-deep water. Flowing water. I ran my fingers through the grooves on the wall, grooves cut by iron implement. This tunnel had been dug by hand a long time ago. Why? I wasn't sure. That secret had been lost with many others.

At this point on my last trip in here, I had switched both Gunner's and my headlamp to a dim red. Red light, while visible to the human eye, was less noticeable than bright white—and given that I had no idea what I was getting into, we needed stealth. This time, I had no need of stealth, so I kept my headlamp on high and lit up the world around me. The flowing water pressed against me in a current pouring from a spring. The water was cold and tasted sweet. I wound through the rock walls, encountering a small shelf every thirty yards or so just large enough for two men to sit on. I had thought then and maintained now that the shelf served two purposes: to give whoever was carving this both a reprieve from the water and someplace dry to put their candle. Working down here in the dark or by candlelight would not have been my first choice. This world was not just dark; it was devoid of light. My eyes would never adjust because there was nothing to adjust to.

Two hours after I left the Zodiac, the narrow tunnel ended in another cave. This one mostly dry. Stalactites dripping minerals from above. Stalagmites rising up from the deposits raining down. The current of water I'd been walking up flowed from a spring pouring out of the rock in front of me. The volumetric flow had held steady. Thousands of gallons a minute. The underground river caused by the spring flowed along the left side of the cave, allowing me to walk on dry land on the right.

I followed the water until it disappeared, then followed the path through the rock. It was here, upon our first visit, that Gunner had jerked to a sudden stop and sniffed the air. At the time, I didn't know it, but he had caught a whiff of Bones. I followed the tunnel another fifty or sixty feet until it ended at the headwaters of the spring, where the water rose like a fountain out of the rock with such force that swimming against it would prove difficult. Then, ten yards away, just as quickly as it appeared, the water ducked below a shelf and disappeared again in another ancient shaft that apparently turned into the flow I'd been walking through. The world in which I found myself was a wonder, and it was also a wonder some opportunistic entrepreneur hadn't set up shop outside, sold tickets, and turned this into a vacation destination.

For my part, I was glad it had not been discovered. Bones had been buried here. It was hallowed ground. I wanted to keep it that way. Bones's map had ended with a specific detail: *Once you reach the headwaters of the spring, look up.* So, as I had once before, I did again.

Doing so confirmed I was standing at the bottom of the circular shaft of a well just wide enough for a man to touch both sides. Maybe six feet in diameter. I pulled off my pack, tied one end of the 120-foot, eight-millimeter rope to my pack, and tied the other end to me. My pack contained stuff to help me if I got lost or hurt or cold, and while it wasn't heavy I had no desire to climb with it. I slid my foot into the first carved hole on my right and was about to step into the second when a wet, furry, slobbery dog latched hold of my pant leg and pulled gently.

CHAPTER 67

I let myself down, slid to my butt, and let Gunner lick my face. He was whining both his apology for not doing what I told him and his stern rebuke of me for leaving him. I let him get it all out, then pulled him to me, hugging him. "Of course I'm glad you came. I really wanted you to come, but I was worried about you making it. I know . . . he was your partner too. And yes, I'm sorry I left you. No, I won't do it again. Yes, I'm still grilling you a steak. Of course I'll cut it up."

Not only had he swum all that way and found me, but he'd brought his vest. I had no idea how he'd managed to swim with it clenched in his teeth, but he had. When I strapped it on him, I realized how glad I was to see him and how I was dreading climbing up this well without him.

I clipped the straps on my vest to his vest, then slung him over my shoulder like a backpack. "Hey, pal."

Gunner whined as I climbed, and I noticed he'd beefed up a little. Evidently running up and down to the Eagle's Nest and back had put some muscle on him. "I gotta put you on a diet. You're pushing ninety pounds."

He did that Scooby-Doo thing and wagged his tail, which slapped me in the face and shoulder. I climbed and knew I'd reached a hundred feet when the rope tethered to me tightened to the pack I'd left on the rock shelf below. Bones had added a PS to his map, which I spoke out loud in my best imitation. Poking fun at him just a little. "If you slip, don't worry—the water's deep beneath you. But it's also flowing with a force like you've never known, so hold your breath because it's about to take you on an underwater ride that not even Disney could imagine, and it will either drown you or save you."

I could feel Gunner's heart pounding through his vest. Despite the fact that I'd recovered and regained my strength and, thanks to Summer, then some, my legs were shaking. Holding on to the rock face, breathing, trying to maintain purchase, I felt Gunner looking at me as if asking, "What's the holdup?"

I spoke out loud and began climbing again. "I don't like this any more than you do."

Then he passed gas to let me know what he really thought. "Thank you. That's just perfect. I'm stuck in a hollow stone tube with no airflow."

He looked the opposite direction and did it again.

One advantage of climbing in a dark world was that I couldn't see below me—which was good. I climbed three more steps and heard an echo, telling me we were about to exit into the larger chamber. I reached to my left, feeling for the worn iron rod I knew had been sunk into the stone. When my fingers found it, I latched on and lifted us out of the well. I unbuckled Gunner, lifted the pack, then secured the rope to the iron rod and allowed the rest to fall free back into the well. Rappelling down would be much easier and certainly more fun.

At this point on our first trip, I'd turned to Gunner and said, "Bones. Find Bones." This time, I rubbed his face and said, "Hey, thanks for coming with me."

He leaned into my shin and scratched his back on my leg. I looked around, took an inventory, which convinced me nothing had changed, then climbed back up to the crypt where I'd found Bones. I can't say why. I just wanted to remember. I found the underground chapel dark, dusty, and unmoving. Just as I'd left it, other than some dried blood where Bones had lain the few days he holed up in here. Below me, Gunner walked in and out of the cell into the larger open cavern. Following his nose through this underground church turned prison of hell.

I sat dangling my legs over the edge of the upper crypt and studied the underground cave, which was easily the size of a European cathedral. It was massive. Smoke markings showed where constant cook fires once burned as well as rock collections demarcating one space from another. Judging from the ruins, along with the size, it was feasible that several thousand people once lived down here. And given the fresh supply of water, along with the channels carved in the rock that looked like they served as drains, conditions down here could maintain some measure of cleanliness if the people were of a mind to do so. At the far end, a wide section of stone steps led up into the world of sunlight above. Bones's letter had told me he was certain Frank would hold him down here. A punishment meant to jog Bones's memory. Bones wrote that while that had been the case early in his life, this hole in the ground had become more briar patch than prison. He felt quite at home.

Staring into the crypt, I was reminded of the moment my headlamp bathed him.

His eyes had cracked open. They were little more than slits, and he had feigned a smile, managing, "Hey, Murph."

I remember thinking how his sense of humor was gone, no doubt beaten out of him. Bruises covered his face, leaving his eyes mostly swollen shut. His breathing was shallow and painful, suggesting broken ribs. I had pushed the lid farther to the side and reached in. Sliding my hand beneath his. My friend and brother.

Bones. I had found him. Then and now I wanted to scream at the top of my lungs.

At the time I had leaned in. He had smiled. "Thanks for coming."

"Can you move?"

"Not much."

His mouth was dry and cracked and covered in blood, meaning internal injuries. I gave him a sip of water. "How'd you get up here?"

"Same as you."

"And Frank?"

Bones sipped and shook his head. "Has no idea about this place. Always been afraid of the dark. I figured either you'd find me or I'd die"—he attempted a smile—"already buried."

I tried to sit him up. "Can I move you?"

"You can try."

I did, lowering him down, and that was when I knew how bad it was. Somebody had gotten ahold of him. Worked him over more than once. The gurgle and the cough told me he was bleeding inside. The less he moved the better, but I had to get him out.

When I got him down, Gunner licked the blood and salt off his face, then lay down next to him like a sphynx. Posting guard. Bones had lain very still, focused on his breathing. "You found . . . my map."

A question posed as a statement. I knelt. "Sorry I didn't get here sooner. Frank . . . kept me busy."

He grabbed my hand. "He's like that." His grip was weak, and only then did I realize there was no way Bones could exit the way I entered. The swimming would kill him. Not to mention the current, which he could not fight. Bones had to go out the front. I remembered telling him I had to get him out and it was gonna hurt. He only nodded. He knew.

Then I said the thing I needed to say. "Bones." I had spread my hand across his heart, both checking his pulse and letting him know I was here. "I'm sorry it took so—"

He tried to smile and shook his head once, and then he said the words that only Bones could say. "There's nothing to forgive."

Even though I knew he would not speak out of the darkness, I said the words again. "I'm so sorry it took so . . ."

Below me, the only noise was the sound of the tide coming in.

I knew the clock was ticking. Bones had needed medical attention three days ago. I lifted him to a seated position. "You ready?"

He wasn't, but he nodded anyway.

I stood him up and said, "Drape your arms over my shoulders."

Bones did as directed, and I lifted him, grabbing a leg in each hand. Some would call it piggyback. I'd call it rescue. Bones would call it ugly.

I lifted him to a deep moan of pain and began walking, carrying his two hundred pounds plus my gear. I made it through the bars and back down the corridor inside the massive cavern. We made it to the stairs and I willed myself to think of the Eagle's Nest. *You've done this a hundred times. Just put one foot in front of the other . . . and dig deep.* So I had.

The next few moments were foggy in my memory. We had climbed the stairs, exchanged fire with Frank's goons, and then I wanted to go up the stairs, make a stand, and then make an exit. Bones said no, and then he said the two words my heart needed to hear. "Follow me." So I had.

He had stepped behind a column, pushed on it, and then said, "Help." When I did, it gave way, exposing a hidden tunnel and stairwell. A spiral staircase. Smooth stone walls.

Now, Gunner and I retraced our steps. Following smeared blood that still stained the once-exquisite walls. It wasn't hard to follow. Before, when we reached a T-intersection, Bones had tapped my right shoulder and pointed. In his absence, I followed the tap again.

CHAPTER 68

Maybe it was the hard granite or the damp echoes, but standing there in the darkness, I heard Bones's whisper. I saw him in my mind's eye hanging by a single line, suspended between this world and the next. Snow and granite.

"People in darkness don't know they're in darkness because it's all they've ever known. It's their world. They navigate primarily by bumping off things that are stronger. Immovable. They don't know darkness is darkness until someone turns on a light. Only then does the darkness roll back like a scroll. It has to. Darkness can't stand light. And it hasn't. Not since God spoke it into existence. The problem comes when you turn on a light and find those in darkness who, having seen light, prefer the dark. Who retreat into the shadows to do their deeds in secret. They are the ashen-skinned, amber-eyed, fork-tongued servants of evil. Pawns who do the devil's bidding. Who don't think twice about 'owning' another person and who, without conscience, profit off another's flesh. Time after time after time.

"They live convinced of their independence. Their power. Their lack of accountability. Truth is, they are. Accountable. From the beginning of time, light has shone into the darkness, and since that first spark, darkness—no matter how hard it tries, no matter what sword it wields or scheme it perpetrates—has not been able to overcome it. Ever. Which means, at the end of the day, there's an overcoming. A reckoning. And if there's a reckoning, then there's a record. Those of us who stand in the light wonder sometimes, *How much longer can it last? This onslaught. How much more can we take? This constancy.* Those of us who walk in the light grow weary. Our hope wanes. Fades. Darkness rages and threatens to drown us. We look around and wonder what happened. *Where'd it go? Where's the light?*"

When Bones had spoken those words that would become my anchor, we were hanging off the side of a frozen granite face in a whiteout. The wind threatening to rip us off the face of the earth. He hung unfazed. Almost at ease. Like a window washer ninety stories up in downtown Manhattan. Somewhere in there, Bones had smiled and paused for a long minute, then he clicked on his headlamp and tapped me just below my heart. "You bring it with you."

Now, leaning against the cold, hard granite in that underground labyrinth, I heard Bones's echo: *Bring it with you.*

Maybe that was my last lesson. Maybe Bones had held on long enough to school me once more. I remembered being shaken from my thought as he coughed, gurgled, and spat. Dark red blood. Frothy. The clock was ticking faster and not in our favor. He had tapped me on the shoulder, then taken my right hand and placed it on the wall in front of me. With what little breath he had, he was pressing toward the light. How many had he saved? How many had he brought home? How many faces, blind and hopeless, had awakened one day to find him holding a flashlight, patching their wounds, beginning to mend their broken heart, and offering freedom? At no cost to them. He'd already paid it. How many children walked freely now? How many parents, once slaves who were afraid to hope past the next minute, now hoped for their child's future? His skin bore the scars. Entry and exit holes. Bullets. Knives. Rebar.

Payment extracted. Payment made.

I stood there now, Gunner sitting at my feet in this dark stone world, and realized he'd taught me all of this. With his life, Bones had walked up beside me, clicked on the light in his chest, and showered me in it. Then he'd taught me how to read it. How to keep it. That it mattered. That it was the only thing that mattered.

Bones was the light keeper. He'd kept it all along. And his body bore the record.

From there we had walked into Frank's office, so I pressed on the wall, the cavity gave way to a handle, and I pushed again, allowing colder air to blow through the crack. The last time I'd walked in here, the room was glowing from the yellow and blue light of multiple screens. Now the only light was the one I'd brought with me. *Fitting*, I thought. Frank's kingdom lay in ruins. Cobwebs. The absence of light. And yet here I was, rolling away the darkness with nothing more than a headlamp. Strange how so small a light can pierce darkness.

Frank had been sitting in his chair. Surprised but not. A Glock 19 on his desk. I told him to stick it under his chin and pull the trigger. Frank was threatening to broadcast to the world that Murphy Shepherd was David Bishop. Populate the internet and answer all the theories. Rob me of my anonymity. Rob David of Murph. Frank was drawing on a cigar, the glow-plug end matching the color of his eyes. In my head I heard the clock ticking and knew Bones was fading. Walking a narrow ridge.

Finally, Bones gave Frank what he wanted. Actually, he'd given it to him years ago, but it was there in that room that he told him where he'd hidden it. *The Storm on the Sea of Galilee.* The painting had been stolen years ago and never recovered, and then had become one of the most valuable paintings in the world.

Bones had interrupted him. Almost a smile. "It's more valuable than you think."

That was about the time Frank had put all the pieces together. He walked around the painting, studied the frame and the canvas. Then he turned to Bones. "Because you knew I'd steal it back. You kept it safe . . . with me."

Bones had nodded.

At the time, I'd missed it, but standing there in the memory, I heard it. Frank had muttered, "I guess I'm not the only one." Frank broke the frame on the stone floor, then studied the canvas. Finally, he picked at one corner of the canvas, eventually peeling back a layer. A false canvas. When he'd peeled it halfway, a document emerged between the two. The real and the false. Frank's eyes lit. He shook his head. "Genius." Gently, he slid the paper from between the two. An envelope. Standing over Bones, he had read the inscription out loud: "'This will not help you.'" He stared down at Bones. "How would you know? You abandoned me."

Bones lay slumped on the couch. No response. I was losing Bones. But there in the memory, I saw it. Bones wasn't done. He wasn't in a hurry to save himself. His eyes were elsewhere.

Frank extracted the single page, read it, and then tore it in two. Then again. Then threw the pieces. He straddled Bones. "You knew and you didn't tell me!"

Bones never opened his eyes. "It changes nothing."

CHAPTER 69

I could hear Frank's echo reverberating off the stone. And I could hear the crack as Frank's hand struck Bones's face. Bones had deflected the blows, spun his brother, and ended up behind him, one arm around his neck. Rear naked choke. In two seconds, Bones could put him to sleep. Then I'd have shot those two guys in the corner, and we'd have been out of there.

But Bones didn't. Just as quickly as he'd submitted him, Bones let Frank go. Yielding his superior position. I'll never forget the look on Frank's face. He sat ghost-white. Astonished. The revelation was too much. Frank sat in disbelief. "How did you not tell me?"

Bones strained to sit up, blood trailing out his mouth. "Doesn't change who you are."

Frank had laughed a painful, soul-splitting laugh. "'Male One.' My name is Male One. My own mother couldn't come up with anything better than Male One."

Bones nodded. "Yup."

"Did she name you?"

Bones nodded again.

"What?"

Bones lay breathing. Tapped himself in the chest. "Male Two."

Frank laughed. "That's us. A couple of nobodies from nowhere."

Bones shook his head.

Frank, his face just inches from Bones's, shouted, "What?!"

Bones was calm. "That's not who you are."

I could still hear Frank screaming. "Then who am I?"

"My brother." Bones swallowed. "Always have been."

Frank sat motionless. Finally, turning to me, he demanded, "How'd you get in here?" He wanted to know how his impenetrable fortress had been penetrated.

"I climbed."

"Up what?"

"The well."

He turned to Bones. "You leave him a map?"

I answered for Bones. "Yes."

More pieces were gathering in Frank's mind. When the last piece clicked into place, he turned to Bones. He could not hide his surprise. And this was the moment that Frank saw the enormity that was and is Bones. The magnificence for which he had no rebuttal.

"You found a way out?"

Bones nodded.

This was inconceivable to Frank. "And yet you stayed in this hell?"

Bones nodded again.

Frank was spitting as he spoke. "Why?"

Bones had opened his eyes and focused on his brother. "You."

The revelation was too much. Frank had no box for such sacrifice. "You stayed in this hell on earth for me even when you had a way out?"

Another nod.

Frank began punching Bones in the face. After the fourth or fifth time, Bones reached up, grabbed his brother's hand, flipped them both, and submitted Frank a second time. Frank couldn't move. Bones had him on his belly, his arms tucked beneath him.

I was still in the dark as much as Frank, evidenced by the fact that I'd whispered, "Snap his neck."

The next words were a shock to both Frank and me. Bones had rolled off him and lay breathing. "Brother. Every day I climbed down, made my

way to the outside, stayed long enough to glimpse daylight, and then returned to Hell Squared. And there's only one reason."

Disbelief spread across Frank's face. "What? What could possibly make
you stay?"

Bones turned, held up one finger, and stared at his brother. "You."

Incredulous, Frank shook his head. "But why?"

Bones looked at me. Then back to his brother. "Because the needs of
the one outweigh those of the ninety-nine."

Frank came unglued. "After all they did to you . . ."

Bones nodded.

The revelation was sinking in. Frank couldn't hold it anymore. "But I
don't love you that much."

Bones eyed the growing puddle beneath him. "I don't love you because
you love me." He coughed, his eyes rolled back in his head, and his head
bobbed to one side. Shaking it off, he focused again on Frank. "Love is
given, not earned."

Frank was shouting now. "What are you saying?"

Bones coughed, the blood frothy. The clock was winding down. His
lungs were filling. He grabbed Frank by the collar and pulled. "I love
you . . . because I love you!"

Frank had no box for this. He sat back and studied his brother, shaking
his head. For the first time in his life, he was paralyzed by indecision.

Now, I closed my eyes and let the darkness wrap itself around me like
a blanket. The air was damp. Smelled pungent. I thought how it was easy
to love someone who loved you back. But it was much tougher when they
were evil. And in my mind, Frank was and always would be evil. Not so
for Bones. He never let himself think that way. He'd always held out hope.

That was the thing that ate at me. Bones had hoped. I had not.

And therein lay the difference between us.

As Bones had been speaking, six men had broken through the door. I
shot the two in the corner, released Gunner on the man closest to me with
the "Choctaw" command, then turned my attention to the five along the
wall. They missed. I did not.

Gunner had his teeth clenched around the man's throat, crushing his windpipe. The man lifted his rifle and was about to shoot Gunner, but nobody shoots my dog, so I'd sent a single round through the man's chest.

As the room fell silent, I turned to Frank, who stood in the center of an empire crumbling all around him. The astonishment was something he'd not expected or experienced. He'd lost control. Bones had taken it, and had done so without firing a single round. Bones's revelation sent Frank tumbling to earth. Kryptonite. His voice took on a pleading tone. "You didn't leave . . . when you could."

Bones spoke with a shallow breath. "You're my brother . . ."

"But they . . ."

At Frank's weakness, I seized my chance. I lunged, grabbed him by the throat, and forced every ounce of my strength, every reserve, into crushing his esophagus. Preventing him from breathing. Forcing him to suffer. As his throat collapsed in my hand, his eyes growing wild and exhibiting fear, his life fading into darkness—I felt a calm hand on my arm.

Bones.

CHAPTER 70

I could still see him there. Shaking his head. Frank was little more than a gnat, weakly fighting my hand. But I had him. We'd won.

I closed my eyes and listened closely, and there it was again. Bones's whisper. "Bishop . . ."

When I opened my eyes I could just barely see him. "Sheep are lost without a shepherd."

I didn't let go. I squeezed harder and felt something being crushed. Frank's face was turning blue, and his eyes were bulging.

"But he's—"

Bones tapped me. "Bishop."

I looked at Bones like he'd lost his mind. "He's not one."

Right here was where I'd learned the lesson I didn't want to learn. Bones's final class. Last exam. Spoken in two soft words. "You sure?"

It struck me now the same way it struck me then. A freight train to the chest. The pieces fell into place, and for the first time in my entire life with him, I saw the enormity that was Ezekiel Walker. The towering, unfathomable completeness. Hatred had filled me. Revenge consumed me. But not Bones. The inescapable truth was Bones had come back. One last rescue. He'd walked down into the slave market, eyed his brother held in chains behind prison bars, and told the slave master, "I'll buy him back."

When the master huffed and said, "With what?" Bones had simply said, "With me."

And he did.

I, David Bishop, write love stories for a living. But I'd never dreamed of a love like that. It was inconceivable. If I'm honest, had I not seen it and felt its breath on my face, I would doubt its existence.

Bones was coughing now. Almost uncontrollably. Dark specks on his chin. I lifted him and was headed for the door when I felt the bullet tearing through my left shoulder. The impact spun me. I dropped Bones, and then Frank grabbed him and disappeared through the passageway that had brought us into this room. Gunner and I bolted through the door and began running back down into the hell from which we'd emerged. We reached the bottom, found the other door open, and continued down the wide stone stairs and through the massive underground cathedral. Oddly, a string of lights lit the walkway. At the far end, under the orange glow of an overhead light, Frank had dragged Bones's limp body back inside his childhood prison of bars. Gunner and I hurdled a stone table and bench as Frank filled the air with a wall of 9mm rounds headed in our direction. Seeing Frank pick up a rifle and level the muzzle, I grabbed Gunner by the collar and rolled behind a stone outcropping as .226 rounds showered our position. When the rifle ran empty, Frank threw it down and continued dragging Bones back into his prison.

Where it all started.

Frank dragged Bones's body to the edge of the well and used him as a shield to protect himself from me. For several seconds, Frank knelt, staring at his brother. I knew if I didn't make a move now, I'd lose any opportunity. Just one shove, and Frank would send Bones down that well and I'd never get to him fast enough. Bones would never survive the impact with the water a hundred feet below, nor the half-mile swim to the Zodiac. If I had a chance with Bones, we had to go out the front door. Not the well. Slowly, I stepped out from behind the stone base of the bars, unlatched the prison door, and stepped inside. Offering Frank a target.

I walked toward Frank, closing the distance, leveling my rifle muzzle at him, my laser held steady on his forehead. If he twitched a muscle in my direction, I was going to blow the back of his head off. But doing so would cause him to fall backward, taking Bones with him. I had to separate Frank from Bones. Gunner crept along behind me, growling. Frank sat on the edge of the well, holding Bones's body across his lap. Cradling his head and shoulders. Bones's left arm hung limp, dangling in the empty air of the well, while his right arm was wrapped around Frank's waist. I tried to will Bones's fingers to move, to send some of the signals he'd learned to make in this very room. But he made no such motion. For several seconds, Frank just stared at his brother. Then he looked at me, shook his head, and struggled to speak, proving that I'd crushed his voice box. He tried again but could only manage a whisper.

"This was no rescue mission. It was a prisoner swap."

I was confused. "Swap?"

He studied his brother, then me. "Him for you."

Realizing his brother was dead, Frank reached into his shirt pocket, pulled out a picture, and stared at it for a long moment.

I had closed the distance to within five feet. Bones was almost within arm's length. But I could not, and on that day, I did not. Frank set the picture on the ground, to make sure I saw it, then he pressed his forehead to his brother's, kissed his cheek, and without warning pressed the Glock beneath his own chin and pulled the trigger.

Standing over the well, Gunner quiet at my feet, I jerked as the memory echoed again. Frank's head had rocked backward, launching his body over the edge and into the blackness, dragging Bones with him. One brother intertwined with the other, so much so that discerning who was holding who was impossible.

I stared down into the well and saw again the horror that haunted me. I had lunged, reached for Bones's leg, but he was too heavy. Given the bullet that had passed through my shoulder, I couldn't hold him. I stared at the fingers he had slipped through. Trained to save. To rescue. I couldn't when it counted the most.

The indomitable man I knew as Bones disappeared into the darkness. Seconds later, I heard the splash.

As much as I hated Frank, I was like him in one regard: my identity was inextricably tied to Bones. I was Bones's protégé. Friend. Partner. He had saved me as a kid and, on two occasions, given me a reason for being. I was both *who* I was because of Bones and *what* I was because of him. I could take credit for nothing. Everything about me tied back to Bones. He made me, shaped me, and he was not just my mentor—Bones was my hero. With him gone, I was floundering. Proving once again that identity flows out of ownership. We can't know who we are until we know whose we are.

Staring down into that dark shaft descending into the earth, I knew whose I was. And whose I'd always be.

Gunner lay at my feet, his head resting on the rock. Whining quietly. He, too, remembered. I lifted the silver coin from my pocket. The one the mysterious, riddle-speaking man had given me as a child when we'd met at the Seagull Saloon. It was worn. Hand-oiled from decades in my pocket. I read the inscription. The eleven words that had changed my life: *Because the needs of the one outweigh those of the ninety-nine.*

It was time. For this reason I had come. I turned it one last time, then opened my fingers. Releasing the coin. I let it go. It turned, flipped slowly in the air, and disappeared in silence into the dark below, splashing several seconds later. In that moment, I finally told my friend Bones goodbye. But I could not use words. Because I could not speak.

CHAPTER 71

I clipped onto the rope, latched Gunner to my back, and began the rappel down. When I landed on the stone shelf, I noticed two things. First, the shelf was wider than when I left it, and I'd come to the end of the rope. Meaning, I'd descended almost 120 feet. Not the original hundred I'd ascended. This confused me. And I had no explanation for the change in water level. Although the water was fresh, the only factor to which I could attribute the change was the tide outside somehow affecting the water level in here through a change in volumetric pressure.

In order to return the way I came, I now had to climb back up twenty feet to the original shelf. So I put my foot in the rock and took one step. Then another. For reasons I couldn't articulate, I took one look behind me. Over my shoulder.

This was the second thing I noticed, and the sight surprised me. I was not expecting what I saw: an empty cavern. Much like the one I'd walked through to get here. I climbed down, unclipped, and knew if and when the tide returned, I did not want to get caught in here—but as of now, it was empty. Not dry, but empty. A worn walkway within a carved tunnel led the opposite direction of the one I'd entered. With my headlamp on high, I pulled a second light from my pack and clicked it on. The path led out of the well and up a slight ramp, which meant it remained above the water-line. It then leveled out into a pathway carved by hand through stone, the circular implement scars on the stone telling the story. I followed the path and, fifty feet in, saw the first thing that took my breath away.

Dried blood. Smeared on the wall. Shoulder high. Then again. Splattered. As if by coughing. Fifty feet and there was more. By now I was jogging. I'd seen the bullet exit the top of Frank's head. That meant only one other person could have smeared that blood. I lifted Gunner, let him smell the dried and caked blood, then held his muzzle and said, "Find Bones."

If his body was down here, maybe I could find it. I knew he'd be badly decomposed by now, but at least I'd know. At least we could bury him properly. Put something other than memories in his coffin.

Gunner began sniffing. Then jogging. I struggled to keep pace. We ran what I could only guess was close to a quarter mile. Winding slightly downhill. Dried blood here. Dried blood there. When the tunnel finally turned right, I saw another thing I did not expect.

Daylight.

We ran the last hundred yards full out. Gunner leading the way. Following his nose. By now, the blood was caked along the floor. Bones had been dragging both himself and his brother. Trying to get to the water. To set them both free. Where they had started. Two boys in the ocean.

The mouth of the tunnel exited into a small, protected bay. I squatted, squinted into bright light, and followed the trail where Bones had slipped down into the water. Dragging Frank with him. At the water's edge the trail disappeared.

Washed by the water.

The tears came again. This time more easily. Something about this felt good. Felt right. Bones had not died in some dark tunnel. He died with the sun on his face. In the water. Arms wrapped around his brother. He'd done it. He'd rescued Frank. And for reasons I didn't understand, something about that warmed me.

I lay in the mouth of the tunnel, Gunner alongside me, his ears perked and listening. We studied the world around us. As the breeze cooled my face, I realized I'd lost count of the days. Had it been eight weeks? Two months? I couldn't say.

As I tried to do the math, I couldn't shake the thought that something looked oddly familiar. That was when it hit me.

I dialed the number. He answered after the second ring. "How are you, my friend?"

It was a good question. One I'd not considered. "I'm well, I think. I was wondering if I could ask a favor."

"Anything."

"The video you showed me of the large yacht moored in the small, protected bay. Can you bring it up?"

Keys typed in the background. "Done."

"Wasn't there a sailboat exiting that video shortly after it began?"

He studied the video. "Yes."

"Can you tell me anything about the boat?"

A few seconds passed as more keystrokes sounded. "Forty-two feet. Name on the hull reads *Nun Taken*, with *Nun* spelled N-u-n."

I considered this.

"Anything else?"

"Can you estimate how fast it was traveling on exit?"

A pause. "Sixteen-point-seven knots. Probably max speed for a craft like that."

"Thanks much." I hung up and scratched my chin. Gunner looked at me like he was hungry. We climbed up and walked across the bare rock outcropping. Surrounded on three sides by water as far as the eye could see. If Bones had wanted a better burial spot, he'd have to look long and hard to find it.

I spent the afternoon staring into the water. Bones's grave. I didn't want to leave. But when the sun dropped below the horizon, something in me gave way. Something in me whispered a farewell. That was when I knew. I'd done it. I'd told Bones goodbye for the last time.

CHAPTER 72

We returned to the mainland in the Zodiac, moored at the marina, and rented a room at a hotel along the water where I sat long into the night thinking. Whether or not anyone called, I couldn't say, as I'd turned my phone off. But a strange thing happened. I sat at the desk, opened a new document on my laptop, sipped soda water, and stared at the screen a long time. Then I wrote, "The." When I did, the rest of the words came in a torrent. I couldn't have stopped them if I tried. Many times I cried so hard I couldn't see the screen. Truth is, I cried my face off. So much so that it startled Gunner. Several times he climbed into my lap to lick the salt off my face. Before the sun crested the skyline, I had written ten thousand words. The most I could remember writing in one sitting.

As I read back through it, I thought to myself, *It's a start. Maybe even a good start. What was that attorney's name who found us on the beach?* If I'm honest, following Bones's death, I had been content to never write another word. But something happened in that crypt. Something I couldn't explain. I had walked into that dungeon looking for peace, closure. Some way to tell my friend, Ezekiel Walker, goodbye. Yet no sooner had I laid Bones to rest than I'd bumped into David Bishop. Lying cold and damp in a dark stone world, silent and shackled in bronze fetters. Rather than leave him to die and bury him alongside painful memories at the bottom of a well, I sensed him stand up and walk out beside me. Sunlight on his face. Free.

Ten thousand and one.

Daylight found us back in the Zodiac, perusing the marina. There were very few sailboats. Most were anchored out in the shallow yet open water just off the marina in another protected bay, but I did not find the *Nun Taken*.

With Gunner having assumed his normal pose on the bow, we idled the coastline of the Bay of Palma, passing just offshore of the Castell de Bellver, a 1300s circular castle. We continued west to southwest, never more than idle speed. I was at home. Back on the water. I'd missed it. We inquired of the harbormaster at Port de Portals Nous, a protected marina with more than a hundred vessels. But no forty-two-foot sailboat. Farther down the coastline, we crept by the St. Regis Mardavall Resort, and I made a mental note to bring Summer back. She'd like it. Plus, it'd give her a chance to model that bikini she'd been talking about.

I laughed quietly to myself and realized the fact that I was making jokes was a good sign. We anchored at the St. Regis, and I drank a beer at a shoreside bar where I quickly realized Majorcans don't wear much at the beach, so if Summer did bring that bikini she might be overdressed. Gunner seemed entertained, and they seemed to like him. I didn't understand much of anything people said, but when the bartender pointed at Gunner and asked me what he'd have in broken English, I said, "Ribeye?"

He nodded and one appeared fifteen minutes later. About then Gunner decided he liked Majorca. After lunch, Gunner snored in the bow, paws pointing into the air, while I continued following the coastline. I couldn't tell you why. I just did. Something about Bones's body floating out into these waters only to finally sink into the depths. I just couldn't leave. But it wasn't sadness that kept me. It was peace. Peace I'd not known for some time.

As we idled out of the harbor, my thoughts wandered home. I wanted to check in with Eddie, Jess, and BP, given that Maynard was never far from my mind. I pulled out my phone and was about to dial Eddie when another thought occurred. *What good would that do?* Did they really need me checking in? Micromanaging their process from across the pond? I knew they were into every system he had. If it was electronic, they owned it. And if they found something, they'd call me. But they also might like to hear my voice. Just to know I was keeping my finger on the pulse.

I was about to speed-dial Eddie when somewhere in the recesses of my brain, I heard Bones's echo. Once again, the memory returned. We were sitting around the firepit. He was sipping wine and doing something he didn't often do. He was talking about leadership and one of the things that makes a good leader. "Find out what people are good at, and let them do more of it." At the time, he was talking about him and me. I stared out across the water. The boats. The smell of outboard motor mixed with coconut suntan oil. Sails flapping loosely in the breeze. Would I learn this lesson? Would I let Bones school me from the grave? Because he was. I closed my phone and, to make sure it didn't tempt me, turned it off. Truth was, Eddie, Jess, BP, and Camp could catch Maynard without me. I didn't like to admit that, but they could. As my phone cycled down, I found myself smiling. Class was still in session. Would it ever end? I hoped not.

We skirted the southern tip just off El Toro, then Santa Ponsa, then turned northwest by northeast, and eventually northwest again along the Costa de la Calma.

Late afternoon brought us to a well-populated beach. A couple of RVs lined the parking lot. Tents on the hillside and boats anchored in a protected cove suggested overnighters. We anchored, and Gunner was giving me the indication he needed the beach. Ribeye always gave him the wind, so we swam to shore and began walking the water's edge. Beneath a tree sat a dark-haired man in his mid- to late forties. Gold necklace. Gold watch. Gold rings. I tried not to make eye contact and heard myself saying, "Don't do it."

Too late.

He stood from his chair, managing not to spill his wine over his ginormous stomach, and approached me. Under the cover of a whisper and a thick European accent, he pretended to be my best friend. "My friend, that is a good-looking dog."

It was always the dog. I nodded while Gunner sniffed his legs. Gunner sneezed, which told me he didn't like him either.

He sipped. "You on vacation?"

Here we go. "Something like that."

"You alone?"

I held up the leash.

"Would you enjoy some refreshment?"

I was pretty sure he wasn't talking about wine. "Define *refreshment*."

He inched closer. "Would you like to relax?"

I studied the sun. The clouds. Tried to play stupid. "I'm pretty relaxed."

"Ah, my friend. We men can always relax more. I think I can help with that."

I smiled. An American with an ulterior motive. "Help?"

"What would you say to a great, one-of-a-kind massage? Would you be interested?"

I pointed at him and shook my head. "You're not my type."

He laughed comfortably. He knew he had me. "I can give you your choice of three. All are young but very good at helping men like you relax."

His life was about to change. I hoped he liked prison. "I like to see what I'm buying before I decide. And . . ."

He waited.

"I usually shop for BOGOs."

The American phrase was lost on him. "Bogos?"

"Buy one, get one."

He nodded knowingly, then stepped to one side. "Follow me, please."

CHAPTER 73

H e led me to the far end of the parking lot, then up a small lane to a private campground. Back where the noise didn't travel. A nicely appointed travel bus, like something used by rock stars, sat quietly, shades pulled, under the shadow of a rock cliff. "Please."

I pulled on the handle and stepped inside, where I was met by three scantily clad girls. Maybe early teens. Each was tethered or cuffed to anchors in the wall. By the looks of them, Fabio had beaten the screaming out of them. They were silent as church mice.

"How much?"

He poured more wine. "For you? Fifty."

"Fifty?"

"A piece."

I didn't like him. Immensely. "And what if I wanted to sample the goods before I purchased?"

Gunner's ears had perked forward. He'd been in enough rooms like this to know what was about to go down. Evidence of this was the fact that his tail had stopped wagging and he was singularly focused on me.

The man's face changed expression. In a measured movement, which I was convinced he'd practiced in the mirror, he opened his shirt to reveal the butt end of a pistol. "You pay first. No returns. No exchanges." A smile. "All sales final."

The girls didn't move. I couldn't place their nationality, but it was not Spanish. Maybe Brazilian. Whatever the case, they looked to be a long way from home. I considered my options. The looks on their faces told me the girls didn't like him any more than I did. I turned to Gunner. "Choctaw."

As if launched from a cannon, Gunner shot at the man's groin. When he latched onto what was once the man's manhood, the prepubescent boy still in there elicited a bloodcurdling scream. Within two seconds, Gunner had his muzzle around the man's throat and had him pinned to the floor, where he was crying and pleading and bleeding.

I lifted the Glock from his waistband, dropped the magazine, emptied the chamber, pulled down on the disassembly pins, depressed the trigger on an empty chamber, evidenced by the *click*, then slid the slide forward and off the frame. I removed the guide rod, then the barrel, and threw all the pieces into the sink above him.

To say I had the girls' attention would have been an understatement. "Do any of you speak English?"

The man below said something, but my foot in his mouth prevented him from saying any more.

The girls just looked at me. I might as well have been from Mars. I dialed the number. She answered after the first ring. "Hey, you. What're you doing?"

I could hear her lips smile. "Planning a wedding?"

"How's your Spanish?"

"*Muy bueno.*"

"I need you to ask three girls in front of me if they want to be with this man."

Casey, who knew about a dozen languages, said into the phone, "*Alguno de ustedes quiere estar con este hombre?*"

The girls still looked at me like I had three heads, although I had a feeling they understood what she said but were still afraid to speak up. So, I turned to Gunner. "Release."

Gunner did. When the man sat up, I turned out his lights. He lay in a limp, bleeding pile on the floor. I spoke again into the phone. "Nope. How about Portuguese?"

Without hesitation, Casey spoke again. *"Algum de vocês quer ficar com esse homem?"*

All three of them shook their heads.

Thought so. When I spoke next, I was looking into the girls' eyes, wanting them to know that while I was speaking to Casey, I was talking with them. "Tell me your names."

Casey translated my request and, one by one, they spoke their names.

"Maria."

"Francisca."

"Margarida."

Such beauty. Such hope. Such innocence shattered. I glanced at Fabio, and my anger flared. I spoke again to Casey. "Thanks. Gotta go."

"Love you, Pops."

I pulled Fabio's keys from his shorts pocket and unlocked the cuffs. When I did, each girl stood, looked briefly at one another, stomped on the man's face and privates, then spat and said something that, based on the tone, was some sort of cussword.

An hour later, the ambulance drove Fabio to a hospital where he would be treated and taken to jail. After I gave my statement, a woman detective took the girls into custody. The last time I saw them, they were on the phone, talking with their parents. Tears all around. The woman detective sized me up, leaned against her car, and offered me a cigarette.

"No thanks. Trying to quit."

She inhaled, then blew a long-practiced spiral of smoke above our heads. "You want a job?"

I laughed. "I got a job."

She studied me. "We have no record of you entering this country legally."

"That's because I didn't make one."

"You know I can have you arrested for that."

"I do."

Another puff. "And I imagine a guy like you would be free before we arrived at jail."

I nodded.

"Figures."

She smiled. "You sure I can't offer you a job?"

"I'm sure."

A sly smile. "How about dinner?"

I held up my left hand.

She shook her head once. "Lucky girl."

She drove out the winding gravel road, escorting the three girls. I had their names in my pocket. Only then did I notice the cut on my knuckle.

Gunner and I ate dinner at the Hotel Coronado, where I rented a dog-friendly room and we sat on our patio staring out across the water as the sun slipped behind Frank's island due south. Gunner, quite satisfied with our little vacation, ate another ribeye from room service while I had the fish. Both were excellent.

I drifted off after midnight, laptop on my lap, and, oddly, slept until room service knocked on the door at 10:00 a.m. Gunner, stomach aimed at the ceiling, didn't move. At the knock, he just looked at me. "I'm not getting it."

CHAPTER 74

We checked out, returned to the Zodiac, topped off the fuel, and idled out. Heading southwest, we encountered another clothing-optional beach at an unspoiled cove called Caló d'en Monjo. The gin-clear water was calm, the beach dotted with sunbathers, and off to my right kids jumped off high rocks, splashing into the water with screams of delight. Another half mile along the craggy coastline and we encountered another cove. This entire landscape looked like something out of one of Summer's favorite movies, *The Count of Monte Cristo*. We navigated into the cove around massive underwater rocks the size of semitrailers and found ourselves alone in one of the most beautiful spots on planet earth. We moored in the shade of a tall cliff, napped on the bow, swam in the warm water, and watched the world go by. An unusual treat for us both.

I missed her and I wanted to hear her voice. She picked up after half a ring. "Hey, you."

I loved the sound of her voice. "Hey, I was just missing you and wanted to . . . well, I wanted to hear you say, 'Hey, you.' I've always loved how you say that."

She giggled. "Hey, you."

"Yeah, like that."

"You good?"

"Yeah."

"Really?"

"Yeah, I think I'm doing okay."

"You go back?"

"I did." I told her about the tunnel I found and how Bones made it to the ocean with his brother.

She listened and said, "Back where they started."

"Yep."

I turned the mirror. "What're you doing?"

"Shep and I are coloring, and he's eating a grilled cheese. And Casey's trying on wedding dresses while Angel, Ellie, and Clay give their opinions."

I liked the thought of that. My family. Together.

She continued, "I'm not pushing you, but you got a return date?"

I told her about the beach, the water, the sand, and how I wanted to bring her back. "Just us," I said. "It's maybe one of the more beautiful places I've ever seen."

"I'd like that a lot."

"It's a date."

A pause. I could hear Ellie giggling in the background along with Clay's deep voice. Summer broke the silence. "Hey, Shep wants to say something."

She held the phone for him. "Hey, Dad?"

I sat on the beach and sank my head in my hands while the water lapped over my ankles. "Yeah, buddy?"

"When you get home, can we build a fort?"

"Yes." I smiled. "When I get home, we can build a fort."

"Okay, I want to build one up in the trees. Like Robin Hood."

"I think that's a great idea. You got a tree picked out?"

"Yep. It's up on the hill behind the house. When we build it, can we roast s'mores?"

The memory returned. I was a kid. Not even a teenager. Sifting through the sand, looking for artifacts, when I met Marie on what would later become my island. In the evening, we would build a fire and roast s'mores beneath the moonlight, accompanied by the sound of cicadas. The memory was sweet and there was no pain in it. "Definitely. A tree fort is no tree fort at all if you can't roast s'mores."

"Can we get the big marshmallows?"

"Definitely."

"Okay."

Summer's voice again. "He's gone. Back to coloring."

"Summer?"

I could hear her smile. "Yeah."

"You're a good mama."

She said nothing. We just sat there listening to each other listen to each other.

"Summer?"

"Yeah."

I wiped the tears. Then I wiped my nose on my sleeve. "I just wanted to tell you . . ."

A moment passed. Then another.

"I just wanted to tell you . . . that I love you. And I can't imagine my life without you. And . . . I know that you carry a lot, and . . ."

I broke off. Another moment passed. Tears long stored up flowed freely. I didn't try to hold them back. I let them fall. I'm not ashamed to say my shoulders shook as they did. Shaking out the pain.

"Murph?"

"Yeah, I'm here."

"You sure you're okay?"

It was *the* question. I palmed my face and tried to breathe. In. Out. "I been wrestling with something."

She waited.

"I knew coming over here who I needed to be. Who Bones had trained me to be. I just didn't know if I wanted to be him without Bones. Didn't know if I could be, but something about seeing that trail of blood . . . Seeing Bones not die at the hand of another but on his terms. His way. Seeing the marks on the rock where he'd slid his brother down into the water, and the two of them floated off home. In each other's arms. Something about that healed something in me that had been broken a long time. I can't explain that. It just did."

She was crying now. I could hear it.

"I'm sorry. I didn't mean to make you cry."

"These are good tears." I could hear her blow her nose and the rustle of a tissue. "There's no hurt in them."

"Hey, Summer? I need to say something to you and I'm not sure how to say it."

She waited.

"So, if I don't say it right, just tell me and let me come at it a second time."

"Okay."

I tried to find the words. When a few settled, I put them together. "I'm . . ." A pause as I doubted my delivery. "I'm not me without you."

More tissue rustling. More sniffling. Finally, the background noise disappeared, which meant she'd stepped outside. "Bishop?"

I loved when she called me that. "Yes?"

"I'm ready for you to come home. And if it doesn't happen soon, I'm getting on a plane and coming to you. You hear me?"

I did. "Yes."

"Okay. Now, I've got a little boy in there who needs me to help him color Robin Hood's hat. He says it needs to be green so we're searching through 128 colors to find the best one. And Casey . . . my goodness, I've never seen such a beautiful bride. You just won't believe it. Poor Camp doesn't stand a chance. He's gonna pass out at the altar. And . . ." She paused. "Even with all of this, you are all I can think about. I miss you. And I need you. I don't care if you're here with me or I'm there with you, but I need you."

The breeze dried the sweat off my skin. "I'll see you soon."

She hung up, and I sat there in the water. Shaking my head. Staring at what my life had become. What I had become. I wrote stories for a living, and yet I couldn't have scripted this one.

CHAPTER 75

Despite the fact that Gunner and I had enjoyed our lazy afternoon in the Count's hidden cove along the craggy coastline, I could feel the tug. It was time to go home. I scheduled the plane for later that evening. Putting me back in Colorado sometime tomorrow. Dinner with my family. S'mores around the fire on Main Street. The thought prompted a question I could not answer: Was I headed back to the return of the life I had once known, or the beginning of one yet to be born? I didn't know. Regardless, I knew something, and someones, awaited me. And I missed them. I missed them a lot. As the sun began to drop behind the cliff, casting long shadows along the beach, I freed our moor line and was about to crank the engine when I spotted a small S-shaped canal of sorts leading out of the protected side of the cove. Maybe fifteen feet wide, it looked to have been carved out of the rock by an ancient river that no longer flowed. Smooth walls reaching some sixty feet in the air. A cliff diver's dream.

We poked our nose into the beginning of the S-turn and marveled at the water and sea life below us. Bells sounded somewhere in the distance. Beautiful. Signifying something undefined but signifying it nonetheless. Making the last turn, we spotted a private beach. Less than eighty yards in length. A true private beach. On one side sat a worn and ancient stone bench. Hundreds of years in the wearing. Long ago caves had been cut into the base of the rock. Whether they were homes at one time or just someplace to get out of the sun I knew not, but given the soot marring the walls, they'd been here a long time. Across the beach, a single set of footsteps imprinted the sand. Some in the water. Some not. Once a meandering figure eight, now a faint half of a three. I studied this place. How it felt so far from my life. What I wouldn't give to set up two chairs and watch the sun rise and fall over Summer's shoulder as she fussed over sandcastles and nonexistent cellulite and stared up at me from beneath that ginormous straw hat that flopped around and swallowed her beautiful face. Also carved into the stone wall were stairs, zigzagging to the top of the cliff some seventy feet above us. Other than the bells, I knew not what waited there.

When I glanced up for the first time, I lifted my eyes toward the rock cliffs above me and found a setting sun, trees growing out of the rocky crags high above, and dozens of large white birds circling in the updrafts. Eden on earth. That's when it caught my eye. The glisten. The reflection. A single pole, spiraling up and out of the trees along the cliff. At first I confused it with an antenna, but then I saw the rope. Adding to my confusion. What surprised me was the illusion. The rock wall closest to me actually sat twenty feet out from the actual outer cliff wall, providing a natural hidden cove inside a hidden cove. In directional terms, we had exited the bay through an S-turn into a larger cove, turned left into the private cove with the stone bench, then turned left again where I spotted the mast. The optical illusion had been created by the trees that had grown out of the false wall and reached across to the actual wall.

I hopped out of the boat and walked the beach in shin-deep water, craning my neck, Gunner at my heels. Reaching the far end of the beach, a walk of about thirty yards, I was able to peer behind the lesser of the two rock walls. The distance between the two might have been twenty feet, but the natural cave made the perfect berth for a sailboat. Which was exactly what I found. And if I had to guess, I'd say she was about forty-two feet long.

Moored to several stainless anchor bolts drilled into the rock, as if that were her home and had been for a very long time, the *Nun Taken* sat quietly, water lapping her light blue hull. Oddly, I sat there staring at her hull like a monkey admiring a Rubik's Cube. Just behind me and standing on the water's edge, Gunner perked his ears and jerked his head as if he'd been shot with electricity. Before I could say, "No," Gunner bounced and hit the stairs at a dead run. In three seconds he was topside and out of sight.

The only thing that would make him disappear like that was a girl-friend he could smell but had yet to meet. I grabbed a shirt and began climbing the steps, trying to figure out how to apologize in Spanish for the fact that my dog just had an unsanctioned date with someone else's. Never an easy conversation.

My legs were burning when I reached the top of the stairway to heaven. Staring down at the more than one hundred steps I'd just as-cended, it hit me that someone really had to love sailing to make that trip. Trying to find my dog before someone shot him, I was met by a world I'd not expected. Meticulously manicured landscape, a sprawling lawn made up of the type of grass used on golf courses, hundreds of roses in bloom, a grape orchard along a hillside, all of which was stretched out below a massive stone building that looked to be a thousand years old. Surrounded by smaller outbuildings. Castle and fortress might be one description. Cathedral might be another. Atop sat a bell tower. Whatever it was had been here a minute, and I doubted seriously these people received many guests. I had a strong sensation I needed to find Gunner and get gone and do so quickly.

Too late. Behind me, I heard a female voice ask, "May I help you, sir?"

I don't know what I expected, but as with everything else here, when I turned I was met by another surprise. She was midfifties. Tall. Slender. Crazy beautiful. Bronzed Spanish skin. Jet-black hair. A pair of pruning shears in one hand. Couple of roses in the other. None of which was un-usual. But what was unusual was her dress. While most folks I'd seen in the last day or so were wearing skimpy bathing suits or no suit at all, she was wearing a habit. As in, she was a nun.

Which might explain *Nun Taken*. Which meant I was now trespassing in a convent. I wanted to crawl under a rock.

I stammered, "I'm so sorry. I lost my dog." I began illustrating with hand signals. "'Bout this tall. Dirty yellow. Goes by the name Gunner. Was once obedient. Now, not so much." I wanted to say something about him being rather uncontrollably attracted to females in heat but figured it might be wise to skip that part.

She laughed and waved me on.

CHAPTER 76

I followed at a safe distance. "Ma'am, if you've taken a vow of silence or something, you can just point and I'll leave you alone. Really, I'm so sorr—"

She laughed again. "I did take vows, but not of silence. That'd be tough for me as I'm a physician."

"Really?" I didn't know why, but that surprised me. "What kind?"

"Trauma."

That, too, surprised me. Not that I doubted her; it just wasn't what I thought when I saw a lady who looked like someone out of *The Sound of Music*. She pointed at the monstrosity of a fortress. "The Sisters here treated returning crusaders, so it's in our blood. We serve several hospitals around. They call us when things don't look good." She pointed at me. "By the looks of you, you know a thing or two about trauma."

While I had grabbed my shirt before climbing the stairs, I had not put it on. Which escaped me since we'd been talking. I pulled it on quickly. "Again, ma'am, I'm so sorr—"

She laughed. "I've seen worse." A pause. "But not much. What's your line of work?"

That was a difficult question. I figured I'd throw her the softball answer. "Um . . . I work for a nonprofit in Colorado."

She did not look convinced. "Oh, really?"

I gathered by her tone of voice that she didn't believe me. "We house and take care of boys and girls who have been trafficked."

318

This piqued her interest. "How do they get to you?"

Another softball. "They're rescued out of some pretty bad places. Then we fly them to Freetown and nurse them back to health."

"Freetown?"

"Yes, ma'am, it's the name of our, um . . . home."

"Where is it?"

"Rocky Mountains."

She studied me. "But that's not the only one, is it?"

"No, ma'am." I shook my head once. "We've broken ground on a place in Spellman Bluff. Coastal Georgia."

"And what do you call it?"

"Hopetown."

"Why there?"

I paused. "It was the childhood home of a friend. We're building it in his honor. Thought maybe in buying it we could drain the darkness out and offer—"

She interrupted me. "Hope."

"Yes, ma'am."

"Why?"

"That goes back to that same friend. He used to tell me, 'We're in the hope business,' so . . ."

"And are you?"

"I'd like to think so."

She stepped closer. Eyeing the scars my T-shirt didn't cover. "And when these beautiful children of God pray for someone to kick down the door, are you the answer to that prayer?"

I figured about here it was probably time to tell the truth. "I'm one of 'em."

She nodded affectionately. "You do this alone?"

"Well . . ." The answer was more difficult than I thought, because I had to hear myself say it. "I do now. But I didn't used to." I couldn't understand why I was opening up to her, but I was. "When I was young, a man befriended me. Put me through school, trained me, and gave me a choice. Life

319

on a silver platter—white house, picket fence, Volvo in the driveway—or I could walk through door number two."

She chuckled. "Can't really see you driving a Volvo."

I shook my head. "No, ma'am."

"How many people have you saved?"

"As of last week, 259."

She smiled. "And I'll bet you can recall all of their names."

I nodded but felt no need to show her my back. "Yes, ma'am."

"Would those happen to be the names inscribed on your back?"

I didn't think she'd seen that. "Yes, ma'am."

"So you made a record?"

I nodded.

"Why?"

I considered how best to answer this. "Because people who've been treated like that have a singular need to know they are of value. That they matter."

"I would imagine they know that from the moment they lay eyes on you." She paused. "You have kind eyes."

"Don't tell the bad guys."

She pointed to a cut on my right knuckle where I'd turned out Fabio's lights. "Recent?"

A nod. "Yesterday." I gestured to the coastline. "A beach back that way."

"You save someone?"

"Three girls."

"Just like that?"

A shrug.

"Where are they now?"

"On a flight to Brazil."

"Never stops, does it?"

"No, ma'am." A single shake.

"Do you?"

I read between the lines. "Did my wife put you up to that question?"

She laughed. "I'd like to meet the lady who can corral you." She studied me. "You didn't answer my question."

"Not very good at that."

"I can see that."

"Occupational hazard, ma'am."

She smiled. "I'm starting to pick up what you're putting down."

I liked her. Liked her a lot.

"And this man who taught you, does he save people too?"

The verb tense caught me off guard, but explaining it was too much to go into. "Yes, ma'am."

"How many has he saved?"

"Nobody really knows." I shook my head. "Thousands."

"Does he carry scars like yours?"

I paused. Figured I'd better come clean. "He did."

"Oh, I'm sorry, I thought . . ."

A tear surfaced that I could not hide. "It's why I'm here. To say good-bye. See, we, uh . . ." I pointed out across the water. "We . . ." It was too much. I didn't know how to break it down. Put it into words. "We walked into some darkness out there and it was pretty dark." A pause. "Darkest I'd ever seen."

"But . . . ?" She waited.

I wanted her to know his story. The truth. The magnificent magnitude that was Ezekiel "Bones" Walker.

"Ma'am." When the memory returned, one half of my face attempted a smile, while the other half shed the tear. "Bones walked in and . . . that darkness did not comprehend it."

This brought her pause. And she almost nodded as if saying something to herself. "Bones?"

"That's his name." I swallowed. "Was."

She nodded. "But he didn't make it out."

"No, ma'am."

"Why?"

"Evil is good at being evil. And sometimes evil wins."

Another nod. "I know a thing or two about that. But that's not what I was asking."

This lady was a steel trap. Nothing got by her.

She continued, "Why'd he do what he did?"

I said the only thing I could think. I said the only thing that mattered. The thing that told the world "I am Bones."

"Because . . . the needs of the one outweigh those of the ninety-nine."

She nodded and couldn't hide the smile. "Seems like I've read that somewhere."

Just then, Gunner started barking his head off. "Ma'am, I'm sorry, but that's—"

She waved me off. "Come with me."

CHAPTER 77

G unner was sitting on his butt, barking at the building. "Gunner, come." He looked at me and kept barking. "Now! Get your—" I bit my tongue, realizing I didn't need to cuss in front of a nun. "Fanny over here. Right now."

Gunner tucked his tail, jogged to me, circled my new friend, sniffing her feet, and then sat beside me. She smiled. "You two must work together."

"Yes, ma'am, we're sort of a package deal."

She waved me on. "You hungry?"

"No, ma'am. I've inconvenienced you enough." Gunner was whining at my feet. "We should probably . . ."

She stepped closer. I could feel her breath on my face. She was studying me. After a minute, she said, "You are welcome to leave, but if you'll stay . . . I have a few questions for you." She forced eye contact. "David Bishop."

The words were like a sledgehammer to my face. "Ma'am?"

She turned and beckoned me to follow. So we did. We walked through the back door, through the kitchen where something delicious sat simmering on the stove, through a breezeway, past a library, then up a flight of stairs, down a hallway, and up another flight. At the top, we turned right, walked a long hallway, and entered a smaller library where several David Bishop novels lay in a stack. It was obvious someone sat here a lot staring out over the water. This was someone's safe space. Where they made sense of what didn't make sense. Then she approached a door that was shut and leaned against it, listening. She studied me, or better yet measured me, and then gently pressed the door open.

I'd heard of and seen people in trauma not being able to differentiate between real and not. Of slipping into and out of a break in reality. Living half here and half there because their heart, mind, and soul couldn't make sense of the pain. Not knowing the difference between what was dream and what wasn't. In that moment, I didn't know if I was still in bed at the hotel, with room service knocking on the door, or not.

The door squeaked and soft late-afternoon sun showered the room. And the bed.

Where a man lay sleeping.

He was bandaged, and an IV dripped into his left arm. His face was partially obscured by a pillow, so she walked to the bed and moved it. When she did, the sunlight bathed his face.

CHAPTER 78

I inched forward, staring, but I could not make sense of what my eyes saw. I studied his face, his arms, the scars, then his hands. I studied his chest. Rising. Falling. Measured. I knelt. Afraid. Fearful I'd wake up. Sure the dream would never return.

And something in me that had died began to press against the stone.

I checked again. The chest rose. Fell. Rose again. Then I noticed his temple, a vein pulsating there. Something inside had to be doing that. It couldn't be a dream. Couldn't be an illusion. The footprints on the beach? I knew if I moved, if I whispered, if I blinked, the cloud would dissipate and the image would be gone. But what about her? Was she real? Was this place?

Was I losing it? Was my trauma greater than I thought? I closed my eyes, squinted as hard as I could, and then opened my eyes. The bed was still there. Man resting. Chest rising. Falling. One breath. Two. He was still there. Now or never. I gambled. I entered the dream. There in that thin place where heaven kisses earth, where light rises and darkness fades, I slid my hand beneath the man's and forgot to breathe.

And there in the dream, in that place between here and there, I managed, "I'm sorry. Bones, I'm so sorry. Forgive me. I should have . . ." I broke off. Tried again. "I should have . . ." Still no better. I buried my face in the sheets and cried at the top of my lungs. Crying from a place in me that I did not know existed. Below the pain. Down where my love lived.

My shoulders shook, and I didn't hold back. Whatever it was that I'd been holding, whatever had started on the phone call with Summer, I let it out. All of it. I cried a long time. I wasn't sure how long. Long enough for the tears to run dry. To soak the sheets. Afraid to look up, afraid I'd lose him again the same way I'd lost his boot prints in the sand, I shook my head and kept my eyes closed. If I stayed there, maybe the illusion would stay. Just a few more minutes, then I could let him go. But this, this was my last goodbye. My apology. My last attempt to tell him that I was sorry, that I loved him, and that I'd never forget him. That he was the best friend I'd ever had and that there was nothing in this life that didn't point back to him. That I was lost without him. That . . .

I stayed in that place until my lungs remembered to breathe and I could hear myself again over the wails coming from inside me. It was a painful place. Maybe the most painful of places. But I was making it through. Or maybe not. I could not tell dream from reality, and honestly, I didn't want to. Didn't care. Only one more step to take. To let him go for sure. The finality. So I opened my eyes. When I did, would I find myself in a hotel room or on a plane? Reality had slipped away.

Bed. White sheets. A man. Chest rising. Falling. Scars. IV dripping.

I'd not woken from the dream. Somehow, despite entering my own dream, the man was still here. I sat on my heels and rested my head on the bed, closing my eyes. That was when the dream got weird. She knelt alongside me, one hand resting on the man's arm. I opened my eyes, afraid the dream would stop, but it was stretching the bounds. It wasn't like other dreams. In this dream, tears and snot smeared the sheets. I tried but couldn't make words.

Then the dream changed again. What had been an illusion, a woman in a habit, reached across the thin place and put a hand on top of my hand that held his. When her lips moved, I could hear her speak. "He spent several weeks in a coma. When he did wake, infection had set in. We treated him, and given the extent of his internal injuries and loss of blood, I put him back into what you might call a medically induced coma to allow his body to rest." She stroked his arm. The same forearm that had seen a K bar enter one side and exit the other. "He talks in his sleep." She nodded. Smiled. "His first words were 'David Bishop.'" A pause.

Why was she telling me this? That was when it hit me: she wasn't real. And of course I'd be David Bishop in my dream.

She continued, "So I read to him. Every now and then he'll wake up. Sometimes he's aware of what's going on. Sometimes not. I think he's healing of more than just physical wounds."

Now I was sure it was a dream. Earlier she'd called me "Bishop."

"Please don't wake me up. Please don't wake up. Please, just a few minutes more. I won't tell anyone . . ."

I buried my face in the sheets and pressed his hand to my face. "I won't tell . . ."

Her arm wrapped around my shoulder. It was the first time I'd ever felt warmth in a dream.

"He likes it when you talk to him."

"I can't."

"Why?"

"Talking wakes you up from dreams."

A chuckle. "So what do you call this?"

She had a good point. "Yeah, but you're not him."

Another smile. "Agreed."

"Are you real?"

"Yes, David, I'm real."

There it was again. "Prove it."

CHAPTER 79

S he opened a closet door and there, folded and neatly stacked, were his clothes. Complete with bullet holes. Alongside lay his empty Milt Sparks 55BN holster absent his Sig 220, which Frank took somewhere along the way. But what almost had me convinced were his boots. The laces had been cut, as if someone had to get them off in a hurry. One lay on its side, the bottom of its sole exposed.

I shook my head again. I'd been down this road before. On the beach. It hurt too much the last time. I couldn't do it again. Something in me was playing a trick on me. Some place of pain just could not or would not let him go.

I sat up, unable to make sense of my world. Gunner was staring at me. And staring at the man in the bed in my dream. And because dreams are weird and don't make sense unless you're dreaming them, he climbed up on the bed, sniffed the man's face, licked him gently, then curled up alongside his left arm, resting his face on his thigh, whining.

Next to the bed, resting on the nightstand, lay seven spent bullets in a stainless bowl. Evidence of the extraction.

The letter. That was when I remembered the letter. Bones had told me in his postscript: "If you slip, don't worry—the water's deep beneath you. But it's also flowing with a force like you've never known, so hold your breath because it's about to take you on an underwater ride that not even Disney could imagine, and it will either drown you or save you."

Did the water save Bones?

I melted into a puddle, crying a long time. Deep sobs. My shoulders shaking. And she stayed with me. When I had cried all I thought I could and then some more, she said, "He talks about you. About Freetown. Angel. Ellie. Casey. And Shep, I think. And"—she petted Gunner—"he talks about you."

I shook my head, not wanting to wake. Trying to will the dream to continue. "How?"

"My father taught me to sail. Have since I was a kid. I had spent the day in a protected cove, reading, trying not to think about the last week. At sundown I was raising my anchor when I saw a man emerge from what looked like a cave dragging a body into the water. One sank; the other floated. I grabbed the one floating. Here we are."

I nodded. "That was Frank. He was . . ."

"The darkness?"

"Yes, ma'am."

She eyed the man. "But he loved him."

"Brothers."

I turned back to the man beneath the sheets. Never had I known greater disbelief. "Is he gonna be . . ."

She finished my sentence. "Okay?"

I nodded, knowing the dream was coming to an end.

"Don't know. Some days are good. Some days not so much. I've never seen one person carry and shed so much hurt. So much . . . pain." She eyed the stainless pan and the bullets. "I don't know how he's made it this far. He's flatlined three times but always manages to return. I'm not even sure he knows I exist." She paused. "I've been around the block a few times. Seen a lot I wish I hadn't. But in all that time, I've never been so aware of such a deep reservoir of love in one human being as in this one." She studied him, almost as if she'd done it for hours on end. "Do you mind if I ask you a question?"

That was good. Keep her talking. I couldn't wake if she was talking. I nodded slowly.

"Can you tell me his name?"

I nodded. "Ezekiel Walker. But we all call him Bones."

I tried to speak again but couldn't. It was too much. But not as much as what was about to happen.

The man's finger twitched. Then again. Then, in what is still the most amazing moment of my life, his indomitable, tender, magnificent hand squeezed mine. Tight.

I'd never felt that in a dream. Dreams don't squeeze back.

Then in the second most amazing moment of my life, his lips moved. When they did, I heard the faintest of whispers. Not understanding, I leaned in, pressing my ear to his face. When I did, he said it again. This time louder. At first I couldn't understand. Too garbled. The words swam around my brain, and when they finally settled, I heard them and my eyes opened.

"Tell me what you know about sheep."

That was when I wondered if the dream wasn't a dream.

I pressed my forehead to his temple and gently pulled him to me, whispering, "They're totally lost without their shepherd."

Then a strange thing happened. A tear landed on my left arm. Her tear. She, too, was crying. And dreams didn't cry.

Feeling the image fade, knowing my dream was ending, I felt the man's body warm. I felt heat. I tried to stay in the dream, but I'd lost it. He was fading. I couldn't see him anymore. And just before he left, that man, that magnificent teddy bear and rescuer of the lost, the epicenter of everything good in this world, the keeper of the record, the keeper of the light, reached up out of the liquid grave in which he'd buried himself and hugged me. Those big, muscled arms wrapped around me, and I watched in wonder as the darkness in me disappeared.

Somewhere in there I woke up.

Only to realize I'd not been dreaming.

Then Bones.

CHAPTER 80

My heart stopped. I couldn't speak. Couldn't think. Couldn't breathe. Couldn't hope. What was real? What was not? Life was coming at me faster than I could process, so I looked at her, and she nodded and smiled. So I turned back to him and rested my face on his cheek and wept like a baby while Gunner licked the left side of his face off.

When I'd been shot with my own crossbow, I rolled down a cliff, crashed into the water, and then floated downriver several miles, eventually spending several days dying in a cave. I had to seal up my own wound, so I heated my knife and did just that. Starting the clock ticking. The clock of infection. Several days later, when the infection was raging and I was more dead than alive, I'd read the letter from Marie. The one Bones had given me. And there in that mostly dead place, I came partially alive. Hours later, or a day, maybe two, I'm not really sure, I passed from here to there. In and out of consciousness. In and out of life. My hope that they'd find me had waned. I had resolved myself to passing out of this life and into eternity. I remembered being thirsty, so thirsty I would have given anything for a sip of water, and then I wasn't thirsty. Then shivering. And being so cold. I couldn't remember thoughts so much as perceptions. Cold. Dark. Hot. Fever. It was a thin place.

Just before I closed my eyes for the last time, a hazy fog seemed to cover my eyes. Blurring what I had been able to see before. That was when I knew. When I knew I was much more dead than alive. So I closed my eyes and waited. Waited for my turn.

But my turn didn't come. Instead, a man dressed in white appeared at the foot of my bed. Or whatever you might call the thin thing upon which I was reclining. Then he inched closer. Finally, his breath on my face, he came into view. I saw him. I saw Bones. He'd found me. I didn't know how but he had, and in that moment I came back. I passed from there to here. He brought me back.

I stared at the man before me. The frame and face I knew well. Together, we'd traveled a million miles. Was this the last one, or just one among the many? But then he breathed. The man inhaled. And exhaled. Both. One following the other. Followed by another. And dead people didn't breathe.

Somehow, despite being shot seven times, bleeding out, and falling more than a hundred feet down a well with his arms latched around his dead brother, Ezekiel Walker had not died. Was not dead.

Bones was alive.

An inconceivable, incomprehensible thought. How could that possibly be true?

I shook my head. Cleared the tears. Then stared again, and he was still here. The vision had not lifted. I stayed there a long time. Crying my face off some more. Shaking my head. A place with no words. What words could I say? Where could I start? How could I begin? So I didn't. We didn't. Some things were just too much.

But in that moment, one thing became clear. Ezekiel Walker had not died on that island. He was a little bit alive. And a little bit alive was not dead, for dead people were all the way dead, and even 1 percent alive was still not dead.

We sat there. Me holding his hand. Him holding mine. Still no words. I couldn't find them. He couldn't speak them. But his muscled hand, the hand that had caught me, saved me, lifted me when I couldn't, felt warm. Even strong.

She stayed with us. Sitting alongside. Not intruding, but monitoring. He'd been touch and go. She wasn't about to lose him now. After an hour, Sister Catalonia, who went by Lonnie or Lon for short, tapped my arm. "Is there someone you need to call?"

I palmed my face. "Yes, but how do I . . . ?"

Bones lay propped up, resting, his eyes closed, Gunner tucked up along one side. He cracked a smile, a hoarse whisper as his vocal cords had spent more than eight weeks making no or little sound. "You'd better make the call. He'll only mess it up. He's no good with words."

She smiled.

Just before I dialed the number, he spoke with his eyes closed. "Murph."

There it was. Crashing back in out of the stratosphere. My name and the one who'd named me. I nodded, trying to control my uncontrollable emotions.

He spoke slowly. "Outside of family, tell no one." A pause. "Not a soul."

Even now, one foot still in the grave, Bones was calculating. Barely able to stand, and my teacher was still taking me to school, standing seven steps ahead.

Summer picked up after half a ring. "Hey, you. You in-flight?"

I cleared my throat and tried to force out "He's . . ." but didn't get very far. I tried again. "He's . . ." This time the whisper sounded.

Summer said, "Hey, honey, you're breaking up. Say again."

I was trying. But it was too much. "Summer, he's . . ."

Bones chuckled and managed a whisper. "Told you."

Sister Catalonia smiled and waited patiently. Evidence of her training.

Summer again. "Bish, you good?"

Bones smiled. He was enjoying listening to the sound of Summer's voice.

"Summ . . . He's . . ."

Summer paused. She knew something wasn't right. Her tone changed. "Hey, it's okay. I'm here. Just take your time."

This time the whisper broke, and I managed two words as one. Hearing myself say the words cracked me even further down the middle. "Heeee's-uuuuh-liiiive."

"What, baby? It's hard to hear you."

I cleared my throat, inhaled, and said, "He's alive."

"Baby, you're talking nonsense. Who's alive?"

I stared at him. Shook my head. And the tears flowed again. He smiled, raised an eyebrow, and rubbed Gunner's muzzle. This time when I spoke, I was crystal. "Bones is alive."

"Did you say, 'Bones is alive'?"

I held the phone inches from his mouth and nodded.

"Hey," he said. "How's my girl?"

The next few minutes were the most fun I'd ever had in my life.

CHAPTER 81

With the plane on its way, Lonnie relayed the details of Bones's rescue and ensuing eighteen hours of surgery. How the Sisters lined up to give blood. When I joked around saying that was a good thing because Bones had never been very good at keeping in touch with his feminine side, he quipped, "Yeah, trust me, at this point I'm having hot flashes and pretty well convinced I'm single-handedly putting the 'men' back in 'menopause.'"

Every few seconds, I'd touch Bones's hand or foot or just put my hand on his shoulder, because the utter inconceivability of the moment was larger than my brain could process. Bones told me of falling into the well and how the water had receded, offering him a shorter way out. Less distance to the outside. Which, as his letter had predicted, helped save his life. Then he told me about Lon, as he was fond of calling her. How in the really tough moments, she pulled him back. Back from the brink. Which had been often. Not to mention he loved the sound of her voice when she read to him.

I filled him in on Ashley, his girls, Maui, Jerusalem, and Ariel. To which Bones nodded, saying, "Good man." I told him about Words with Friends and the break. The anonymous request to play. Alaska. The rough plane landing. The cabin. What we found. I also told him about Maynard. His farmhouse in Virginia. How Clay, Camp, and I had pretended the drunken crash to install cameras. And my phone calls with Maynard.

Bones listened and processed. Finally, he said, "Does he suspect you suspect him?"

"Not sure. I've tried to hide it, but my disdain is palpable."

"And Ashley?"

I shook my head. "Not good. Sequestered in Georgia. The knowledge of what happened to his girls was too . . . well, he has submitted a letter of resignation. The president has issued a replacement to the Senate. They're scheduled to vote in a week."

Bones's face told me he did not like what I just told him.

"And the nominee?"

"I'll give you one guess."

"Figures."

Bones had tired, so he napped while Lonnie showed me the grounds and Gunner kept watch over Bones. Evidently he'd smelled Bones, which was why he'd bolted up the stairs and started barking his head off. He'd done exactly what I'd told him to do. "Find Bones."

That evening, as Bones faded off, Lonnie tapped my shoulder. "He's tired. We'd better let him get his sleep."

In the kitchen, I asked Lonnie, "There a butcher shop nearby?"

She drew me a map. "Tell them I sent you."

I returned twenty minutes later, fired up an ancient outdoor stone grill thing, and watched Gunner salivate. When the steak was ready, I let it cool, cut it into small pieces, and, to Lonnie's audible delight, lay on the floor with him and fed him piece by piece. Twenty minutes later, Gunner had returned to Bones's side, stretched out, and snored the drunken-sailor snore of contentedness.

I slept a few hours on the sofa in his room. Lonnie brought me coffee at daybreak, and we walked the grounds while she told me her story. Late fifties. Studied medicine in school. Engaged to be married in her early twenties. Her husband-to-be, an Italian race car driver, died in a crash. Heartbroken, she'd joined the convent, and they'd encouraged her to finish her studies. She did. Excelled in surgery. And in trauma. She'd obtained specialties in war-torn parts of Africa, Serbia, and Iraq, traveling with various NGOs but always returning here. Both to her hospital, where she served as chief of surgery, and to her boat. The *Nun Taken*. Always had a thing for kids. Especially the tormented ones.

The plane landed late afternoon on the second day. Everybody came. Knowing she was about to be invaded by a lot of people, I started making hotel reservations. Watching me struggle with the language barrier, Lonnie waved me off. "Sisterhood isn't as popular as it once was. We have a few empty rooms. Take your pick."

To protect Freetown in their absence, Camp had called in a few favors. The reason? A much-needed vacation for all of us. Given that the pay was really good, guys lined up, making a wait list. Freetown was well guarded and cared for, but no one outside of us and Sister Catalonia, who had insisted that I call her Lonnie, knew of Bones's resurrection.

I met them at the plane with the convent van and was immediately bombarded with ten thousand questions. I just held up a hand and shook my head. What could I say? The smile on my face told them much of what they needed. We unloaded, they followed me single file, and then one by one we walked into the convent where Lonnie had Bones sitting on a porch overlooking the water. When they saw him, a hush fell. They all covered their mouths and stood at a distance. Then Bones stood and said, "Well, don't just stand there. Bring it in." And I watched in amazement as Bones walked back into our lives.

There were several moments in my life I'd never forget. That moment was one of them.

Ellie, Angel, and Casey cried like teenage girls who'd just watched *The Notebook*. Summer wasn't far behind. Clay didn't even pretend to hold it together, just bear-hugging his friend. Camp stood to one side and nodded. "Sir."

Bones laughed and noticed his sidearm concealed within his jacket. It was the CZ I'd given him, which was actually Bones's to begin with. "Nice choice."

Camp pointed at me. "It's his." Then he thought about it. "Well, actually it's yours."

Bones looked at me with a comical and disapproving look. "I guess this means you've been sampling my cellar."

They all nodded, and Clay spoke up. "Every chance he gets."

Jess, BP, and Eddie were next. Followed by Shep, who stood pressing himself to my thigh, holding my hand. Bones saw his reticence, stooped down, which took no little effort, and held out his arms. I whispered, "It's okay."

Shep gingerly stepped forward, unsure if Bones was real or a ghost. Bones gathered him to his chest and, after a little help getting settled in a chair, pulled him up on his lap, where he tickled him. The laughter was pure tonic.

And Summer? After hugging his neck and smearing tears on Bones's face, Summer locked arms around me. Pressing herself to me. Blurring where she ended and I began. Which was just fine with me.

We spent an unbelievable week. Feeling guilty like we'd overstayed our welcome, we made plans to leave, but when Sister Catalonia found out, she would have none of it. So we stayed two more. Bones improved, taking slow walks with each of us, and given improvement, Lonnie agreed he was healthy enough to fly. Which he was eager to do as he had a wedding to attend. Casey was beaming.

That Bones had a thing for Lonnie was evident. He was smitten. But how smitten could he be? She'd been promised to God. So he kept his feelings to himself. Watching them was tender. She'd saved his life. They were forever bound in the uncertain eight weeks they'd spent while she single-handedly pulled him back. I'd met some fine doctors in my day. She was in a class all by herself.

Two weeks in and we found them in the garden, sharing a glass of red wine. I thought about interrupting and pouring two more, to share in the moment, which is what wine is—a moment shared—but Summer tugged on my sleeve and shook her head. She was right. They were learning to say goodbye. Which would not be easy.

In our third week there, amid the bliss of a Majorcan afternoon, Summer squinted one eye and said, "You busy?"

I shook my head.

"Boat ride?"

"Love to."

We loaded into the Zodiac, with Gunner assuming his *Titanic* pose at the bow, and I showed her the coastline, retracing my path. Explaining Fabio, the restaurant, and the beaches. Studying the clear water and white sand beaches, she pointed. "Like that one?"

It was deserted. Not a soul in sight. High cliffs on each side made it accessible only by boat. "Yep."

She raised an eyebrow and nodded, that sneaky smile bubbling to the surface. I laughed, anchored up, and we walked the shoreline. Her hand in mine and my heart in hers. Then Summer did what only Summer could do. She took off her cover-up, revealing the bikini she'd been telling me about. And pointed out her cellulite.

Which she did not have.

As the sun faded, I pulled the anchor and cranked the engine, which should have brought Gunner from wherever he'd been sniffing, but he didn't show so I cut the engine and called out, "Gunner! Here, boy!"

Nothing.

So I called again.

Still nothing.

We listened for several seconds when Summer tilted her head and said, "You hear whining?"

Come to think of it, I did. The sound was coming from the rocks above us.

I slid a Glock 17 behind my back, and we followed the sound up and into the rocks where, after winding through some granite boulders and crawling on our knees through thorns and briars, we found Gunner. He was lying on his side, his body wrapped around something small, black, and furry. "What you got, boy?"

Gunner was licking its head. The rest of its emaciated body was a mess of abrasions, scabs, and tics. Whatever this thing was, it was a mess. Fortunately for it, Gunner didn't think so.

I lifted its head and the cutest half-open eyes I'd ever seen looked back at me. It was too weak to whine, so it just blinked and waited for the inevitable. Which, again, thanks to Gunner, didn't come.

Not more than a couple weeks old, the little furball must have been dropped off by somebody traveling the highway higher up, and it had either crawled or rolled down here. Given his condition, he wouldn't make it long without assistance. He had twice as much skin on his face as he needed, which produced ample folds. Square head. Small ears. A mutt for sure, but from what I could tell, he looked to be part boxer, part terrier, and part shar-pei. Whatever it was, he was a cute combination.

I looked at Gunner. "What you want to do, boy?"

Gunner nosed the puppy toward me. I lifted him.

"You sure?"

Another nudge, then Gunner stood and began walking circles, herding me toward the boat. Summer stroked the puppy's back. "What if he doesn't make it?"

I glanced at the rocks and the hawks flying higher up. "Better he not make it with us than not make it out here on his own."

We washed him at the water's edge and began pulling tics. The attention brought him to life. He cracked his eyes open a little further, and despite what certainly had been a life of hardship thus far, he began licking us. Little guy was a bundle of affection. Having cleaned him as best we could, we set him in the water and let him wobble, trying to catch his balance. Finally, he just sat in the cool water and alternated licking each of us. Gunner circled around, standing between the puppy and the deeper water while Summer fed him crushed-up pieces of Gunner's food, which I'd had in a bag in the boat. The little guy devoured every piece.

Gunner stood alongside, letting the puppy lean against him. Every few seconds he'd stoop down and lick his head or back. And when he fell over, Gunner nudged him upright so he wouldn't drown.

After we fed him, I climbed aboard the Zodiac and set him on my lap. Where he fell fast asleep. Snoring within seconds. Noticing the speed with which he'd taken to me, Summer put an arm around me. "You got a plan for our new little buddy?"

"Still trying to figure that out."

She ran her fingers through my hair, which was one of her ways of telling me she knew something that I did not. And that I needed to know it. I'd never been all that quick in the ways of women, but I wasn't an idiot either. I smiled. "I have a feeling you know something I should probably know."

She smiled. "Every little boy should have a puppy."

"Yes." I laughed. "Yes, they should."

CHAPTER 82

Sister Catalonia took us to a vet in town who checked out the puppy and gave him a few shots. She said he was probably five or six weeks old and wasn't long for this world when we found him. Another twenty-four hours and he'd have died from exposure and starvation, but from what she could tell, he would recover. TLC, a steady diet of good food, and some medicine and he'd be on the mend. Good as new. Thanks to Summer's Google-sleuth skills, we then wound our way to Puppy Heaven because she thought he needed a few things. And evidently he did, because in about fifteen minutes we checked out with two hundred fifty dollars' worth of puppy food, a collar, a leash, and little treats that promised strong bones, nails, and teeth. Loading into the van with Sister Catalonia, who was laughing out loud at the sight of all our bags, Summer said, "Oh, one more thing," and ran back inside only to reemerge moments later with two little stainless steel bowls, a chew toy, and some more treats that she thought smelled good. That's when I starting laughing out loud.

Returning to the convent, we had two hurdles. Well, three actually. The third was how to get this little guy back into the United States without any kind of paperwork whatsoever, but since we were flying private, I figured we could hedge that little problem. Worst case, I could slip him into a backpack and escape across the tarmac. Getting him home was the least of my worries. It was the first two I needed some help with.

I found Shep at the water's edge. He was fishing with Uncle Clay. They were in the process of filling a cooler for tonight's fish fry under Bones's watchful eye. When I sat down next to Shep, the shiny, black, mostly sleeping furball in my arms piqued his curiosity. He set his pole down and looked up at me, asking without asking. So I set the puppy in his lap. The puppy, finding another gullible sucker, climbed up, or rather fumbled up, Shep's chest and immediately began licking his face, which brought the most delightful and innocent giggle out of Shep. At this point, I knew our troubles were over. I just needed Shep to know that. By now, Shep was lying on his back while the puppy licked his face off.

"I was wondering if you'd do me a favor?"

Shep looked at me around the dog, who was now standing on one shoulder nibbling on an ear. "Sir?"

"I was wondering if maybe you'd keep an eye on my little friend here."

Shep sat up and looked at the puppy, then back at me. "Really?"

"Yep."

"For how long?"

"Well, see, that's the thing. I don't know. I travel a lot and he's pretty young and going to need a steady buddy. Somebody who's there all the time. Somebody to feed him. Take him out. Bathe him. Somebody to hang with. You know, be a pal."

The puppy had circled back and was now licking his nose. Shep nodded. "I can do that."

"You sure it's not too much trouble?"

Shep shook his head amid the giggles.

"Well, if you get tired of him, you can just give him back."

He considered this. "I think I'm okay."

The knot between these two was getting tied pretty fast. "But." My voice took on a serious tone. "We have one problem."

Shep clutched the puppy as if he were afraid someone was going to take him away. "Sir?"

I stroked the little guy's head. "We can't go around calling him Puppy. Or Dog. Or whatever. The little guy needs a name. Names matter. It's one of the most important things ever. So I was thinking maybe you'd like to name him, seeing as how you'll be taking care of him."

Shep looked at the puppy, rubbed his head with both hands, then lifted him up and held him eye to eye. Sizing him up. Causing the soon-to-be-named puppy to slobber on his cheek. Shep asked me, "Where'd he come from?"

So I told him the story, starting with Gunner and finding him in the rocks, then taking him to the vet and ending up back here.

"He was all alone?"

I nodded.

Setting him down, Shep looked at Summer, then me. Then Summer again. Then back at me. I could tell he wanted to say something but wasn't sure if he should. "It's okay. You can say it."

He held the puppy inches from his face, then kissed his wrinkled muzzle and tucked him like a football under one arm where he fit perfectly. Finally, he said, "Atlas. I think we should call him Atlas. 'Cause . . ." He was quiet a minute, then he looked up at me. "Him and me . . . We were both alone and carrying a lot when you found us."

I choked back a flood of emotion and wrapped my arm around him. It was perfect. "I like it. It's a good name." Shep smiled, and I thought I saw his chest expand an inch or two. Like he'd done something. Which he had. "A really good name."

After about five minutes of rolling around in the sand, Shep lifted Atlas and said, "Dad?"

The word bounced around my chest, finally coming to rest inside my heart. "Yeah, big guy?"

"If you like"—he paused, finally nodding with certainty—"I can keep him for you." Another pause. "Forever."

"I'd like that." I kissed his forehead. "And I think Atlas would like that a lot."

When I looked up, Clay was standing over us, his handkerchief wiping his face. He blew his nose, folded the handkerchief, and returned it to his back pocket, all while shaking his head. "Somebody's cutting some onions up in here." Summer was in even worse shape while Bones sat smiling, sipping wine, and staring out across Majorca.

CHAPTER 83

O ver the following days, Bones relayed more of what he'd learned while under Frank's "care," as he liked to call it. Snippets here and there he picked up on. Frank never thought Bones would make it out alive, so he wasn't too careful in what he revealed. In fact, the opposite was true. In an attempt to let his brother know how smart he was, he shared quite a lot. Frank was, in fact, a genius. That was never in doubt to us. Only to Frank.

His seven generals were still out there, and while Bones had been laid up, he was pretty certain they were vying to keep their spot, if not to grab the top spot. All-out war would soon erupt—if it hadn't already. He even thought one or two might forge some sort of alliance, probably based on region or ethnicity, until the opposition was defeated. I told him that sounded a lot like politics. He nodded but made no verbal reply.

Otherworldly power and money were at stake. People weren't going to let those things slip through their fingers. That's when I told him again about Maynard. The phone calls. My suspicions. Bones considered this. "When we get home, I need to show you something." I knew there was more to his statement, but I let it go. We had time.

He wanted to know about Alaska and what we found. Specifically. So I told him. Ending with the rooms containing ropes, pulleys, and cameras.

"An arm's-length voyeur." He nodded.

"Looks that way."

Finally, he wanted to know about me. And when he asked, he made sure I was looking at him. "How're you?"

"Good."

He paused. "How long we been knowing each other?"

"Long time."

"So you'll understand if I don't believe you."

I smiled. A shrug. "Until a few days ago, not well."

"Why?"

"Because I watched you fall down a well and your leg slipped through my hand. You were gone. I'd failed you. We'd lost. And I'd lost you." I paused. "I had this recurring dream. Every night. Couldn't shake it. Frank shot himself and pulled you back with him. Then I lunged but I was always a microsecond too late. And then you were gone. The splash would wake me."

He stood, shuffled to me, wrapped his arms around me, and hugged my neck. This was no bro-hug. This was the real thing. Not father and son but in the same category. When he did, his strong arms making a vise like a bear, he whispered, "Love is a crazy thing. It's the most powerful thing in this universe or any other. Hell has no counterpart. But love is also the most painful thing. Has no equal." He placed both hands on my shoulders and stared at me. "And if it ever stops hurting, it's not love." He poked me in the chest. "Knowing the pain you will face as you lace up your boots, and yet you do, proves the immeasurable depth of your love. Which, in the end, is all that matters."

I waited.

"Bishop, you love well." A nod. "And I love you for it."

Summer walked in and found us having a moment. Rather than walk away, she joined. A group hug, just the three of us. "Bones?"

He smiled. "Yes."

"Need to talk to you about my man Murph here."

Gunner rolled over and put his belly and paws in the air, letting out a grunt.

Bones looked amused. "Been a little moody in my absence?"

"Just a smidge." Summer held my hand. "He's been carrying the weight of the world on these big, broad, beautiful shoulders, and the ridiculous thought that he somehow let you down. That he failed. More specifically, that he failed you. I need you to let him know that your trip back to get Frank was a one-way trip. Was from the beginning. You let him take you. And . . ." Summer looked at me and stroked my hair. "That he's not a fail-ure." She kissed my cheek. "Never has been."

Bones was listening to her but looking at me. For the first time since he woke up, a tear formed in the corner of his eye. After a minute, he spoke. "The longer we do this, the higher the stakes. The greater the hurt. The more at risk. Evil doesn't know what you know." He tapped my chest gently. "Doesn't have this. And the only way we defeat the darkness that rages is to love furiously. With all we got. All the time. Nothing held back. Never counting the cost." The tear broke loose and trailed down his face, where he wiped it with the back of his hand. "You do that better than anyone I've ever known. The names on your back and your books on the shelf are Exhibit A before the jury."

A pause. "I knew at your graduation, when I offered you options A and B, that A would lead to prosperity, a white picket fence, 2.5 kids, fast track to Admiral, three stars, joint chiefs. Consulting. Speaking. Power. Prestige. People would put you on a pedestal. Pay you a lot of money to speak to their organizations. Pat you on the back. Light your cigar. Life on a silver platter. I also knew you'd be miserable. You could excel in that world but you weren't cut out for it. But option B? I didn't sleep at all that night because I knew what option B would cost you. The toll it would exact. A big part of me wanted to protect you from that. Save you the pain. I knew it would be easier for you in this life if you never knew the pain of that life. But every time I decided to rescind the offer, I watched you in my mind's eye free the girls, escape the boat, only to hear the muffled scream behind you, then without hesitation run back. Back to fight a man you knew you couldn't best. To a fight you knew you'd lose." A single shake of his head. "I can't train that." He poked me in the chest. "Either that's in there or it's not." He shook his head again, then waved his hand as if gesturing to the whole world. "They'll never know what you know. The inexplicable joy of walking into the slave market, thumbing your nose at a master with no mercy, then ripping a door off its hinges and carrying a slave to freedom. And no one, not one single person either at Freetown or inked across your back, would fault you if you wanted to step back. Take a break. You've earned it. You need to hear that. It's okay to walk away. You've done more than most will in a hundred lifetimes."

I shook my head. "Bones, I don't want to walk away. My love has not grown cold. I just don't want to do this without you."

A nod. "I know. Me too. But that, too, is the risk we take. We risk hurt. Pain. Not coming home. We risk everything. Every time. This is what we do. 'The needs of the one . . .' isn't some pithy catchphrase I placed on a coin because I found it written in a book. I wrote it down and kept it close because it's true. Because when everything goes wrong, when my plans fail, when darkness is all I see, there is a truth that is more true than my circumstances. Very few people will leave the safety and security and comfort of the flock, of their family, of those they love, to walk across a battlefield to find the one sheep who's lost and then carry 'em home. Return them to the arms of those they love and who love them. This thing we do is a selfless act. The most selfless. And there's no one I'd rather do it with, but—and this is important, so listen up—we risk each other. Every time we walk out that door, we risk one of us not coming back. It's the hard truth. Evil doesn't care. In fact, it would like to use our love against us."

He stared out across the water. Toward the island where he was held in the dungeon as a boy. "Right now, somewhere on this planet, some evil nobody has kidnapped an innocent somebody and they're selling them to anybody with enough coin. Usually a wealthy, perverted miscreant who thinks they're entitled to do what they want, when they want, with whomever they want, and they ask no one's permission. What is lost in the transaction is that innocent somebody is raped for profit forty times in a week. Every hour on the hour. Some every thirty minutes. This is the evil of our age. Possibly the worst evil one human can commit upon another. We're not going to stop it, but we can make a dent. We can walk down in the basement and shine a light.

"Right this second, those innocent, tormented somebodies, those magnificent children of God, are lying on their backs praying that God would just kill them. End it right here and now. Why go on? Why live? What's the use? When He doesn't answer that prayer, they pray for someone to kick down the door. To lift them out of that hell. To make the bad man stop." He poked me in the chest again. "You are that answer." He looked at Camp. "Him too." He turned back to me. "In all the rescues, all the names inked across your back, name one who wasn't worth your life or mine. Just one."

I shook my head. "Can't."

"Correct."

I waved my hand across the same world before us. "So what do we do with the bad guys?"

The question surprised him. "What do you mean, 'What do we do with the bad guys?'"

I hesitated. "Frank got a pass from you. Why?"

He nodded in admission. Then he saw the bigger picture. How the experience with Frank had confused my conception of justice exacted. "Frank was the exception. My brother. I saw what he'd endured. I knew who he was before he became the Frank you knew. He also had information we needed, and I was never going to get it from him if I met power with power."

"Information? What are you talking about?"

"Later. The point is, there was only one Frank."

"But what about—"

He cut me off. "All the other Franks?"

I nodded. "Yes. What do we do with them?"

"Make the bad man stop. They don't go home. Don't pass Go. Don't collect two hundred dollars. Never rape again. Every last one. Send them to God. He can sort them out."

"Does this mean you're getting back in?"

He looked at me like I'd lost my mind. "Back in?" He chuckled. "I never got out."

I pointed over my shoulder at the island barely visible in the distance. "So Majorca changes nothing?"

"Not one thing." He held up a finger. "But only if I get to do it with you." He cracked half a smile and shot a glance at Camp. "I'm too old to start training somebody new. It was hard enough the first time."

The room had grown pin-drop quiet, and we had everybody's attention. The girls had quit giggling and Gunner's tail had quit wagging. Bones studied all the eyes staring at him. Then he spoke to all of us. "We are in the hope business. That is what we do."

I felt a presence behind me. Sister Catalonia. She'd been listening at the door. She put a hand on Bones's arm. "Time for meds."

Bones took the paper cup, obediently swallowed, and then let her check his vitals. When finished, she gave him an injection of something, then stood to leave. In an uncharacteristic move where he pressed into her personal space, he reached for her hand. Which she allowed him to take. It was an invitation not to leave. His voice was calm. "When you save someone's life, you become family. Our conversations are your conversations."

CHAPTER 84

Our presence did much for Bones's rehab. Lonnie said that medically, while he needed several months to heal fully, he would be ready to fly in a week or two. Bones heard that, put his feet on the floor, and began walking. We took turns. Laps up and down the hallway. Around the yard. Finally, after a week, he braved the steps down to the water. He made it to the beach, collapsed into the water, and soaked for an hour. "I can't believe I was stupid enough to walk down those steps."

I carried him on my back most of the way back up. And I loved every minute of it.

The Senate was scheduled to vote on Ashley's replacement in forty-eight hours. Bones kept staring at his watch. Finally, he stood, wobbled a little, then steadied himself. "Might be a minute before I get back up to the Eagle's Nest."

"Ride the lift. Much easier."

He began pulling on a shirt.

"We going somewhere?"

He nodded. "Georgia."

"Why?"

"Time to see an old friend."

"I don't think it'll do any good."

After a pause, he said, "You and I need to run back across the line one last time, to a man who thinks he's too broken to finish."

He was right. We had to try.

"He's got to rescind his resignation. Stop the vote. There's too much yet to be done. And we can't give the world to Maynard on a silver platter."

"You could just call him." I turned to Sister Catalonia for confirmation. "I'm not sure it's safe for you to . . ."

By now he was feeding one leg through his jeans. "He needs to see my face." Unexpectedly, he turned to Lonnie, knowing she wasn't about to let him out of her sight without passing him over to another qualified doctor. "You ever flown private?"

She shook her head. "No."

"Well, it'll ruin you for the ordinary, but it's something everyone should do."

She smiled but said nothing.

He started again, "Ever seen Colorado?"

Another shake of her head.

He fired a third shot across the bow. "Ever thought about treating trafficked children?"

She considered this. "I've acquired some leave time, but I would need to find a priest. Someone to hear my confession."

By now, he was putting on his boots. When he stood, he buckled his belt, adjusted his holster, press-checked the Glock 17 he'd borrowed from Camp, then reholstered and said, "I also priest."

I guess that was when I knew. Lonnie was married to God. Had been. He wasn't asking her to betray that. Nothing of the sort. But something was going on here at a deeper level. Something had happened in her rescue of him and, in some odd way, his rescue of her. The wound of her fiancé's death had never really stopped bleeding. Then she dragged some guy out of the ocean, hauled him home, patched him up, and read to him over the weeks—and somewhere in that mysterious exchange, Sister Catalonia unexpectedly fell for one of her patients. And her patient fell for her. Which neither one expected. I didn't know much about much, and I wasn't sure how things worked for priests and nuns, but I had a feeling Bones was about to ask God for her hand.

CHAPTER 85

Shep slept in my lap most of the flight. Drooling on my shirt. Must have been the ice cream just prior to takeoff. Summer said she liked that look on me. So I said, "What look is that?"

"The 'with kid' look."

It was the first time she'd ever really suggested she'd like children of our own. "Are you saying you want us to try to do that?"

She smiled. Raised both eyebrows. "I did wear that stupid bikini."

"It's not stupid."

"Well, I'm never wearing it in front of any other human being. It's for your eyes only."

She looked like she had something else to say but didn't. I pressed her. "So are you saying you want to try?"

"Well, you've had a lot on your plate, and I didn't really know the right time to—"

"Honey." About here I realized I was a little slow on the uptake when it came to women, especially those within my own house. I needed both a manual and a keeper. I whispered, "Do you want to try to have another child? One of our own?"

Summer tried to hide her true feelings. She bit her lip.

"I mean, can you? We're not spring chickens."

She weighed her head side to side. "Technically, I still can."

At this point, Angel saw us whispering. "What are you two lovebirds talking about?"

I had no idea how to communicate this. I gestured to Summer. "All yours."

Angel smiled. "Oh, you're talking about the thing, aren't you?"

Summer pulled her knees into her chest and tried to hide both tears and a smile. Her face was flushed. Angel shook her head. "You two should get a room."

"How is it that everyone knows the details of my personal life long before I do?" I guess I spoke loud enough to be heard by those around me, because Casey laughed.

She pointed at me. "'Cause when it comes to romance, Mr. Kick-Down-the-Door, you're dumb as a bag of hammers."

Lonnie, sitting to my left, laughed out loud.

Admittedly, I realized my skills were deficient when it came to "reading" the female species. I looked at Clay, who was about to say something. "Nope. Don't. I can't take it from all sides right now."

CHAPTER 86

The plane touched down in Georgia where Camp had a large SUV waiting. As we taxied to the hangar, I had a few lingering questions about Atlas but kept them to myself. Didn't want to worry Shep. I wasn't quite sure what Customs would do if they discovered his origins. When the door opened and Customs asked the pilots for passports, Shep wrapped Atlas up in his arms and, escorted by Gunner, marched off the plane like he owned the tarmac. Nobody said a word to him as he crossed the distance and then climbed into the SUV. Confirming the notion that no one in their right mind would challenge a kid, his puppy, and his dog. Watching them disappear, I heard Summer whisper, "Atlas . . . welcome home."

The ride to Ashley's farm was short. We were met by heightened security, though when the guards saw me, they tripped over themselves opening the gate. We rolled down the drive and parked in front of the antebellum house. Summer, Casey, Angel, and Ellie piled out first. It had been several weeks, and Summer and I thought the girls might welcome their presence. Somebody to talk to who wasn't a therapist and wasn't their folks. Somebody who'd been through it.

Clay and I exited next. Bones and Lonnie did not.

We were welcomed at the door and ushered inside. The girls upstairs. Clay and I to the office, where we found Aaron staring into the fire. Quietly. What looked like a cold, and full, cup of coffee in his hand. He had shaved and was smartly dressed, but his eyes were dark sockets, sunk in his head.

Evidence he hadn't slept in weeks. Tormented by a memory he couldn't shake, he'd aged a decade. The moment I looked at him, I knew I couldn't lift him and carry him to the finish line. That would require something or someone stronger than me.

He tried to speak, but his voice was a raspy whisper. "Hey, Murph, good to see you."

I put my hand on his arm. "You too, sir." The fire crackled. "How're the girls?"

He nodded. "Resilient. But sometimes they scream at night. We lay awake half the night waiting for the next one. Run in there to find they're still asleep." He shook his head. "We don't sleep much."

Beyond the door, I heard the rhythmic sound of a cane tapping hardwood floors.

Ashley spoke without looking at me. "Murph, if I forgot to thank you . . ."

"You did, sir. More than once."

A pause. "They vote in two days. Should be quick."

"Yes, sir. That's what I hear."

"It's good for the country."

That was not true, but I didn't tell him that.

He was staring and slowly started shaking his head. "I just can't shake the idea that they did all that to my girls while I sat here twiddling my thumbs. One of the most powerful men in the world, powerless to help my own family. What kind of a dad does that make me?"

"It makes you the kind that loves, sir."

His eyes never left the fire. When the door opened, Ashley continued to stare. He was lost. We'd lost him. When he did speak, I heard the depth of his pain. "We lost. Evil won. On my watch, evil . . ." He trailed off.

Then a hand touched his shoulder. A voice sounded from the stratosphere. "We don't fight because we always win, sir. We fight because . . . who else will?"

Ashley heard the voice, then slowly turned and looked upward. Seeing a ghost, he sat in silence several seconds. Then he stood, put his hand on Bones's arm as if to test whether it was real, then fell into his arms.

Like the rest of us, my friend Aaron could not control his emotions. Nor did he try. He didn't have the strength.

We talked for hours. Ashley coming to life before our eyes. His color returned. He even regained a hint of strength in his voice. Bones told his story. Then I relayed mine. Ashley sat shaking his head, staring at Bones as if he could not believe it. Which put him in good company. None of us could. Look up "too good to be true" in Webster's 1828 and you'll see a picture of us. Lonnie reminded us Bones needed to get his blood flowing, so we walked Ashley's pecan orchard and circled the lake. Bones's strength was returning, but he was by no means strong. He had a long way to go.

Dinner was an amazing moment. All of us, girls too, gathered around a ginormous picnic table. Fried chicken. Mashed potatoes. Sweet tea. I was a stuffed tic at the end. After key lime pie, Bones stood. The day had been long and we could tell he needed rest, but as was his nature, he was pushing through it, which he'd no doubt pay for tomorrow.

"I realize we popped in unexpected. But to be quite honest, this wasn't entirely a social call." Miriam, Ruth, and Sadie sat wedged between their mom and dad with Sadie sitting on her dad's lap. From what little I'd heard, she'd had the roughest go at the cabin. But from what I could tell, whatever had happened had done nothing to diminish her tender affection for her dad. She sat legs across his lap, arms around his neck, eyes trained on Bones. "I realize, maybe as much as anyone, that this is going to come across as insensitive given everything that has happened. But I don't have the luxury of time that would allow me to be more sensitive. So." He nodded at Esther as if asking her permission. "Please allow me to be blunt."

She nodded once. An offering. We all waited.

He turned back to Aaron. "Given my past, I have some idea what you're going through. Not entirely. Never had girls of my own. But I've . . . endured such hostilities. So I'm somewhat acquainted with the pain. That said, I'm here, we're here, to ask you, bluntly . . . to rescind your resignation. The president will gladly accept. The country will understand. Sir, I have information that you need to know. And if we ever needed you, it's now."

Bones let that settle and sat. Letting the focus of the room shift to Aaron. Sadie, who'd been resting her forehead on his chest, raised her head and looked at her dad. Finally, she placed a hand on his cheek and turned his face toward hers as only the child of the vice president could.

"Daddy?"

"Yes, angel."

"Are you quitting because of us?"

He considered this. As he did, I realized he had flinched when she said the word *quitting*.

Finally, he nodded. "Yes, I am."

"So the bad guys win?"

Evidently Aaron, whom I'd long thought to be one of the smarter individuals in any room he'd ever entered, had not considered it in those terms. Nor had he heard it communicated with such innocent honesty. "It means I'll get to be with you more."

Sadie didn't budge. "But are there other girls out there going through what we went through?"

Aaron nodded. "Yes."

"And you're a fighter pilot? Shot down planes?"

Another nod.

"And if you're vice president, you can help them?"

A third nod.

"So . . ." Sadie had always been the sassy one. Right here she was about to show why she'd earned the nickname Sass. "Why are we having this conversation?"

At this point, Esther laughed out loud, releasing an emotion that had been pent up for some time, suggesting she'd been having this same conversation with her husband but getting nowhere. Sadie pressed her forehead to his. "Daddy, we're safe. We're okay."

Ashley shook his head and palmed his face, finally sucking through his teeth. Then he kissed his daughter and quietly motioned to Stackhouse, who seldom left his side. "Call him."

Stackhouse handed him the phone. Ashley cleared his throat. "Yes, sir, good to talk with you, sir." A pause. "Yes, sir, they're doing fine. Healing up. Little by little. Well, yes, sir, I know they intend to vote. That's actually why I'm calling—"

The president said something that interrupted him. Ashley started again. "Well, sir, I realize this has been a bit of a roller coaster, but if you'd allow me, I'd like to rescind my resignation. Yes, sir. I still think there's some work yet to be done. Yes, sir, I'd like to continue to serve if you will let me. Yes, sir, I can be there first thing. We'll do that." The president said something that took Ashley by surprise. "Well, sir, if you wish, we can do that as well. I know Esther and the girls"—he eyed me and Bones—"along with the rest of my family, will be glad to see you. Yes, sir. See you then, sir. And yes, sir, she'll have some made for you."

He hung up the phone and turned to Esther. "The president was hoping you'd cook a key lime for breakfast."

The room laughed.

"He's coming here." He turned to his girls. "Wants to see all of you."

CHAPTER 87

Our working theory was simple. When Maynard did not get what he wanted—that is, the nomination—he'd let his hair down slightly and medicate his frustration. We thought he'd do that in a place where he was comfortable, where he had friends to pat his back and cry in his beer, and where he knew he would not get caught. Or at least, we had the feeling he'd be open to the opportunity in that place if it happened to present itself.

Which, thanks to Jess and Clay, it would.

In my absence, the team had attacked every piece of electronics tied to Maynard and his associates and anyone who worked for him. Most had been turned into listening devices. Which the team had been doing 24-7. Chances were good they knew more about Maynard than Maynard. And Maynard was starting to glance around the corner. At what was coming. At that amount of power. Which meant the freedom to do what he wanted, when he wanted, with whomever he wanted. The hints were subtle, but they were there if you knew what to look for. We not only had his texts, which were cryptic but slightly disturbing; we also had his sound. His tone of voice. Maynard sounded like a man who knew he had the winning lottery ticket but had yet to declare it publicly. Jess and BP had put together a montage of sound bites. In poker language, they were "tells." To Maynard, his plan had worked and he knew what no one else knew. That he had won. He was just waiting patiently for everyone else to come to that realization. He was about to summit the Everest of his own life. To conquer that which for so long had been off-limits.

His language took on a giddiness he was growing unable to mask. This was what we wanted. This euphoria. Because we had the notion it would turn to rage when we pulled the rug out from under him. And a raging man would do things he wouldn't otherwise.

To trap Maynard, we had to offer him something he was unlikely to resist at a time when his guard, which he had spent a political lifetime building, was down. A momentary lapse brought on by bitter anger with no outlet. No way to vent. We knew when the trap was sprung, Maynard would face a choice. Rage publicly or swallow it privately. We also knew he was far too controlled in public to ever open the valve of the pressure cooker, allowing others to see his weakness. To know the truth of him. But privately? He would want to satisfy an appetite. A sick miscreant like Maynard saw no difference. For that type of person, both prepubescent children and ice cream were simply tastes that satisfied. Something of little or no value to be enjoyed for one's own pleasure, eliciting no emotional connection, that once mostly consumed was best dispensed in the nearest trash can. Offering a few hours, or minutes, of satiation. That was all.

We knew for the trap to be enticing he had to overhear something he was not meant to hear, and that whatever he heard would have to pique his particular interest and offer zero risk. We also suspected it was highly possible that Maynard didn't arrange his own fetish pleasures. He might very well employ a staff member to do that for him who was just as perverted as he. But that, too, brought risk. What if the staff member ever tired of running that errand? That interference? Whoever that person was, he or she, and in earnest it was probably a he, must have committed some serious sin and Maynard kept the evidence as leverage. And that sin must have been so egregious that the errand boy would be continually willing to provide unwilling suitors for the senator, because the alternative of Maynard turning in that evidence or revealing it to the proper authorities brought with it the very real threat of life in prison—and even prison was not kind to child rapists. Proving once again that evil people used evil tactics to coerce other evil people to acquiesce to their evil demands. Fear of consequences was a powerful motivator. And among the evil, it may well have been the most powerful.

Stackhouse delivered the silver key and instructed us on how it was used. It wasn't inserted into a lock so much as presented to an attendant at a small desk, who then punched a button and opened a door, allowing access to the downstairs portion of the pub. If you had the key, you could go anywhere and take anyone with you. No questions asked. Just don't lose the key. Which was one reason they were about the size of a human palm. Made them harder to misplace.

The Gilded Kilt was famous for its location—an alley tucked between two old warehouses that had been converted to upscale condos and townhomes with starting prices north of a million. Across the street sat a long-forgotten and badly dilapidated theater that, thanks to Maynard, had received federal grants and now stood like a towering sentinel in a thriving artistic culture.

Jess and Clay rehearsed and dressed and had an Uber drop them off, which was not unusual. Maynard himself often Uber'd back and forth between the Capitol, the pub, and his apartment when it was late or he'd had one too many, which wasn't often but did seem to coincide with the passage of some legislation he'd helped draft or sponsor. When not hiring a car, Maynard also liked to walk, which, based on the data from his phone, involved multiple underground private tunnels frequented only by the people who owned the real estate above them. This back-and-forth pattern suggested Maynard either had paid off a lot of people, which was unlikely, or had hired some kid to hack a few systems and create an access code. Probably the latter. By following his phone, we established that Maynard could traverse ten blocks and never see daylight. Welcome down underground.

We also found something else of interest. He often stopped at one or several of the private residences above ground, where he would spend an hour or the night. The pattern was rather random but limited to one of seven condos. Ownership of the condos was registered to a Florida-based company that, when we peeled back all the baloney wrapped around it, was owned by none other than Waylon Maynard, proving that the senator had done well for himself. No, better yet, he was a real estate genius who owned somewhere north of, by conservative estimates, fifteen million in real estate. Which was a testimony to the power of compounding interest or suggested that maybe Maynard had other sources of income.

When Eddie and BP circled back around and revisited Maynard's cell data, crossing it with the numbers of his staff, an interesting pattern surfaced. One number had an uncanny ability to precede and follow Maynard at every condo. He'd arrive less than thirty minutes before, spend at most fifteen minutes, and then, just moments before Maynard arrived, retreat to a nearby condo or back to the Gilded Kilt until Maynard exited the premises. Then he'd return, spend maybe five minutes, and exit in a vehicle by way of the belowground parking deck.

Eddie tapped the screen revealing the pattern and said quietly, "Delivery and cleanup."

I knew what he was saying so I didn't ask him to explain.

Looking like elevator servicemen, Camp and I poked around and discovered that all seven condos were sparsely furnished. Each had a bed, a couple had a chair, one had a desk, but that was it. Nothing in the kitchen other than some wine and spirits, with emphasis on expensive single malt Scotch, and no food. Nothing to go bad or spoil. And while there were towels in the bathroom, there were no clothes. No pictures. No artwork. Nothing of a personal nature. The suggestion was that while someone might stop off here, no one lived here. These places weren't inhabited. They were used. Infrequently at most. The only items of interest we did find were cameras. Each condo contained at least four either tripod-mounted or arm-mounted telescoping cameras extending from the walls like lights in a dentist office. Lastly, multiple anchor bolts and pulleys had been sunk into each wall and ceiling, and various lengths of rope hung from each. The locations of the anchors puzzled us until Camp suggested that not only were the ropes to tie people down but to support people who couldn't support themselves.

"Heavily medicated kids?"

He nodded. "Drugged."

The setup mirrored what we found in Alaska although, in comparison, the Alaska setup had been thrown together last minute. This was more permanent.

Camp shook his head in disgust and spat. "This joker's going down."

I studied the room and wondered what horrors had been committed here. Who had suffered. How long. I spoke without looking at Camp. "I need you to do me a favor."

"Name it."

"When we kick down this door, I need you to stop me from killing this guy."

Camp considered this. "Okay, but since we're asking something of each other, I need you to do me a favor."

I looked at him.

"Keep me from doing it before you do. And"—he paused—"given that I'm younger, more agile, and quicker on the draw, you need to be on your A-game. I'm liable to be reholstered by the time you clear leather."

I chuckled. He had a point. "Maybe we should call Stackhouse."

Camp shook his head. "Nope. Those three girls are like family to him. Stackhouse would enjoy it too much and then we'd all be in federal prison together."

"Clay?"

Another shake of his head. "Bad idea. That man's got sledgehammers for fists."

"Maybe we should just dial 911."

He considered this too. "Well, who's gonna hold him and who's gonna dial?"

"That's easy. I'm holding. You're dialing."

A wrinkle appeared between his eyes as he studied the circus contraptions around us. "Maybe we could take turns."

I nodded as Gunner walked around the room, sniffing the walls, the hair on his back standing up. He didn't like this place any more than we did. We pulled the door closed behind us and the waiting began.

CHAPTER 88

Clay, an elderly, tall, white-haired, chisel-chinned, and handsome black man, and Jess, a young, fit, and incredibly beautiful white woman, would normally attract some second glances in most surroundings. Which the Gilded Kilt was not. As a result, the duo walked in the front door of the pub and actually fit right in. They found a booth with a bird's-eye view of both the front and back doors, along with the door that led downstairs into the key-holding-members-only club, and settled in for what we suspected would be Maynard's victory lap. Word had spread. Several hundred of Maynard's closest friends came out of the woodwork and packed every square inch, hoping to tilt one back with everyone's favorite senator and soon-to-be president.

Admittedly, our plan hinged on one thing over which we had no control. With the vote tomorrow, and the tally a mere formality, we felt certain Maynard would make one or two prime-time evening news shows, stop in at several political dinners or fundraisers where he'd slap backs and promise favors, and then possibly visit a late-night talk show. But not too late, because after he'd kissed enough babies and patted enough backsides, he'd end up here. Where he really wanted to be all along. Along with several other close-knit legislators who knew the real conversations, including cabinet appointments, would occur downstairs when the crowd wore thin. This meant timing was critical. We had to catch Maynard at his strongest, then crush him and capitalize on his weakness.

Ashley would be the nail in the coffin, and what better place to drive it in than the front steps of the house where Maynard planned to spend the next eight years. So Summer, Bones, and Stackhouse had returned to the Naval Observatory with Aaron to await our call. Which was a strange thought. The future POTUS awaiting our signal, who would then communicate with the current POTUS so that the two of them could tell the world that Vice President Aaron Ashley was not stepping away. Far from it. In fact, he was stepping back in the ring. We knew, given the story that had spread like wildfire of Ashley's heroic landing on the ice—in which he'd risked his own life to save his daughters—that Maynard could not compete. He'd have to bow out. Defer. Once again play the obedient servant, which was what he'd been all along, though we did not know his master.

Maynard thought his time had finally come. Ashley was about to tell him it had not. And while we thought he'd play nice in public, we hoped he'd come unglued in private.

Maynard arrived at 10:47 p.m. Earlier than I'd thought, but I guessed he was eager to celebrate. He'd made the rounds on the news channels, dropped in at two diplomatic dinners, and literally poked his head into one of the earlier nighttime talk shows before asking his driver to reroute to the Gilded Kilt.

Maynard entered to a prolonged and rousing standing ovation, but most were standing already as it was standing room only. A few of the news outlets had parked trucks out front in anticipation of adding to the 11:00 p.m. news cycle. Maynard, who was not necessarily a tall man, was ushered to the bar and then lifted on shoulders and set on top of the bar so that he might be seen by those in the back. Camp and I had thought we'd wait out Maynard's internal combustion from one of the private residences two or three blocks away, but then I realized I wanted to see the look on Maynard's face when Ashley pulled the rug out from underneath him. So we surfaced, donned ball caps, fake eyeglasses, and Georgetown hoodies, and watched with some enjoyment as Waylon Maynard, lifelong politician and the man destined to be the next president of the United States, was carried on the shoulders of staffers and placed on his bar-top pedestal amid shouts and earsplitting whistles.

When the applause quieted, the bartender, obviously a longtime friend, handed Maynard a microphone that would amplify his voice to the growing crowd outside. An unconventional site for a celebration of one of the most powerful men in the world, but organic nonetheless.

In interviews, Maynard had praised Ashley, his service, his commitment, his integrity. He'd also said how he had wished we as a country were not in this place. Replacing a broken man. He teared up talking about how he mourned the events of the last few weeks, and said continually how he was praying for the girls and knew firsthand that they were getting the care they needed. He then turned the corner and began speaking of himself. How, during his more than fifty years in this city, he'd always wanted to be the "people's president," which was just what he intended to be. A statement that brought down both the house and the ever-growing crowd outside.

"I believe there are some things we can do, and we can do them quickly, to get better. Be better." Maynard then listed those things as if he were reading them off a teleprompter in his head. Each one bringing more applause than the last. Finally, he said, "Honestly, I never thought I'd be here. Thought my time had passed. But if Vice President Ashley cannot serve, and I wish to God he could, then I will take up the mantle. I will serve."

Given the choice, polls showed people chose Ashley two to one over Maynard. But that was not an indication that they didn't like Maynard. They did. A lot. They simply adored Aaron. After what he and his family had endured, and how he'd come through it, they loved him all the more.

As the applause drowned Maynard out, I called the vice president. He answered, and given the noise, I had trouble hearing him. "Sir, this would be a good time." A pause. "And, sir, we're all pulling for you."

The line went dead just as Maynard loosened his tie, an action commensurate with the president of the people, and announced he'd like to buy the house a round, his first gesture that he was extending his hand across the aisle. "With a good beer." The crowd went nuts and then launched into a raucous chorus of "He's a Jolly Good Fellow," followed by three cheers. At the end of the third cheer, the forty-seven televisions mounted on every wall and angle in the pub flashed a "Breaking News" banner along the bottom. Every screen then switched to a nighttime shot of the front steps of the White House, where the president, in dark slacks and a sweater and ball cap, stood in front of a microphone. Next to him stood Ashley, wearing a lambswool fighter pilot jacket, with Esther at his side, her arm locked inside his.

CHAPTER 89

T he president was the first to speak. "We as a country have known some difficult times." He glanced at Ashley. "And some of our people have endured what I can only describe as inhuman trials." A pause. "There is no pain like the pain endured by our children. But out of pain, great men arise. And out of hardship, great leaders emerge. Ladies and gentlemen, my friend Aaron Ashley."

Now that the third cheer had faded away, the pub fell pin-drop quiet. No one whispered. No one shuffled. No one sipped. All eyes were trained on the screens.

After the obstacle course, when I really got to know Aaron, I saw a reservoir of strength in him that I'd rarely seen in other men. A deep well. Quiet confidence. While the last two months had chipped away at it, they had not cracked it. Nor had they cracked Ashley. In the spotlight, under the shadow of the people's house, my friend Aaron told the world of the unspeakable horror he and Esther had endured. That their girls had endured. Of the evil that lurked in the shadows.

"I've been tempted, most every day, to walk away. Circle the wagons around my wife and girls and live out our days quietly on our farm in Georgia. But a good friend of mine asked me the other day, 'What about all the other girls? The boys. Those praying for somebody to kick down the door and lift them out of hell. So . . ." He turned to Esther and allowed the cameras to focus on her. "We, I, have decided that as long as I am able, I will serve out my term. And, if you will allow me, take the baton from my good friend"—with that he put a hand on the shoulder of the president—"and serve as your next president."

I could not count the gasps inside the bar. Or the involuntary curse words muffled below and above breath. Maynard, still standing on the bar, turned three shades of purple. Then Ashley put the cherry on top. And I have to take some credit here, because I told him this would be the pièce de résistance. Further, I asked him to say it because I wanted to see the contortions of Maynard's face. "To my good friend Waylon Maynard. Since I first stepped foot in this great city, you befriended me. Showed me the ropes. Helped me, a man with little to no political experience, navigate this world. In over two decades of friendship, I've valued your wisdom. Your service. Your love for this people and for this country. And now, more than ever, I'm going to need your help. You have championed me every step of my career, and you have my heartfelt thanks and gratitude."

While the room was watching the screen, I was watching Maynard, who looked like he wished a hole in the earth would open and swallow him. He looked like he wanted to be anywhere but where he currently was. He also looked like his blood pressure was nearing dangerous levels and like he would soon explode. The crowd, sensing the tension but loving Ashley more than Maynard, raised an obligatory glass to Maynard, who slithered off the bar and sought to disappear into the crowd, which he obviously couldn't do. So he did what we were quite certain he would. He went downstairs. Where it was safe. Where there were no cameras. Only allies. Where he could switch from beer to something a good bit stronger.

To a not-so-rousing round of applause, Maynard waved to the crowd, approached the door, which was quickly opened, and descended the steps to the belly of the Gilded Kilt. Where presidents and legislators and cabinet members and judges had been quietly making decisions and laws and helping run the country for close to two hundred years.

Camp and I did not have a key, but we didn't need one. We didn't think he'd be there long. We exited out the back and began following what we surmised would be Maynard's path as he tucked tail and disappeared into his predetermined set of tunnels, which would keep him out of the public eye, where he could lick and medicate his wounds. Jess and Clay, on the other hand, had watched the news conference from downstairs. From the very bar where Maynard would receive his first and second Scotch. Both doubles. Normally, Maynard controlled his consumption, waiting until he was alone to dive into numbers two and three. But not tonight. And who could blame him? Maynard received his third, then settled into the large booth along a far wall with several other consoling men. Close confidants. Maynard sat with his back to Jess, who was sitting shoulder to shoulder with Clay. This meant their whispers could be heard by Maynard. When Maynard leaned back and began to sip, she made her move. We knew we couldn't just bait him once. In order for the hooks to be set deep, we'd have to tempt him, then bait him, then set the hook.

Jess whispered, "The client didn't show."

Clay responded. "And the product?"

"Medicated. Unaware."

Clay paused. As if calculating a next move. "Ages?"

Jess hesitated, as if making sure no one could overhear. "Eight and ten."

With that, Clay exited the booth en route to the bar while Jess sat staring through sunglasses in an already dark room. We knew we had his attention when he shot a glance at Jess, who pretended not to notice nor be impressed. Her mind was elsewhere. She was not focused on Maynard. She was focused on how to fix a problem. A big problem.

When Clay returned, she scribbled a series of letters and numbers on a napkin, followed by two codes. One beneath the other. She did so at an angle that allowed Maynard to see that she was sharing a secret with Clay and no one else. Finally, she slid the napkin to him. "You have about four hours before they wake and make life difficult." An intentional pause. "They are pristine and untouched. I will find another buyer. I just started the auction. I don't know what happened to the last. Fifty thousand is a lot to walk away from."

Clay nodded.

"Can you hold and monitor off-site until we close the auction tomorrow evening?"

Clay read the napkin, crumpled it, and nodded in the affirmative. "Yes, but it'll be two hours before I can get there. Need to attend to something else first."

At this point, Jess herself nodded and then left without so much as a goodbye. Leaving Clay to sip alone and paying no attention to Maynard, who according to Jess had become a peeping Tom. She could see from her new vantage point that Maynard was paying close attention to the napkin.

We knew that in order for Clay to leave a crumpled napkin with information on the table where it could possibly be found by someone bussing the tables, that information had to make no sense to anyone. Just a row of numbers and letters. Unless you owned a condo three blocks away and were familiar with how the rooms were lettered and designated. Eight floors were A–H, and the rooms were every ten with the added twist of north or south. So B20S was second floor, second room, on the south wing. E100N was the fifth floor, tenth room, north wing. And so on. But getting in was equally as complicated. The parking deck and elevator shared the same four-digit security code, while the room had its own six-digit code. So G60N followed by a four-digit and a six-digit code would only make sense to someone in that building. Otherwise it was Greek. Fortunately for us, we knew Maynard owned two units in that same building.

Clay finished his drink and, occupied with thoughts elsewhere, left his seat while allowing the napkin to fall onto the booth. Where Maynard could see it out of the corner of his eye.

Clay exited the room while Maynard's hand discreetly reached and clasped around the napkin. He held it several seconds before glancing at it. When he did, he leaned his head back, seemed to smile slightly, then pulled out his phone and sent a text.

Which we thought he would.

Ten minutes later, a middle-aged staffer left the pub having never said a word to Maynard, walked through the underground, and then took the elevator up to G60N. He used the combination and let himself in. Camp and I knew we couldn't very well use two live children as bait, so we did the next best thing. We made it look like we had two young children asleep side by side in a king-size bed in the massive master suite. The man, whose name was Bob Ladstrom, a nearly thirty-year staffer who'd been by Maynard's side for the entirety, entered the room and spied the two child-like lumps curled up in each other's arms beneath the massive down comforter. The covers had been pulled up so that only the wigs showed above the edge. Ladstrom tiptoed to the edge of the bed and was in the process of pulling back the cover when my right fist encountered his left jaw.

Thirty seconds later, after having read a few of the back-and-forth messages shared by Ladstrom and Maynard passed through the end-to-end-encrypted Signal app, I did my best to sound like Ladstrom as I sent Maynard a text. Which, in reality, was little more than a cut and paste from several previous. "All clear. Enjoy."

Jess then reported that Maynard polished off his drink, slapped a few backs, and left in a hurry. Out the back door. Through the tunnels.

We had set the hooks. Deep.

CHAPTER 90

Maynard scurried like a rat through the tunnels without being told where to go. He knew them by heart. He rode the elevator, exited on the seventh floor, and turned north. He was wasting no time. He entered the condo quietly and walked directly to the master suite, where the lights were dim. He saw the two figures in bed, but unlike Ladstrom, he did not investigate. That had already been done. By his trusted friend. So Waylon Maynard, respected senator and friend of the people, undressed to his birthday suit and then walked to the bedside where he stood looking down. Having been conquered but still able to conquer.

Right about there, my fist broke his jaw.

Smart and powerful men are not always smart when it comes to their physical desires, especially after they've been made to feel less powerful. Add to that a sense of entitlement and a healthy dose of anger, and you have the perfect recipe to convince a six-term senator with bad intentions to stand naked over a king-size bed where two innocent children lay sleeping under a heavy haze of medication. He thought he could get away with it.

My fist convinced him he could not.

I had him tied to a chair at the foot of the bed and limited his movements to facial expressions. When he came to, he was not happy. He was also as naked as the day he was born. Which, once he realized he was being recorded, he liked even less and began touting the magnitude of trouble I was in holding a sitting senior senator and future presidential candidate against his will. Then he said something about how I would not like the federal prison system and how he would use every lever within his power to make sure they put me next to some horrible people. I tuned him out and let him spit all over himself.

Senator Vesuvius oozed hatred for several minutes. Kicking. Screaming. Promising retribution to the third and fourth generation. Add to that a goodly amount of alcohol, along with a little something Camp injected into his system to help loosen his tongue even further, and he was fit to be tied and had to stop and catch his breath. At which point I suggested he might want to consider adding some cardio to his nonexistent fitness routine.

After ten minutes of speaking some of the most evil words I'd ever heard in my life, the senator finally took a moment to look around and realize his predicament. When he saw the picture more clearly, he turned to me. "How much?"

Camp spoke for both of us. "Hundred million."

"Done. Account number?"

Camp sat typing into his laptop. "You tell me yours and I'll tell you mine." Amazingly, the senator obliged without hesitation. Gave Camp the account and routing numbers and passcode. Camp, curious to see if it actually worked, entered all the numbers and pressed return. When he checked the account seconds later, it read, "Pending." He nodded. Almost in surprise. "I think it worked."

The senator huffed. "Of course it worked, you moron. Now cut me loose. And get the . . ." He rattled off several cusswords that expressed his great displeasure.

Thanks to Bones, Freetown had set up accounts worldwide. This allowed us to seize assets pretty much anywhere and use them for whatever purposes we deemed necessary. Without government interference. Were we acting above the law? Yes. Of course we were. Something I had no problem with when I was staring at degenerates like Waylon Maynard. Camp was accessing one of our Swiss accounts, and although I highly doubted Ashley would let us, we had talked about giving the money to Miriam, Ruth, and Sadie. I figured we could have that conversation later.

When the word changed to "Executed" and the account balance showed the nine-figure increase, Camp nodded. "Done."

I pulled a chair up in front of Maynard and turned it around, resting my arms on the back rest and staring quietly while he sat there exposed to the world. He did not like the silence. That was when he really started bargaining. "He told me about you."

Of course I wanted to know who "he" was, but I waited. I figured it'd spill over eventually.

"Said you could ruin everything." He laughed. "Which of course you did." More laughter. "Which we were all so glad to hear. I couldn't wait for that demented sick man to die."

I thought that was the pot calling the kettle black, but I kept my mouth closed.

"I was there the day you showed up. Frank finally had Bones."

There it was. The piece I'd been waiting for. I kept quiet.

"I don't know how you got to him, but I'm so glad you did. Wish I'd been there."

This was about to get good. I almost wished I had popcorn.

Maynard began to see the writing on the wall. "I'm one of the seven. Does this make sense to you?"

I nodded, while also slightly amused. Breaking his jaw hadn't affected how much he talked, but it had definitely changed the sounds coming out. They sounded more garbled. Less controlled. Maynard was coming apart. Fraying at the seams. And he knew it.

"The other six are even now jockeying for position. To secure, expand, and eliminate. If you want to know everything, and I do mean everything, what can you offer me?"

With that, the door opened and Aaron Ashley walked in. Fresh from his press conference. Still wearing his lambswool jacket. Maynard turned, his eyes focused, and all the color drained out of his body. "Aaron, I didn't know. I swear to—"

Aaron raised a hand while Maynard sat in a cold, frothy sweat. I studied the juxtaposition. One man had spent his life hell-bent on power. Now his house of cards had come crashing down and he sat here humiliated, realizing he was not in charge and all his conniving had come to nothing. His only goal had been to dominate, subjugate, and control. The other man had never grasped for power. Had never assumed anything. He had served. Fought for, with, and alongside. Yet here he stood. He had ascended. Soon to be one of the more powerful men in the world. A striking contrast.

I stood, and Aaron sat in my chair. Eye to eye. Staring at Waylon. I wondered what he'd do and how much physical restraint it took to not physically destroy the man who had paid for and personally violated his daughters. Whatever the case, Aaron didn't lay a hand on him. Which said a lot. He turned to the table next to him and spun Camp's computer so Maynard could view the screen. Then he pushed Play.

Having backdoor access to the computers in Maynard's Virginia farm-house, Eddie and BP had uncovered a treasure trove of videos of Maynard doing unspeakable things, which, we can only assume, he had stored for his later enjoyment. Maynard's problem was simple. The current montage would put him in prison for the next thousand years. After several uncomfortable minutes for Maynard, the images switched to the Alaska cabin. Jess had crafted the video in such a way that Ashley was not forced to watch sadistic actions committed on his daughters but Maynard was forced to watch himself commit perverted and demented actions upon the daughters of the very man sitting in front of him.

I wasn't sure how Ashley refrained from hurting Maynard. But he did. He exercised a restraint I didn't possess.

When the video looped through a second time, Aaron stood and pressed Return. Doing so transmitted the video to local news agencies. The faces of all the girls and boys had been blurred. Maynard's had not. In ten minutes, the court of public opinion would be calling for Maynard's head on a platter. Camp then opened the door, and Bill Stackhouse walked in with local police. About then was when Maynard's world crashed to a halt. The plan was to allow the legal process to unravel all of Maynard's hopes and dreams, and then we'd offer him a deal to move him to a facility where very talented people could mine him for information, all while being watched over by my cell-phone friend Steve. Steve said he'd be delighted. Things did not look good for Maynard.

Camp, Gunner, the vice president, and I walked out into the cool night air as Bones emerged from the shadows. Bones was the first to congratulate Ashley. "Congratulations, sir."

Ashley had aged. And while his strength was returning, he had not escaped the DC swamp unscathed. The internal scars showed on his face. He nodded, made almost no expression, and stared at the three of us. "You three will be receiving a commendation. A medal. Our nation's highest. I'll hang it around your neck in my office. You get to touch it. Stare at it. Then hand it back and we'll keep it for fifty years, at which time, if you're still alive, you can have it back. Tell your grandkids about it." He paused, looked each of us in the eye. Ashley had come far. The light was returning to his eyes. "I am in your debt. More than you'll ever know."

While Stackhouse loaded a kicking and screaming and naked Maynard, which was not a pretty picture, into a van, I made a phone call. He answered after seven rings. And then, only a whisper. "Yes, sir."

"In about a week, you're going to get a new cellmate. Presidential directive. He's an unlikable fellow. In fact, you won't like him at all. But if you've ever wanted a shot at redemption, this is it. Let me know what you find out. I have a feeling the longer he stays and the more uncomfortable he becomes, the more he'll say. He'll use it as leverage. Thinking somehow his information will give him access to more comfort. Eventually it will, but in the short term, he's yours."

"He got a name?"

"You'll figure it out."

A pause. "Hey, Murph."

"Yeah."

"I know I'm on thin ice, but can I ask a favor?"

"You can ask."

"My daughter. She's . . . well, let's just say she didn't win the lottery in the dad category, so she's a bit of a tough nut to crack. Anyway, she's crazy brilliant smart. Can code anything. Never seen a computer she couldn't hack. Having some trouble getting into a few colleges because her test scores are subpar."

"I thought you said she was smart."

"She is. She hates tests. So she answers a few questions and walks out."

"So she's got authority issues?"

"I'm to blame for that. I was never there. Anyway, she can't afford the good schools. She pretends to be a Georgetown student, wears the sweatshirt, works at a coffee shop, lives on somebody's couch, goes to lectures, but she's not. She hacked their system, got herself accepted, awarded herself a tuition scholarship, and is somewhere in her junior year, but she's bored out of her mind and flirting with darkness and dark people. Can you help her? Anything is better than what she's doing. I'm afraid if she continues down that path, it'll be a while before she gets off. By then, it'll be too late. I've tried but she won't listen to me, which is understandable. I was not, am not, a good dad. She's had a rough go but she rescued every stray cat in our neighborhood when she was a kid and never met a bully she didn't stand up to. She's a fighter. And she deserves a chance. I realize I can't do anything for you—I have no right to ask you—but she's my daughter."

"I make no promises."

"Thanks, Murph."

"Stay in touch."

CHAPTER 91

The coffee shop doubled as a bar under the unique and catchy name of "Caffeine and Alcohol." I pushed open the door and found a single barista making espresso with one hand and pouring draft beer with the other. She had green and purple hair, a mixture of tattoos, black fingernails, and a "don't even think about messing with me" look on her face. She also matched the picture Steve had texted. When I sat at the bar, she stared at me through sunglasses and never asked what I wanted. When I didn't order, she moved on. I'd seen people treat mosquitoes the same way.

"I hear you're pretty good with a computer."

She chuckled but felt no need to respond.

I pointed at her Georgetown hoodie. "Hacked the mainframe. Awarded yourself a scholarship."

She stopped wiping down the bar and lifted her sunglasses, which revealed beautiful eyes. Causing me to wonder why she ever covered them up. But then, I knew a thing or two about people who didn't want to be seen.

She did not look impressed. "What do you want?"

I raised my phone and held up a picture of Steve.

To which she held up her middle finger and told me that both I and her dad were number one in her heart.

I was tired, and it'd been a long few days, so I cut to the chase. "Where does your road end?"

The space between her eyebrows narrowed and a wrinkle appeared. "What do you care?"

"You're wasting your skill set. I'm here to offer you a place to put it to good use. A place to belong."

She paused, pushed her sunglasses back down over her eyes, and then emptied the tray from the dishwasher and loaded another.

"How do you know I won't rob you blind?"

"I don't."

She chuckled. "Who are you and what do you want?"

I handed her a card with a phone number. That was it. "I work with a team of people, and we help rescue those who are in bad places with bad people who can't rescue themselves. We could use your help."

"If you're so good, why do you need me?"

"Honestly, we don't. We have better people than you. People who can code circles around you and without all the drama. But they might be able to teach you."

She huffed but didn't give me the finger again, which suggested I'd at least intrigued her. "Why?"

"Because I know your dad."

"Know him?"

"I caught him when he was doing bad things."

"You put him in prison?"

I nodded.

"Then you have my thanks."

"He asked me to come see you. Asked me to help you find your way out of this dark place."

"What if I like it here?"

"People in hell like it until they get thirsty. When they find there's no water, they tend not to like it anymore."

"Did you practice that? Because it sounded rehearsed."

I waited while the rest of the vinegar drained out.

"Look, dude, I don't go home and hook up with older men." She pushed my card back across the counter. "And I don't want anything from you."

I left the card. "If you change your mind, call this number. We'll fly you out. Give you a tour. A place to live. And maybe, in your case, we'll give you a reason for being you. Not to mention, we're about an hour and a half from your dad's prison."

"Why would I ever want to see him again?"

"Look, I put him there. He deserves to be there. At least for now. He also made some bad choices and he's trying to help you not make the same ones. But he asked me to come here, so I did."

This time something glistened in the corner of one eye. A break in the dam? "Why?"

I stood and zipped up my jacket. It was cold outside. I could see my breath. "Because the needs of the one outweigh those of the ninety-nine."

CHAPTER 92

It was 4:00 a.m. and I was way past tired, but Bones had a bee in his bonnet. So Camp drove while Bones sat quietly in the back. En route to the hotel, he rerouted us. To Arlington National. Even though it was normally closed this time of morning, Stackhouse led the way and opened it for us. We unloaded and climbed the small hill while Gunner sniffed the surroundings. He didn't like it now any more than he did the first time.

The air was cold. Night quiet. Grass damp. Moonlight on marble. We stood staring at the stone while Bones studied the ground. Brow furrowed. Slightly comical look on his face. Trying to come to grips with the surreal thought of his casket sitting empty six feet below. "What'd you put in there?"

"Mementos. Stuff to remember you by."

"Anything valuable? Maybe we should dig it up."

"You sure you want the attention?"

Camp spoke next. He dug in his pocket and extended a large silver key to me. "Maynard's. Lifted it off Ladstrom. Figured he wouldn't need it where he's going."

I hefted it. Years in someone's or several someones' pockets had worn it smooth. I tried to read the names of who had given it to whom, but several letters were worn and it was difficult to read under the moonlight. "You figure out who gave it to Maynard?"

"Guy named Beetle Baswell."

The name meant nothing to us but evidently meant something to Bones, who chuckled and shook his head. "What a tangled web we weave . . ."

I waited.

Bones looked at each of us. "Beetle Baswell was one of Frank's many aliases. He liked first and last names that started with the same letter. Something about the alliteration." A pause. "Richie Rockwell and Cory Coxbury were two more. There were many others."

It felt weird to be talking with Bones while staring at his grave. Felt like we were cheating something. "You mean to tell me that your brother Frank gave Maynard his membership to the Gilded Kilt?"

Bones spoke without looking at me. "Makes sense. Frank prized information above all else. He knew this was where to get it. He also knew he had Maynard on a string so he could leverage whatever video evidence he had to keep Maynard on a short leash. Which he did. For over twenty years."

We stood quietly a minute while the enormity of what we were staring at stared back at us. Bones was quiet. Finally, he looked at me. "We have kept David Bishop a secret for a long time. And his secret is safe with us. Likewise, it would be best if we could keep Ezekiel Walker dead until such time as we want to let our enemies know he is not."

I understood. It made good sense.

Bones again. "When I show you two what I'm about to show you, you will understand that it will be best for us and bad for our enemies if they all think I'm still in that box."

We nodded.

"If I'm dead, I can operate more freely in the shadows. Which will help when you two are kicking down doors." Bones had taken to Camp. A burgeoning relationship I enjoyed watching. He turned to face him. "I've been out of the loop awhile, but are you about to be late for your own wedding?"

Camp nodded. "T-minus thirteen hours and counting."

Bones turned, put his back to his grave, and walked away. "Then we should probably hurry."

PART III

"You shall be called the repairer of the breach,
the restorer of streets to dwell in."

—*Isaiah 58:12*

CHAPTER 93

The chapel was packed. Not having to reserve venues meant the planning came together quickly. All of Freetown had dressed for the occasion and filled every square inch, while Camp was a nervous wreck. He was wearing his dress whites and his chest was covered in medals. Something else he didn't feel the need to explain. His groomsmen were all fellow SEALs who had served in his platoon. Alongside. A unique brotherhood. I felt fortunate that he'd chosen to work with us. Camp was special. One in a million. Which was exactly what Casey deserved.

When the music started, Bones seated Summer and then sat alongside her. The only person in the room with more medals than Camp. Which I thought fitting. Summer, meanwhile, was stunning. I had a difficult time taking my eyes off her. She was glowing. How that beautiful and magnificent woman ever married me I'd never know. When she winked at me, Camp noticed. He whispered, "You're blushing."

I wasn't prepared for what happened next. The wedding party. Angel and Ellie. The two processed down the aisle arm in arm, causing me to wonder if I'd be able to stand up when I was asked, one day, to give either of them away. I was pretty sure I wouldn't be able to make it through that.

Rounding out the party, and taking his ever-loving time, strode Gunner, cheeky as ever. He was escorting Shep, who was escorting Atlas, who was still trying to figure out how to get his big paws to move in a straight direction. Attracted to everything that glittered or moved or breathed, the ring bearer walked a pinball path toward the altar, stopping at every hand for a pet or a stroke. The levity was good for the soul. Gunner led Shep and Atlas to Summer's side, where she lifted them onto the pew and tucked them in close to her. Then Gunner took his place next to me.

The music changed to "Canon in D," and Clay appeared at the back of the chapel. I whispered to Camp, "Your turn's coming."

It was a fun, and beautiful, moment.

Everyone stood, and Casey—a vision—took Clay's arm, and the two began that long, slow walk into the rest of her life. I wouldn't soon forget it. Watching Camp watch her. His tears. Hers. It was one of those beautiful moments when the sun stopped and all the world held its breath.

I remembered the shower and lifting Casey off the floor. Her faint pulse. The way she laid her head on my neck. Breathed once. Then twice. How she clung to me while her life departed. Then returned.

I remembered the hospital and how she held my hand. In disbelief. Given her past, given all the men who had used her and discarded her, who would rescue her? Who would ever value her? Who could? She walked slowly. Elegantly. Was anything more beautiful than a bride presented to her groom?

Then there was Clay. The statesman, the gentleman of Freetown. Tux. Black patent leather shoes. White beard. Beaming. A man who understood freedom. And who better to present the bride?

Halfway down the aisle, Casey's tears broke loose. Clay, ever watchful and not the least bit hurried, stopped, pulled out his handkerchief, and handed it to her. Casey, in perfect self-effacing fun, accepted it, wiped her face, blew her nose—which brought much laughter—and then waited for him to resume their walk. Which he did.

When they reached me, Casey stood like an angel who had flown too close to the ground. Camp, teetering on my left, was close to hyperventilating, while Clay had become our anchor. He held us all together. We made a beautiful patchwork. A mosaic of broken shards now indistinguishable from the whole.

I spoke to the audience. "You may be seated."

While they did, I marveled at Casey. A revelation. Never had I seen a bride so brilliant. So full of life. So deserving of that dress. She was a mixture of smiles and tears and laughter and a wadded-up, snotty handkerchief. A beautiful expression of a messy life in bloom. Which she was. Which we all are.

The music stopped, and it was my turn, so I spoke. "Dearly beloved, we have come together in the presence of God to witness and bless the joining together of this man and this woman in holy matrimony. The bond and covenant of marriage was established by God in creation, and our Lord Jesus Christ adorned this manner of life by His presence and first miracle at a wedding in Cana of Galilee. It signifies to us the mystery of the union between Christ and His church, and Holy Scripture commends it to be honored among all people.

"The union of husband and wife in heart, body, and mind is intended by God for their mutual joy, for the help and comfort given one another in prosperity and adversity, and when it is God's will, for the procreation of children and their nurture in the knowledge and love of the Lord. Therefore, marriage is not to be entered into unadvisedly or lightly, but reverently, deliberately, and in accordance with the purposes for which it was instituted by God.

"Into this holy estate, Camp and Casey come now to be joined."

While part of me spoke, part of me watched. Maybe it was the writer in me, but I'd always been pretty good at people watching. The audience was mesmerized. Completely absorbed in the moment. One of their own did it. Casey was living the fairy tale. Most everyone in that room had been rescued from hell and lived to tell about it, and every single one dreamed the dream. The impossible dream that said, "Maybe someone will love me too. Maybe I'm lovable." And Casey, whose story was as bad as was conceivable, showed them that the fairy tale was possible. That happily-ever-after could happen. That each of them not only deserved to but *would* wear white. Which was their heart's cry. To wear white and not only *not* feel guilty in the wearing, but feel like they deserved to.

Because there was a difference. A big difference.

"Casey." She never took her eyes off Camp. "Casey Bishop." She shot a glance at me and cracked half a smile. "Will you have this man to be your husband, to live together in the covenant of marriage? Will you love him, comfort him, honor and keep him, in sickness and in health, and forsaking all others, be faithful to him as long as you both shall live?"

"I will."

"Camp, will you have this woman to be your wife, to live together in the covenant of marriage? Will you love her, comfort her, honor and keep her, in sickness and in health, and forsaking all others, be faithful to her as long as you both shall live?"

"I will."

Next I spoke to all of Freetown. "Will all of you witnessing these promises do all in your power to uphold these two persons in their marriage?"

"We will."

I couldn't hide the smile. "Who gives this woman to be married to this man?"

Clay tried to speak, could not, and tried again. This time, he looked across the audience and then back at me. "We do."

Maybe that was the moment. The moment when I knew Marie had been right. My life had meant something because she'd made one singular decision.

I closed my book and spoke to Camp and Casey. "Okay, you two. This is 'that day.' It's here. Take a deep breath. Nobody's in a hurry. You're sur-rounded by friends and family. Every single person here is pulling for you. We can't mess this up. And even if we do, they'll never say a word, so take a deep breath."

They did. Which was good, because Camp was about to pass out.

CHAPTER 94

I continued speaking to Camp and Casey. "I don't really expect you two to remember what I'm about to say to you, but you can watch the video."

Then I told the story of the shower, the hospital, and me telling Casey that someday some guy would come along, and he'd be crazy about her. His palms would sweat and his heart would palpitate and that moment was now. He was here. Casey, meet Camp. They all laughed. While I spoke, Gunner broke rank, circled me, and sat alongside me. Which elicited more laughter, which was what he wanted.

Then I talked about Camp and how we'd lured him to Vegas and he'd not taken the bait, and how I admired him and how he had yet to tell me a single thing about this chest full of Purple Hearts and Bronze and Silver Stars, which said a lot about him. Finally, I told them about the rescue, how he was cool under pressure, and then how he'd asked me for Casey's hand and why. Because he knew her tether was attached to me. And how in this moment, it was being loosed from me and placed with him.

Finally, I turned to the audience. "When Casey walked down this aisle and took Camp's trembling hand, each of us watched with expectation and joy. None more so than Camp. And while you might be listening to me, right this second, all of you—me included, and none more so than these two—are wanting me to get on with it so they can say their vows and kiss. Why? Because this thing we're doing, this hope, this expectation, this joy written on our hearts, is a picture of what's to come. The bridegroom returning for his bride."

After my sermonette, I turned back to the two of them. "You may face each other." Then, because Camp forgot, I whispered, "You can lift the veil now."

Laughter bubbled up from the audience.

"Hold hands."

More laughter and they did.

I looked to Casey, who repeated after me. "I, Casey, in the name of God, take you, Camp, to be my wedded husband. To share with you in God's plans for our life together, united in Christ. To be a loving wife to you with God's help and strength, seeking Him always no matter the trial, to love and cherish, in sickness or health, in joy or sorrow, for richer or poorer, until we are parted by death. I give you all that I have and all of my love. This is my solemn vow."

Then I turned to Camp. "I, Camp, in the name of God, take you, Casey, to be my wedded wife." It was at this point that I began hearing sobs from the audience. "To share with you in God's plans for our life together, united in Christ. To be a loving husband to you with God's help and strength . . ." The sobs grew louder. "Seeking Him always no matter the trial, to love and cherish, in sickness or health, in joy or sorrow, for richer or poorer, until we are parted by death. I give you all that I have and all of my love. This is my solemn vow."

The percentage of people crying was near 100 percent. Summer was a wreck. Bones was thumbing away tears. Clay had entirely crumpled his second handkerchief, refolded it, and then handed it to Summer, who smeared makeup all over it and then handed it back. Jess, normally stoic, was halfway into a box of Kleenex, and poor Eddie was almost inconsolable. It was a beautiful picture. A beautiful moment. And while I wanted to get these two married, I also wanted to sit in the beauty for a minute. To stay right here.

Gunner knew we needed a tension breaker and a bit of a laugh, so when I turned to him, held out my hand, and said, "May I have the rings to seal these vows?" he rolled over onto his back, stuck his paws into the air, and whined. Which was Gunner-speak for "Here, scratch my belly."

Everyone laughed. Which we needed. I stared at all the faces. The smiles. Tears. The total contrast to when I first saw them. Dark hotel rooms. Trunks of cars. Cabins in the woods. Hostels in Europe. Mansions in Russia. Townhomes in New York City. While the locations might have differed, their facial expressions when we kicked down the door were all the same. They all spoke of the horror they'd experienced, wordlessly pleading, *Get me out of here*. Their expressions also spoke one more thing. And it was the worst thing. Given what had happened to them, the evils that had been committed upon them, and the rejection they had known every hour on the hour for weeks, months, or years, their hearts were broken. Shattered. Ten trillion pieces scattered across the floor. And when I tried to lift them up and out of the hell in which I found them, most of them whispered, "Who could ever love a used-up, discarded piece of flesh like me?" Because that's what was stolen. They'd come to believe they were of no value. Worthless. At some point they'd stopped hoping. For each one, hope had died. I saw it in their eyes. And maybe that was the most evil act inflicted upon a human. To not kill their body but to kill their hope and force their soul to wander through life hopeless.

But staring out across that crowd with heads on shoulders, arms wrapped around shoulders, snotty tissues, puffy eyes, red cheeks, knees tucked into chests, smiles stretched ear to ear—I saw it return. When it did, I turned to Bones. He saw it too. Maybe he was looking for it. Maybe he'd seen it before me. Whatever the case, he held Summer's hand and mouthed these words: "We are in the hope business."

And he was right.

I knelt, untied the rings from Gunner's collar, and scratched his tummy. Standing, I returned to the two of them. "A cord of three strands is not easily broken. Lord, bless these rings to be a sign of these vows by which this man and this woman have bound themselves to each other through Jesus Christ our Lord. Amen."

Camp's hand was shaking. A man who had commanded combat missions around the globe, and he was nervous putting a ring on a finger. It showed the extent of his love and depth of commitment. Evidence he was all in. I whispered, "Repeat after me."

He nodded but never took his eyes off Casey. "Casey, I give you this ring as a symbol of my vow, and with all that I am and all that I have, I honor you. In the name of the Father, and of the Son, and of the Holy Spirit, with this ring I thee wed."

Then I turned to Casey and placed Camp's ring in her palm. When she received it, she stepped to my side, kissed me on the cheek, and said, "Thank you."

Until that moment, I had done a pretty good job of holding it together. After that, not so much. That was when I started crying. Her tender kiss pretty much broke the dam. I stood amazed at this woman. Whole. Healed. Strong. Giving herself completely and without reservation to this man. Heart full of hope. Eyes full of light. Spirit full of love.

I used the handkerchief Clay had given me to get my act together and compose myself while everyone in front of me laughed. Another much-needed tension breaker. "Casey, place this ring on the fourth finger of his left hand and repeat after me."

Casey did and stood waiting. "Camp, I give you this ring as a symbol of my vow, and with all that I am and all that I have, I honor you. In the name of the Father, and of the Son, and of the Holy Spirit, with this ring I thee wed."

They stood staring at each other. Smiles. Tears. Hearts pounding. I placed my hand on top of theirs and said, "Now, may the Lord bless you and keep you; the Lord make his face to shine upon you and be gracious to you; the Lord lift up his countenance upon you and give you peace."

Every wedding came down to one point. All of us, me included, wanted to get through the vows and the rings because we were all here to see one thing. Sure, we cared about the dress, the decorations, the ceremony, all the stuff—but we were here to witness one act. The kiss. It was universal. Every face in front of me was singularly focused on that one final act. For the kiss was what sealed it.

"Camp and Casey, in Christ you have become one. Now that you have given yourselves to each other by solemn vows, with the joining of hands and the giving and receiving of rings, in covenant before God and all of us, I pronounce you husband and wife. Those whom God has joined together, let no man put asunder."

The audience inhaled a singular collective breath, held it, and sat unmoving in a room without sound.

"Camp, you may kiss your bride."

And he did.

And the world breathed again. "I'd like to present to you Mr. and Mrs. Jay Middlecamp." The two turned, and Camp offered his arm to Casey. But just before she took it, she extended her hand to my face and thumbed a tear. Then she smiled, locked arms with her husband, and let out a fist-pumping "Woo-hoo!" shared by everyone in attendance. Camp waited as his saber bearers got into position, starting with the first pew. One of them then ushered a quiet "Center face" command, and all the men turned and faced one another. This was followed by "Arch sabers," at which point each man drew his sword with the right hand and extended it in an arch across the aisle until the tip of one saber touched the tip of the opposing saber. Cutting edge up. Once safe, Camp led his wife beneath the arch and into their new life while the audience chanted, "Camp, Camp, Camp . . ."

The raucous applause drowned out the beautiful music. Only then did I notice Sister Catalonia standing in the back corner. She, too, was crying. And I couldn't say for certain, but something in her demeanor was different. Not bad. Not painful. But wishful. And I wondered.

CHAPTER 95

The last time we held a reception at Freetown things did not go as planned, so our security for this one was a bit over the top. The wedding party walked from the chapel to the reception. Winding path. Cool evening. Summer clung so tightly to me I couldn't tell where she stopped and I started. Which I liked. When Summer and I married, she gave me a gift. A most precious gift. She gave me an empty picture frame and then filled it with the image of herself. Live. A priceless offering. And just like last time, without notice, she pulled me into our private little room where someone had lit candles. A bottle of champagne sat on ice and a small box sat wrapped in red paper on the table.

I surveyed the room. "I didn't think we were exchanging gifts at Casey and Camp's wedding."

She rolled her eyes.

"I must have missed that memo."

She smiled, proud of herself. She'd surprised me again. She was never one to stay in heels for very long, so she slipped them off and tiptoed barefoot to the champagne where she struggled with the cork, eventually popping it to the ceiling. The bubbles overflowed the bottle. She poured two glasses, then handed me the box.

Summer, usually confident, was sweating on a cold night, and the vein in her temple was throbbing. I didn't know what I was getting into or quite where this was headed, so I did the smart thing and kept my mouth shut. That way I didn't put my foot in it.

She clinked my glass. "To us."

"To us."

She sipped. "Now open it."

I felt like I was being baited, but I had little choice, so I slowly unwrapped the perfectly wrapped package, which, incidentally, was about the exact same size as the last package. I pulled back the paper, revealing a cardboard box. Nothing fancy. So I opened one end and slid out a picture frame. I smiled, anticipating holding it up and finding my wife filling the frame in the beautiful, selfless way she had the first time—but what I found was Summer holding a mirror.

She said, "Hold it up."

I obeyed and held the frame like I had before so that she filled it. Only, unlike last time, she then held up the mirror, which filled the frame . . . with me.

Again, I knew better than to open my mouth and prove how utterly incompetent I was in the ways of romance, so rather than speak and confirm her suspicions, I said nothing.

She sipped and smirked. "You like it?"

I nodded. Expressing how underwhelmed I was. "Yes, very much."

She laughed out loud. "Liar."

"Well, okay, maybe I did like the last one a bit more."

"Good answer."

She secured the mirror in the frame and handed it back, forcing me to look into it again. "Who do you see?"

I figured this was a trick question, so the less I said the better. "I see me."

"Who is he?"

"Murph."

"Good. Here, have a sip from your sippy cup. Maybe it'll loosen your tongue."

I did as ordered.

"And who is Murph?"

"Just a dude."

She shook her head. "Nope. Here, drink all of this. Now, try again. Third time's a charm. Who do you see?"

"I see your husband."

Both eyebrows rose. "Hmm. Closer. Doing better." She poured me a second glass of bubbly. "Have some more liquid courage. Evidently you need it when it comes to romantic talk."

"Lest you've forgotten, I've written a handful of rather successful books that have been pegged as 'romantic thrillers,' and I do have a rather large worldwide following of primarily female readers."

She downed her own glass and poured herself a second. "Yep. And if they saw you in this moment, they'd quit reading. So it'll be our secret. Keep going."

This was making me uncomfortable, so I thought I'd try the honest approach. "Honey, I know you're trying to get at something, but the chances of me saying something stupid are nearing 100 percent and I don't want to blow it."

She giggled and tapped her teeth with her fingernail. "Strange how you are so good at kicking down doors, but when I open one for you, you're all thumbs." She returned the mirror to my eye level. "Keep going."

"Repeat the question."

"You're stalling. Who do you see?"

"I promise I just see me."

"And who is he?"

"The one who loves you with his whole heart?"

"Close. And nice try. I'll even give you a B for effort. But try again."

About here, I got an inkling of what she was digging at. The same thing she'd been digging at for months. She'd just had to peel off the layers to get at it. "I see a man who has spent his life walking back across the battlefield to rescue the wounded."

She nodded. "Now we're starting to get it. And did I fall in love with that man?"

"You did."

"Has anything changed?"

"No."

"You sure?"

"Yes."

"And come tomorrow morning, what is the man in this mirror going to do?"

"Same thing."

"Correct." She scooted around beside me, her cheek pressed to mine. Our faces filled the frame. "Now what do you see?"

"I see us."

"Anything wrong with this picture?"

"Nothing."

"Now, no matter what I do, don't take your eyes off the image." With that, she turned, held my face in her hands, and kissed my cheek. Then she kissed it again, holding it a long time. "What do you see now?"

"I see you kissing my face."

CHAPTER 96

She laughed. "Good." Then she pressed her cheek to mine and stared with me at us.

"And now?"

"I see us again."

"Where do you end and I start?"

"Tough to tell."

"Good answer." She took the framed mirror from me, set it on the table, took my hands, and then did that little twirl dance move she liked to do when she was happy. Then she wrapped one arm around me while placing one hand on my heart. "David Bishop?"

"Yes, ma'am."

"You're not alone. Not ever. Not even when you feel it and the darkness tells you that you are. You're not. You carry me with you. I'm yours. I'm with you. Where you go, I go. I'm not leaving. I'm not tapping out. No matter how much it hurts." I was struck by how, once again, my incomparable wife was fighting for my heart. Truth be told, she was a better fighter than me. "We are in this thing together. In this frame forever. If you ever look in this mirror and my face is not alongside yours, then something is wrong in the universe." She wrapped both arms around me. Her heart was pounding. My drumbeat. Once again calling for me. "You picking up what I'm putting down?"

"Yes, ma'am."

"I'm not kidding." She stiletto-poked me in the chest. "You've come through a hard place. One of the hardest places. First Marie. Then Bones. I wasn't sure how much more your heart could take, but we're still standing. And while we're standing, I want you to know this. This one thing." She held my face in her hands. "I'm yours. I'm all in. I've got you. You've got me. And . . ." It was here that she teared up and choked back the emotion that had been building. "If the darkness comes for you. If he rears his ugly face. If he so much as lays a finger on you, I will remove his head from his shoulders and post it on a stake outside the city walls. I'm not playing. He can't have you. I am the repairer of the breach. Standing guard on the wall that is us. And if the darkness comes, he's gonna have to get through me, and when he does, I'm gonna tell him . . ."

Oh, how I loved this woman. A hundred and thirty soaking wet, and here she was taking on all of hell. Standing between me and anything that threatened to drown me.

"Repairer of the . . . ?"

"Breach. It's a break in the—"

"I know what it is. I just wanted to hear you say it again. I like the way it sounds when you say it." I pulled her closer. "Just what are you going to tell him?"

She was getting hot now. "I'm gonna tell him he can pound sand. He can go back to hell where I hope it's hot and the maggots eat his face off."

She was really fired up. "Summer?"

"Yes."

I reached in my coat pocket and pulled out a small wrapped package. About the size of a man's wallet. Shiny blue wrapping. White ribbon. Neat corners. The works. She eyed it with suspicion. "What is it and where'd you get it?"

"Honey, gifts are surprises. It's part of the reason we give them. Some of the joy is in not knowing."

She palmed her face, holding the gift in her other hand. "And you've had this in your pocket the entire time?"

"No, I just flew to Jerusalem real quick while you were storming the gates of hell, wandered the streets of the Old City real quick, and came back."

She raised both eyebrows and contorted her lips like she was thinking. "Well, somebody has to. And I'm not playing."

"Are you going to open it?"

She slowly unwrapped the package that had taken me over an hour to wrap. "Who wrapped this?"

"Me."

She examined the corners. "No way."

"Honey, I have parachuted out of planes in the middle of the night over countries I'm not supposed to be in. I can wrap a gift."

Evidently I was making good points and I had impressed her, in that she thought she was the only one who remembered this room and what this little moment had meant in our life. But I'd had a feeling she might pull me aside after the wedding and before the reception and sort of run the same play a second time. Contrary to popular opinion around Freetown, I am not totally romantically ignorant. I do have a few things to say.

She pulled off the paper and sat staring at the small box. She shot a glance at me and then lifted the lid, where she found a single smooth stone. Like something you'd find in a stream. Polished from eons in the water. One of several trillion on planet earth but unique with its own size, shape, polish, and color. She hefted it and let it rest in her palm, waiting.

"It's a two-part gift. First, it represents a moment. I was in Jerusalem. We were meeting with Ariel. Nighttime. Walking the streets of the Old City. Moon was high. And I stepped over this roundish, oblong thing that caught my attention. I stooped down, picked it up. A simple rock. How many people had stepped over it? How long had it been there? The more I held it, the more the dust wore off and the more it shone. Actually, it had a high polish. Meaning, it had spent its life under constant pressure. Constant wear. Bumping up against other hard things had worn off its jagged edges."

She raised an eyebrow. Not impressed with my pet rock. Having a difficult time believing I'd come to this realization on my own. "And you want me to do what with it?"

I laughed. "Remember, I said it's a two-part gift."

She waited.

"If you'll reach beneath that table there, you'll find part two."

Now I really had her guessing. The idea that I'd planted a gift in this room, anticipating that she'd bring me in here, was blowing her mind. She never expected that I'd one-up her. It had never crossed her mind. She thought she was going to give me the mirror, kiss me, get her point across, and then we'd attend the reception. And I loved her for that. But I wasn't a corpse. I did have a pulse. And my heart actually did beat—always for her and her alone. So that's what this was about, and she was about to realize I'd been thinking about this moment for a little bit longer than the last five minutes.

She reached below the small table and found a second perfectly wrapped box. This one wrapped with brown paper. The box was about the size of a ream of paper. Because it was. Unable to hold both, she handed me the pet rock and held the second gift on her lap, awaiting further instruction. I smiled and set the rock on top of the gift. "It's a paperweight."

For a split second, I saw the confusion set in. Then it cleared. And when it did, her eyes lit and she realized what she might be holding, but the thought was almost too good to be true, so she was afraid to hope it.

So I fed it a little. "A long time ago, when I was in pain, I found that if I could 'write it out,' it didn't go away and it didn't really hurt less, but something happened in the writing. It's like God used my own pen to probe the wound. A scalpel to get rid of the dead stuff. Then He sutures up what remains. Something happens in the writing. Something I can't quite explain. So I did. I lived by that then. I live by that now. So"—I tapped the package—"I did that here. And given that you are David Bishop's number one fan, I thought maybe you'd want to read it first." She was about to rip open the package when I placed my hands on hers. "Sometimes I think

I live in a strange world where, whether I like it or not, I hold the power of life and death in my hands. After so much death, I needed life. And this"—I tapped the manuscript she held once more—"is life. And you, Summer Bishop, breathed life into me when I could not breathe."

Tears trickled down her face, and she started bouncing. She didn't know whether to kiss me or rip the paper off the box. And the fact that I'd done all this was still blowing her mind.

We spent the next day at the Eagle's Nest. Summer reading. Me watching her read. She laughed, shook her head, tucked her knees into her chest, tapped her teeth with her fingernail, huffed, and sat amid a pile of scattered sheets of paper. It was a beautiful read. And when she finished, finally reaching the last page, she set it down, took off her readers, shook her head, and placed her palm flat across my heart. "I don't know how you do it . . . only that you do."

EPILOGUE

B ones placed his palm flat on the scanner, the reader confirmed his identity, the air lock hissed, and the giant blast door inched open. At nearly ten thousand feet elevation, the former nuclear bunker was well hidden among the mountains of Colorado. Bones had retrofit it last year after Freetown was blown up in the event that we needed to move everyone to high and safe ground. Once an underground retreat for America's leaders, now it was an empty, well-stocked ghost town awaiting habitation. Every few months we came up here, poked around, marveled at the sheer sight of something dug down into the earth, and then talked about how glad we were that we didn't need it, because needing it would mean something had happened that caused us to need it. Which would undoubtedly be bad. Bones had awakened me early and we'd set out. He wasn't strong enough to make the hike to the Eagle's Nest, but if we rode the chairlift, he could walk the ridgelines. So the three of us—him, me, and Gunner—had watched the sun come up over the Collegiates. And while a lot of things are wrong with this world, witnessing the sun light up the skyline over the Rockies is not one of them.

The loss of his venerable Sig 220 was felt sorely by Bones. It had gotten him out of more than one bad spot. It had gone "bang" when he needed it to, and it had never failed him. While he was very much a fan of the CZ, and appreciated it, his hand had been wrapped around the grip of the Sig so long that anything else felt awkward. Knowing this, I contacted the manufacturer and explained our dilemma. Save the fact that I could not tell them he was alive. I told them it was for me. In memory of. Bones had a bit of a storied reputation among the Sig folks, so their response was quick. The custom shop cooked up a singular creation. A Sig 220 Legion made special for Ezekiel Walker. They even stamped "Bones" on the slide. They made one change not before seen on a Legion. A lanyard loop. The lanyard loop saw wide acceptance on 1911s and Browning High Powers through World War II and earlier iterations as far back as World War I. Originally intended for use among cavalry, since bouncing around on a horse or crawling through a trench was a good way to lose a pistol. As it turned out, so was traversing a dungeon in Majorca. The loop was a thoughtful nod toward the history and résumé of all the storied .45s and early 9mms that came before. Bones started as a .45 man, and even now, after all the developments in ammunition, he was still a .45 man. You could take the .45 out of his hand, but not the .45 out of the man. It was a thing. Bones had taken to the new sidearm and was in the process of breaking in a new Milt Sparks VM2. Maybe the best holster ever created.

Gunner and I followed down a long corridor of lights through a series of giant caverns and hallways and intersections. The bunker was designed to hold a small city. Some two thousand people. The insides accommodated movement of large numbers of people. Two walking through made the entire place seem cavernous. Which it was. Not to mention the echo.

We made it to the server room. The brains of the place. Bones once again held his palm to the scanner, it confirmed his identity, and the glass doors slid open following another air lock hiss. He leaned on his walking stick, catching his breath, and stared at the servers. "Just before he took his own life, Frank told me two things. The first might make our job a little easier." He pointed at the servers. "We've been stumbling over ourselves, wracking our brains trying to find Frank's data vault. Where he kept the trillions of bytes that contained all his secrets. All the info he used to leverage and blackmail world leaders, rock stars, actors, politicians. We didn't look here, where it's been all along."

"What?"

"This is an intranet. No hardline to the outside world and the internet, therefore it can't be hacked remotely. Frank knew it would be safe here. So once he knew I'd retrofit this space, he worked twenty-four seven to dump all the data. Tedious work. He had to physically stand here and upload all that data. Took some time I should think."

I looked at the rows of black boxes and multicolored cables that daisy-chained the untold amount of terabytes together. "You mean the key to Frank's generals was sitting right here, under our nose, the whole time?"

"Evidently I wasn't the only one hiding a secret in plain sight."

Just as Bones had kept the birth certificate safe with Frank all those years, Frank had kept all his data safe with Bones. Maybe identical twins do tend to think alike.

"What do you think we'll find?"

"Bunch of stuff we probably don't want to know."

"You think Maynard is in there?"

He nodded. "It's why he never accepted the nomination while Frank was alive. Frank couldn't have someone more powerful, or equally as powerful, working for him. It evened the odds too much. Plus, in Frank's world, Maynard was more useful as the power behind the throne. Not the power on it. Power on a throne draws attention. Power behind it does not. Soon as Frank died, Maynard executed a plan he'd hatched long ago."

"Kidnapping Ashley's kids?"

"Taking out his opponent. Clearing the way. That way he could run unopposed. Assure victory. Ashley just happened to be the one standing in his way at that particular time."

"You got the team on it?"

"Eddie, Jess, and BP are headed up here now. Gonna spend a few days digging into the code."

"Think we can ID Frank's generals?"

He nodded. "Not to mention the chips Frank installed. Eddie thinks he can make sense of it. Which, honestly, is the easy part." He shook his head once. "Tearing down their playhouse? Not so much. Powerful people don't like it when you take away their power."

"Or their money. Or freedom."

Bones nodded.

We exited the bunker. I gathered some dry wood and sparked a fire, and the two of us plus Gunner stood staring into the flames, warming ourselves as the sun began burning off the cold. We were for silent several minutes. Finally, Bones said, "Got plans tonight?"

A rhythm had returned to life at Freetown. I wouldn't say "normality," but at least I woke in the same bed every morning with Summer wrapped around me like a vine. Which was just fine with me. "Date night. You?"

He weighed his head side to side, trying to find the right words. Which I found telling. "Eagle's Nest. Wanted to show it to Cat before she leaves."

Cat had become Bones's way of referring to Sister Catalonia. "And the wine?"

He smiled but didn't look at me. "Something dusty."

"I've been accused lately of being a little thickheaded when it comes to anything romantic, but that sounds like a date to me."

A nod. "Me too."

"You wrestled that out with God?"

Another long silence. Finally, he looked at me. A content half-smile. "He didn't say no."

I put my hand on his shoulder. "Of all the people on planet earth, you deserve happiness. I'm pulling for you."

I was about to speak when my phone dinged. An encrypted message on the Signal app. I studied it.

Bones pried. "Who?"

"Ariel."

"A good man." He studied my face. "But it's not a social call, is it?"

I studied the picture and shook my head once.

"Bad?"

"It's not good." I held up the screen and showed him a picture of Ariel's daughter. Below it, the one-word message read, "Help."

Bones was in no condition to jog, but we jogged anyway, Bones grunting with every bump. I spoke over my shoulder. "You explain it to Summer for me."

He shook his head. "Nope."

That was unusual. "Why not?"

"'Cause I'm going with you."

"But you're in no condition to—"

He held out a stop-sign hand. "I didn't walk out of that watery grave to let you leave me here."

"I can handle it."

Another shake. "You can come with me, but I'm not *not* going."

I knew this, but I just wanted to hear him say it. "And the Eagle's Nest?"

"Have to wait."

"Will she?"

He shrugged and continued grunting. "Don't know."

Minutes passed. He sounded like somebody getting punched in the gut. I raised an eyebrow. Unlike Bones, I might have been in some of the best shape of my life. "Starting to feel your age?"

He kept grunting but kept his eyes focused on where his feet needed to touch down next.

We jogged another mile as I marveled at the man running alongside me. Bones had physical strength for sure, but he had an inner strength that was unmatched. I'd never seen its equal. I was pretty sure he had a red cape tucked down inside his shirt. "What was the second thing Frank said?"

Bones was quiet a minute. His face told me he was back in the dungeon, his back pressed to his brother's chest. Only seconds remaining. We reached a peak in the ridgeline. All of Colorado spread out before us. We could see eighty or ninety miles in any direction. "He said, 'I love you.'"

The inconceivability of that struck me. I didn't think Frank capable of that.

Bones began jogging again.

"You think he meant it?"

A nod. "I do."

We rounded the last corner to the Eagle's Nest, loaded into the ski lift, closed the door, and began the ride down while Bones pulled on a KUIU down puffer so he didn't cool off too quickly. He sat opposite me, barely breathing, staring off into the horizon. When he spoke, he did so beneath the surface. "It's what we fight for."

We rode down in silence as the weight of his words hit me. I didn't believe Frank capable of love, yet Bones had. All along. He had never quit believing. The picture focused. Bones had walked back down into hell, out across the battlefield, to rescue the one dumb sheep that got itself lost. And when he found it, he put it on his shoulders and walked it home. Bones had done that. He'd done that with his brother. He'd done it with Frank.

My back was sore from the recent ink: *Maria, Francisca, Margarida, Ruth, Sadie, Miriam.* For each of them, I wondered how long before their love returned. Their hope. Their willingness to trust. They were young, and I was hopeful, so I felt strongly that it would. I just didn't know when. In some ways, it already had. As we descended out of the clouds, I sat and studied Ezekiel Walker. My friend. Bones. There in that thin air, I saw what I'd not expected again: my mentor taking me back to school. One more time.

"Bones?"

"Yeah."

"Thank you."

"For what?"

"Not dying."

He chuckled. "Not sure I had much to do with that."

"You sure I can't convince you to let me go solo on this one, and you spend the evening at the Eagle's Nest?"

Bones considered this. A minute passed. "Maybe I could take a later flight. Join you when you've reconned and put a plan in place."

I smiled. "You gonna get down on one knee? Girls like it when you do that stuff."

Bones sucked through his teeth and raised an eyebrow. "Don't know. Honestly, I'm not sure I know how to ask a nun not to be a nun anymore."

"Maybe you should just start by taking her by the hand and asking her to go for a walk, or ride, up this mountain."

"Good idea."

"But don't forget the wine."

He did not look amused. "Believe it or not, unlike you, I do have a romantic bone in my body."

"Why is everyone always accusing me of not knowing diddly about romance? For the record, I do write love stories for a living."

"Yeah, about that."

"What about it?"

"Summer says it's her favorite. Your best yet. Read it in one sitting."

"She says that about all of them."

"What's it called?"

I smiled. "*The Piece Keeper.*"

His lip curled. "That's a dumb name. Why'd you call it that?"

"Because when my world shattered and I couldn't hold all the pieces scattered about the floor, I found that Summer could. Piece by piece, she put me back together."

"Okay, maybe it's not such a dumb title."

"And because when I look across Freetown, I see all that was once lost now restored. Returned. Made whole. I see the smiles. I hear the laughter. I realize you did that. You dreamed it. You hoped it. You risked everything for it. You took all the broken pieces and crafted a mosaic we call Freetown."

He sat quietly a second. "You should definitely keep that title. It's a good title."

"That's what I'm thinking."

We reached the landing, unloaded, and found Clay sitting in the truck with the engine running, waiting to ferry us to the runway. Any minute spent saying goodbye to Summer was a minute spent not trying to find Ariel's daughter. The clock was ticking. I'd have to call her from the air and rain-check date night. We jumped in, and Clay rushed us to the basement where we loaded gear and then to the tarmac where the plane sat waiting. With one addition. Summer stood there zipped up in a puffer, bracing herself against the cold.

Summer stood between me and the plane. I tried to explain. "I was gonna call."

She nodded as the pilots finished their pre-check. "Two things."

I nodded. Waiting.

She looked up at me. "Find her. Do whatever, and I do mean whatever, it takes."

I studied her. Summer. Once again standing on the wall. Taking all comers.

She shook her head once. "Don't take any foolishness off anybody. If they bow up, knock 'em down."

The jets sounded. I nodded. I had a good idea what she'd say next, but I just loved hearing her say it. "And two?"

She placed one palm flat across my heart, the other flat across my cheek. "Murphy Shepherd?" I could feel her breath on my face. Her eyes were bright. Full of light. "I need you to bring David Bishop home . . . because he's the keeper of my heart."

Then she kissed me, and I boarded the plane.

To find the one. And bring her home. Back to the ninety-nine.

And the Shepherd.

DISCUSSION QUESTIONS

1. Murphy says that Bones was motivated by the "real kind" of love. "The kind that says me for you." Do you think you could rescue someone who wanted evil for you? What do you think it would take to have that kind of love?

2. Bones had Murphy write his seminary thesis on Matthew 18:12, and he clearly modeled his life around leaving the ninety-nine for the one. What characteristics might one need to possess in order to be able to accomplish such a mission?

3. When Murphy is questioning Steve about his role in the kidnapping, he realizes he could have ended up like Steve were it not for Bones's influence on his life. While not excusing Steve's mistakes, he could see how a broken man chose the wrong path. Is there anyone who made a difference like this in your life or the life of someone you know?

4. Murphy is nervous for Camp to revere him the way he did Bones because he knows it could end in heartbreak. He says that to love is to risk. What do you think about that statement? Have you experienced deep hurt because you chose to love someone or something, and would you do it again?

5. Murphy tells Ellie, "Love doesn't halve—it doubles." Where in your life have you found this to be true? Were you surprised at your heart's capacity for love?

6. Bones told Murphy, "A name is the singular thing that separates us from the ninety-nine. A name makes us the one." Have you ever felt the power and significance of someone knowing your name? What kind of difference did that make in your life?

7. Bones teaches Murphy that it's crucial to learn which orders to obey and which not to. He said the voice inside each of us is always speaking, and the question is whether we're listening. Have you felt stuck in a place before where you weren't sure what to listen to? Do you have any experiences of listening for that voice and hearing it?

8. Were you surprised when Murphy found Bones alive? Did you expect that to happen? What significance do you think there is in the timing of when Murphy found Bones?

9. Bones says, "The problem comes when you turn on a light and find those in darkness who, having seen light, prefer the dark." Why do you think some people choose to stay in the darkness?

10. Bones teaches Murphy that to be a good leader, you need to "Find out what people are good at, and let them do more of it." Have you had or been an example of this kind of leadership?

11. Bones tells Ashley, "We don't fight because we always win . . . We fight because . . . who else will?" Are there places in your life where your influence might make a difference? What do you need to do in order to have the courage to fight?

ABOUT THE AUTHOR

Photo © Amy S. Martin

Charles Martin is the New York Times bestselling author of more than 15 novels, including his most recent, *The Last Exchange*. His work is available in 35+ languages. He lives in Jacksonville, Florida, with his wife and their three sons.

Learn more at www.charlesmartinbooks.com.
Instagram: @storiedcareer
X: @storiedcareer
Facebook: @Author.Charles.Martin